# Readers love Anton Du Beke's sparkling fiction...

'Beautifully written'

'What a triumph'

'A story full of true emotion, heart, poise and survival'

'I was enthralled from start to finish'

'Anton Du Beke has done it again'

'A truly fabulous read'

'The story of The Buckingham just gets better and better. Couldn't put it down'

# A DANCE *for the* KING

# ANTON DU BEKE

Signed first edition

# ANTON DU BEKE

# A DANCE *for the* KING

*A Buckingham Hotel novel*

ORION

First published in Great Britain in 2024 by Orion Fiction,
an imprint of The Orion Publishing Group Ltd.
Carmelite House, 50 Victoria Embankment
London EC4Y ODZ

An Hachette UK Company

1 3 5 7 9 10 8 6 4 2

A CIP catalogue record for this book is
available from the British Library.

ISBN (Hardback) 9781 3987 2225 5
ISBN (eBook) 9781 3987 2227 9
ISBN (Audio) 9781 3987 2228 6

Typeset at The Spartan Press Ltd,
Lymington, Hants

Printed and bound in Great Britain by Clays Ltd,
Elcograf S.p.A.

www.orionbooks.co.uk

*For Hannah, Henrietta and George.*
*Your support and love means the world to me.*

*London, Summer 1942*

Have you ever visited the Buckingham Hotel?

There it sits, in the very heartland of London: seven storeys of glimmering white, overlooking the verdant oasis of Berkeley Square. Beyond the surrounding townhouses, London is at war. Barrage balloons are strung up in the skies; nightly, the brave boys of the RAF soar across the city, repelling Mr Hitler's rapacious hordes. On Oxford Street, the grand department store of John Lewis remains in ruins; the craters of Piccadilly are slowly being filled in; rolls of barbed wire and sandbags have turned Horse Guards Parade, and Parliament's approach, into a military command. London is a city that is brutalised yet defiant, its people crushed but never cowed. From the north to the south, east to the west, London *endures*...

But here, here in the heart of Mayfair, here sits a fortress defiant.

Come through its doors...

In the ballroom, dancers waltz and turn. On the stage, the Max Allgood Orchestra trumpets out its joyful music, heedless of bombs. In the kitchens, chefs and underlings concoct delights that show no sign of the privation of war. In the rooms and suites, guests are treated as royalty. Indeed, some of them *are* royalty – for the Buckingham Hotel is a home away from home for the exiled kings, queens and governments of Europe; a shining light of fortitude, a bastion of hope that goodness shall soon win out against all that is wicked in this world.

But come upstairs, into the smoky environs of the Candlelight Club.

Here sit lords and ladies, men of money and men of power; here, glasses are raised and cocktails composed; here, over martinis and Veuve Clicquot, brave men make the decisions that might yet turn the tide of this insufferable war.

You would not think it, not in an establishment as esteemed as this, but someone raising their glass in here tonight is plotting to sell out their king.

Someone toasting their loved ones in here imagines a future where Great Britain has fallen, becoming nothing more than a protectorate of the Reich.

Someone who waltzes in the Grand Ballroom, someone who dines in the Queen Mary Restaurant, someone who walks the halls of this hallowed institution, believes they can bring about the end of this island nation's valiant fight.

Sometimes, the enemy is not really out there at all.

Sometimes, they're right *here*.

Sitting beside you.

Clinking their glasses against your own.

Dancing in your arms...

# *January 1942*

# Chapter One

After a lifetime in the deserts of North Africa, after countless weeks at sea among the invalided and exiled, after the bombs that pulverised the port city of Liverpool where his transport came into dock, Lieutenant Raymond de Guise was grateful to be sitting in a crowded train carriage, surrounded by a hubbub of English voices, making the final approach to the city he loved.

London: the city where it all began.

He hadn't expected to see it again – not so soon.

There had been plenty of long nights, eking out rations inside the besieged city of Tobruk, when he wondered if he'd see it at all.

If he'd ever lay eyes upon his darling wife, Nancy, or cradle their newborn son in his arms.

And yet here it was, appearing by degrees through the window. For hours now, the train had been grinding through the stations and sidings of London's approach, stopping and starting again with frightening regularity. More than one train had been derailed in the damage from the Luftwaffe's bombings last year – nowadays, it was part of the job for the driver and conductors to check the integrity of the tracks up ahead – but Raymond had waited a long year to see Nancy; he could wait a little longer. In his hands were letters she'd sent him along the way. Some had been lost to the oceans, some to the desert sands and the hastened retreats from one billet to the next – but some he'd carried with him across the long arc of the war, and here, right here, was the letter she'd sent when their son Arthur was born. Eight months old, now, and not once in this life had Raymond laid eyes upon him. The boy had taken Raymond's late brother's name, but what he smelt like, what he looked like, how he sounded or felt sleeping in his arms, Raymond did not know.

But he was going to find out.

This very day, he was going to find out.

The train juddered to a halt.

Raymond heaved a sigh. Some of the other travellers – none of whom looked as if they'd come as far as Raymond, for this train was filled with office clerks, day-trippers, railwaymen and other city workers – looked exasperated, casting aggrieved glances at the conductor, but Raymond sank instead into his letters. Nancy neither knew nor hoped for his coming. Right now, she was either at home nursing their son – or she was rallying her girls in the housekeeping department at the Buckingham Hotel, that esteemed establishment sitting on London's Berkeley Square where she and Raymond had first been drawn together. Wherever she was, her day marched obliviously on. The longing, the yearning, was Raymond's alone.

'My dearest Raymond,' Nancy wrote, 'when Arthur babbles I am sure he is calling for his father. Sometimes, when I sleep, I am calling for his father as well...'

There was commotion further along the carriage now. One of the other passengers seemed to have provoked mirth in a group of city clerks clustered at the end of the carriage. Raymond tried to block out the noise. Here was London, right in front of him. Another half hour, another hour, and he would lay eyes upon her.

He wondered how motherhood had changed her.

He wondered how much a year in the desert had changed him.

He wondered about all the lies he was going to have to tell to explain to her exactly *why* he had been summoned back to London; exactly *why*, though his war with a rifle was over, his part in the battle went on.

'*I haven't heard from you in two long months,*' Nancy had written, '*but when I sleep, I still feel you beside me. And that is why I know you are out there still. That is why I know, one day, you will be coming back home . . .*'

In her heart, Raymond thought, she had reconciled to not seeing him for years.

But tonight, she would be in his arms.

Moments earlier, further along the carriage, a youth had flurried suddenly out of sleep. He was a young man, nineteen or twenty years old, with coils of black hair and a slightly deranged look in his eyes – and, as he blurted out 'Where am I?', splutters of laughter rose up from a group of middle-aged clerks. His reflection in the window glass revealed a man who looked as if he'd spent the night in the back booth of some alehouse, not in a station hotel on the Salisbury plain. He wore a brown suit, which had seen better days, a shirt open at the collar, and carried a trumpet in a beautiful leather case in his hand. But it was not the fact that he was Black that drew the eye – even though he was the only Black man on the train this morning. No, it was his accent, rich and honeyed and dripping with the sounds of his native Chicago, that stirred attention.

'We're outside London, sir,' the conductor said, as he passed. 'Waiting for an inspection of the tracks up ahead. We're being held here by the wardens until we can keep going, but it shouldn't be long.'

The young man shook his head like a dog rising up from the river. 'About time,' he cheered, and shook the conductor's hand so vigorously that the man backed away, unnerved. 'London's calling. London at last. London, here I come!'

The group of middle-aged clerks were still staring. The young Black man got to his feet. A more spindly kind of man would be difficult to imagine. Now that he stood, it was obvious his suit was too big for him, and that he still carried with him some of the gangliness of youth. He stood over six feet tall but was thin as a rake. Whistling, he took off along the carriage.

He was loping past the clerks when one of them called out, 'You're a Yank, then?'

The Black man inclined his head, his face still split by a dazzling smile. 'And proud of it!'

'With the army? I didn't know you'd landed yet.'

The Black man swivelled on his heel and flashed his smile at every one of the clerks. 'Gentlemen, I'm a musician, not a fighter. I'm a man of peace ... except when I get on that stage!'

He was already sauntering on, eager to be the first off the train and into the wild promise of Paddington Station, when he heard the clerks start snorting. 'There'll be more like *that* coming,' one of them said. 'Trust me, we'll be inundated. A plague like you've never seen. I heard, back in America, they're not allowed to ride the same trains.'

'It's a good system. It rather makes sense.'

The young man stopped dead.

His smile died.

His scarecrow body seized up.

'Oh yeah,' one of the other clerks snorted, 'they'll be sending them over in droves. You think they'll be letting them have free rein? Or keeping things nice and orderly, like they do back home?'

The young man turned on the spot, marched back towards the clerks, and seethed, 'What did you say?'

'That was a private conversation, sir,' the first clerk said. 'You'll be learning some English manners while you're over here. Eavesdropping is hardly the behaviour of a welcome guest, so if you don't mind—'

'Move over,' the young man said, 'I want to sit down.'

The clerks looked at him, horrified. 'There's not a seat to be spared.'

'I don't know, I reckon I could fit. Might even sit on one of your laps, if you'll have me.' Without hesitation, he started inveigling his way between two of the clerks.

'Sir, this is outrageous!'

'I'll tell you what's outrageous,' the young man snapped, when the clerks – finally finding their brio – jostled him back into the aisle between seats. 'You think you're better than me – and there you sit, on your big round backsides, just pouring dirt on others. Yes, sir, they keep *my* type separate where I come from. Don't mean it's right. Don't mean it's fair. But look at you, with your ruddy smug faces – you're closer to pigs than you are good, honest men.'

'That's ENOUGH!'

One of the clerks had shot suddenly to his feet. Now he extended a finger and jabbed it at the young man's breast.

'You're a guest in this country, not even a soldier by your own admission, and—'

'You touch me again,' snarled the man, 'and you'll see what happens.'

\*

It was those words, 'you'll see what happens', that tore Raymond out of the letter he was reading. He'd seen enough fights break out in billets and barracks to develop an instinct for the approaching storm. Nancy's words – *write and tell me you are safe; write something I can read to our son* – faded out of thought and mind as he folded the letter back into the little leather case where he'd been keeping them, then stood up to see a young Black man puffing out his breast while a portly city clerk jabbed him with a finger.

Each man was appraising the other, daring him to move.

Raymond marched along the carriage until he was almost on top of the altercation.

'Young man,' the plump clerk declared, 'you won't get far in this country with an attitude like—'

The Black man sighed. 'I gave you fair warning,' he said rue-fully, then brought back his fist to let it fly.

And he might have done exactly that if only, at that moment, a shadow hadn't fallen across him, a hand hadn't clasped his shoulder – and, under the pressure of its fingers, he hadn't turned round to come face to face with Lieutenant Raymond de Guise.

The young man seemed ready to brawl with Raymond too, but something in Raymond's demeanour quelled his rage. His ability to calm another man, especially in the theatre of war, was second to no other. It might have seen him become a commander if he hadn't received that mysterious phone call from the old hotel director, Maynard Charles.

'We're almost at London,' Raymond began, fixing the man's deep, black eyes with a benign look. 'Perhaps it would be wiser to just go on your way.'

'Hear, hear!' one of the clerks exclaimed. 'Throw the rabble out. See what a good, upstanding soldier can do, young man?'

Raymond bristled. He could sense the young man bristling too. He'd almost pierced the boy's outrage and mollified his ire, but suddenly it was erupting again.

There was nothing else for it.

Raymond stepped in front of the young man, making his way into the middle of the altercation.

Then he cast an excoriating eye over the clerks and said, 'You ought to be ashamed. The boy did nothing to you – nothing but happen by. It's war, gentlemen – or have you forgotten what that felt like? We're meant to stick together.'

Taken aback by Raymond's waspish tone, the clerks slumped into their seats, sharing looks of outrage. Not that Raymond cared; he was already bustling the young man back along the carriage, into the vestibule at its end.

'You ought to have let me show 'em,' the young man said. 'I've dealt with sorts like that before. They don't got any courage, not when it comes down to it. I could have left him on the carriage floor, and no mistake.'

Raymond had to admit that he liked the young man's bravura. He could have made something of a man like this if he'd been part of the company in Cairo. But it was different back home. Sometimes, being brave was only a whisker away from being foolhardy – and Raymond was quite certain that this young man couldn't tell one from the other.

'I think you timed it right. Walking away doesn't lead to war.'

'Hey, man, I heard they called that *appeasement.*'

Then the young man's face opened in laughter so infectious that Raymond grinned too.

'The name's Nelson,' the younger man said, and grasped the soldier's arm in a brotherly half-embrace. 'You look like you been in the wars, sir.'

'Well I'm home now,' Raymond replied. 'I'm Raymond,' he added, 'and you're … a trumpet player?'

Nelson was still swinging the black leather case at his side. 'I can toot a horn, but it's not my thing, you know? Problem is, you can't go carting a grand piano around – so a man's gotta find himself a second instrument. This here,' and he hoisted up the trumpet, 'is on loan from my uncle. Now *he* can play. You ought to hear him with his trombone. Lucille, he calls it. A man's gotta have a name for his instrument. It shows he's in love.'

Nelson was grinning wickedly; it was difficult not to join in.

But the train had started moving at last, and the conductor's voice hollered up and down the carriage. 'Next stop, Paddington Station! Paddington Station, coming up!'

'You want some advice, since you're coming to London?' Raymond began. 'You keep your head down, you stay out of trouble, you work hard – and you walk away from the fights. And, boy, you might just about make it in this city. That is, if the bombs don't get you first …'

Raymond waited on the platform until Nelson had barrelled away, making certain first that the rabble of city clerks didn't mean him some further mischief in the station. Then, and only then, did he shoulder his packs and make haste for the station entrance. Outside, the morning was growing old. A throng of passengers just disembarked from their journeys were clamouring for taxicabs lined up by the roadside – but Raymond just hovered at the entrance, took in his first glimpse of London in the January chill, and started to march. After so many weeks of voyaging, he was quite sick of travel – and home was just a short walk away.

Nancy, just a short walk away.

Arthur, waiting for the father he'd never known.

There'd be questions, so many questions, of that there was no doubt. But he'd received his briefing at the Liverpool dock, and there'd already been two weeks of intensive training at a military retreat off the Salisbury Plain – the kind of place that didn't appear in military manuals, and which didn't exist in the public record – so at least he felt well prepared. What he didn't feel prepared for, he realised now, was the rush of feelings that had started coursing through him. When you were away at war, it was easy to enter a strange limbo state – you missed your loved ones, of course, but for a time you existed in a separate world from them, and that made it easier to box your feelings away. Now that he was in London, those rules hardly applied. Nancy was just a quick march away. His son, who knew him by blood but not by body, could be in his arms inside half an hour. His world, changing and then changing all over again.

A voice hailed him from the side of the road.

'Sir?'

When he looked round, the window of a black taxicab had been wound down and the driver – who looked a cut above the usual London taximan, dressed in a charcoal-grey suit and navy-blue necktie – was piercing him with a look.

'I'm walking from here,' Raymond said, his heart filled with imagining that one holy moment when he would step over the threshold at home, that little house in Maida Vale which he and Nancy had made their own.

'No, Lieutenant, you're not,' the driver replied.

He loaded the word 'Lieutenant' with such meaning that Raymond immediately understood this was no ordinary taxi driver. Most men might have inferred his rank from the uniform he wore, but there was a knowingness in this man's eyes, an air of imperial command that did not befit him.

'Sir, I'm headed home,' Raymond insisted.

The taximan stepped out of his vehicle, picked his way round and opened up the passenger door. 'I'll drop you there myself, but you've a little detour first. Step this way, Lieutenant. It would pay to remember: your time isn't your own; you haven't been decommissioned, not yet.'

Seeing his family was like a mirage that kept slipping away, the closer he got. He'd known a few mirages like that in the desert. All you could do was steel yourself and accept them for what they were. So it was with a profound sense of resignation that Raymond got into the taxicab and sat there in silence as the driver took him across London, along thoroughfares at once familiar and strange, around the fortified environs of Buckingham Palace, and onto the long boulevard of Piccadilly.

The Buckingham Hotel was only a stone's throw from here. How strange it would be to see it again.

Yet, the moment he allowed himself to imagine that that was where he was being taken – for wasn't the Buckingham the very reason he'd been summoned back from Cairo, wasn't it at the Buckingham Hotel that he was needed the most? – the taxicab pulled into a side street, just beyond the dazzling lights of the Ritz, that fierce rival to the Buckingham Hotel, and the driver shepherded him out.

'The Deacon Club,' he announced, approaching a nondescript black door between a leather goods' shop and a gentlemen's outfitters. 'You'll be attending this place a lot, sir, but mind you don't mention it to another soul – not even your wife.'

Raymond was already aware there would have to be secrets he kept from Nancy. Such, he was told, was the cost of coming back home and spending the war in her company.

'Come with me, sir.'

The door to the Deacon Club opened up at the driver's touch, and Raymond followed him into a narrow hallway, where a concierge waited at a stark desk. This man, with his beak of a nose, did not have the look of a regular butler about him; his eyes told a different story – that lingering under the polite, officious façade was a well-trained, deadly sort of man. He ushered them deeper into the club, and onward Raymond came, up a narrow staircase, along hallways garlanded with portraits of days gone by – until, finally, he was ushered into a dining room with a bar, where gentlemen of dour appearance were taking their meals in abject silence or whispered conversation. Here the butler left them, and the driver – first instructing a waiter to pour Raymond a drink – said, 'You'll wait here, Lieutenant, while I make sure your officer is ready.'

It was too early for the whisky they poured him, but its golden hue was so appealing that Raymond allowed himself the indulgence. It slipped down like honey. There were still riches in London, then, even in this age of austerity and rationing.

Some moments later, the driver reappeared.

'You may come through now, Mr de Guise.'

Beyond the bar was another staircase, and at the top of that another hall. Raymond was ushered through the door at its end, his whisky glass still in hand, and there the driver left him with a final knowing look.

The drawing room he had entered was not so very extra-ordinary. Dominated by an enormous desk, its walls lined in books – and one particularly savage bear's head, mounted on dark, stained oak – it smelt of dust, the barbershop scent of Pinaud Clubman, and the smoke from the copious White Owl cigars which appeared to have kept the man he was visiting company through a long night.

There stood Maynard Charles: once the director of the Buckingham Hotel, now an officer with MI5; once, the man who hired Raymond to be a ballroom dancer in the fêted Grand Ballroom, now the man who was about to hire him as a spy.

'Raymond,' Maynard intoned, in his deep, plummy voice, 'welcome to your new war.'

# Chapter Two

In the Hotel Director's office, at the end of that warren of passageways behind the check-in desks of the Buckingham Hotel, a man lay dead.

Frank Nettleton – reliable hotel page, stalwart member of the hotel fire watch, sometime ballroom dancer in the glittering environs of the Grand – had only arrived at the office to deliver Mr Knave a note. It was not in the job description for a hotel page, nor a demonstration dancer, to discover dead bodies – particularly when that body had once belonged to the eternal spirit of Walter Knave, the man who had been so calmly navigating the hotel through the choppy waters of war.

The note that Frank had been holding, just a hurried memo from Douglas Guthrie – the Scottish laird currently occupying the Continental Suite – slipped free of Frank's fingers, then floated like a feather to the floor. 'Mr Knave?' Frank whispered, though it was already clear the man was dead. There he lay, in front of the desk that dominated the office, arms and legs splayed out, his face turned to the side and tinged in blue. 'Mr Knave, can you hear me?'

The note finally touched the carpet at Mr Knave's side. It had opened up as it fell. There lay the invitation to a dinner Mr Knave would never make. 'I should be honoured if you were to dine with my wife Susannah and I, at a restaurant of your choosing.' The venerable guests of the Buckingham Hotel often wanted to curry favour with management – many of these guests came time and time again, and it always reaped dividends to know the hotel director by name – but Walter Knave would not be sending an RSVP.

Frank crouched at his side. The old man had always had pallid features, but not like this. He'd run the hotel in his pomp, steering it through the unprecedented circumstances of the Great War a generation before, and only returned to his post at the outset of this fresh catastrophe.

He reached down to close the man's eyes. He'd died with them open – but apparently, closing them was more difficult in real life than it was in the pictures. Some sort of rigor must have set in, which meant the poor old man must have met his end the night before.

Frank found a blanket on the armchair by the office fire and covered him gently. He took one last look, then hurried out of the office.

It was difficult to know who to tell. In a daze, Frank picked his way along the long corridor, round the audit office, past the Benefactors Study – and out through the doors that led to reception.

The reception hall of the Buckingham Hotel was buzzing on this early winter morning. He hurried past the ornate marble archway that led into the Grand and straight down the newly restored Housekeeping hall.

He was already at the Housekeeping Lounge, where each morning chambermaids gathered to receive their rotas, when the doors opened. Immediately, the corridor was filled with dozens of chattering chambermaids. A good number of the girls cuffed him around the shoulder and said hello as they passed – for

Frank was often to be seen, of an evening, in the chambermaids' kitchenette, high up in the Buckingham's rafters, taking tea and toast with the girl he one day intended to marry.

There she was now: Rosa Bright, her heart-shaped face framed by hair as dark as her eyes. He'd been stepping out with her ever since he first came to the Buckingham Hotel, dancing with her in the clubs, sharing stolen moments, dreaming about the life they would one day live together. Rosa was a little older than Frank, though she seemed eternally sixteen – fiery, impassioned, and eager to embark upon every adventure life gave her. Her face lit up upon seeing Frank – 'I can't wait for dancing at the Midnight Rooms tonight!' – but, when Frank did not immediately respond, she clutched his hand and said, 'Frankie?' Her accent had softened of late, but there was still the estuary twang of sunny Southend in her voice. 'Frankie, what happened?'

'I – I c-can't say...'

Frank looked to move past, squeezing her hand in reassurance, but Rosa already knew something was dreadfully wrong; Frank had conquered his stammer, but it always crept back in when he was agitated.

'Is N-Nancy through there?'

Rosa put her arms around him and whispered in his ear, 'Come and find me later. I'm on the fifth floor.'

He kissed her on the cheek as she drew away, looked back at her as she hurried down the hall – and only then did he bow into the Housekeeping Lounge.

The breakfast things were still laid out across the long wooden table around which the chambermaids gathered each morning. Then he was on the other side of the Lounge, ducking through the doorway into the office.

There sat Nancy, her head in her papers, poring over budgets and rotas – all the manifold tasks that it fell to the Head of

Housekeeping to fulfil. Nancy de Guise, née Nettleton, his older sister – and the only maternal figure he'd ever known, for Frank's mother had died in childbirth, leaving Nancy to bring him up. She was a mother now herself, a working mother no less, and already carried the weight of worlds upon her shoulders – but to Frank she was the only one who would know what to do.

Upon hearing his footsteps, Nancy looked up.

She was more lined of late, weary from work and young motherhood, but immediately she knew something was wrong.

'Frank, what happened?'

So he told her it all.

Some time later, having shed the weight of responsibility, Frank shivered in the cold out on Berkeley Square, waiting for the black cab to arrive. Standing in Michaelmas Mews, the little alleyway that led from the glorious environs of the square, around the side of the hotel and to the old tradesman's entrance, he was not as sheltered from the January wind as he would have been if he'd stood beneath the hotel's grand marble colonnade – but Frank had been drilled in propriety, and knew that a simple hotel page should not be seen where lords and ladies took in their first impressions of the glorious establishment. Consequently, here he waited, in the slush and biting cold, until – what felt like an hour later – a black cab came round the square and parked only feet away from where he stood.

Frank hurried out and opened up the door.

John Hastings – the American industrialist who had become the Buckingham's principle investor and, last year, the head of the Hotel Board – hardly wanted Frank's help disembarking, but accepted it all the same. 'And you're the one who found him, are you, boy?'

Frank nodded. 'I went to deliver a note. Lord Guthrie wanted to introduce Mr Knave to his wife at dinner. I hardly thought...' He swallowed. 'I'm sorry, sir. I did the best I could. I covered him with blankets and – and – and...'

Mr Hastings, thirty-something and portly, stopped and slapped him on the back. 'I'm sure you did valiantly, young man, but I'll take it from here.'

By the time they reached the Hotel Director's office, it was late morning and the Buckingham was alive. But the news of Mr Knave's demise had been properly contained – a concierge stood at the door, tasked with sending away any who'd come to see the director. The concierge nodded at Mr Hastings and Frank, then stepped aside to permit them to enter.

Inside, the reverential hush was broken only by the voice of Doctor Evelyn Moore, narrating to Nancy – who stood, a willing doctor's assistant, against the outer wall, taking notes. The good doctor, who was paid a retainer's fee by the hotel and attended to its guests' every ailment, crouched on the floor by the cadaver, taking measurements, making inspections, and thinking out loud. Aside from Nancy and Moore, only two other figures were in attendance: the audit and night managers, the most senior left on site. The secret would have to be revealed – and quickly, before rumour took hold – but at least the narrative might be controlled. That was as important in an establishment like the Buckingham as it was in the halls of Westminster itself.

'Mr Hastings,' Doctor Moore began. He was a wispy fellow, towering at more than six and a half feet, with dignified greying hair and a kindly undertaker's look. 'We can rule out foul play, I'm pleased to say. Mr Knave was a man of a certain vintage. Eighty-four years old this summer, and still toiling hard. His ticker hasn't been in the finest of conditions for some time – and a man's sense of duty can keep him alive only so long. I'm afraid he went to his maker before midnight last night. By the look of things, he'd stayed to keep up with his paperwork.' Doctor Moore gestured to the files and papers still open on the office desk. 'My guess is he didn't know much about it. Here one minute, gone the next. There are worse ways for a man to go.'

Mr Hastings crouched at Knave's side, and whispered some prayer of his own.

'Have we notified his next of kin?' he ventured.

'Not yet, sir,' the audit manager replied.

'And do we have procedures for death?'

The audit and night managers only looked at each other glumly. In the end, it was Nancy who weighed in. 'There are protocols for deaths in the suites.' A hotel had to have them, and every lowly chambermaid was made aware of them from their first day on the job. Secrecy was of utmost importance, for no new guest wanted to learn that, days before, a man had gone to sleep in their suite and not woken the next morning. Death, or rumour of death, left an indelible stain that it was difficult to shake off – so secrecy was taken very seriously indeed.

'What are they?' Hastings enquired.

'A judgement call is made: when can the body be removed, with the least visibility? It tends to be the dead of night, or else when dinner is being served.' Nancy sighed, sadly. 'Times when decorum is most easily maintained.'

'He'll be missed long before the day is out,' said Hastings, thinking out loud.

'He's due to take luncheon with Mr Bancroft at one,' chipped in the audit manager. 'Mr Bancroft's a regular guest – he's staying with us off and on until the end of summer.'

'Then he's meant to address the dancers in the Grand,' Frank recalled. 'To talk about our plans for the ballroom this summer.'

Hastings drew himself back to his feet. 'Then we must act swiftly. Frank, those plans will need cancelling. Blame it on sickness for the day. Can you do that, boy?'

Frank nodded.

Mr Hastings gazed around the room, fixing each of his audience with a pointed look. 'I say it too often, but we sit at a critical juncture in the life and times of this hotel. My countrymen are coming to the war. That means they're coming to London in their droves – and bringing with them all the might, and money, of the New World. I'm quite certain Mr Knave would understand and forgive us for thinking of the hotel in this moment. It was, after all, the work of his life to keep this establishment afloat. But the Buckingham must win this custom. I will not let the Savoy take the spoils. I will not come second to the Imperial or the Ritz. I will not let this fine man's death derail us from our duty to each other – nor expose any weakness for those lesser establishments out there to exploit.' He closed his eyes, kneaded his forehead, lost himself in thought for but a few moments. 'Go back to your posts,' he finally declared, 'and spread the word: an all-staff meeting after the kitchens and bars have closed tonight, every soul in the Buckingham Hotel to gather in the Grand, after the last dance. And Nancy?'

Nancy looked at him and nodded.

'I'm afraid you're the one I trust most, so I'll have to ask you to help with the grisliest matter at hand.' Hastings paused. 'I'm going to need your help to remove Mr Knave, for the very last time, from his office.'

# Chapter Three

Maynard Charles had not aged considerably since the last time he and Raymond met, but that was only because nature had, from his earliest years, blessed him with the hangdog countenance of one much older. If anything, he had grown into his lugubrious – yet dignified – air. Now he stood in oak brown trousers and braces, an off-white shirt open at the collar, his sleeves rolled up like a man who had been attending to some unbecoming business just moments before. Evidently he'd been wearing a dark red tie at some point, because there it lay, pooled on the desk between mountains of files.

'It's strange to see your face again,' Maynard began, drawing on the fat cigar in his hand, 'and in such different circumstances. But my officers tell me you performed admirably in your initial instruction, so at least our business is already begun.'

Raymond was caught off guard. It seemed, then, that there were to be no pleasantries; that his return to active service in Great Britain was to be every bit as swift and efficient as his time at war. It would be far-fetched to call Maynard Charles a friend, but he was surprised by how urgent and brusque the older man was being.

'They were very efficient, sir. Your officers were waiting for me at the dockside to whisk me away to their camp in Salisbury. I'd imagined I might get to go home first, sir. My wife gave birth while I was in the desert. I'm yet to meet my son.'

Maynard Charles merely arched an eyebrow. 'I'm aware of your family situation. It is my business to be aware of every tiny detail. You need not worry, Raymond. Your son is in good health. Your wife stands on her own two feet. She always was a strong woman. You'll see them soon enough, but I'm afraid you'll have to wait a little longer. You're in my service now, Raymond. King and Country comes before home and hearth.'

Raymond said, 'They made that very clear to me in Salisbury, sir – and I don't question it.'

Two weeks he'd been there, two long weeks of training quite unlike anything he'd done before. Basic infantry training drilled your body, but this had been the kind of training to drill the mind, to make a liar out of an honest man, to show him every underhand technique; training designed to turn a soldier into a spy.

Maynard Charles reached for the decanter on his desk. Apparently there was to be no tea this morning – for meetings like these, only brandy would do.

'We've come a long way since our days at the Buckingham Hotel.'

Sometimes it felt as if that esteemed establishment, with its glorious white façade and the copper turrets that made it look as if the building itself was wearing a crown, was the centre of the world. Raymond could still remember the day he'd been summoned to the hotel – the rumour already spreading around London that the Buckingham Board had invested in construction of a new ballroom – and been shown into the cavernous interior of the Grand. 'I should like it were you and Hélène to be my stars,' Maynard had said. Hélène Marchmont: the glacial beauty, Raymond's partner in dance, who had shared in his greatest accolades. Maynard didn't understand dance; he didn't understand song, and spectacle – nor even, really, joy – but he *did* understand that you had to treasure a prized investment, and Raymond was his greatest asset in the Grand. They'd worked together for nearly ten years, ending only with the onset of war – when both were called to take the King's shilling, albeit in very different worlds.

'Has it really been three years?' Maynard said, with the world weariness that came so naturally to him.

'Less, sir – though time feels very different these days.'

'It does indeed. It slows down and speeds up at the will of this war – and now, Raymond,' he tipped back his chin and took the brandy in one big gulp, 'it's changing again. You've been fighting your war in North Africa – but there's war here in London as well. And I don't mean the bombs from above…'

Now it was Raymond's turn to take his brandy. It warmed every corner of him.

'I know, sir. They explained my commission when I got to Salisbury. The shadow war, they called it. One fought with whispers and rumour, not guns and tanks.'

'The war against our own,' Maynard said, with a sigh. 'You were still stranded in France when we first rounded up Britain's own fascists. There were plenty who slipped the net, of course. Money always buys freedoms. And since then, I'm afraid, we have seen no shortage of men preparing for our new Nazi rulers. God willing, the story of this war will be one of Britain rising triumphant from the darkness, but there will be a litany of untold stories – stories of traitors and turncoats in our midst. It's those stories I'm tasked with putting a stop to, before the full tale gets told.'

'I'm ready for the fight, sir. You don't need to doubt it.'

'Things have moved on since the beginning. Back then, every traitor in Britain was happy to *advertise* the fact they hated our way of life. Mosley and his Union of Fascists. Ramsay and his Right Club. They were *proud* of it, waving their flags for the future they wanted.' Maynard paused. 'These days they play a quieter game. Sedition is not as spectacular as once it was, but it's still sedition. Mr Churchill might have the Empire lined up behind him, but there are others working to rout him. Admiral Domville might be interned, but there are still plenty who would see him installed as Mr Hitler's puppet if Britain was to become a Protectorate of the Reich. Don't believe for a second that men don't congregate in London with the express intent of bringing Mr Churchill to heel. Don't believe there aren't people here who want to see stormtroopers goose-stepping down Horse Guards Parade.' Maynard smiled. 'Which brings me neatly back to you, and our beloved Buckingham Hotel.'

'It sometimes seems as if all roads in my life go back to the Buckingham, sir.'

'It is the business of my department to have eyes and ears all over London. I have men working for me in places low and high. I have my men in the munitions factories and railyards; I have men in universities and churches. But, right now, I have no eyes and ears in the Buckingham Hotel – and it has become of paramount importance that this is corrected.' He paused. 'The Buckingham Hotel is a playground for the powerful, the wealthy, the elite.'

'Ever since its inception,' Raymond returned. 'It's what I was hired for. To win their custom with elegance and poise.'

'Well, now you must win their confidences in the same manner – then bring their secrets back to me.'

Salisbury had been full of it: every conversational gambit and tactic interrogated in intimate detail, drilling Raymond so that he might open up hearts and minds, then plunder every secret.

'Unfortunately, as you have seen, men of high standing are not always immune to the temptations of treachery. A certain Lord Tavistock has been using the Candlelight Club of late, hosting his nefarious meetings. His are the purse strings behind various fascist causes we seek to undermine. Or take a trip over to the Savoy. I'm breaking protocol here, Raymond, but I do it to impress upon you the importance of our crusade: a certain young US diplomat was recently intercepted trading thousands of private communiqués between the leadership of this nation and the White House. So you see, I need a man on the ground. You're of more use here than you ever were in North Africa. There are a hundred others who can serve in your stead out there. Only *you* can give me what I need in the Buckingham Hotel. That playground of princes has become a sorting house for spies.'

At that moment, the door of the little drawing room opened and a lean, angular man, with dark, darting eyes shuffled in, a pile of papers in his hands.

'Ah, Mr Charles, I see I've kept you waiting.'

'Not at all, Mr Croft,' Maynard replied – and, standing, sought to introduce the man to Raymond. 'Mr Croft, meet my old compatriot, Raymond de Guise. Raymond's been fighting the Boche between Tripoli and Tobruk much of this last year, but as you know, his skills are needed elsewhere.'

'Well, Mr de Guise,' smiled the man named Croft, offering Raymond the limpest handshake of his lifetime, 'I'm the one tasked with bringing you home without questions.'

Raymond wasn't sure he understood. 'I'm already home.'

'Oh yes, but there'll be people asking *why*. Not just your family and friends, though you'll be required to keep them in the dark as to your true purpose. There are authorities to satisfy. The conscription board, for one. I have your replacement papers here.' Mr Croft splayed out the papers he'd brought with him and started detailing them to Raymond and Maynard, one by one. 'An honourable discharge, so that your history shows you as the hero you're going to be. How confident are you at keeping a cover story, Raymond?'

Raymond's eyes darted around. He was about to reply when, suddenly, Maynard Charles waded in: 'When I first approached Raymond to be my star dancer in the Grand, I was under the impression he was the minor son of some French aristocrat. Raymond *de Guise*, you see. Little did I know, back then, that he was really one of the sons of Whitechapel – a rabble rouser in the East End, who'd simply been tutored for the ballroom by a Frenchman. It was that Frenchman who convinced feral Ray Cohen he should become the debonair *de Guise*. Yes, I'd say Raymond here is adept enough at sticking to a story.'

'Well,' Croft said, guardedly, 'this one mustn't be exposed – not even to your nearest and dearest.' And he moved on to another set of papers. 'Your medical report, from doctors stationed at the barracks at Kasr-el-Nil.'

Raymond hadn't once been to the field hospital, except in the service of injured friends.

'Mr de Guise,' Croft went on, 'you are now completely deaf in your left ear, and the hearing in your right has been impacted as well. You'll find the details of the incident in which you sustained these injuries on pages three and four. Memorise it before you leave this room. You'll be telling the story over and again, and I'll be testing you on it before the day is done.'

Raymond's eyes roamed over the paper. Something about a bomb overturning the military convoy in which he'd been travelling.

'You understand why?'

Raymond nodded. 'You need an injury that gets me discharged, but doesn't require me crippled for life.'

'I need you dancing,' Maynard Charles chipped in.

Raymond nodded. 'Deafness at this scale might easily impact my timing in the ballroom, but I think I could make it look real.'

'A champion, triumphing against the odds,' smiled Mr Croft, warming to his theme. 'I'm sure an artiste of your calibre can sell that story. Count yourself fortunate: one of my colleagues suggested a little surgical adjustment, to make one of your eyes blinded and milky. You might have ended up wearing a patch.'

'I need him handsome,' Maynard cut in. 'People spill secrets to the beautiful. It is an unfortunate facet of human nature, but we distrust those to whom we're not attracted.'

Raymond looked up from the paperwork. 'Nancy's bound to see through it.'

'You're to see that she doesn't,' Mr Croft snapped, and stood to leave. 'Come downstairs when you're finished, Mr de Guise. I'm afraid there are some more tests we have to work through before we can set you loose. I need to know how well your story holds up. I need to poke and prod at it from every angle. We'll have you back to that wife of yours by day's end, I'm sure, but not until we're satisfied your head's where it needs to be.'

As soon as they were alone, Maynard softened.

'I know it's going to take some adjusting to, Raymond, but you truly will be a valuable asset.'

'I hope so, sir.'

'You'll never be able to say what you did for King and Country, but there's a certain pride in that. You'll come to feel it in time.'

Raymond nodded, 'How am I to get back into the Buckingham, sir? Things have moved on since I left the ballroom. The troupe is different now. It has new leadership, new direction.'

'Make overtures, as soon as you can, to the management at the hotel. Use your wife if you must. Bully and cajole them, if that doesn't work. Use your nous and find a way. But I expect you to be dancing again long before this winter beats its retreat. I expect you to be dancing, listening, and reporting to me – and me alone.' Maynard Charles reached out and gripped him by the hand. 'I know it won't be easy, Raymond. We are under no misapprehensions about that. Much has changed in London since you left. Your home, your work, your old world – much of it will feel unfamiliar in the weeks and months to come. But this is how you serve, Raymond. Find a way back into the ballroom. Find a way back into the glitz and the glamour of the lifestyle you left behind.' Maynard released his hand. 'Welcome back to the war, Raymond. Welcome back to the dance.'

# Chapter Four

Max Allgood, the fêted – though still, he liked to think, *improbable* – leader of the Buckingham Hotel's orchestra, was proud of his jowls. Though it hadn't been scientifically proven, he devoutly believed that the quality of a trombonist's musicianship correlated directly with the quality of his jowls. Right now, as afternoon ticked towards evening in his new lodgings at No 62 Albert Yard, he was admiring both the girth of his jowls and the polish of his trombone in the upright mirror. He'd be glad to get back to playing tonight. The Christmas festivities at the Buckingham Hotel already seemed a long time ago, and the first slow weeks of January had passed in a blur. There was spring to look forward to, a ball for Midsummer's Night – his first full year in charge of the orchestra in the Grand Ballroom. So many things had slipped through Max's fingers on his rise to the top, but he meant to make this year count.

He put Lucille to his lips.

Her song rang out, through the open window, over the rooftops of Lambeth. London sat under a grey shroud as evening drew near, but Max's music spoke of long summer nights, raucous dancing out under the stars. He'd been determined to bring something American to the music of London ever since he was summoned to the Buckingham. The news that the

Americans were at last joining the war, and that platoons of them would soon be coursing into London, only gave him yet more conviction: the future was the jitterbug, the jive, the wild jazz and swing he'd played in the bars of the Bowery, Chicago, New Orleans.

So engrossed was he in making Lucille take flight that he didn't hear the engine, at first. Indeed, it wasn't until a car door slammed, and he heard a familiar voice remonstrating with its driver, that the music died, and he carried Lucille to the attic window, there to look down upon the street below.

Albert Yard had been devastated in the bombings of two Christmases ago, and the scars could still be seen up and down the street – but the ugliest thing on show was the young man who, having climbed out of a taxicab, was now ungraciously explaining why he didn't have the money to pay for the fare.

Max was still watching him, his heart growing heavier with each volley from below, when the bedroom door opened up – and in marched his cousin Ava. She was a big woman, bold in both body and soul, and the floorboards quaked where she trod. She'd been his companion across the ocean, across the dance halls of the Continent – the mastermind, he wasn't embarrassed to admit, of their ascent at the Buckingham Hotel. Max was as talented a trombonist as any who had ever played, but his musical flair was matched by his business ineptitude. Ava, meanwhile, had an acumen honed in the less salubrious quarters of New York.

She jostled Max out of the way, looked down out of his window, and stoutly shook her head.

'Here comes trouble. You'd think he might have the good grace and gratitude to not cause a *situation* before he's even put his foot through the door. Nelson!' she cried out, her voice big and brash, as loud as Lucille. 'Nelson Allgood, you stand to attention down there! That man don't deserve your cursing.' Then she withdrew her head from the window and declared, 'Fish some farthings out o' your pocket, Max. We'll bail him out of this one, but after that he'll have to pay his way.'

Max waited until his cousin was gone, then placed Lucille tenderly back in her case. 'I see he's brought my trumpet, at least,' he told her. 'You don't need to get jealous now, Lucille, but it'll be good to have Tommy back. You got to keep your family around.'

With Lucille happily at rest, Max waddled – he'd been a little bow-legged ever since birth – out of the bedroom and down the attic stairs, following Ava to the ground floor. It had been mere weeks since he and his cousin had taken up residence here, and the truth was he still felt like a guest – so, when he passed Mrs Orla Brogan in the hall, he bowed down to her like a good lodger should. The Brogan family were stalwarts of the Buckingham Hotel, with two of their children working there – the others were out in Suffolk, where they'd been sent at the start of the war – and had been happy to take lodgers into the big, empty house. They'd told Max, more than once, to treat the place like his own – but if they'd seen the way he used to live, back in Chicago and New York, they might have thought twice about that particular instruction. Max might have been the leader of the orchestra at the grandest hotel in London, but he'd grown up in lice-infested flophouses, done a long stint in a juvenile penitentiary, and slept in too many barns and bus stations to mention. The road to the top was not as gilded for a Black musician from New Orleans as it was for an upper-crust Englishman born to titles and wealth.

Ava was already out of the front door and into the gathering dark. By the time Max waddled through, she had managed to placate the taxi driver – though Nelson still fumed, bouncing from foot to foot, by the kerb.

'See, I *told* you we were upstanding. I *told* you you'd get paid. Uncle Max,' Nelson called, as Max shambled past, 'these people got no respect for an upstanding man. Pay him his fare, won't you? I promised him *double* if he'd only stop yapping.'

'You did *what?*' sighed Max, who wasn't remotely surprised.

'I got to get that devil off my back. This is new beginnings, Uncle Max – but it's same old attitudes, everywhere you turn!'

Max could smell the liquor on his breath – so, he supposed, it wasn't *really* a new beginning after all. The boy was supposed to have come in on the morning train; they'd thought him delayed, but evidently it was an alehouse in London town that had delayed him. Thank God some ne'er-do-well hadn't taken off with the trumpet.

Max palmed every coin he had in his pocket to the driver and tried not to grizzle too much at his nephew as he retreated into the house. 'Same old attitudes sure is right,' he muttered. 'You know, Nelson – you ever heard what the English say? You always bring the weather with you.'

Nelson slumped through the front door. 'What do you mean, Uncle Max?'

'It means … *you're* the storm; wherever you wander, the rain comes down. But I suppose you ought to come here,' and he opened his arms. 'We've missed you, boy.'

Max was still holding Nelson in a bear hug when Ava came back through the door, dusting her hands down. 'Good riddance to bad rubbish,' she said, as the engine of the taxi flared outside. 'Was he that rude to you on the journey, Nelson?'

'Oh, *worse*,' Nelson grinned, emerging from his uncle's arms. 'These English don't know *manners*. They just know the idea of it. It's like they practised being polite so much they've forgotten who's real people and who's...'

Nelson blanched, for another face had appeared in the living room now: Orla Brogan, pale and white, with a great basket of laundry in her arms.

'I beg your pardon, ma'am,' he ventured, bowing ridiculously low. 'I didn't mean nothing bad against your countrymen. I'm sure there's good English too.'

Orla rolled her eyes. 'Oh, you don't need to worry about that. I'm *Irish*.' She walked on through, deposited the laundry in the kitchen, and peeked her head back round the corner.

'So this is home?' Nelson said, taking in the cluttered front room, the staircase tucked behind, the great hearth where the embers of last night's fire still glowed. 'You know, I figured that, when I finally came to join you, I'd be getting my quarters at the Buckingham Hotel.' He eyeballed his mother and uncle searchingly. 'I figured I'd have some palace of a suite. There'd be a chambermaid to turn down my bedcovers. Maybe a concierge to feed me grapes.'

Ava clipped him round the ear; she'd been doing that ever since he was knee-high, and it didn't look like she'd be stopping it any time soon. 'Things changed,' she said, 'but you can be grateful for this place. We sure are.' She made sure Mrs Brogan had heard before she went on. 'The Brogans have put a roof over our head – and yours – and all they ask for is a little in board, and that we pool our rations. It's a *very* nice living – nicer than you've had this past year, I shouldn't wonder, sleeping on floors and in closets, by the look of you. Billy works up at the Buckingham with his sister Annie – they can get just about anything we might need, even off ration. Don't ask me how – the job comes with perks – but that Billy, he's got the golden touch.'

38

In the kitchen doorway, Orla Brogan smiled, 'We wouldn't even have this house without our Billy.'

'So you're to treat the place with the same respect you'd treat your own.' Ava paused. 'On second thoughts, you're to treat the place with *more* respect than you'd treat your own – much, *much* more.'

Nelson had the look of a curious dog about him as he prowled the edges of the room, seemingly sniffing every corner. 'It's better than Bristol,' he said. 'Better than those digs in Manchester when I was playing at the Ritz.'

Max's eyes goggled. 'You played piano at the Manchester Ritz?'

'I stepped in for some lag who'd had too many whiskies.'

Max said, '*You* smell like you've had too many whiskies, and it's not yet five o'clock.'

'A little toast to coming to London town, that's all it is!' Nelson beamed. 'The Manchester Ritz is a swish ol' place, Uncle Max. Almost every dance band worth anything's played there. I'm just not sure they were *ready* for these . . .' And he lifted up his hands, to wiggle his fingers.

So, thought Max, he'd not lost any of his obnoxiousness since they'd been apart. Nelson had been playing in clubs and dance halls wherever he could, anywhere that might pay him enough for his supper – and, if he was lucky, a roof over his head – but hard times hadn't drilled the bad manners out of him.

'I'll bet it's not nearly as fine a gig as the Buckingham Hotel. Now, *there's* a place you'll remember. They don't pay you in rum at a place like *that*.' Nelson looked from his mother to his uncle with a radiant smile. 'So, when do I start?'

There was silence in the front room. Max slumped into one of the armchairs, kneading his brow wearily. Not even Ava could meet her son's expectant eyes. As for Orla Brogan, she had decided that now was the right moment to get on with that laundry.

'See, there's been a problem with that,' Ava began. 'Max, why don't you tell the boy?'

'*Me?*' baulked Max, who wished suddenly he had Lucille back in his hands.

Nelson's smile was suddenly a little less radiant. 'You're starting to sound like those dance-hall managers I been dealing with. They always deal bad hands. Ma, what's going on?'

Ava just looked at Max – and Max had never been able to weather that demanding look for long, so at last he said, 'I gotta get there soon. We're playing tonight. Nelson,' and he stood up, making for the door, 'we can talk about it later. I won't be back until midnight, mind – and that's gambling on the sirens not singin'…'

Max was hurrying for the stairs to collect Lucille from above, but Ava slipped suddenly into his path. 'The boy deserves the truth.'

'You ain't holding out on me, are you, Uncle Max? I thought we had a deal? You and Ma get yourself settled up at that hotel, and then you find a place for me so's I can follow. That's what you *said*, isn't it? And – and I know for a *fact*, a god damn *fact*, that your old pianist's on the out. He left before Christmas, and you had to fill in, Uncle Max. They're talkin' about it everywhere. Max Allgood put down Lucille and tinkled the ivories for the Christmas Ball. Well? *Didn't* you?'

Max had the heaviest of hearts. 'It's not been simple, boy. Now's not the right moment.'

Nelson's eye had started twitching, just as it did when he heard those clerks making certain vile inferences on the Paddington train. 'Then what in the name of hell did I come here for? No,

Uncle Max – no, you *owe* me. You can't flake out on a promise. You said you'd make me a star.'

'Star?' Ava clipped him round the ear again; she was the only one who could get away with it. 'You been in the gutter so long, and you're still thinking about stars? No, Nelson. We ran into a little trouble last year. It may have escaped your notice, but we're not bunking at the Buckingham Hotel any more. Things got a little strained. Max here's been fortunate to keep his job, and that's only because management figures they need some American pizazz now our countrymen are coming to the war.' She was tempted to give Max a clip round the ear as well, because he had slipped past her and was already hoisting his way back up the stairs. Instead, she exasperatedly went to hug her son. 'I know it's disappointing, but we've got to keep our hands nice and clean, got to prove to management we can be trusted. If there's one thing these English hate, it's *drama.*'

'Ma!' Nelson yelled. 'I'm hardly the sort of man who makes dramas!'

At that moment, Max reappeared, cradling Lucille in his arms. 'Uncle, you *promised.*'

'And I ain't reneged on that promise. I don't intend to. But this is the situation we're in, so we've got to contend with it. Look, I'm going to help you, Nelson. London's the place for you. It's where those God-given talents o' yours can shine.' He crossed the room, until he was almost at the front door. 'But it ain't at the Buckingham Hotel – not now. This isn't New York. We stuffed it up in New York. Good Lord, boy, we've crossed half a world to start again – and right, smack, into the middle of a war. Let's not stuff it up again.'

'Well, it's nice my own family have so much *faith!*' Nelson crowed.

'Oh, I got faith in your music,' Max told him, one foot already out of the door. 'It's the rest that takes some convincing. Let's not get started on the wrong foot here, boy. You get work in the clubs round here, you show what you're worth, you get yourself a reputation for wild, magnetic shows on stage – and *clean livin'* off of it – and then *maybe* we can talk about you joining us up at the Buckingham Hotel.'

With those words, Max skedaddled out of the door, dancing his way down the street as fast as his bowed legs would carry him.

In the sitting room, Ava looked – with some modicum of sympathy – at her son.

'You got that look about you again, the one that says you've been hard done by, that the world isn't giving you what it ought.'

Nelson threw his arms open wide. 'Story of my life, Ma! The one and only story of my *life!*'

Max was grateful when he reached the Buckingham Hotel, the winter dark now smothering Berkeley Square. It wasn't that he'd been dreading Nelson's arrival – the boy, after all, was family – but there'd been a certain trepidation which came with knowing he'd have to break his promises. The fact was, Nelson was a whirlwind on the piano. A prodigy, no less. It was his character that was lacking. Now, Max was understanding about that as well; he'd hardly led an exemplary life – but at least his periods in peril had been born out of circumstances, not weakness and temptation. Nelson was as talented a musician as Max – but the difference was, Max hadn't really *known* how talented he was, not until some of the wildness of youth had already passed him by. Nelson, meanwhile, had grown up with the surefire knowledge he was one of the greats – and, with that, came a sort of moral weakness. He was given to flattery, too easily slighted, too prone to being led down dark alleys. No, there wasn't any way Max could trust him here at the hotel. This post, the job of a lifetime – the one that might save him from penury and privation, the fate of so many old musicians – mattered too much. One day, Nelson might be ready – but that day was not today.

Backstage, the other musicians were already gathering, tuning up ready for the evening's entertainment. Among them came Jack Lovegrove, the first of the early season's guest pianists. He wasn't as good as Nelson – Max was distinctly aware of that – but inspiration wasn't what he needed, not right now; no, what he needed was dependability, reliability, a solid work ethic – and Jack brought all three.

The dance troupe was gathering too. At their head stood the titanic Marcus Arbuthnot, a champion from days gone by. Marcus stood as tall and statuesque as a fairytale prince, with a mane of russet-gold hair. At his side stood the Austrian beauty Karina Kainz – and, behind them, the elfin Mathilde Bourchier, lost in conversation with her partner Frank. Max wasn't certain, but there seemed a strange atmosphere in the dressing rooms tonight.

The hour was almost nigh. Max rallied his musicians, marched them to the doors, and declared, 'Gentlemen, the hour has come!'

Across the dressing rooms, Marcus Arbuthnot nodded too. The champion dancer was the scion of a family famed in repertory theatre, and had inherited some of his father's grandiose gestures. 'This New Year has much to be hopeful for,' he had declared, his booming voice reaching dancer and musician alike. 'A new beginning in the ballroom, and a new beginning for the world. It is dark out there, my friends. January casts its shroud over this city we love. But let us conjure light and magic, for a few short hours. Let us remind the world what lies beyond war!'

Max was not the kind of man to get swept up in such ostentatious speeches, but he admired the theatricality of it. He admired Marcus's mastery of the troupe as well. He'd only been in station a little longer than Max – coming to the hotel to take over from the Grand's long-standing king, Raymond de Guise, when war was declared – but he had refashioned the troupe in his own image. It belonged to him now.

It was the musicians who filed out first. Before he opened the doors to meet the applause, Max caught Marcus's eye and said, 'Maybe we should take a little tipple after the show tonight?'

'I'm not sure there's scope for a drink this evening, Mr Allgood, as delectable as that sounds,' Marcus purred, his voice dripping with honey. 'There's an all-hands meeting, to be held after the ballroom's clear. They're summoning every soul.'

Max rolled his eyes. 'Mr Knave didn't tell me.'

Marcus looked at him with deep, thoughtful eyes. 'The strange thing is, Max, it isn't Mr Knave who summoned us.' Then he paused, meaningfully – as if here was some secret to which neither of them were privy. 'It's Mr Hastings, of the Hotel Board.'

But there was no more time to speak of it then, for the moment had come.

Max opened the doors.

He led the musicians out.

Here stood the Grand in all its glory. Across the sprung dance floor they came, parading in front of the great and the good, the lords and ladies and ministers for the Crown who made this place their playground. Chandeliers glittered. Champagne corks flew. The applause was like a storm, leading Max and his musicians to the stage.

As soon as he climbed onto the stage, he put Lucille to his lips, and as she sang, out came the dancers – in twirling pairs, each presenting themselves at the head of the dance floor, before the music truly began.

Then, all the worries about Nelson, all the curiosity of the evening's meeting to come, simply faded away.

This was why Max was here.

This was why he was in the business at all.

He lost himself in a frenzy of music and dance, for all the hours to come.

And the Buckingham's garlanded guests?

Well, they lost themselves as well.

# Chapter Five

London by night. Was it wrong that Raymond had missed this?

He'd been confined, most of the day, to the back room of the Deacon club on Piccadilly, while Mr Croft and other members of B Branch assessed his capabilities, and especially the tenacity with which he might maintain his cover. And yet, every time he'd turned his back and they'd tossed out some other question, he'd answered without hesitation. 'That's the challenge,' they said. 'That's where the cracks will start to show. You're half-deaf now, lieutenant. You need other prompts to understand. If someone calls your name from the other side of the Candlelight Club, you mustn't flinch. If some guest is talking to you in the hubbub of the ballroom, you must absorb everything they say – but only ever respond as if it's on the very edges of your hearing. Do you understand?'

Raymond wasn't arrogant enough to believe he would be exemplary from the start. Nor was he worried about maintaining his cover at large; it was lying to Nancy that was needling at him. He'd been a whole year away from his marriage. In that time, his child had been born. The world, *his* world, had moved on without him – and he didn't like the idea of how it would feel, trying to build bridges across the chasm of the last year, and yet lying to her all the time. Not quite fitting in in the ballroom was one thing – but not fitting in with his family was quite another.

As he left the club and strolled through the blackout, marching in the shadows of the barrage balloons above Green Park, he tried to imagine how it would be.

His life was being handed back to him.

He just didn't know how to feel.

His feet had taken him north, through the townhouses of Mayfair, onto the very edge of Berkeley Square. A few short years ago, you could have seen the lights spilling out of the Buckingham Hotel. Now, it sat in its own cloak of darkness – but the faint swing of the orchestra could be heard through the ballroom walls. Beyond the blackouts, they drank and danced.

A lifetime had passed since he went through those doors.

A lifetime, since he thought of it as his own.

Even the music was different now. It wasn't Archie Adams leading the orchestra beyond those walls. It had a new stridency, a new urgency, all of it led by a wild trombone solo. It would be interesting to dance to that, thought Raymond.

He hadn't expected its pull on him to be so great. In that moment, he wanted nothing more than to stray through the doors, to glide into the Grand and let the old sensations wash over him again.

But no – he stopped himself.

His time to venture back through those doors would surely come.

But tonight?

Tonight was for family. Tonight was for the people he cherished most of all – and, by this late hour, Nancy was surely already at home, tending to their infant son.

There'd be nothing to interrupt him this time.

He was going back *home*.

With the faint music from the Grand still echoing in his ears, Raymond backed away from the Buckingham Hotel and continued his long march north.

Only a few songs after Raymond vanished from Berkeley Square, Max Allgood led his orchestra to their final triumphant number of the night, then they stood together on stage as the dancers and musicians soaked up the applause.

Frank Nettleton's heart had been soaring but, as soon as the music ended, reality resumed. He wasn't yet off the dance floor, Mathilde gliding giddily alongside him, when he *remembered*. It had been easy to pretend none of it had happened while he danced, but now that he skipped back into the dressing room, it was only too clear:

The day had started in death.

The secret was growing heavier by the hour.

'Mr Nettleton,' Marcus Arbuthnot declared, grasping Frank as he came back through the dance-floor doors. 'A fine evening, young man. I've some notes to give you on your footwork during 'Heaven Sent', but these are the most minor of details. Mr Nettleton, were this war not occupying every hour of every day, you might be championship material.'

Marcus's words melted some of the worry in his heart. 'Really, sir?' *Championship material*. It was what he'd been dreaming of, ever since he started doing the demonstration dances in the Grand. 'I think it's Mr Allgood's music, sir. It just... moves me.'

It was more than that. It was Marcus as well. Frank had grown in confidence under his tutelage, grown stronger and leaner and more technically capable too. There'd been a time when Frank was at his best dancing in the clubs of Soho with Rosa in his arms – when dance was just wild and instinctive and free – but the ballroom demanded more polish and elegance

than a young man could cultivate without the steadying hand
of a mentor. If Max Allgood's music inspired Frank, Marcus's
technical knowledge kept him improving.

'Perhaps, Frank, once this war is over…' Marcus winked.

'Yes, sir?'

'Well, the world will be needing some joy. I still remember
the years after the Great War. I'd never known headiness like
it. There might be opportunities for you, young man. Perhaps,
after all the death, the world just needs to dance.'

All the *death*…

It wasn't Marcus's fault – he didn't yet know what had happened in this hotel – but Frank's mind tumbled back to the
morning, and the meeting about to be held in the Grand. He
supposed he'd feel lighter once the secret was shared. He didn't
like lying, and lying to Rosa felt the worst of all. Here she came
now, slipping tentatively into the dressing room to find him, as
all of the chambermaids came down from their quarters above.

'How was it tonight, Frank?' she said as she sashayed over.

'Mr Arbuthnot said I could be championship material.'

It seemed to thrill Rosa even more than it had thrilled Frank.


Raymond had often walked down these streets before – but
tonight it felt as it had when he first stalked the night-time
streets of Cairo: like he was the proverbial stranger in a strange
land.

It didn't help that the roads between Mayfair and Maida Vale
had been refashioned by bombs. The diversions he followed took
him down neighbouring roads he'd never followed before and
it struck him, as he approached his own street, that Blomfield
Road might easily have been obliterated without him knowing.
The world was such a vast place, its lines of communication

so often broken and slow, that he might be about to turn a corner – and be faced by nothing but ruins.

And yet, the moment he stepped round the corner, he did not find the smoking ruins of his mind, just the old familiar street, preserved exactly as it had been on the day that he left.

He hadn't appreciated how nervous he'd be, not until he was striding past his neighbours' homes, not until he was at the black wrought iron gate outside number 18.

He looked up.

Through the gate he came, up the garden path, onto the step directly in front of his own front door. This was *home*, but it felt so unreal. For twelve long months he'd slept in barrack buildings, makeshift camps, outposts out in the desert. How long had it been since he'd last spoken to a woman?

He didn't know why, but he realised he was lifting his fingers to knock on his *own* front door.

Inwardly, he smiled.

At least he would be making an entrance. Raymond had been good at that once: twirling into the Grand Ballroom, shoulders back and statuesque, presenting himself for the whole ballroom to see.

Footsteps tolled on the other side.

Raymond's heart lurched – and then the door opened.

But it was not Nancy who stood there. It was dark within, shadowy in the ill-lit hallway, so it took Raymond a few moments to realise who this was. She'd changed too: his sister-in-law Vivienne, short and elfin, her striking red hair now cascading around her shoulders. She looked at him inscrutably, each one of them hesitating before recognising the other. It must have been, thought Raymond, like she was seeing a ghost – and there'd been plenty of those in Vivienne's life, for she'd been married to Raymond's brother just before the start of the war, widowed by the time of Dunkirk, and haunted ever since.

'*Raymond?*' she exhaled, her accent betraying the whisper of her native New York.

'Vivienne,' Raymond replied. Behind her, he saw his nephew – Vivienne's son, Stan – burst out of the sitting room. By God, he'd grown big. At three years old, he stood nearly as tall as Vivienne's waist, and had the wolfish, rangy look that Raymond recognised so well – for Stan was a spitting image of his dearly departed brother Artie.

Vivienne reached out and took his hand, as if to make certain he was real. 'You're here,' she said. 'But Raymond,' and she had to scoop her son into her arms, for Stan had stopped dead, his bottom lip trembling at the sight of this stranger amongst them, 'what are you doing here?'

A thought hit Raymond: perhaps now was the moment to begin his act. He inclined his head, as if he hadn't quite heard, and instead of explaining straight away, he asked, 'Is Nancy here?'

Vivienne realised she was blocking his passage. Still discombobulated, she stepped back, ushering him inside.

'She's still at work. She sent word – management called everyone together, after the dancing tonight. Not just the heads of departments – everyone, from big to small.' She paused. 'Something's happening at the Buckingham – but Raymond, what on earth are you doing here? I thought – *we* thought you were still in Cairo.'

Raymond could hardly believe where he was standing. The disappointment of not being met by Nancy had hit him hard, but still it seemed like he was floating through a dream. He allowed his fingers to dance lightly across the walls, lingering on every photograph. There, framed in perfect black-and-white: an image from his wedding day, Raymond and Nancy in the centre, Vivienne and Artie just to the side.

The Grand Ballroom.

At the bottom of the stairs, he stopped and said, 'Vivienne, I'm afraid my war is over. I've been sent back home.'

Vivienne asked why, but now was not the moment; Raymond relied on his cover, and feigned that he hadn't heard. Instead, he took one step on the stairs, peering into the soft glow that came from the landing above.

'Vivienne ... my son?'

'He's sleeping. He's a good boy, Raymond. He never lets me down. Not like this one,' and she tickled Stan under the chin, 'making a riot, all day and night. Arthur's like Nancy – he's quiet, he's reflective, he's ...'

'My own son. My flesh and blood.'

Raymond supposed he ought to wait for Nancy. That was the dream of this moment: that Nancy should be the one to introduce him to their son. But his feet had other ideas. Up one step he came, then up another – until, at last, he had picked his way along the landing at the top of the stairs and hovered, breathless, at the nursery door.

He'd been a father for seven long months.

But only now would he see his son.

Raymond could hardly keep himself from smiling as he opened the door.

Nancy was among the last to reach the Grand Ballroom. As the chambermaids and concierges, the check-in attendants and kitchen staff, the pages and porters and cocktail waiters all gravitated towards the Grand, she remained hidden in the Housekeeping Office – nominally going through that day's stock-take, but in reality just resting in front of the fire. It wasn't often that she had to stay so late at the Buckingham Hotel, but the day had drained her. She'd been awake with Arthur half the night, had been longing for the empty evening ahead – but here she was, still tied to the hotel. Nancy was no stranger to the dead – she could still remember saying goodbye to the waxy body of her mother, then, many years later, closing her father's eyes after he had breathed his last – but there was something unsettling about knowing Mr Knave was gone. He'd been an old-fashioned man, steeped in the traditions of several generations before – but he'd been the one who agreed that she might remain in post as Head of Housekeeping after she fell pregnant. There weren't many men who would have made such an allowance.

He'd been the steadiest of hands on the Buckingham tiller. There had been few surprises with Mr Knave at the helm, but there'd been dependability, reliability, a spirit of *endurance*. And wasn't that what the Buckingham needed, while the world tore itself apart?

Nancy straightened her papers, locked the Lounge up behind her, then picked her way into the Grand.

The ballroom heaved.

She'd seen the ballroom at its most frenzied and energetic, but even then it wasn't as thronged as this. A chance to step into this hallowed hall did not come around very often, and the various chambermaids, porters and concierges who never ventured through its doors were enjoying gawping at the radiant chandeliers, or taking each other in hold to waltz around the dance floor. Nancy waded into the crowd, seeking out her chambermaids – and found them only when she spotted Frank. There he stood, with Rosa beside him, the group occupying one of the tables above the dance-floor balustrade.

'Stay together, girls,' said Nancy when she approached. 'I don't want to hear reports of us treating the Grand with any less respect than she deserves. I'm afraid this is going to be a very serious meeting.'

'Oh, hark at her!' Rosa laughed. 'You know what this is, don't you, Nance?'

Nancy gave her a cautionary look. Rosa was a friend, as well as Frank's sweetheart, and as a result she was often overly familiar in front of the other girls. Nancy worried that it chipped away at the respect in which the other girls held her. She made a mental note to talk about it later, and was about to tell the girls to take seats, when the great oak doors beneath the Grand's marble arch opened up, and in walked John Hastings, followed by the rest of the Hotel Board.

Hastings was the youngest of them by almost a generation. The others predated his investment in the hotel and had always, it was said, resented him for wading in with his showy American money and occupying a seat at the high table – but they followed him, now, like sub-lieutenants. Their faces were impassive as Mr Hastings reached the head of the balustrade, urging the Grand to silence with an imperiousness entirely at odds with his unremarkable appearance. Here was a man who wielded power quietly, a man of few airs and graces, a man who prized order, rigour, and the basic tenets of good business. He was not, on the surface of it, a man to bring somewhere as ostentatious as the Grand Ballroom to a standstill – and yet, that was what he did.

Up on stage, even the dance troupe and musicians were held rapt.

'Hush now, girls,' said Nancy to her staff, 'and listen to every word.' Then she threw a consoling look at Frank. She knew her brother inside and out – and Frank had been feeling the heavy load of this secret all day.

He flashed back a weak half-smile – and then Mr Hastings began.

'Ladies and gentlemen, loyal members of the Buckingham Hotel, my thanks to you for attending this meeting tonight. I can scarcely imagine what you have been thinking today, as you've been awaiting this most unusual summons – so, if you'll allow me, I am simply going to cut to the chase.' Mr Hastings took a breath, studiously surveying the crowd. 'It is my solemn duty to announce that Mr Walter Knave, whose own life story has been entangled with our beloved hotel for many long decades, passed away yesterday evening. The physicians tell us it came suddenly – that one moment he was hard at work in the service of this magnificent institution, and the next he was gone.'

John Hastings paused, and Nancy's eyes flickered around the ballroom. A strange, reverential hush had descended. Not a soul said a word. Glances were exchanged, hands were held, but not a whisper broke the silence of the Grand.

'Mr Knave was an unfussy gentleman, the kind of man I most admire: a man devoted to service, given to few personal ostentations, fastidious with detail – and eager to acknowledge, in others, the deep reserves of talent that make our Buckingham so great. When history was at its most perilous, he returned to our hotel with the methodical, understated brilliance of a man who knew he needed to prove nothing – who had a job to do, and immediately bent himself to it.

'Looking at you now, I can see the questions bubbling behind your eyes. But Mr Knave wanted no calamity in this hotel. He knew that the Buckingham's greatest strength was in providing safety, consistency and confidence – not just to our guests, but to you, our devoted staff as well. And so I have come to a decision.'

Now the whispering started – only the merest mutterings at first, thought Nancy, but soon it was spreading all around the Grand.

Mr Hastings held up his hands, inviting further silence, and continued:

'The Hotel Board met this afternoon and ratified my decision. We will not embark upon a lengthy process to hire a replacement for Mr Knave. Instead, as of this moment, I am assuming personal responsibility for the management of the hotel. To wit, ladies and gentlemen, from this moment, and until the cessation of hostilities with Nazi Germany, I am your new director. I do this for two reasons. Firstly, consistency is key. We are at a critical juncture in the story of this war, and you deserve certainty in your leadership. If war has taught we men of business anything, it is that swift, sharp decision-making is key to success. And, secondly, I hope that my own nationality will be a useful weapon as we seek to win the custom of my countrymen, even now flooding into London.' He looked around the ballroom. 'Mr Knave's family have asked for privacy as they come to terms with his loss, but they have asked me to pass on their thanks for following him with such steadfastness across the last years. We will, in due course, raise our own memorial to a man we all valued. But, until then, we have work to do – and it begins now.' He stopped, clapped his hands, and declared, 'Thank you for joining me here tonight. Sometimes, our lives are punctuated by days such as these – when everything *turns*. But tomorrow is a fresh day, and I thank you all for your service. I shall see the heads of department in the Benefactors Study at 10 a.m. Until then, goodnight, my friends.'

Then, still cloaked in the deep silence of the Grand Ballroom, John Hastings marched back through the marble arch, the rest of the Hotel Board following solemnly in his wake.

In the ballroom, the silence continued.

It was several stunned moments later that the gossiping began.

Nancy listened to the conversations flurry up around her, but tried to shut them out. Some concierge was lamenting poor Mr Knave, while a group of kitchen hands chattered on about the looks on the faces of the Hotel Board. 'They never wanted John Hastings in the first place.' 'And an American! The Yanks might like it, but there'll be plenty of toffs who don't.'

The chambermaids were slow to join in the chatter. By the time Rosa exploded, 'What does it matter for us anyway? It's still just bedsheets and brass polish. You could make a goose hotel director and we'd still just be turning down beds,' the ballroom was emptying, its attendees taking their gossip to all four corners of the hotel. Annie Brogan had scampered off to be with her sweetheart Victor, who slaved his days away in the Queen Mary kitchens. Mary-Louise and the rest just stood, awaiting instruction.

'Back to your rooms then, girls,' said Nancy. 'We've got an early start.'

Frank was about to go with them when Nancy caught his eye. 'Are you all right?' she asked.

'I don't know why it moves me so much,' he said. 'It's just one death in thousands.'

'But it's somebody we know,' said Nancy, warmly. Then she let him go. 'I'll get a taxicab, Frank. You find some corner for the night. Tea and toast, upstairs with Rosa.'

Frank had been known to steal a night's sleep on the sofas in the chambermaids' kitchenette, though he'd never crept into Rosa's room – no matter what the tittle-tattlers might say.

'Thanks, Nance,' he said, and Nancy watched him go.

The hotel had been providing taxicabs for Nancy ever since Arthur was born. That was Mr Knave's promise. She was dead on her feet tonight, and there'd be precious little rest at home.

It was quite possible that Arthur was already awake, keeping Vivienne busy by squalling for milk.

The taxicab was waiting for her by the hotel colonnade. Thank goodness the sirens weren't singing tonight, for the last thing she needed was a night in the shelter; no, what she needed was warm water for her feet, her son clutched to her breast, and hot tea to lull her to sleep.

When she reached number 18 and began to pick her way up the garden path, she heard music coming through the walls.

*Music* …

Midnight was on its approach. Arthur and Stan must have been in bed for hours. Any other night, Vivienne would be slumped asleep in the chair by the fire. And yet Nancy could hear Raymond's old favourites billowing at her through the walls: the Cab Calloway Orchestra, that record he'd brought back from New York. What was it called again? The *Jumpin' Jive* …

Nancy opened the door.

The music rolled out to meet her, just like the warmth of the fire.

'Vivienne?' she called out. 'Viv?'

But when she stepped into the sitting room, it wasn't only Vivienne she saw.

There'd been life-changing news today, but not like this.

For there sat Raymond, in the chair by the fire, their infant son asleep against his breast.

# Chapter Six

Nancy's gaze flashed madly around the room, as if she was looking for reasons not to believe her own eyes. She took three faltering steps. By now, Raymond was on his feet, and her son's eyes were opening up. Even at this distance, Arthur recognised her. In a moment, his hands were reaching out, grappling for her like he always did. It had been too long since she'd seen him.

It had been an infinite time longer since she'd seen Raymond.

Nancy dropped her bag at her side. She felt as if the room was reeling around her. 'But this doesn't make sense!' And for the first time she smiled. She couldn't stop herself. It twitched in the corners of her lips, until it broke wild and free. 'You were in Cairo.' Without looking, her hand floundered for the last letter he'd sent, propped with the others on the cabinet just behind the door. She knew, because she read them to Arthur each and every night. 'You're not meant to—'

'Oh but I am,' beamed Raymond, and dared to march across the room to meet her. 'It's me, Nancy. It's real.' Their son was between them, so he could not embrace her, not at first. 'I'm back and I'm not going anywhere. They sent me home.'

Nancy could find no further words, not until Vivienne swept between them, coaxed Arthur back into her own arms, and promised to get him settled. 'You two need a minute.' Moments later, she could be heard taking him back up the stairs – and, for the first time, Raymond and Nancy were alone, with only the sounds of Cab Calloway's Orchestra to envelop them.

'It doesn't make any sense.' Her disbelief, perhaps even trepidation, was giving way to the giddiest of feelings. Her head had been lying snugly against Raymond's shoulder, but now she looked up, trying to find his eyes. Her fingers ran around the contours of his face. 'You didn't send word. There was no telegram, no letter, no...'

'I wanted to, but it hasn't been... straightforward.' *I've been back for two weeks*, he wanted to tell her. *They've had me billeted in Salisbury, sitting in seminars, listening to lectures, drilling me in the tradecraft of spies.* But instead, he just held her. He owed her an explanation, but the longer he put it off, the longer he didn't have to lie.

Then the Cab Calloway recording came to an end, and in the sitting room there was a silence that needed to be filled.

Raymond kissed her on the top of her dark waves of hair, then slipped out of her embrace to reach his greatcoat, hanging on the stand just inside the hall. From its pocket, he produced a simple manila envelope. It would be better that she read it herself. That way, it somehow seemed a little less than a lie.

He handed it to Nancy.

Nancy was shaking already, a heady cocktail of exhaustion, bewilderment and elation making every corner of her tingle, but Raymond was quite sure she started shaking more fiercely as she took in what the letter had to say. Her eyes showed her fear, her panic, her sweet release at the idea that he'd come so close to death and yet survived. It was as if he could see the whole sorry story unfolding in her: the attack on the convoy in the desert that hadn't taken place; the military Jeep turning cartwheels under the incendiary's force; Raymond, dragging himself from the wreckage – deaf, now, and unable to hear the rattle of the machine guns that sought to take out any survivors.

The letter strained beneath her fingers. She let it fall to the floor, then threw her arms back around Raymond. 'My love,' she told him, with such ferocity and tenderness all at once. 'My love.'

Those words ought to have filled him up, and in lots of ways they did. Now that she was hanging around his shoulders, his body had started to remember the shape of her; they still tessellated, he told himself; she still fitted him, like one dancer does another. And yet, in the aftermath of that warm feeling, there came a bitter coldness. It was all a lie. The fact that he'd been instructed to lie by his superiors, that the lie was in the service of His Majesty and the country he loved, leavened the sense that he was himself a traitor only a little. This was Nancy. She could be trusted with a secret – of that he was absolutely clear. And yet, when he'd asked Maynard Charles to permit him one single confidant, he had looked at him with scorn. 'These are the pacts we make, Mr de Guise. We lie to our loved ones because it is required of us. Your first duty is to your country, Raymond. See that it's so.'

Yet now, looking at Nancy's pained expression, he wondered if he had the strength for it. There were different duties in life. What did you do when one diminished another?

'It's not as terrible as it seems,' he told her, though his whole body revolted against the lie. 'I can still hear you, Nance. I can still hear Arthur cry. It's just... you feel a little far away, that's all.'

It was how Mr Croft had described it, that afternoon at the Deacon Club. Being partially deaf, he said, might feel a little like being underwater: the sounds might still reach you, but perhaps they've been dulled along the way. The trick was to keep it vague. If you're loose with your descriptions, they'd told him, you'll be less easily caught out in a lie. Your situation is flexible, Raymond. The damage might grow worse or get better. Don't anchor yourself to the details; anchor yourself to the feeling instead.

Nancy lifted herself to kiss the dark stubble that lined his jaw.

'I'm still here,' he told her. 'I'm still *me*. And listen to me, Nancy: they tell me my war's over now. I'm no good to them, out in the desert. What use a commander who can't hear his own commands? I've been discharged. I have the papers right here. An honourable discharge, and back to civilian life. Back to *you*. Back to ...' his eyes flashed at the hallway and the staircase leading above, 'our son. I can be a husband now. I can be a father. I'm here, here until the end.' He hesitated; it was time to soothe the worry etching lines upon Nancy's face. 'It's going to get better. I can feel it already. And until then ...' He bowed to kiss her on the cheek. 'A family, like we should have been at the start.'

Vivienne must have settled Arthur, then gone to join Stan in the room across the hall, for she was nowhere to be found when Nancy led Raymond upstairs, and together – hand in deceitful hand – gazed upon their sleeping son. Raymond marvelled at the boy's black hair, with the same high crown as his own; his long fingers, which he had surely inherited from Nancy; his full lips, his tiny nose.

'He's been a good boy,' Nancy whispered, 'the best we could hope for. Oh and Raymond ... Vivienne! I couldn't have done it without her. Not with Housekeeping as well. Not with the Buckingham Hotel.'

Raymond knew his lies had to start here. He looked at her askance, as if he'd only half heard. 'Vivienne?' he asked.

Nancy's face flickered, and Raymond could tell she was working hard not to show the pain she clearly felt at his news.

The depth of the lie struck him like a spear in the side. He would never be able to tell her; for the rest of his days, he'd have to spin the mistruth, dancing around it in every interaction they had.

'She's been a godsend,' Nancy said, on her tiptoes so that she could breathe the words into his ear. 'But now you're here and … Raymond, I just can't believe it. There's so much I have to tell you. So much I haven't been able to say. Everything that happened last year. The ballroom and … there's big news from the Buckingham. Mr Knave—'

'I must go to him at once,' Raymond interjected, still staring dreamily at his sleeping son.

But Nancy breathed out, 'He's dead, Raymond.'

This time, when Raymond said, 'What?', it wasn't because he hadn't heard, nor because he was keeping up the deceit; it was genuine surprise that scored lines across his face.

'Frankie was the one who found him. Just lying on his office floor.' Nancy took Raymond's hand, nestled herself against his shoulder, still needing his touch to believe he was truly here. 'He was old, Raymond. And the stresses of the last two years … Maybe it was just his time, but I can't help thinking it was the war that took him, just like it's taken so many others.'

As if he could suddenly sense his mother's discomfort, Arthur started scrabbling in his sleep. His little feet kicked as if he was lost in some dream – but, when Raymond went to soothe him, Nancy stayed his hand.

'Trust me. Let him dream on. Once he wakes, we'll be up all night.'

Raymond whispered, 'I'm not sure I can sleep anyway,' but he trusted to Nancy's words, and soon husband and wife were closing the nursery door, stealing together along the landing to the door of their own bedroom.

On the threshold, Raymond paused. Some invisible force seemed to be slowing him down, keeping him from going through that door. In there, he thought, lay a foreign country. A ridiculous notion, perhaps, but he'd had the feeling before. It seemed a different aeon, but he'd made it home late from Dunkirk, had to find his own way from the seas outside conquered France – and leave his brother Artie behind, six feet under the ground. He hadn't known how to hold Nancy back then, not while the grief and anger were still coursing through his system. He wondered if it would be the same right now, what chasm the lie might have carved out.

Inside the bedroom, Nancy checked the blackouts, then lit the candles she kept on the dresser. In the mirror she hardly looked like herself: the day's exhaustion showed on her face. 'I've got to be back at the hotel before dawn,' she said, stepping behind the partition as she disrobed. Something held her back as she squirmed out of her Buckingham day clothes and reached for the nightdress. The shyness of newlyweds, she thought – and she already married for three years, with a baby next door.

When she stepped away from the partition, Raymond was still standing there, seemingly uncertain what he should do.

So she showed him.

Across the bedroom she came, to unbutton his collar, loosen his cuffs.

'It's OK, Nance,' he said, with some reticence, and sat himself on the end of the bed to take off his boots. 'Maybe I'll come with you in the morning. There's no time like the present. I should go to the Hotel Board. There might be a use for me yet.'

Apparently Nancy wasn't certain whether she should go to him again or not. Instead, she just turned down the bedcovers on his side, the side that had lain empty and untouched for more than a year.

'Mr Hastings declared he was going to take the directorship.'
Of all things, this was what startled Raymond.

'Mr Hastings?'

It was Raymond who'd brought him to the hotel, all those
years ago – Raymond who'd been on commission to romance
the businessman in New York, then accompany him back across
the Atlantic. There'd been an understanding between them ever
since.

And that might make it easier, thought Raymond. Mr
Hastings had always approved of Raymond's role in the hotel.
There'd be a future for him there, if it was down to him.

'You're only just home,' Nancy said as she slipped into the
sheets. 'Maybe you need a little more time.' She was trying not
to watch as Raymond disrobed, but her husband had always held
some magnetic force for her. When he caught her watching, a
smile played on his own lips. And: yes, thought Nancy, *that* was
good, *that* was encouraging. Raymond had come home broken in
body, but not in heart. She reached for his hand. This time, as he
slid into the bedcovers, he took it. The chasm remained between
them, half the bed like a barren field, but at least their hands
were joined. 'It doesn't have to be tomorrow, does it, Raymond?'
She lay on her side to face him. 'Mr Hastings has only just
stepped up. He's calling the heads of department together by
mid-morning. Why don't you spend the day with Arthur? He
needs to look on you, Raymond. He needs to know his father.'

Raymond turned on his side so that he was facing Nancy too.
Part of him wanted to pretend he hadn't heard, for perhaps that
would make it easier to disregard what she was saying – but
the greater part of him rebelled at the lie. Besides, he knew she
was right. Making his return to the Grand feel reasonable was
more important than rushing it. Perhaps he oughtn't to force

it. Perhaps a day or two at home with Arthur might be right for everyone.

He was so lost in those thoughts that he genuinely didn't hear what Nancy said next. He had to ask her to repeat it, which only made pity illuminate her eyes. That sympathy, the depth of Nancy's feeling, would be a thorn in his side across the coming days. Every supportive look was just another reminder of this fiction he was spinning.

'Raymond, will you even be *able* to dance?' she asked. 'If the music feels so distant...'

It must have seemed the cruellest of punishments for a man whose life story was so tightly enmeshed with music. But Raymond consoled her now, tightening his grasp on her hand. 'It might take a little work, but I'm not so far gone, Nancy. I'll find my way back in. King of the Grand again... Perhaps, when the time's right, you might tell Mr Hastings I'm back from Africa? Perhaps he might take a drink with me, in the Candlelight Club? I should like to see the old place again. I should like to feel like I'm part of it.'

'You're part of *this*,' said Nancy, and rolled towards him.

There he was: her husband, her wounded warrior returned from the war. They slid together, like two old dancers always will.

Raymond closed his arms around her, and for a moment they lay there, entangled, hearts beating in syncopated time.

He didn't need to hear what she was saying for this.

Nor did he even need to pretend.

And perhaps it would have been like a second wedding night, perhaps it would have been love renewed, every fumbling step of the way, if only, the moment their lips met, the sound of Arthur squalling hadn't echoed through the walls.

Nancy loosened her hold on Raymond, slipped out of his arms and threw on her dressing gown. 'Duty calls,' she grinned as she trudged across the bedroom.

It really does, thought Raymond, as he lay there in the dark. Duty calls in the most unusual of ways.

*February 1942*

# Chapter Seven

'This is the place,' said Max Allgood, trembling in the frigid February air. There was damage up and down this particular Fitzrovia boulevard, but the Ambergris Lounge looked pristine. 'You'll know plenty of places like this, Nelson. Now, there's bound to be a different vibe through these doors than there is back home. You won't find any mob boss pulling the strings here. But you'll get the feeling of it soon enough. They dance different in London. The music plays different too.'

Nelson, who'd been sauntering languidly in his uncle's wake, suddenly seemed a fountain of energy. 'It won't play different long, Uncle Max. Not when I get my fingers on those keys ...'

But that was the attitude that had earned Nelson a good walloping outside the Jinx in Harlem one night three or four winters ago. It was the attitude that had seen the gendarmes threaten to throw him out of Paris, that long, unforgettable summer before the war. Europe had seemed like a new start when Max, Ava and her son fled the Americas and tried to make Paris their home – but Nelson's impatience and overconfidence had derailed them even before war swept their Continental ambitions aside.

'Now, listen here,' Max said. 'We're guests in this country. It's different here. There's no Jim Crow here. The English got rid of their laws a century ago. They won't kick you off the buses here. They won't toss you off the trains. But it doesn't mean there aren't *opinions*. It don't mean there aren't *attitudes*. Orla Brogan tells me there's still alehouses with NO BLACKS NO IRISH written on 'em. NO DOGS too – which goes to show what some still think of us. So lesson one, Nelson: don't go provoking folks; don't go chasing the wrong reputation. You can stay out of trouble here. It's a fresh start.'

'You don't need to tell me, Uncle Max. I'm ready to let loose.'

'That's exactly what I'm afraid of. You still aren't listening. So, lesson two: just let the music do the talking. You've got the talent in spades. But talent at the piano don't mean a thing compared to talent with people. Just play what you're told to play when you're told to play it. A few months of calm, dedicated playing—'

'*Months!?*' baulked Nelson.

'…and then maybe, just maybe, you might have proved you can do this. Nelson, this isn't just about music. You've got to play the game now, boy. When in Rome…'

Max strode past Nelson and had already ducked into the shadowy interior of the Ambergris Lounge when Nelson sighed, 'We're not in Rome. This is London, old man. You been drinkin' too much gin.'

It wasn't yet showtime, so the Ambergris Lounge was at peace when Max picked his way inside. The bar manager was sorting out his cabinets, one of the clerks sat at a booth with his papers spread out, and up on the stage a figure was reorganising the drum kit. By the time Nelson sauntered in, Max was already hoisting himself onto the stage and approaching this man.

'Freddie, I'm sorry we're late. Now that's my fault, not the boy's.' He pointed his thumb back at Nelson. 'I'm not as fast on these legs as I used to be. But, listen, here we are.'

Freddie Riordan had been playing the clubs of London since the end of the Great War, one of that generation of young men who'd come back to civilisation with just about enough vim left to try something *new*. Though he'd been a competent horn player during the war, no serious musician would have paid him a second thought – but there was something about coming back home, alive and unharmed, that made a man eager to reinvent his life. By the end of the Roaring Twenties, Freddie had become a bandleader of no insignificant note, leading orchestras across the north country – and eventually bringing his sounds to London. He might not have had the distinctiveness or pomp for a place like the Grand, but there wasn't a dance club in London that didn't respect his name.

'Him?' Freddie asked, eyeing Nelson.

'He's young, but he's good. He deserves a chance.'

'Piano, you say?'

Max nodded.

'There's you, hunting around London for a pianist to join the Grand, and you're sending him to me?'

Max held up his hands. 'It's not that he isn't good enough for me. It's ...'

Freddie rolled his eyes. 'You're sending me a wild child.'

Max shrugged. 'He needs to pay some dues, you know?' He floundered to find the right words. 'Listen, I can't have my orchestra thinking he's a shoo-in, just because he's blood. I'm still earning their respect. I don't want to put noses out of joint. There's been enough of that already. Nelson needs a reputation of his own.'

'It looks like he's already developing that,' said Freddie, and inclined his head with a grin.

Max followed his gaze. Apparently Nelson had got bored of waiting by the balustrade, because while Max had been speaking he had moseyed his way over the dance floor to meet one of the cleaning girls, tidying up in the corner. The girl hadn't yet stopped working, but it looked as if she was about to; Nelson was charming her with his winsome smile, breaking down her defences bit by bit. One moment, the girl was sponging the stickiness off one of the tables. The next she was shrilly laughing and flicking the water from the sponge straight onto Nelson's freshly ironed shirt.

'Just one moment,' Max said, with the best impression of calm he could possibly muster.

By the time Max had crossed the Ambergris, Nelson and the girl were embroiled in conversation. The girl had abandoned her mop against the back of a booth – and, though she was telling Nelson that she really had to work, she didn't appear to be making any effort to pick it back up.

'You see, that's how it goes in New York city,' Nelson was saying as Max made the approach. 'A boy can go places, if he's got the right pair o' hands.'

Max grabbed Nelson by the wrist and wrenched him away from the startled girl. Instants later, she seized her mop and resumed working, as if to pretend that Nelson hadn't been there at all.

Nelson was still grizzling when Max hauled him to the stage. Up there, Freddie Riordan had opened up the baby grand piano that sat centre stage. He struck a few chords before vacating the seat, then merely winked at Max.

'Well, go on,' said Max, 'show him what you can do.'

Nelson didn't say a word. All he did was flash a look back at the cleaning girl in the corner. Though she was feverishly scrubbing one of the tables, she did look up and flash him a smile. That seemed enough for Nelson. Max shook his head wearily at the boy's attitude – but then he started playing, and all his reticence was blown clean away.

It wasn't exactly the *right* sort of music. Nelson had started playing a ragtime blues, the sort of thing they soaked up along the rivers in New Orleans – but it filled the Ambergris with its rolling rhythm, Nelson's left hand pumping like a piston as it kept up the bass. His right hand was *dancing* – there was no other word for it – and the music flowed out so powerfully it was like he didn't need an orchestra at all. In the corner, the cleaning girl abandoned her mop once again. The bar manager set down his papers and started drumming his fingers on the countertop.

'Stop, stop, stop!' Max said, and battled Nelson's fingers away from the keys. 'We talked about this. What plays good on the delta doesn't play good in the city. It's different notes for different folks. And that isn't *quite* the thing they'll appreciate in here on a Saturday night.'

'Not yet it ain't. You just wait until those GIs get into London. Now, there's a crowd who'll appreciate real music. You gotta cater to taste, Uncle Max.'

Behind Nelson, Freddie shrugged.

'Just play what I showed you,' Max told him, with fresh steel. 'You got to prove you can adapt if you ever want to play in the Grand. Lords and ladies don't want ragtime. You won't find a crown prince bopping along with your honky tonk. Just show him, Nelson. Show him what I showed you.'

Nelson's eyes darkened. His look could have pierced Max like a knife. But he reached out his fingers again, cracked his knuckles across the keys – and, moments later, Max's own composition, 'Sweet Home from Home', was flowing out of his fingers. It was a slower number, though still fast by the Buckingham's standards – a song that Marcus Arbuthnot and the Buckingham dancers had often performed a quickstep to.

There was space in it for a guest vocalist and Nelson somehow found a way for little right-hand flourishes to fill in where a vocalist might have been. The song simply *soared*.

While Nelson was still playing, Freddie joined Max on the edge of the stage.

'The boy can play. It's whether he can play along with others that I doubt. I've known his sort before. They rub folks up the wrong way. They know how to play music, but they don't know how to play people. They're slow to respect. If he was to join my band, even for the night, he'd be on the bottom rung – no matter his quality. A boy like this just doesn't understand that.'

'Now, Freddie, don't he deserve a chance to show it?'

'But *you're* not giving it to him, are you? All those guest pianists you're working through and here you have one of the city's superlative talents, just chomping to sign up with you, and instead you're offering him to *me*. Max, I like you, but I can smell a scam a mile off.'

'It isn't a scam,' Max insisted. 'He just needs... breaking in. They already got *me* numbered as a wildcard for the Grand. Imagine what might happen if I brought Nelson down there unpolished.'

Nelson broke into the song's larger-than-life finale.

'I just need him to grow up a little,' said Max. 'I need him to learn London and what it's all about. He can do that out here. He won't cause you trouble, Fred. Or, if he does, he can feel the consequences of it himself – throw him out, dock his wages, make him see he's not the centre of the world.'

Fred shook his head. 'Sometimes a musician needs that kind of confidence. It's when it butts up against reality that things get sticky.'

'Pay him a half wage,' Max suddenly blurted out.

Freddie just stared at him, intrigued.

'Call it a trial. A few gigs, no more. Pay him a piece rate, then don't invite him back if it isn't working. But Fred, the boy's right about one thing. Us Yanks really are coming. And, if he plays right, if he stays out of trouble and just lets loose on a Saturday night, my nephew Nelson might be the sort of thing to bring you some pizazz. It's all the talk of the Buckingham Hotel – how to win American money. Well, it's the same out here in the clubs, isn't it? And there, right there, is your weapon. I'm gifting him to you.' Max paused, for he had seen a flicker of interest in Freddie's eyes. 'Those American boys like a drink and a dance. They're coming to join the war, and they're bringing plenty of dough with them. They'll be in want of a little entertainment – and what better than doing it the good old American way?'

Nelson hit the last chords, and couldn't stop himself from playing a dramatic trill all the way up the piano keys. Then he stood to take a bow, as if the Ambergris was full – and full for him alone.

Fred looked at Max, whose heart had suddenly dropped.

'I'll have a word with him. I'll tell him he's not the star of this—'

But Freddie Riordan had already grabbed his hand.

'One gig at a time, Max,' he grinned. 'Let's see if your boy's got more than just talent.'

# Chapter Eight

'Raymond, they're here.'

Outside, the late winter dark was descending – but in the house on Blomfield Road, Raymond sat at his son's crib-side. He'd set up the small gramophone in the corner, and right now it was softly playing an old Dorsey Brothers record Raymond had found in a New York thrift store. It had been a long time since he'd listened to music, and he'd found much joy in sifting through the boxes of old records, dreaming about how and when he would introduce each to Arthur. So far, the boy seemed to like Glenn Miller – but, then again, who didn't?

Raymond half turned, as if he'd only just heard something on the very edges of his perception. Then, upon seeing Nancy, he said, 'Is it time?'

Nancy nodded; she'd been getting used to this strange new distance between them. She felt closer to him when they lay together in silence, in those moments when words weren't needed. At least, then, there was no chasm to cross.

'Come on. The pot roast's nearly ready too.'

What Nancy called a pot roast was not nearly as extravagant as it sounded – more of a broth, thick with roast potatoes, to make what mutton they had go a long way.

Frank and Rosa were still taking off their coats, stamping the winter slush from their boots, when Raymond came down the stairs. Frank, who ordinarily lodged with Nancy, had kept himself scarce since Raymond's return – bedding down back at the Brogans', where his old room had been taken over by Max Allgood's nephew – but, the moment he saw Raymond, he gambolled over and gripped his hand like a long-lost brother. Rosa, who hadn't known Raymond as well, was more reticent – but grinned from ear to ear when Raymond kissed her cheek.

'Frank, I can't tell you how good it is to see you.'

'We thought it would be years,' thrilled Frank, as Raymond led them into the kitchen, where the dining table had been lavishly set. 'There's so much you ought to know!'

Raymond was eager to hear it – not just because Frank spun stories of the Grand Ballroom with such *joie de vivre*, but because anything he gleaned might be useful in inveigling his way back into the hotel.

Soon, the family – for family it was, no matter how higgledy-piggledy it had become – were gathered around the table. Raymond said a few words as Vivienne filled plates and handed them round.

'My friends, I can't begin to explain the way I feel.' This much, at least, was true; the lies would come later. In the days since he'd returned, Raymond had sold the lie over and over again – not just to Nancy, not just to Vivienne and now Rosa and Frank, but to his mother and aunts, and their adopted daughter, who still lived in their terrace in Stepney Green. If it was getting more natural, that didn't mean it felt any easier. 'I didn't think to look on your faces for many months and years. And here you all are.' He raised his glass. 'To every one of you – to family!'

Dinner began. Three mouthfuls later, Nancy was rocketing upstairs to tend to the squalling Arthur. Talk turned, as it always did these days, to the Americans. The first general infantrymen had already landed in Great Britain, filling the barracks while military plans were drawn up.

'I don't know what all the fuss is about,' remarked Vivienne, when Frank brought out a copy of *The Times* taken from the Buckingham Hotel. 'American GIs are friendly and simple,' she read, 'not Hollywood stars or two-gun Texans.' She looked up. 'I remember them being flashy and superior – but I'd wager these aren't Manhattanites coming to fight for the King. Boys from the country, I should think.'

'They'll have money,' said Rosa, who seemed titillated by the prospect. 'It's all they talk about at the hotel. American money – how can we get hold of American money!'

'They haven't been rationed in America. They haven't been under a blockade,' said Nancy.

'Well, me and Frank will get to go out there and jive,' said Rosa. 'That's what they're all saying, isn't it? American music to entertain American soldiers. The Midnight Rooms has already announced a jitterbug. Well, you're the one who introduced it to Frankie, aren't you, Raymond? Cab Calloway, the Cotton Club, all that jumping around? You'll be out there with us, will you, dancing all night?'

'Maybe we should put on some of those records after dinner?' said Frank, eagerly.

Raymond seized the moment. Any little hint of what was happening in the Buckingham Hotel would do. He wanted to be fully armed when he finally arranged his return. 'I imagine Mr Allgood's bringing some American flair to the Grand Ballroom, is he?'

'Oh, it's hardly *wild*,' Frank shrugged. 'But there's a different feeling to the place. It's not that anything's changed in the fixtures and fittings – but as for the *atmosphere*... Do you think you might come one night, Raymond? I'm sure Mr Hastings would have you, for a guest.'

'As a matter of fact, Frank, I'm hoping to—'

Suddenly, Nancy clutched his hand. Apparently she didn't want him to speak about his hopes and ambitions. She'd already spoken to Mr Hastings, already organised him an audience with the Hotel Director, but sometimes he got the sense she didn't want him there – as if, somehow, Raymond's return to the Grand felt *wrong*. Perhaps she was only afraid for him. He hadn't yet worked it out, so he simply caressed the back of her hand and smiled.

'Perhaps we *should* put on some records,' he said. 'There's room for a little dancing, isn't there?' And he winked at Frank. 'As long as things don't get *too* wild.'

The sitting room was hardly a dance hall, but it had seen enough dancing. Raymond chose a record by the Ink Spots – it wasn't what they'd play in the Grand, but it was good to get an atmosphere building. Frank had no inhibitions about leading Rosa around the room, nor lifting her and turning her around when the music reached its giddiest heights. After that, Raymond searched out something more soulful, Don Bester and Victor Young – the old classics that had first been played in the Grand, music to take him back to a different era.

At first, Nancy seemed reluctant to slip into his arms. 'Nance, I'm going to need some practice if I'm to convince Mr Hastings tomorrow,' he whispered to her – and, after he smiled like that, Nancy could hardly resist. It took her a little time to slide into the rhythm of it – but Raymond, it seemed, still had his dancer's instincts, even if his hearing was damaged beyond repair. Their box-stepping grew livelier as the song reached its chorus; there was no room to glide gracefully across a dance floor here, but enough to feel as if they were out there, in a world without war, spirited and carefree as midnight approached.

At some point, Nancy opened her eyes to see Stan, half a potato still in his hand, gazing upon the madness unfolding in the sitting room with a child's ceaseless wonder. 'Raymond, I've got to ...' she said – and, kissing him, she slipped out of his arms to sweep up Stan instead.

'Trumped by a three-year-old,' Raymond grinned, as Nancy deposited the half-chewed potato into his hand, then danced gaily on with Stan's fingers wrapped within her own.

Raymond found Vivienne in the kitchen, the table already cleared, the roasting pan half scrubbed in the sink.

'Vivienne,' he ventured, 'you're not the maid. Come and dance.'

Vivienne looked up from her work. 'I think you'll discover I'm the official housekeeper here, Raymond.' She smiled. She took off her washing-up gloves and rested her back against the counter. 'I don't want to dance. I just want to ...'

Raymond crossed the kitchen and folded his arms around her.

At first, Vivienne was not sure what to do. She stiffened in his grasp, but the longer he held on, the more she softened – until, when he let her go, her brittleness was gone.

'I haven't said thank you, Vivienne.'

'There isn't any need. It's my family too. *You're* my family – not that either of us ever dreamed it would end up this way. I need this place, and I've needed Nancy, as much as she's needed me. It works.' She shrugged. 'I know it isn't ordinary, but it's real.' She put her hand to her mouth. 'I miss Artie,' she said, voice cracking with emotion. 'You look so much like him. Less handsome, of course. You're like some portrait artist's impression of Artie – all the edges smoothed off. But you still look like him – and there you were, knocking on our door, coming back from the dead for the second time. It's silly, but I almost thought it was *him*.'

Raymond had so few words to console her. 'Nancy couldn't have kept working without you,' he said. 'You kept her safe and secure while I've been gone. But this is your home too, Vivienne. Nothing changes, just because I'm back. But ...' He stopped. 'You don't need to cook and scrub and clean for us. You were made for bigger things.'

Vivienne had run a charitable foundation once: the ill-gotten gains of her fascist stepfather, surreptitiously siphoned off into something good. The Daughters of Salvation, as it had been called, was where she and Artie first became lovers; it was where she had turned her life around. There'd been a time, not so very long ago, when she'd envisaged it being her life – but it had died in the first year of war, razed to the earth when bombs laid waste to the East End, and since then she'd been a mother, a nursemaid, a housekeeper, a friend.

'Do you ever hear from your mother, Vivienne? Your step-father?'

Lord Edgerton was locked up as a fascist sympathiser now, but he'd once been Head of the Board at the Buckingham Hotel. Vivienne looked at Raymond. 'They're not my family any more.'

Their eyes locked, and Raymond feared he'd pressed too suddenly on a bruise.

'You'll always have my thanks – and, Lord help me, my love as well.'

Vivienne rolled her eyes. 'Artie was twice as charming,' she said, good-naturedly, and turned back to her scrubbing.

As Raymond picked his way back across the kitchen, his thoughts returned to the Lord Edgerton of old. After he'd come back from Dunkirk, Edgerton and all of his ilk had been expunged from the hotel. It felt as if the place had been scrubbed clean of traitors in their midst. And yet now he knew: the game went on. He was about to enter the fray. When he met with Mr Hastings tomorrow, he'd have to make it count.

'Raymond?' called Vivienne.

Raymond turned around. 'Yes?'

Vivienne faltered. She'd been about to say something, but a curious look had come across her face. Raymond knew what it was: he'd turned instinctively as she called out his name, looked over his shoulder without any thought. A truly deaf man might not have heard her at all. All of that training was coming unstuck – and Vivienne, somehow, had sensed it.

After a moment's hesitation, however, she seemed to shake away the feeling that something was wrong. She simply looked at him and smiled. 'Raymond, I'm glad you've come home.'

But as Raymond returned to the dancing, he couldn't shake the feeling that she'd *noticed*.

He'd have to buck up from now on.

He had secrets that needed keeping.

'I have to say,' said John Hastings the following morning, 'when your wife came to see me, I didn't expect her to be arranging *this* particular meeting.'

Raymond had felt some trepidation as he approached the Buckingham Hotel for the first time in a year. He entered as a guest and, when he last worked here, it had been the tradesman's entrance every time. Then, the staff at the front desks – so few of whom he recognised, for the old hands had gone off to war – kept him waiting for some time. When the concierge came to escort him to the Hotel Director's office – when had Raymond de Guise *ever* needed escorting around the Buckingham Hotel? – he recalled Frank's words of the evening before. 'There's a different feeling to the place. It's not that anything's changed in the fixtures and fittings – but as for the *atmosphere*...' He'd been talking about the ballroom, but perhaps it applied to the rest of the hotel too.

'Nobody expected it less than me, sir,' said Raymond. 'I'd made peace with leaving this world behind. And yet ... here I am.'

'Our lives present many and varied twists and turns.' John Hastings paused. 'And here you are, a man in want of employment.'

'I don't intend to be a weight upon my family, sir. I've been sent home with a modest stipend, and I'll join the ARP again, I shouldn't wonder, but I want my life back, sir.'

Mr Hastings smiled. 'And that means the ballroom?'

'The Buckingham Hotel has been my life. It's in my blood. I should like to serve it again.'

Mr Hastings picked up the phone receiver from the cradle on his desk and dialled a single number. 'Collect him for me, James. It's time.' Then he set the receiver down again. 'You can imagine, there's a lot happening in the hotel. Mr Knave's death does not leave us without ruffles that need ironing over. The hotel has been in rude health, but the well runs dry so quickly these days – there's no room for complacency. I've set myself the challenge of winning fifty per cent of the American custom that's coming into London. That would put us so far ahead of the Imperial and Savoy that we need hardly remember they exist. I need everybody bent to it. There's a chance we can *thrive*.' There came a tapping at the door. 'Ah, here he is. Mr Arbuthnot, if you could come in?'

Raymond knew Marcus, of course – not just from that winter after Dunkirk, when he'd last graced the Grand, but from the ballroom circuit and competitions of the decades before. He hadn't, however, expected to meet with him today. In he strode, a titan in shirtsleeves, russet-gold hair brushed back in a wave. Marcus was broad of shoulder, Herculean in stature, a dominating presence in the ballroom – and so he dominated the Hotel Director's office too. Raymond stood and shook him by the hand.

'Mr de Guise, from the bottom of my heart, from all of my troupe, I'm so pleased you're well. When we heard you'd been invalided home...' He placed an enormous palm over his heart.

'Mr Arbuthnot,' John Hastings began, 'I'm certain you must know why I've asked you to join me here. What we have in front of us is not only the former King of the Grand Ballroom, not only our old colleague and friend. What we have in front of us is an *opportunity* – and I should very much like your thoughts on how best we exploit it.'

Marcus's eyes flashed. 'Am I given to understand Mr de Guise is offering himself for hire?'

John Hastings inclined his head, inviting Marcus to go on.

'Sir, I understood that Mr de Guise had suffered damage to his hearing?' At last, Marcus looked directly at Raymond. 'Is it not so?'

'I mustn't tell a lie,' Raymond said, knowing he was about to do exactly that. 'The world feels a little duller now, everyone a little further away – but I'm not too far gone, Marcus. I can hear the music.'

'Be that as it may... The troupe is in order, Mr Hastings. I've trained them to the new music. We're ready to put on the best shows in London. Raymond, you're a fine dancer – one of the greats, no less – but you've been away from the ballroom for more than a year. It's two and a half years since you led in the Grand. The world – *our* world – isn't the same. And now... your hearing?' He looked him up and down. 'Your body? You've a soldier's physique, not a dancer's.'

Mr Hastings took off his silver glasses and polished them in silence.

'My troupe is finely balanced, Raymond. Karina and I at the front, Mathilde and Frank as our seconds; the troupe revolves around us. You remember how delicate the balance of a troupe like ours is. I have no partner for you, Raymond – even if you were at the peak of your ballroom powers...'

As he spoke, Raymond sensed Marcus's resistance hardening. He hadn't wanted it to come to this. He'd wanted to slide back in, quietly and only half noticed, willing to pay his dues for a second time – anything to fulfil his obligations to King and Country, and perhaps experience a little of the old magic along the way. But if Marcus was going to resist then perhaps he had no choice.

'I understand, Marcus,' he said. Then he stood.

'I'm glad we see eye to eye,' Marcus declared, and shook Raymond's hand.

Raymond ambled to the door. 'I'm sure I'll find something, Mr Hastings,' he said. 'The ballroom at the Imperial isn't quite as starry as the Grand, but a man could dance in worse places. Or, if there's no room at the inn, then perhaps... the Savoy?'

John Hastings seemed to know Raymond's game. He suppressed a wry smile as he said, 'I didn't tell you to go anywhere, Raymond.'

Raymond turned back.

'Mr Arbuthnot, I've been clear with everyone in this hotel – we must grasp every chance at winning the custom of my countrymen. To wit: I will not have us send away a man of Raymond's calibre, not if it means the Imperial or the Savoy take him into their ranks. Remember, sir: the ballrooms of London are engaged in their own private battle now. I intend to win it.'

'Mr Hastings, it isn't as easy as you think to—'

John Hastings held up a hand, commanding Marcus's silence.

'The most successful enterprises in the world are the ones that can adapt, the ones that embrace change, the ones constantly reinventing themselves. That's what we're doing at this hotel, Mr Arbuthnot – and I need to see it happening in the ballroom as well.' He clapped his hands. 'Raymond, I'll sort out a retainer fee while we work through the nuances of what your role here will be. I won't have you put in front of guests if you're not up to standard, but nor will I lose out on the opportunity to deploy you. Marcus, you're to make what accommodations you must – but without compromising our offer in the ballroom. Do I make myself clear?'

Both dancers said, 'Yes sir,' in unison.

Mr Hastings reached for his jacket. 'Then, if you'll excuse me, gentlemen, I must adjourn. I'm to meet with Lord Guthrie and his wife. I'm afraid they were rather left in the lurch when Mr Knave left us, and I'm keen to keep their custom. They're with us, off and on, across the year.' He brushed past the dancers, then led them out into the hall. 'You see, we must all do our bit, gentlemen. We must romance these guests in every way we can.'

Mr Hastings strode ahead, leaving the dancers to follow in his wake.

'I never imagined John Hastings would become a man to talk about romance,' said Raymond, if only to break the spell of silence cast over them both.

'Indeed,' was all Marcus replied.

Marcus said nothing further as he marched along the director's corridor and into the throng of the reception hall. By the doors of the Queen Mary restaurant, Mr Hastings was already meeting with Lord Guthrie and his wife. The Scottish laird was a tall man, a rake with dark hair and immaculately styled whiskers. Balding at the crown, he had trained the rest of his hair around his pate. What he lacked on top was made up for by the thatch of his eyebrows, the lustre of his moustache. Dressed head to toe in charcoal grey, he was the precise opposite of his wife: Susannah Guthrie was petite by her husband's standard, as golden as he was dark. The ivory dress she wore made her look like the day to his night.

As they passed, Raymond saw her take Mr Hastings' hand. Inwardly, he smiled: yes, both hotel director and guest needed to romance each other. That was the way an elite establishment like the Buckingham made its business.

Marcus was already some way ahead of him. Through the ornate marble arch he stepped, down the gently inclining corridor that led to the Grand. Raymond felt a familiar shiver as he walked in Marcus's wake.

Through the doors he came.

Here he was: back home.

And yet... did it *feel* like home? Did it even look like home, any more? The chandeliers had been replaced, the balustrade refashioned. On the dance floor, Mathilde and Frank were preparing for the afternoon demonstrations – while, up on stage, the silver lettering above the grand piano read THE MAX ALLGOOD ORCHESTRA. Archie Adams had ruled the roost when Raymond last danced here. It was unnerving how quickly the world moved on.

Marcus was about to march down to meet his dancers when Raymond said, 'I know what I'm asking, Mr Arbuthnot. I know it must feel wrong. But it's your troupe. I know that, in my bones. I've no intention of derailing what you've accomplished here.' He looked up, into the glittering chandelier light. 'I just want to find my way again. I want to see if dance still calls for me. I'll play third fiddle, Marcus. I'll be a loyal sergeant-at-arms.'

Marcus had had a flinty look in those winsome eyes, but now he softened.

'I'm sure we can find a use for you, Raymond. We are all servants of this hotel, after all.'

Raymond watched him march down to meet Frank and Mathilde. The fact was that in everything he'd said, Marcus was right. Dancing required dedication, and Raymond hadn't danced in a year. He'd scarcely danced in two. His body was different now and the ballroom wasn't his – and he wondered if his heart was as eager as it had once been to glide out onto that dance floor.

Once upon a time, that had been his sole purpose, the centre of his life. But now, he wasn't here to dance for the hotel. He came here to dance for King and Country.

Raymond sashayed down to the dance floor, just in time for the music to stop and Frank and Mathilde to come apart.

'Here he comes,' declared Marcus, his theatricality this time sounding forced. 'May I introduce you to the newest member of our dance troupe?' His smile was forced too. 'Ladies and gentlemen, Mr Raymond de Guise...'

*March 1942*

# Chapter Nine

'Here they come, Frankie...'

Spring came early to London, and with it the feeling of fresh hope. On the edge of Hyde Park – itself upturned by the war, for shelters and trenches now pockmarked its beautiful surrounds – Frank and Rosa saw it coming: hope and excitement, in the shape of the six hundred American infantrymen now marching through the Marble Arch.

The sun had come out for them. So had the Londoners. Frank and Rosa had thought to get here early, to see the proud American boys waving their 'stars and stripes' as they started their parade in Hyde Park, then marched round Buckingham Palace and on into the east – but, by the time they arrived, the route was already thronged.

Frank didn't want to admit it, but there was a little part of him that felt jealous. He'd been one of the first to the War Office in 1939, eager to do his bit and march off to France like so many others – but the Medical Board had dismissed him, and instead he'd found himself beached at the Buckingham. There were valiant things to do on the home front, but nothing looked quite as valiant, right now, as marching with so many hundreds of your brothers, all united for the common good.

It didn't help that Rosa was thrilling as well.

'Let's follow them, Frankie. I mean, those trumpets are hardly what you're used to – but it would be fun, wouldn't it?'

Rosa's joy was infectious. Hand in hand, they jostled their way along the parade route, following the brass section until they were almost at the Wellington Arch, the fortified entrenchments of Constitution Hill half hidden between fluttering Union Jacks.

'I wonder if we'll see the King, Frankie?'

She often liked to stroll down by Buckingham Palace and daydream about looking up to see the King framed in one of the windows, gazing out over his kingdom. But even Buckingham Palace hadn't been spared the bombs – by Frank's count, it had already been struck seven times.

A great cheer was rippling through the crowd, and Rosa joined it now.

'Hey, look – there's Annie!' cried Rosa. Some of the other chambermaids from the hotel were at the edge of the parade route now; she cantered to meet them, dragging Frank behind. 'It's *something*, this, isn't it, Annie?'

Annie had to stand on her tiptoes to see through the crowd.

'You two follow the rest of the route,' Frank grinned. 'Marcus is expecting me in the Grand.'

'Oh, but Frankie!' Rosa exclaimed.

Frank shrugged, kissed her full on the mouth, and said, 'Tonight. I'll find you tonight.'

By the time Frank had picked his way through the crowds, crossed Piccadilly and made his way up through the quieter Mayfair streets, the rehearsal was about to begin. Thankfully, he wasn't the only one rushing to make it – because there was Raymond, stepping out of a taxicab beside the hotel's grand white colonnade.

Raymond felt as if Frank was chaperoning him as the young dancer skipped ahead, eager to reach the Grand Ballroom before

Marcus's meeting began. By the time Raymond entered the dressing rooms, Frank had already spirited himself through the ballroom doors. Raymond took a moment to steady himself before he followed. *Remember the act,* he told himself.

The troupe was already here. So too the musicians. Marcus Arbuthnot and Max Allgood stood by the stage's side, conferring with bowed heads.

'Mr de Guise,' Marcus declared, detaching himself from Max and throwing his arms open wide. 'Just in time. Join the troupe, if you will. Let's get this rehearsal under way.'

Raymond marched over to the troupe and took his place among them.

How strange it was, to be part of the rank and file.

He'd been a leader for so long.

'Ladies and gentlemen,' Marcus began, pacing up and down in front of his troupe. 'Spring is dawning, but our attentions must turn to summer. The upheavals in the hotel must not break our stride, and I have this week had confirmation from Mr Hastings that we must plough on with preparations for our Summer Serenade in June. That leaves us three months to compose something spectacular – and Mr Allgood and I have reached an agreement. This summer, our ball is to be held in honour of the New World. A New World Symphony, if you will.' Marcus smiled at the crowd.

'Mr Hastings has been very clear: we are to draw the eyes of London, and especially the Americans who have freshly come to our shores. And, while there will be no revolution in this ballroom, we must embrace something of the American if we are to thrive.' He paused. 'This seems as good a time as any to hand over to our dear Mr Allgood.'

Raymond hadn't yet had the chance to meet Max Allgood, but the man looked an unlikely leader for the Grand. He'd hoisted himself, in an ungainly manner, onto the stage, and seemed to be crab-walking from side to side, wiping sweat from his brow and waving a scrunched-up paper in his hand.

Not as elegant as Archie Adams had been – but there was *personality* up there, and perhaps that was what counted.

'I reckon we've already struck some fear into your faces,' Max beamed, 'but don't go losing your heads. We won't be getting lords and ladies jitterbugging and jiving by summer. No, but we've been thinking – the old American standards. Paul Whiteman, Barney Trimble, that kind of a number. Now, some of those songs are nigh on twenty years old – so me and my boys, we'll be working 'em up, giving them a *modern* feel. But that'll just be the *start*. Because we've been working on some new numbers – Allgood Orchestra originals, to really take things up a notch.' Max looked around his musicians. 'I thought we'd go through one today, just to get the juices flowing. This one's called the Buckingham Bounce. I'll be on the trombone eventually, but today I'll take the piano – you know, while we've not got a permanent player…'

'Let's dance this one by feeling alone,' Marcus announced. Then, as the dancers all gravitated to their couples, his eyes fell on Raymond. 'I'm sorry, Mr de Guise. There are going to be a few awkward moments like these, aren't there? I'm afraid, no partner for you. I've no doubt we'll have you back on the roster for the open dances, Mr de Guise – you'll be out here, romancing the guests as you always did – but it's going to take a little more thinking to get you back into the showpieces. I wonder – has Mr Hastings talked about hiring you a partner?'

Raymond only shook his head.

'You must take the next dance,' Marcus announced, opening his arms to Karina, who slipped automatically into his hold. 'Then we'll see how that body of yours is holding up.'

It was a strong number, breezy and bold – a song for a fast waltz, with a few nods to something wilder. Yes, Raymond thought he could hear what Max Allgood was up to: driving the ballroom in a bold direction, a few little paces at a time. Speed up a song like this, play it with reckless abandon, and it might have suited one of the dance clubs in Soho just as well as the elegant environs of the Grand.

Frank was evidently enjoying it.

At one point, he was so overcome with the feeling of the moment that he lifted Mathilde from the dance floor and pirouetted around.

'Mr Nettleton!' Marcus announced. 'Decorum, please!'

Frank did his best impression of being shamefaced, but winked across the ballroom at Raymond.

'Of course,' Raymond said as the dance came to an end, 'they used to think the waltz was salacious as well. Nowadays, it's the height of propriety. But go back a hundred years... it was the devil's dance.'

'Yes, well, the Grand isn't the place for devilry,' declared Marcus.

'Just the *tiniest* bit of devilry would do,' said Max, from up on stage. 'These lords and ladies, they got the devil in them too!'

Marcus's eyes flashed around. 'Perhaps we can stop speaking about the devil in such glowing terms? I take your point, of course. We are pushing at the edges of things this summer. We must inject some more passion and drama into our Serenade.' He stepped away from Karina. 'Perhaps the song again, Mr Allgood? And this time, Karina, might you do me a favour and dance with Raymond?'

Karina's eyes were glittering. 'Not for the first time, Raymond?'

She'd joined the Grand the year before Raymond left for France. Back then, Raymond had still been working with his partner Hélène – but he could vividly remember the first waltz he'd danced with Karina. It was always so memorable, fitting yourself to a new dancer's body.

The music started again, and Raymond let it flow through him.

How good it felt to be on this dance floor again ...

How strange, to close his eyes, reach for the music, and know he was truly back home ...

'Let's cut it here, shall we?'

Marcus's voice rang out across the ballroom.

Raymond opened his eyes.

Karina slipped out of his hold.

'I think it's the shoulders, Raymond – there's a rigidity about you I don't recognise.' Marcus paced again, musing carefully on the matter. 'And am I wrong, or were you a half-beat ahead? Your posture – it's defiant, rather than refined. It's this soldier body of yours, Raymond. We must do something about this soldier's physique. You're heavy of foot.' Marcus surveyed the other dancers. 'One moment, please.' Then he inclined his head to Raymond. 'A quiet word, perhaps?'

By the stage door, they convened.

'I know it's going to take some time, Marcus. I'm grateful for the opportunity.' What else was there to say? Raymond supposed he hadn't been at the peak of his prowess – nor was he expecting to be – but he couldn't avoid the feeling there was something pointed about Marcus's words. It struck him as a shame – he'd been hoping to dance around any struggles for power in the ballroom. He was meant to go unnoticed.

'Raymond, I have to ask it outright. Posture and poise, the little tricks of elegance and refinement – these things will flow back through you, in time.' Marcus paused. 'But only if you can feel the music, Raymond. And to feel the music, you have to *hear* the music.'

'Oh,' said Raymond, quite simply.

'Am I right, Raymond? I fear that I am. You're out of sync, because you couldn't latch on to it. Now, perhaps, in *time*, you'll know these songs like the standards of old – and perhaps, then, you'll dance perfectly, even when they're on the edges of your hearing. But right now...'

Inwardly, Raymond tensed. Had Marcus just seized an opportunity to put Raymond in his place?

But he knew that, in a roundabout way, Marcus was helping him here.

Helping to establish his cover.

'It isn't easy, Marcus,' he said quietly. 'But I promise I'll get there. And if I can't – well, I'll accept it gracefully, and step aside from the troupe.' He smiled, feigning his dispiritedness. 'Can you give me until the Summer Serenade to prove myself? I just need a little time.'

And Marcus braced his shoulders, eyes blazing with a magnanimity that was surely false.

'Raymond, every single soul in this ballroom is behind you, every single step of the way.'

Later that evening, admitted to the Deacon Club by a sour-faced clerk, Raymond recalled the finer details of Marcus Arbuthnot's expression to Maynard Charles, and threw back his brandy in one.

'You're to row back on any drama in the ballroom, Raymond. The Grand is not to be rocked by disagreement, disharmony or scandal. It's in everyone's interest that the Buckingham thrives – and that it attracts as much American custom as possible. Am I understood?'

'You are, sir.'

Raymond hadn't intended to spook Maynard Charles. Indeed, he'd thought the man might raise a smile at the idea that artistic rivalries still went on, in a world tearing itself apart. But he'd forgotten: the man had been dour as Hotel Director, and he was more serious still in his current capacity.

'It's good that you have until the Summer Serenade to solidify your place. Allow Mr Arbuthnot to think he has the better of you. Pay him fealty – but don't simper. You're to get the respect of the troupe as well as exist among them. You're to become the star attraction, under their very noses. Only then will the guests I have in mind start gravitating towards you in the Grand.'

'Which guests *do* you have in mind, Mr Charles?'

Maynard smiled, for the first time that evening. 'To business, then.'

'To business,' said Raymond – and accepted the folded paper which Maynard had just slipped across the dining table.

'You're to destroy that, of course, once the names are committed to memory.'

Just a list of names, saw Raymond – five or six titled individuals, who had been taking rooms at the Buckingham Hotel.

'St John Bancroft is of particular note,' Maynard began, lighting his cigar. 'A Dorset man. You might have come across him before. There was a time that he wined and dined with our own Lord Edgerton. Before that, he had business associations with Beamish. You recall the name Beamish?'

Raymond did not.

'He would have been in your paperwork, de Guise. You need to keep up. Henry Hamilton Beamish – he was one of those with the Imperial Fascist League, back in the days when an Englishmen could openly declare his Nazism and suffer no ill consequences. He founded The Britons.'

Raymond remembered this. They'd even had some pamphlets published by that contemptible organisation in Salisbury where he was first briefed. He'd already known there were hateful men in the world, but that they were willing and eager to commit their hatred to paper still chilled him.

'Beamish is interned now – at leisure, of course, like rich men are, but he's off the map, as far as we're concerned. He's still in Southern Rhodesia. There are worse places to be. But Bancroft has been using the Buckingham for some months now. You're to develop associations with him however you can.'

'He'd hardly accept a dance from me, sir.'

'No, but his wife will.'

'And Douglas Guthrie, sir?' Raymond whispered, looking at the paper once more. He recognised the name, but it took him a few moments to recall it properly. Then it struck him: it had been this particular Scottish laird who'd invited Walter Knave to dinner on the day of his demise. Raymond had seen him himself, some days later, when he'd first met with Mr Hastings and been swept off to the Grand. There he'd been, with his wife Susannah, waiting by the doors of the Queen Mary restaurant for John Hastings to arrive.

'Guthrie helped fund the Link.'

'Truly, sir?'

'A more cautious bastard than either Beamish or Bancroft, and perhaps doubly as dangerous because of it. The Link were funded by Berlin. Led by Domville – another one of our esteemed officers now residing at His Majesty's Pleasure. They *said* the Link was simply a way of fostering Anglo-German relations, of course – but treachery has many guises. Guthrie's is a quiet one. Hitler's man in the Highlands – that's what we've been calling him. But he's careful and he rarely puts a foot wrong these days, so we haven't had the grounds to lock him away. Raymond, you're to find those grounds – if you possibly can.'

'By dancing with his wife,' Raymond whispered.

'Cultivate them however you must,' said Maynard Charles. Then he caught the waiter's eye and, with a sudden change in tone, said, 'Tear that paper up now, de Guise, there's a good chap. I think some dessert is in order.'

The spiced fruit cake came with poached plums and custard, and was one of the most indulgent things Raymond had eaten all year.

'You've maintained your cover well so far, Raymond. It's time to put your talents to the test. Allow Marcus Arbuthnot to think what he must. Develop a sense that he's *saving* you, if that's what it takes. Yes, a man like Arbuthnot would probably get a rise out of that – the idea that he, and he alone, can salvage the wreck of a dancer you've become.'

Raymond smarted. 'Now, steady on …'

'Oh no, Mr de Guise. If prostrating yourself for Marcus Arbuthnot is what it takes to cement your place back in the Grand, then it's what you'll have to do. If feeling a little humili-ated is the cost of cosying up to Bancroft and Guthrie, then so be it. Be *proud* of how they treat you. Every time it irritates you, it's a sign it's working. Take pleasure in that. Let Arbuthnot rescue you, and he won't want to jettison you from the Grand.' Maynard Charles punctuated each of the next three words by exhaling little puffs of cigar smoke. '*Let – him – win*. Do you hear me?'

Raymond methodically finished his dessert. 'I do, sir.'

'We're all dancing to disaster, Raymond. The question is: how long does the ball go on?'

# Chapter Ten

As Nelson hit the final chords, wrists rolling in arpeggios from one end of the piano to another, he felt like howling at the moon. That's what one of the old blues musicians would have done. They'd have let it rip, and had the whole bar howling with them.

But Nelson knew better.

He wasn't in Chicago any more.

He wasn't in New Orleans.

Lord, how many times had Uncle Max warned him about going too far?

So he kept his howling to himself, pounded the piano, then stood to soak up the applause.

The dance floor in the Midnight Rooms had already come to a standstill. By the look of the dancers, they'd come to a stop some time before. So too had all the other musicians in Freddie Riordan's makeshift orchestra. It hadn't occurred to Nelson, until this very moment, that the trumpets had cut out long before he'd reached that final crescendo – nor even that the drums had stopped keeping time. A hundred sets of eyes were just staring at him.

'An encore, is it?' he grinned, wolfishly, then flung himself back down.

'Nelson,' Freddie ventured, from behind his saxophone, 'I think the bar manager is...'

Nelson looked up. Another man might have seen the Midnight Rooms' manager shaking his head and understood he was calling time on proceedings – but Nelson had always seen a full glass where others saw empty. What *he* saw was a man shaking his head in disbelief at the absolute musical glory he'd just witnessed, begging for another song.

'These folks need something to *dance* to before bedtime,' Nelson grinned. 'I'll take it a little easier on you this time, shall I? Something nice and soothing to lead you into the night...'

Nelson launched into a repeat of the night's first number, 'Home from Home'. He kept it calmer, slowed the tempo, and soon the dance floor was moving again.

At the song's conclusion, Nelson made a more restrained bow to the audience, then hit one discordant chord to say farewell – it was his signature move – and ambled off the stage.

'You're meant to follow my lead, boy,' Freddie said, as the other musicians flocked into the cramped backstage area – where the trumpeters were already setting up a table for a game of cards. 'Whose name is it above the stage?'

'Fred, I was just giving those people what they wanted. They left with a smile, didn't they?'

It was the only thing that saved Nelson from a rollicking. Fred said, 'Just be mindful, boy. You're here on a trial, remember? The showboating doesn't play well with management, not at the end of the night.' Then Freddie pressed a small brown envelope into Nelson's hand. It wasn't as heavy as Nelson might have liked, but it would do; it was always good to earn an honest night's pay.

'Hey, Nelson,' cried one of the trumpeters, 'you staying for a hand?'

The cards were already being laid out. The musicians all took their pay from Freddie, shoved half of it into their back pockets, and stacked the rest in towers on the table.

*Poker.*

Nelson grinned. Maybe these English weren't quite so reserved after all.

'Here, boy, take a shot,' said one of the trumpeters – and poured Nelson a half-glass of the cherry brandy they'd been drinking.

Lord, but it smelled sweet. One drink never harmed a man, so Nelson poured it into his gullet, letting it coat his insides like syrup. Too sweet by far – these English weren't hard drinkers – but it had a certain warmth.

'So, are you playing a hand?'

There were four men around the card table, with a fifth place set for Freddie. One of the trumpeters shuffled aside, as if making room for a sixth – but Nelson just grinned; one drink was hardly enough to blot out the memory of Uncle Max's voice, nor to forget that admonishing look in his mother's eye. He was meant to be on the 'straight and narrow' – which is the name they had for the boring road. But if the way to the Buckingham was paved by boredom, well, maybe it was worth it. Uncle Max had laid him a god damn *challenge.*

'I got a warm bed waiting,' he grinned, then turned to leave by the back door.

Some of the musicians started booing playfully, but Nelson had heard worse. His smile only broadened as he reached the door.

As his fingers hovered over the handle, one of the trumpeters said, 'Just let him go. The kid's got bravado at the piano, but it doesn't go much further than that.'

Nelson froze.

The smile vanished from his face.

'What did you say?' he said, half turning over his shoulder.

It was at this point, sensing some tension in the air, that Freddie intervened. 'Leave the kid alone. We don't all have to play your cards.' Then, saxophone hoisted on his shoulder, he sidestepped past Nelson and out of the door. 'Get off home, kid. Your uncle's waiting.'

'Maybe he doesn't know how to play,' said one of the trumpeters, after Freddie was gone.

'Poker?' Nelson jeered. 'American poker?'

'It's a French game, as a matter of fact. Poque, they called it. And we've been playing it since before you Americans had your revolution. Boy, everything you have, *we* invented!'

He felt the envelope stuffed into his back pocket.

Enough to give the Brogans a little something towards bed and board.

Enough to show his Uncle Max there was hope for him in the Grand Ballroom.

'Just leave us to it, boy – save your pluck for the stage tomorrow night...'

*Enough to show these English what a boy who learned cards in the Bowery could do.*

Nelson slammed shut the door, took his place at the table, and drew out his night's pay.

'Ace is high, right?' he said.

The trumpeters shared a silent smirk before they nodded. The night had just got interesting.

'Go on then,' grinned Nelson, '*deal*.'

The games started slowly. Nelson was a wily player and knew when to fold. 'See, that's what a good gambler does,' he said at the end of the second hand. 'He knows when to take his bow and exit the stage.'

Nelson won the third hand with a pair of knaves. The fourth was a bust, and so was the fifth, but by the time the sixth game came round (and consequently Nelson's sixth taste of that sweet, sweet liqueur), the gods of poker smiled on him so sweetly that Nelson found it hard to keep it in. Right now, there was every chance he was going to let slip that he was holding three queens in his hand. He could hardly stop rising up and down in his seat. He just couldn't put a bridle on the excitement.

One after another, the other players laid down their hands.

In the middle of the table, Nelson's prize glittered. 'Tell 'em to take me on half pay, would you, Uncle Max?' he grinned. 'Just imagine the look on his face when I strut in with *all* your wages for the...'

The game had been called. Only one player left in. He faced Nelson with a smile and opened his hand.

*3...*

*4...*

*5...*

*6...*

*7...*

'Straight flush, beats three queens. I'm sorry, Nelson.' Nobody could claim the victorious trumpeter was being magnanimous in victory; his smile was so wide it nearly eclipsed the rest of his face. 'I suppose you were right. Being vainglorious and cocksure on stage sometimes works. It just isn't as effective with cards in your hand.'

All the effervescence that had been bubbling away inside Nelson suddenly died. The world seemed awash with grey as the trumpeter piled up his winnings. The only music Nelson could hear was the thunder of his own heart, the churning in his ears – as if his head had suddenly been plunged into the water.

That had happened a lot, in the clubs back home.

One wrong word, one wrong look, money owed to some crook – and it had been threats of being tossed into the Hudson river, or his head held deep in some running lavatory pan to show him what the consequences would be.

Nelson stood up, kicking his chair aside. 'You're sharks, the lot of you. You got me. I see it – you got me. It ain't nothing but luck. And there's one place luck doesn't count. Out *there*. And I'll outshine the lot of you. Every god damn night, I'll outshine you!'

'Hold your horses, gunslinger,' came a voice from the back of the room.

Nelson swirled round, to see the bar manager pouring him another glass of brandy.

'I don't see any need for the histrionics. It's just a friendly game of cards. Nobody bent your arm to take part.'

Nelson just strode towards the door. 'Uncle Max is expecting money in his pocket. He's expecting good reports. You sitting here, you lot, with broomsticks up your asses and silver spoons in your cracks – all fun and games to you, isn't it? But I got a *life*. I came over here to make something good of myself, and here's you thieves just…'

'Thieves, Nelson? *Thieves?*'

God damn it, thought Nelson, it was almost like they'd *rehearsed* it.

'You know what I mean,' he said, kicking the wall with all the ferocity those boys in Hell's Kitchen had kicked him in the head with that Thanksgiving.

'Kid, I'll show you how we're not thieves,' said the bar manager, not unkindly. 'I like you, Nelson. You're a bloody forest fire, but I like you. You brought some thunder out there tonight. They mightn't have known what to make of it, but they'll talk about it – you can be sure of that. So, how about I forward you pay for the next three shows. It'll get you back in the game – and, with a bit of luck, Uncle Max'll be none the wiser.'

Nelson gazed around the room. All those eyes were boring into him.

They thought they'd won. These English thought he was a sucker? Well, in a couple of hours, they'd know what a boy from the South Side was really worth.

Nelson slid back into his seat, fresh fire in his belly, fresh belief in his guts.

'It's you who called for us Americans to come, boys. Well, here I am. Deal 'em. There's nothing more dangerous than a man with something to prove!'


Some time later that night, long past the hour when she ought to have been asleep, Ava Allgood heard a cacophonous crashing, and stumbled down, past the room where Orla Brogan and her husband William were sleeping, into the living room of No 62 Albert Yard.

The door was wide open, the electric lights turned on, every blackout protocol completely breached – and there lay Nelson, already sprawled on the sofa where he'd stumbled, one foot trailing in the soot he'd kicked up from the grate.

'Brandy,' Ava cussed, as she hurried to close the door, then checked that her baby boy was still breathing. Lord, she hated herself for this – treating him like he was an infant, when there he was, a man fully grown, and old enough to know better. 'How much have you had?' she said, slapping him about the face. 'Nelson Allgood, you open those eyes right now ...'

Nelson did.

They were bloodshot and raw.

'You've been at it all night.'

'Ma, it was one hell of a show. I stopped the dance floor. They didn't know how to dance to it.'

Ava shook him, but Nelson didn't resist; he just tremored like a rag doll. 'Nelson, look at the state of you. Crashing in here like it's a damn flophouse! These people are being good to us. That's what's happening in London – folks help each other out. But you're not meant to tread on their civility. We're *guests* here and ...'

'Don't worry about it, Ma,' Nelson slurred, reeling across the room now that he'd broken free of his mother's grasp. 'I'll get them their money. I just need a little more time. I almost had 'em, Ma. I had 'em right in front of me. I could have paid and paid and paid – and then, BANG, a royal flush. You can't blame it on me, Ma. A royal flush – now that's a *thing*. You don't see it so often. I've been *privileged*, Ma.'

'What – did – you – say?'

'I told you, Ma. It was within my grasp. You'd have been so happy with me. You used to be. If I came home with winnings, you used to jump for joy.'

'*That* was when we were starving. Not when we were safe and secure, and the only thing stopping us from staying that way is *you* and your ...'

'My what, Ma? My *soul*?'

'It isn't your soul drags you into these things. It's your *weakness*.'

Suddenly, there was movement upstairs. Ava shot a panicked look at the stairs, forcing a hand over her son's mouth to keep him from blurting out some other inanity. 'Your Uncle Max got back from the Buckingham *hours* ago. You damn fool, Nelson, if he thinks for a second you messed this up – and so early! – he'll never have you in the Grand.' She waited some more, still compelling Nelson's silence – and only when she heard no more movement on the stairs did she let him go. 'How bad is it? What's the damage?'

'A total blitz, Ma. I'm not getting paid for the next three shows.'

Ava plunged backwards, to sit upon the sofa beside her son.

'I'll get it back, Ma. You see if I don't.'

There was a genuinely plaintive air to his voice, but Ada had heard it a hundred times before.

Tears welled in her eyes.

She couldn't keep them from falling.

'I'm sorry, Ma,' said Nelson. Upon seeing his mother's emotion, sobriety had hit him with all the power of a freight train. 'I'll set it right. You know I will.'

'That's the problem,' Ava said – and, brushing herself down, got to her feet. 'I don't know it at all.' She got to the bottom of the stairs before she spoke again. 'Go put your head in a water bucket. Do anything you can to clean the stench off you. The stench of brandy. The stench of sweat. The stench of all the lies, Nelson. London's meant to be a new start. I won't go back to how it was in New York. I won't go back to penury and, and...' She couldn't even say it; the way she'd made a living back home was not fit for decent conversation, and she'd made herself a solemn promise never to mention it again. 'I need you, Nelson. I need you to hear me. I'm going to live a proper life in London. I want you in it, and I want you Buckingham bound – but if I have to do it without you, that's what I'll do.'

Nelson was so aghast that he said nothing as his mother took herself back upstairs.

He just sat there, staring at the dead fire, thinking on all that he'd done.

Money in his pocket, a good show beneath his belt – and he'd frittered it all away, and more besides.

And why?

Just because some English had goaded him.

His eyes flashed to the door.

He wondered if it would have been better for everybody if he just ran for the hills right now.

But he was too weak-willed even for that – for the moment he got up, his legs gave way, and after that, it was all he could do to drag himself to bed in the rafters above.

'Two steps forward, six steps back,' he grunted as sleep took hold of him once more. 'Ain't it always the same . . .'

# Chapter Eleven

It wasn't until an hour before his first formal appearance in the Grand that Raymond recognised the feeling that had been growing in his gut all day.

How strange it was to be *nervous*.

Raymond hadn't felt like that since that season in Europe almost twenty years before, his first Grand Tour with his mentor, Georges de la Motte.

In the dressing room behind the Grand Ballroom, he looked into one of the ornate mirrors and slipped out of the brown jacket he'd been wearing. Hanging beside him, his old suit of midnight blue seemed like a skin he'd shed some years before. As he stepped into the trousers, they felt a little too loose; he'd lost weight in the desert, becoming more rangy and wiry than he'd been in his heyday, but the braces would remedy that. Next, he slipped his arms into the sleeves of his evening jacket, fussed with the collar, brushed down the lapels and arranged the ivory silk handkerchief in his pocket. Now, when he looked in the mirror, he was the debonair dancer Raymond de Guise again. It was only in the rough cut of his hair and the hollow of his eyes that he knew anything had changed.

Nerves curdled inside him. But there wasn't a soul he could share his turmoil with, save for Maynard Charles – and what did he care for the unsettled feeling in Raymond's stomach? 'You have a job to do, de Guise.' Dance used to be a calling; now it was just a job, and he needed to bend himself to the task.

There was a guest pianist with the orchestra. Raymond had known Gordie Entwhistle when he used to tour the provinces, dancing in every competition from Brighton to Blackpool and Glasgow beyond. A more stately gentleman pianist would have been harder to find – but, at fifty-six years old, he had a reputation for being stuck in the past. He was hardly, Raymond reflected, the right fit for a new, exciting orchestra that prided itself on living in the moment, embracing the new, touching the *American*.

'What you really need is a wild one,' remarked Raymond, when Max caught his eye. 'That is, if you want to capture a flavour of the Cotton Club…'

Max's eyes danced. He and Raymond had already shared a few offhand conversations about New York, and that hallowed land in Harlem where the jitterbug was born. 'Harlem in Mayfair's not the thing I'm after, Ray – but don't go temptin' me now. A man can get ideas. No, Gordie's enough for tonight. We'll excite 'em, but we don't want to shake things up too much. That's a hard lesson learned, Mr de Guise – I'm in society now. I gotta walk the tightrope.'

Soon, the Max Allgood Orchestra were marching out to the ballroom's applause – while Marcus rallied the dancers to the doors. Raymond joined them, though there was no place for him in the showpiece dance the troupe were about to perform; without a partner to feature with, he'd been shuffled to the side, told he would have to wait until the dance floor was open for guests. It would smart a little to see his old crowd sally out without him – and Marcus had seemed just a little too happy to break the news – but Raymond reminded himself what Mr

Charles had said, and clung on to it like it was gospel. It was a *good* thing that Marcus held himself superior. 'If they steal your thunder, so be it. It's in the quiets of the storm you'll operate best.'

Out in the ballroom, the applause died down. The orchestra struck up.

'Our assignments for the evening,' Marcus pronounced, as the music swelled.

Around went the roster for the evening's dances: every guest who'd reserved a place with their favourite for the festivities to come. Frank, as ever, was to dance three waltzes with the daughter of one of the Free French diplomats who frequented the hotel, a close confidant of de Gaulle.

Raymond didn't recognise the names he'd been allotted. The more starry names were lined up alongside Marcus himself. Among them, one name in particular stood out: Jane Bancroft. He'd already done his research, making small talk with the concierges and learning the residents of every suite. Jane Bancroft was wife to St John Bancroft, whose name had been seared into Raymond's mind that night in the Deacon Club. Here was his first opportunity: ingratiate himself with the wife, to curry favour with the husband.

'Dear friends,' Marcus announced, titanic arms open wide. 'Let us dance!'

The ballroom doors flew open. Raymond sidestepped out of sight. Past him came all the couples of the troupe, led imperiously by Marcus and Karina. In the rear, Frank and Mathilde skipped out to meet the crowd.

The ballroom doors fell closed, and Raymond was alone.

For a time he paced. It was all he could do. Just pace around the dressing room where he used to be King and try to *remember*. But the fact was, Max's music was infectious. It was lively and it rolled, and by the middle of the showpiece song, Raymond had started to feel it. Gordie Entwhistle might not have been inspiring, but the way he kept the song pounding forward perfectly complemented the soaring swoon of Max's trombone. When Raymond heard a wave of applause, even in the middle of the song, he knew he had to catch sight of what was happening out there. He stole to the doors, opened them a crack, and just watched.

Frank sailed on air. Marcus and Karina drew every eye in the house. From this vantage he couldn't see the orchestra, but he could see their cavorting shadows, cast against the blackout blinds behind them. The chandeliers glittered. The air pulsated with promise.

No nerves now – Raymond de Guise couldn't wait.

And nor did he have to. He watched as the song reached its conclusion, as the shadow of Max Allgood held his trombone Lucille aloft, as all the lords and ladies of the Grand Ballroom joined their hands in applause. Moments later, the dancing couples were elegantly parting ways, skipping to the balustrade that ran around the edge of the dance floor to take their allotted guests by the hand.

Marcus took the hand of a slender lady in silks, whose skin was as olive brown as the height of summer. Jane Bancroft, Raymond decided. At least he had eyes on her now. Marcus wouldn't be dancing with her all evening; there'd be countless other guests to romance. Somewhere along the way, Raymond would seize his chance.

Out he strode, head held high. Two strides through the door, on the dance floor's edge, he paused. Behind him, the doors fell shut. He breathed in the ballroom.

The soldier returned.

The dancer reborn.

His charge was waiting for him by the balustrade steps. Raymond felt the dance floor glide beneath him as he sallied forth to meet her. She was tall, lithe, with greying hair that betrayed her age: sixty, perhaps, the wife of some industrialist not given to dance.

He took her hand.

And the words he used to speak every night, just before the music began, came back to his lips like old friends.

'Shall we?' he ventured.

The hotel guest smiled, 'We shall.'

Then the music struck up.

It didn't take long to find the rhythm again. His body was used to the privations of a forced march, to long sleepless nights, the exhaustion of Africa – but every dancer's body is the chronicle of all the music they've ever absorbed, and by the fourth bar Raymond knew he was home.

Raymond danced three songs with his first partner, then moved to his second and third. The music grew a little more raucous as Max's set progressed – Max, he decided, was more astute than he let on; he was *teaching* the Grand Ballroom about the new music by degrees, leading them into it with all the surety of a dancing great – but it never strayed too far from the familiar. Raymond's partners were all averagely adept, but that was enough for him. He had always loved the feeling of taking someone with only a little prowess and making them feel like they could reign supreme at the Hammersmith Palais or the Royal Albert Hall.

The Royal Albert Hall – now, *there* was a venue he'd love to dance in. It was one of the few great establishments across whose floor he'd never waltzed.

The first half of the evening was almost at its close. At the end of Max's original number, 'My Only Runaway', Raymond bowed to his partner and watched her return to her husband above the balustrade, still floating on air.

That special feeling – it was what the Grand was for.

He turned, and there – taking cocktails beyond the dance floor's edge – was Jane Bancroft.

Raymond's roster was empty, no more reservations until the night's second half. An opportunity like this, he decided, would not come again – so, within moments, he was rising from the dance floor, weaving his way deftly through the congregation, and approaching the Bancroft party.

St John Bancroft stood some tables distant, head bowed in conversation with a broad, bearded gentleman with the air of a barbarian trussed up in gabardine. That was a disappointment – it would have been useful to come face to face with the man – but Raymond needed *something* to report. 'Battles like ours are won by degrees,' had been some of the counsel from the analysts in Salisbury. 'Keep the glamour for the dance floor. Your new craft requires no dazzling moments of glory, just quiet, assiduous work…'

'Ladies,' Raymond ventured, as he drew near. 'I wonder, perhaps, if you might care to dance?'

How many overtures like this had he made before? Too many to remember. Such was the role of a hotel dancer: to bring the ballroom to life. There were three ladies in Jane Bancroft's party, and their conversation broke apart at Raymond's approach. One of them he was certain he'd danced with before. A larger lady with auburn hair, her olive-green chiffon gown sparkling in the chandelier light, she greeted Raymond like a long-lost friend.

'Mr de Guise, I feel I'm tumbling back in time. Can it be?' She lifted her hand, as if to stroke his short black hair, though she dared not touch him. 'What have they done to you, sir? Your luscious locks have been burnt back, like a – like a grouse moor!'

Raymond feigned a deaf ear. 'You'll have to forgive me, ladies. My dancing, as you've seen, has suffered only a little – but my hearing is not what it was.'

'You're the returned soldier then,' said the second lady. 'I've heard them speaking of you.' She was petite and golden, and had to reach out to take Raymond's hand. 'My name is Susannah. Susannah Guthrie. I'm charmed to meet you.'

Guthrie, thought Raymond. Yes, he'd seen her at the doors of the Queen Mary, beside her odious husband. Susannah Guthrie radiated warmth; the thought of her and the Scottish laird didn't harmonise, somehow.

Raymond planted his lips gently on the back of her hand.

'If it takes fighting a war for us to meet, it has been worth it.'

'A charming soul, as ever,' said the red-haired lady.

'Ladies, it's my first night in the Grand. It feels something of a foreign country – and yet, dancing down there, I could almost believe France didn't happen. I could almost believe London is as it was before. That I wasn't stationed in a desert encampment just before Christmas.'

'The boy wants to dance,' chortled Jane Bancroft. 'Somebody do him a favour and glide with him.'

Raymond seized his chance, 'Perhaps you, Mrs Bancroft?' He glanced around, to make sure nobody was listening. 'I was King of the Grand, once upon a time. You danced with my heir tonight,' and his eyes glanced at Marcus, down on the dance floor, 'but why dance with a princeling when the old King returns?'

Jane sipped her drink, then took Raymond's hand. 'I've always liked a gentleman charmer,' she said to her companions. 'You ladies will have to take your turn.'

Jane Bancroft was a better dancer than any Raymond had partnered with tonight. She was assured in her footing, confident enough to glide in time with Raymond's body, almost prescient in anticipating his pivots and turns. 'It isn't the first time you've done this,' Raymond whispered – but Jane just smiled. 'You don't need to charm me, Mr de Guise. I'm already in your arms.'

The second song was faster, looser, with just a bit of that dangerous devil-may-care that Max had introduced to the ballroom. Raymond pushed Jane a little, making sure her steps kept pace with the song; turns, pivots, feints – she seemed adept at it all, but when the song came to its end, she was quite breathless, enough that she was forced to admit it was her time to leave the dance floor.

'It's a shame, Mrs Bancroft. I felt as if we were only just getting going.'

'A drink, perhaps?'

Raymond looked around. Marcus's eyes seemed to be fixed upon him, but he pretended he hadn't seen.

'It appears to be time for an intermission, Mr de Guise. Perhaps we will dance again – but for now...'

It was true. Even now, Max Allgood was up on stage, announcing that his orchestra would return in twenty minutes to revitalise the night. The applause that followed the musicians out of the ballroom followed Raymond, too, as he left the dance floor behind and joined Mrs Bancroft's party at their table. A waiter in resplendent white, with gold brocade, had just delivered further martinis to the table. 'One for my friend,' Mrs Bancroft announced, and the waiter bowed in acknowledgement. 'Ah, Raymond, allow me to introduce you to...'

St John Bancroft looked up from his martini, one thick eyebrow arched. He was a man of broad shoulder and the kind of jowls that threatened to obscure his collar entirely. Eyes bottomless and black looked at Raymond over the rim of his glass. 'The dancing man,' he began, in his deep plummy tones. 'Yes, very well, Jane. I'll take his hand, shall I?' He gripped Raymond's hand. 'Good waltzing, of course. Nice to make your acquaintance. But can you kindly go back where you came from? This is a private party.'

Suddenly, Raymond understood why Jane had enjoyed his charm, no matter how contrived it must have seemed. Her husband had not one ounce of charisma.

The Dorset industrialist ignored his wife's protestation – 'Oh, St John, really! We're in the Grand Ballroom, for Christ's sake. We're here to have fun, not talk business.' Mr Bancroft seemed to care not one jot for what his wife thought.

'Every social occasion is a business occasion, darling. If I wanted to fraternise with artistes, I'd have become a collector.' Then he looked, with mock contriteness, at Raymond again. 'I'm sorry, sir. My companions tell me you've been in Africa, trying to keep the colonies in line. Well, I'm grateful for your service – of course I am – and I'm grateful, too, for you keeping my Jane entertained this evening. But honestly, know your place, young man. There are staff in this hotel, and there are guests. One serves the other. One does not fraternise with …'

'You're being a boor,' came a rumbling, Scottish brogue. One of the men beside St John Bancroft had turned – and Raymond recognised the Scottish laird Guthrie at once: rake-thin, dark and balding, his face dominated by that magnificent moustache. 'St John, you're not talking to some porter or page. The dancers are here to spin some magic. They're *here* to provide the charm.'

'Good God, man, you talk as if they're dancing *girls*.'

'Well, I think we owe him a little more respect, don't you? If the word's right, this man's just come back from fighting Rommel.'

That had come from Susannah, Douglas Guthrie's wife.

St John Bancroft's cheeks were turning pink as sunburn. His eyes flashed.

'I appear to have intruded,' Raymond began. 'Gentlemen, ladies, forgive me. I'll retire for our intermission – but I should very much enjoy another dance this evening, Mrs Bancroft. You too, Lady Guthrie, if it appealed.'

As Raymond turned, Jane took his arm. 'I'm sorry for my husband. He treats these evenings like they're board meetings. If we leave a dinner party or a dance and he hasn't *advanced his interests*, he's a pig for a week.' She winked at him. 'Next time – the tango?'

In Raymond's day, the tango was considered too wild, too intimate, too impassioned for the Grand Ballroom. He wondered how much that had changed with Max's coming.

'I shall look forward to that very much,' he declared, then pivoted on his heel to cross the dance floor, back through the dressing-room doors.

His heart was out of time as he left the ballroom behind. St John Bancroft was a brute. Guthrie seemed more courteous – but Raymond already knew what was in his heart, so he tried not to give him too much credit. He just wasn't certain whether the interaction had been good or bad for his cause, what Maynard Charles might make of it the next time they met. On balance, he supposed, he'd progressed his situation. Contact had been made, a rapport (of sorts) established.

There was still time.

It was just as Maynard had said: these were not battles that needed to be won in one fell swoop.

He was still lost in these thoughts when he felt a figure looming over him, and turned to see that Marcus had approached through the multitude of musicians, all enjoying a stiff drink before they returned to the fray.

'How did you feel it went, Raymond – your first night returned to the Grand?'

Raymond smiled, 'I knew it was going to feel strange. I think I just have to dance my way through it. Just let the strangeness slough away, if you see what I mean.' Then, mindful of knowing his place in the ballroom, he added, 'If you've any pointers, Marcus, I should be pleased to hear them. I'm not too set in my ways to learn new tricks. And I know I'm heavier of foot than I used to be. I could feel it as I waltzed.'

'I do have one little observation,' Marcus ventured, 'though it needn't hold us back. Was there a reason you made a beeline for Mrs Bancroft, Raymond? It's only that I couldn't help seeing you cutting a swathe straight to her, disregarding all others.'

Raymond tensed. So, Marcus had been watching him, studying his behaviour in the ballroom. It irked that he'd been so obvious. He ought to have danced around Jane Bancroft more; he ought to have sought a more natural introduction to her party.

'Have things changed so much that we mustn't try and entertain the guests?' Raymond laughed, matching Marcus's smile.

'Mrs Bancroft had already taken a turn on the dance floor. She requested my hand for the first of the evening's dances. It just strikes me as a little *strange* that she would be your first choice too.' Marcus paused, as if cogitating on some intricate matter. 'I hope it wasn't a kind of ... showmanship, you heading straight for Mrs Bancroft? You're used to being the centre of things – I understand it. But Raymond, you're back in the rank and file.'

Raymond had never been quick to anger. But it took all his strength to bridle his emotions right now.

'Marcus,' he smiled, 'I've given you my word, and I'll give it again. You're the leader of the dance. I don't want to feel like I'm the King again. I just want to feel like I belong.'

Marcus gripped his shoulder. 'You do belong, Mr de Guise. You belong at my right-hand side, and I couldn't be prouder to have you as my lieutenant.'

*April 1942*

# Chapter Twelve

April was unseasonably warm, with a balminess that lingered long into the night. In the back garden at the house on Blomfield Road, Raymond's ramshackle family took full advantage of the evening light, with their simple dinner stretched out on the lawn and Stan rampaging around, bellowing 'Happy Birthday' at the top of his voice. Arthur, meanwhile, had decided to celebrate his first birthday by taking his first steps. He might have been able to cross from one side of the lawn to another, from Raymond's encouraging arms into Nancy's outstretched ones, if only Stan hadn't been running pell-mell, chasing imaginary foes.

The blackout was nearly upon them, and it was time for the party to disperse. Rosa, who had been enjoying the unseasonable sunshine – and enjoying a few short glasses of the sherry Mr Hastings had gifted Raymond – had grown sleepy as evening approached, but the promise of night seemed to bring her back to her senses. 'You really ought to come too, Nance. It's Freddie Riordan's band playing. They're *wild*. And Mary-Louise says the club's a hot spot for all the Yanks coming into town.'

Nancy grinned, 'You forget, Rosa – I'm a mother.'

'You know,' said Vivienne, 'it's not as if I don't look after Arthur every time you stay late at the hotel ...' She shot Nancy a look. 'You're allowed to enjoy yourself as well as being a mother. They haven't rationed that yet.'

Nancy looked at Raymond. She remembered going out dancing with him so well. But that was in the days before Arthur; the days before war; the days that weren't lived, from night to frenzied night, wondering when the bombs might come. It had been nice to catch glimpses of Raymond back in the ballroom – but sometimes she wondered if he was all quite *there*. She stole a look through the dressing-room doors, saw him guiding some diplomat's daughter around the dance floor, and fancied his mind wasn't really in the music at all, that his thoughts were still far away. Were they still in the desert, or was it the deafness that had changed him? Had it drawn its veil between him and the music? Did Raymond even *love* the dance any more?

'It might get him going again,' she said quietly to Vivienne. 'Somewhere a little wilder than the Grand. I've seen it before. Vivienne, when he first took me to the Midnight Rooms ...'

'Then go,' Vivienne said simply.

'It's Arthur's birthday night.'

Vivienne took her hand. 'So put him to bed, and take off. I'll watch over him. You see if you can tease some life out of his father.' Together, they looked at Raymond. At least he didn't seem to know they were talking about him; there were some advantages that came with his affliction. 'Listen to me – they'll cut him out of the Grand Ballroom if he's vacant in there. John Hastings is a kinder man than my stepfather, but he'll be every bit as ruthless as a businessman. So go – take him by the hand, lead him onto the dance floor, remind him what it's all *for*. Nance, me and Arthur, we'll be right here waiting.'

\*

The moment Frank led Rosa into the Ambergris Lounge, they were smothered in arms.

The other chambermaids from the Buckingham Hotel had arrived a whole half-hour ago, and already occupied two booths on the dance floor's furthest side. Annie Brogan had brought along her kitchen boy Victor but the rest crowded around a pair of tables already covered in glasses and spilled drinks. Up on stage, Freddie Riordan's After Hours Orchestra were playing a raucous number, full of trumpet and trombone. The pianist, whoever he was, had a devil's fury; his hands moved like a whirlwind over the keys. Thin and angular, he was the only Black musician in the band – but what made him stand out was the way he almost *stood* at the piano, hovering just above his seat, bowed crookedly like some scarecrow, one foot pounding on the pedal, the other just keeping its beat.

'It's like a thunderstorm!' Frank marvelled.

So rapt was he in looking at the dance floor, where crowds of American servicemen skipped and turned, pushing at the edges of what was acceptable, even in a place like this, that he lost his place three times at the bar. By the time he returned with drinks for himself and Rosa, she was already itching to dance.

'Drink up, Frankie, this is going to be thirsty work!'

Frank needed no further encouragement. Moments later, he and Rosa were waiting for a gap between the dancers, then gliding into it to join the throng.

There was nothing like dancing with Rosa. This was fast, frenetic music, matched by fast, frenetic dancing. Men held their partners more closely than would ever have been dared in the Grand; hands crept lower down, resting upon the waist – and even below. When the song reached its height, one of the American GIs dared to lift his partner from the dance floor, throwing her upwards so that, for a fleeting moment, she was flying through the air.

The pace just kept growing, driven to wilder and wilder extremes by the pianist on stage.

And just when Frank thought it could get no more fierce, the song exploded.

The trumpets were like a clarion call, the piano was like wildfire, the trombone urgent and demanding.

Then: just silence.

And the whooping across the dance floor.

Up on stage, Freddie Riordan was grinning at his pianist, as if he couldn't believe the young man had just summoned such a cascade.

'Again!' came an American voice, somewhere in the crowd.

'I'm game, Frank – are you?' asked Rosa.

'Oh yes,' said Frank.

This time he'd hold her closer as well. This time, Rosa's eyes dazzled at him when he held her at the waist, then let his hand start to stray.

This song had a different feeling. It was woozier somehow, more summery – like a languid late-August day, the war a thing only on the distant horizon. The dancing was different, but no less charged. It set the stage, too, for the song that followed – an explosive, three-minute song that had the dance floor kicking, skipping, turning, coming together and coming apart: the dance of the Americas, thought Frank, just like Raymond had described it so many times. He looked into Rosa's eyes, for she was alive with it – as if every nerve ending in her body was dancing to the beat. 'I love you, Rosa,' he said.

'Oh Frank, you're a puppy dog,' she laughed – but when she danced closer and kissed him on the cheek, it was all the reply that he needed.

He wondered, suddenly, if they'd still be dancing when they were sixty years old.

When the song came to an end, Frank was ready to dive straight into the next – but Rosa, sweat beading on her brow, had other ideas. 'I need my drink, Frankie,' she said, 'but look – here's Annie… Show her a wild time!' Rosa grinned, then winked over Annie's shoulder as Frank welcomed her to the floor.

Dancing with Annie would be like dancing with a little sister, thought Frank – but, all through the next song and the songs that followed, he couldn't stop imagining Rosa in his arms.

Outside the Ambergris Lounge, the taxicab opened and out stepped Raymond de Guise.

No suit of midnight blue, but the shimmering gabardine he was wearing was elegant enough. As for Nancy, she had opted for a dark green evening dress she hadn't worn since the start of the war. She'd been uncertain to begin with, but the taxi ride seemed to have changed everything: once the engine was rumbling, and Arthur left behind, the anticipation had started.

She threaded her arm into Raymond's. 'Vivienne was right. We can have *fun*, can't we, Raymond? You were lighter before, Raymond. Even after Dunkirk, you longed for the Grand Ballroom. I know things are different now, but… I'd like to see you longing for it again.'

Nancy stepped into the doorway, leading Raymond on. 'Maybe, through here, you can remember what it's all for. You used to know it: for joy and wonder. To be transported. To leave the world behind.'

Inwardly, Raymond smiled. Nancy was right; that used to be his dictum. The problem was that, this year, when he walked into the Grand, he carried all the problems of the world with him.

And he couldn't tell her a thing about it.

Together, they walked through the doors. The doorman bowed, took their coats, then they were ushered through, into the expansive surrounds of the Ambergris Lounge.

The dance floor was an ocean being wracked by a storm.

Bodies turned, pivoted and spun.

Somebody sailed through the air in the hands of another.

Somebody cheered.

And up on stage, the pianist had accidentally kicked over his stool – and now hunched over his piano, like he was conducting a sermon, his own feet skipping as the song pounded forward.

Nancy noticed Raymond staring curiously at the stage.

She wondered how it all felt for him: everything so distant and far away, his senses out of sync with each other.

'Are you all right, Raymond?' she asked, face lined in concern.

'Yes, it's just that...' Raymond looked quizzically at the piano player again. 'Nancy, I *know* him.'

'Enough, Frankie!' Annie laughed, gasping for breath as another song reached its titanic close. 'Enough!' She slipped out of his grasp, then staggered to the balustrade and up above. As she was going, she looked up and locked eyes with a statuesque, black-haired gentleman above. With eyes wide as saucers, she looked to his left – and came face to face with her manager, Mrs de Guise. 'Crumbs,' she blathered. 'I'll be in on time, Na – I mean, Mrs de Guise. I won't be a second late. I'll set up for breakfast. I'll do an extra shift. I'll...'

Nancy smiled and took Annie's hand. 'You're not at work now, Annie. A little dance isn't forbidden.'

In her wake, Frank rose up from the dance floor. 'I didn't think you'd make it, Nance,' he grinned, and hugged her. 'Come on, Nancy, Raymond – the girls are this way. I'll get you drinks.'

But when he got to the booth, there wasn't a place to sit – for the chambermaids had been joined by a group of young men with short, military haircuts, the tanned complexion of folk who haven't just endured a bitter English winter, and smiles that dazzled Frank as they approached.

'Hey, Frank,' Rosa called out. She was pressed up against the inner wall of the booth, one of the new arrivals at her side. 'Meet our new friends, Frank. This is Greg, and this is Turner, and this is…'

'Joel,' said the thickset young man beside Rosa, standing up to shake Frank's hand with his own brawny forearm. 'Joel Kaplan. I'm pleased to meet you, sir. We been watching you dance. You turn a dervish down there, if you don't mind me saying.'

The man had spoken in an accent Frank had only ever heard on the silver screen. He'd met plenty of Americans in the Buckingham Hotel – or, at least, he'd run errands for countless Americans – but they all spoke with an almost dignified air. Either they were from the moneyed townhouses of Manhattan, or from way out west, the darlings of Hollywood come to London to promote their latest picture. This man had what Frank could only think of as a cowboy's voice.

'Annie couldn't cope any more,' said Frank, with a grin. 'I think I owe her a drink.'

'The drinks are on me tonight, sir,' said Joel Kaplan, back on his feet. 'You all look like you could use some cheering. It's been a long, dark winter.'

Then he sidled off – *just* like a cowboy, Frank thought – to reach the bar.

Frank was about to make space for Raymond and Nancy at the booth, but when he looked round they were already bound for the dance floor. If being in the Grand Ballroom still felt conflicting, thought Frank, being *here* would surely bring out the best in Raymond.

One thing was for certain: no matter how damaged his hearing, he couldn't fail to be overwhelmed by the riot that pianist was conjuring up on stage.

Frank was watching them dance – how strange and wonderful to see Nancy on a dance floor, instead of hard at work in the Housekeeping Lounge, or tending to Arthur back home – when Joel returned with a tray full of drinks. After throwing back the whisky and ice he'd bought for himself, he said, 'Hey, you looking for a dance?'

Frank looked round. Rosa seemed thrilled to have been asked, but she looked at Frank and said, 'I think my Frankie's already dizzied me enough right now. Maybe a little later on.'

'Hey, you don't mind, do you, sir?' Joel chipped in. 'We have a dance club like this, back in Madison. My girl's back there, of course. Full permission to dance with any of those hicks that stayed behind – not that there'd be any to her fancy, but you take my meaning. As a gentleman, sir, I'd just like to dance. Shake a little of this wildness out of me. You'll know what it's like when you're on leave, won't you, sir? You're pent up, waiting for action. You just want to cut loose.'

'Oh,' Rosa said breezily, 'my Frank isn't on leave, he's—'

A strange shame had suddenly erupted in Frank. He hadn't felt such shame since the days before he'd joined the flotilla sailing out to Dunkirk. 'Dance away,' he said, as if to change the conversation. 'Go on Rosa, show him how it's done. Well, I danced with Annie, didn't I? It's only fair.'

Rosa was up and out of her seat in seconds, squeezing Frank's hand as she stepped out of the booth. 'Just one little whirl, Frankie. Keep my seat warm and my drink cold, won't you?'

Joel patted him on the back as they left.

Then Frank sat down and idly looked up, into the faces of all those other American GIs.

'To victory,' he said sheepishly – and raised his glass.

'Are you feeling it?' Nancy asked.

The noise on the dance floor was so overpowering that Raymond felt quite certain he really would go deaf. At least he had the presence of mind to feign that he hadn't heard Nancy. When she realised, she lifted herself onto her tiptoes and spoke directly into his ear.

'Nancy, it's incredible.'

The song had reached its end, and in the calm between storms, Raymond looked again at the piano player. Yes, he was quite certain – it was the same reckless young man he'd encountered on the train coming into London. Apparently, his recklessness in ordinary life was rivalled by his recklessness on the stage – because, right now, the other musicians seemed to be telling him to calm down, to rein in his performance. But, at the moment, Raymond thought there was a lot to be said for recklessness. It had entirely captured the room.

Rosa spun past – but she wasn't in Frank's arms. One of the GIs was holding her, his hands hovering on her waistline.

Wild abandon on stage; wild abandon on the dance floor below. Raymond decided he should probably indulge in a little wild abandon of his own. He'd been holding back too long. Not just because finding his niche in the Grand was vital to his new line of work. No, Nancy was right: he needed to do this for his soul as well. This, exploding everywhere around him, was *life*. What else was he fighting for, if not the promise of this?

The new song began.

No piano yet – just swooping trombone and drums.

But the dance floor was holding itself in anticipation.

Up on stage, the pianist knew what they wanted. Hunched over his piano, already disregarding his stool, he turned to them and beamed.

His fists rained down, ready to unleash a storm…

…and, somewhere in the piano, something snapped.

The song petered out.

The band looked at their pianist in horror.

Freddie Riordan took the trombone from his lips and, surveying a club full of disappointed patrons, said, 'Folks, we'll call that intermission. Half an hour away from the dance floor might just be the tonic you all need for what we've got in store.'

Then, to groans of disappointment, most of the musicians vacated the stage, leaving only Freddie Riordan with his arms shoulder-deep in the unfortunate piano's innards – and the pianist prowling the edge of the stage with the thunderous look of a boy who's been unjustly exiled from his classroom at the whim of his capricious teacher.

Raymond could feel Nancy's hand drawing him back to the booths, but he couldn't tear his eyes away from the pianist.

'Perhaps I can help with this,' Raymond said, squeezing Nancy's hand. 'I've been around a few pianos in my time.'

As the low hum of chatter grew thicker in the room, Raymond gravitated towards the stage. The fact was, he wasn't expecting to help with the piano at all – but he'd seen that incandescent look on the pianist's face once before, and it was certain only his intervention had stopped something much uglier taking place on the train. The boy looked like a coiled spring, ready to snap. But the problem with kicking out at the world was that the world was likely to kick back. And young men with tempests inside them never came out on top.

'You can really play,' said Raymond when the boy looked up.

'I know it,' he muttered darkly. '*They* know it too. All of them back there, and all of them out here as well. Won't stop me getting roasted for that piano string. That'll be wages gone again. I'm indentured. That's what it is.' The young man stopped prowling and furrowed his eyes, as if studying Raymond. 'Hey, I *know* you. You're *him*, aren't you? The stranger on the train?'

'I'm sure I did give you my name, *Nelson*,' smiled Raymond.

Nelson grabbed his hand. 'The god damn cavalry,' he laughed, 'sticking it to those bowler hats in the carriage. Hey, you wouldn't mind talking to Freddie up there, would you? Reckon you can keep me my pay for tonight? I got *bills* I need paying. I got *responsibilities*. And I'm the one bringing all the fire!'

Freddie Riordan looked up from the piano, his eyes glowering darkly at Nelson. Then he dived into its innards again, coming up with a length of sharp string – and a small piece of shattered wood. This he threw to the floor in fury. It seemed the piano was beyond quick repair.

Raymond reached into his pocket, and out came a small ivory card, embossed with the crown and sceptre insignia of the Buckingham Hotel.

'Here's where I dance,' he said, handing it over. 'I know for a fact they're a piano player down in the orchestra. They've guest pianists coming in and out – but there's nobody like you. You'd have to learn a little more elegance, a little more refinement – but it's a place your talent could shine. You'd just need to be a little ...'

'A little less like *me*,' Nelson laughed. 'Yeah, I heard all about it.' But he took the card all the same, and pushed it into his pocket.

'I haven't the influence I used to have, but I could have a quiet word with the powers that be. There might be an audition in it for you.'

But Nelson only scoffed, 'I'm a *long* way from that, Lieutenant. Me? I got a better chance of playing for the King of England.'

And he pointed with his thumb at a poster hanging, framed, by the side of the stage.

In the low dance-hall light, this is what it said:

**INTRODUCING THE ...**

# ROYAL DANSANT

**4th July 1942**

**at**

## THE ROYAL ALBERT HALL

### In celebration of our friends and allies
### The union of Old World and New

**An open dance competition**
**Amateurs and Professionals**
**Competitor Applications Now Open**

### BY ROYAL COMMAND

~

'They've already started putting their orchestra together. Freddie up there's auditioning for cornet. Oh, they're talking about it in all the clubs. A pauper's chance to play for his King. But I reckon my reputation goes before me now.'

Up on stage, Freddie had reared out of the piano and marched purposefully to the edge of the stage.

'Ladies and gentlemen!' he announced. Slowly, the room quietened. A hundred sets of eyes turned to take him in. 'I'm afraid our second set's going to be a little bit different from the first. No more piano tonight, folks.' The groan around the room grew in fervour. 'But we'll give you a storm regardless – I can promise that. Get your dancing shoes back on in fifteen minutes.' Then he looked sharply at Nelson. 'Better come backstage, boy. Your show just ended.'

'Freddie, it's not my fault. It's all in the perils of the game. We're playing with fire – Fred, sometimes, we're gonna get *burned*.'

Nelson's head hung low as he tramped after Freddie – but, before he disappeared through the backstage door, Raymond called out, 'You've got a rare talent there, Mr Riordan.'

'Rare and bloody,' Freddie remarked, then swept Nelson through the door.

Raymond felt movement at his side. An arm was snaking into his. When he looked down, Nancy had reappeared, their drinks in hand. She seemed to be studying the poster carefully, reading and rereading its every word.

'I think, perhaps, that was our cue,' Raymond smiled. 'Arthur's waiting.'

Nancy looked back at their friends, crammed into the booth with that group of American infantrymen, and knew Raymond was right. It was their time to leave.

Outside, a thin spring drizzle was coating the streets – but at least there were taxicabs waiting in the rank. Raymond helped Nancy inside, then slid in beside her. Through the blackout they sailed, past the shadowy ruins, homeward bound.

'You're thinking about it, aren't you?' Nancy ventured. 'The Royal Albert Hall. The Royal Dansant. An open competition...'

Raymond really wasn't. He was thinking about Jane Bancroft and her brute of a husband. About the slight, simpering figure that was Douglas Guthrie, the sorting house for spies that the Buckingham had become. And he was thinking about all the lies he had to tell to get close to them.

Nancy grabbed his hand. 'I think it would be good for you. The Royal Dansant, Raymond. You've never danced at the Albert Hall. If the Grand doesn't feel like yours any more, if you really can't find your way back to the love of it – well, mightn't it be the thing?' She nestled against him. 'I hate seeing you so wrought. It's like you're taut, rigid, all the time. And I know it's the desert. I know it's the war. But ... the ballroom used to transform you, Raymond. I used to see it in you every night, when you stepped into the Grand. Whatever worried you out here didn't touch you in there – and you carried the magic back out with you. You brought it back home.'

Raymond smiled as he stroked the hair from Nancy's brow and said, 'Is it not magical any more, Mrs de Guise?'

She just laughed and melted into him.

'Think about it,' she said, as the taxicab pulled up to the gates of No 18 Blomfield Road. 'It might be just the thing you need. You might be safe in body. But what about your soul?'

# Chapter Thirteen

The band were cooking up another storm. Trombone and trumpet wove around each other, then dovetailed in perfect flight. Nelson could hear the vacuum where the piano ought to be but, when he sneaked a look through the backstage door, the guests seemed to be enjoying it just about enough. It wasn't quite as wild, he saw. That brought him a kind of joy. But it didn't last long – because, here he was, just prowling about backstage, nothing to do and nobody to do it with, fingers itching, feet restless, and already having been told he'd be forfeiting the night's pay. 'Half because you only played a half set,' Freddie had told him, 'and half because somebody's got to pay for those repairs.'

Indentured – yes, he'd said it to the Good Lieutenant, the god damn dancing cavalry, and it was the only word that made sense. These people thought they *owned* him – when he was the thing that set them apart.

On and on the music went...

He shoved his hand angrily into his pocket, only to discover the card Raymond had given him there.

The Buckingham Hotel...

Why was he even dreaming?

What was the point?

Elegance and refinement. Lords and ladies. Maybe Uncle Max needed the safety and security of all that – but was it really what Nelson *wanted*? Was that really what mattered?

Nelson was still prowling, a caged animal, when the last song was played and, to waves of applause – it wasn't quite *rapturous*, he thought – the musicians appeared through the backstage doors. They looked pretty happy with themselves, thought Nelson – but all they'd done all night was ride in the slipstream of what he'd accomplished. As far as Nelson was concerned, they could all go to hell.

He was about to slide off, back into the night and the inevitable disappointment back at Albert Yard, when one of the trumpeters started laying out the cards and said, 'Nelson, you wound them up so tight, they couldn't help but dance. We're all grateful, you know. They'll be talking about that broken piano for weeks. They'll want more of it, the next time they come.'

'I tell you what, Nelson,' another trumpeter said. 'If you bring that fire to the card table, you might walk out of here laughing. You might be able to pay for those repairs *and* take something back to your uncle.'

'I'm out of here. Freddie, you want me to play again, you know where to find me. I'm gonna need paying next time.'

Nelson took a great stride towards the door.

'Let him go,' somebody said. 'The boy's out of bluff. He doesn't want to lose.'

Fire coursed through Nelson. Every sinew in his body seemed to be thrumming, telling him to turn round, to take up a hand of cards, to show them who he was.

But then he *remembered*.

It wasn't these boys he was fighting with.

He was fighting temptation, and temptation alone.

'You boys get stuck in. I got a nice warm bed waiting.'

Through the backstage doors he came, out onto the barren stage. The stage lights were dark in the Ambergris Lounge, but the house lights were not yet up. Apparently the bar manager had decided to eke a few more drinks out of the patrons who remained, even though the dancing was over for the evening. Some groups of revellers still congregated in the booths.

There sat the wretched piano, grinning at him with all its black and white teeth.

There was only *one* missing.

Nelson sat down.

Anyone could play with a missing key.

His fingers rolled up the octaves, building a wave. His left hand started slowly, building a broken rhythm. His right danced around the missing key, playing scales that jumped it.

Find the melody, he told himself.

Yes, this felt good. Feet could stomp to a melody like this.

It was some time before Nelson realised the revellers still left in the bar had all stopped their chatter, and turned to watch him perform. In the same moment, he realised Freddie Riordan had emerged from backstage and was sharing a quiet word with the bar manager, who'd appeared from his office.

They were going to tell him to stop.

Nelson let the song hang in the air. Only the echo of it remained. He looked out at the revellers. Their eyes wanted more. He could see them dazzle.

'You'll have to come back next week, folks,' he said, grinning from ear to ear.

Then, before either Freddie Riordan or the bar manager could castigate him, he jumped off stage and made as if he was about to leave the club.

He was only halfway there when one of the young dancers cantered to his side and said, 'Have a drink with us. It's on me.

Sir, I've never felt as *feral*. I thought I'd danced to everything, but...'

Nelson rather liked the sense that the man was confounded.

'The name's Nelson,' he said, and shook the dancer's hand.

'Frank Nettleton,' he said. 'Come on, I'll introduce you. I want to hear it all.'

Frank's party seemed to spill out of one of the booths on the dance floor's farthest side. One after another, he introduced them – 'This is Rosa, and the girls she works with up at the hotel – that's Mary-Louise, and Sal and, over there, that's Annie. And these – well, we've only met these gentlemen tonight, but this is Joel and...'

Joel Kaplan stood up and grasped Nelson's hand. 'The name's Kaplan.' And, one after another, he introduced his fellows. 'This is Greg and this here's Turner. And that, there in the corner, that's Rick. Larkin, we call him. Don't mind him – he's a little worse for wear.'

The man named Rick, with doleful black eyes which didn't seem to focus on anything whatsoever, just raised his hand feebly in acknowledgement.

'You're from back home then?' Joel ventured.

'Chicago. New York. You know, the places where the music *matters*.'

'I've never been to NYC,' Joel said, 'so I'll have to take your word for it.'

Then the infantrymen returned to the task at hand: romancing the Buckingham's chambermaids with stories of prairies, skyscrapers and wide, open skies.

Frank didn't mind. Now that he had Nelson, America seemed even more fascinating than it had before. Drinks were poured and soon Frank was asking him about Harlem, about the Cotton Club, about the Creole Jazz Band of Chicago.

'Now, I'm nineteen,' said Nelson. 'I haven't seen it all. But there's places underneath New York where the music never dies. It's morning to night in those joints. Old speakeasies that never shook the feeling of Prohibition. You know what Prohibition is, right?'

Frank did not. He simply stared.

'They tried to ban it,' Nelson said, lifting his brandy and gazing into its shimmering glow. 'They did ban it, no less. Something foolish got hold of my country and they made it a sin to have a good time. But folks still did it. They just kept it secret, see? And it's in secrets that the best things are born. You wouldn't have wild music if it didn't feel just a little bit dangerous. You need to walk on the dangerous edge of things, if you're gonna—'

'Dangerous edge of things?' the infantryman named Rick interrupted, suddenly rising from his stupor at the back of the booth. 'You're talking horseshit, but when have your lot ever talked anything else? Why don't you sign up, you layabout? Or is that what you're doing over here? Sneaking out on the draft?'

'Sneakin' out?' Nelson scoffed. 'Now who's talking horseshit? You blowhards hardly want my *type* in the army at all. You want to keep your segregation? Hey, hick, that's fine by me – you can trot off to be cannon fodder, and I'll stick with what I'm good at.'

Rick rose to his feet, even while his fellow infantrymen told him to shut up and sit down.

'Hey, I'm willing to die if I have to,' Rick announced, 'but not before I blow a hundred fascist bastards outta my way first. What are *you* going to do for democracy?'

Nelson just spluttered. 'Hey, you want me and my *type* to fight for democracy, you give it to us first. Until then, padre, I'll let you play the hero. Shit, when my cousin tried to sign up, what did they give him? He's a boot cleaner in some barracks somewhere. Just clerks and storemen – that's what we end up.'

'It's all you're fit for,' Rick spat, and cut his way between the chambermaids until he was almost on top of Nelson.

'Sit down, redneck,' Nelson retorted. 'This is the Old World. They civilised here. You want my lot to fight this war – you give it to us straight, like you got it. A chance to rise up in the world. Shit, no Black man got a chance to be an officer. It's just more servitude, while you rise through the ranks.' Nelson finished his drink, stood up, and turned his back on Rick. 'Hey Frank, I'm sorry, I'm not listening to this shit. I ain't a coward. I don't have to put up with this.' Then Nelson's lips twitched in something of a smile; he inclined his head in a bow and said, 'I apologise for my countrymen. They don't got no manners.'

Two strides later, he was practically preening. His ma would have been proud.

Uncle Max would have been proud.

That was twice tonight he'd walked away from temptation.

By God, the fire was coursing through him – and still he'd walked away.

Then, from somewhere behind him, Rick drawled out, 'That's right, off you go. Spout your horseshit, then just sidle out of here while the rest of us stand up for what's right. You ain't no good. You're just a chicken.'

There'd been fire coursing through him.

Now Nelson's blood ran cold.

'What did you call me?' he said, as he turned round.

'Play your music, boy. Talk about magic and wonder. This isn't a Hollywood movie. This is real life. People are dying. But you? You just want to sit pretty at home, as far from the fighting as you can possibly get. Why? Because you're nothing but a coward.'

That was it.

Temptation could be beaten twice, but a third time was once too many.

Nelson threw himself forward, barrelling Rick backwards. The infantryman crashed into the table, sending the Buckingham's chambermaids staggering – but somehow, despite his stupor, he stayed on his feet. That was why he was capable of throwing the first blow. A meaty fist drove into Nelson's temple, and suddenly the Ambergris Lounge was filled with stars.

But Nelson had been beaten before.

He'd taken his hidings like any kid back home.

One punch hardly mattered.

When the next came, he caught it in both hands, wrenched Rick around, and rode the bastard until he was on the dance floor, crumpling underneath him. By now, Nelson was howling. Straddling Rick from above, he started slapping him with open hands. A punch was too good for this man.

Moments later, when he swung backwards to slap the infantryman one more time, two brawny hands closed around his forearm, hoisted him upwards and thrust him across the room.

Joel Kaplan waited only until he knew Nelson wasn't about to come steaming in for more, then reached down and helped his comrade to his feet. 'Somebody get him a drink!' he called out. 'Rick? Rick, are you OK?'

Rick just teetered, like somebody twice as drunk as he actually was, until the chambermaids helped him back into the booth.

Turner and Greg strode towards Nelson.

'Leave him,' Joel said, his eyes flaring.

'Just let him do that to one of our own?' one of the infantrymen snapped.

'They'll have you court martialled for less,' said Joel firmly. *'Leave him.'*

Nelson looked like a cornered animal. Then his eyes landed on Frank. 'You wanna watch out for this lot, Frankie. The all-American hero isn't quite what he's made out to be, up on the silver screen.'

Then, still labouring for breath, he bolted straight for the exit.

Frank stood alone in the middle of the dance floor, watching him go. Why didn't it seem to matter to anyone that it was the infantryman who started it?

After some time, he turned back round. In the booth, Rick was nursing his bruised ego and battered body with another shot of whisky – while the chambermaids cosseted him, making sure he was OK.

And there, beside all the others, stood Rosa.

'At least you didn't get trampled, Frankie,' she said softly.

But she didn't come over to him.

She just stood there with the rest, one eye on Rick, just in case he was about to keel over.

The other flashing towards Joel Kaplan, the 'all-American hero', who stood so tall and proud, protecting his friend.

Outside the club, Nelson hunched into the rain and kept running. Soon, the streets of London were rushing past. He ran past the ruins and the scaffolds, the dark shopfronts and townhouses, until the breath was bursting out of his lungs. Somehow, he had run as far as the river. There it was, the great Thames, cutting the city in half. He could see the dark outline of Parliament. The barrage balloons, like great black clouds, up above.

The ivory card from the Buckingham Hotel was still in his pocket.

Fat chance of that now, he thought. Once Uncle Max knew he'd not only broken a piano but also lost his wages, and brawled with some servicemen, there'd be no chance of being trusted in the Grand Ballroom.

He screwed the card in his fist and cast it into the Thames' turbulent waters.

'There really is more chance of playing for the King,' he snorted as it flew.

But then he thought...

The Royal Albert Hall.

The Royal Dansant.

They were auditioning musicians, weren't they?

It wasn't just on recommendations and hearsay. It wasn't about reputation, friendships and favour.

No strings needed to be pulled.

It was just about *talent*, wasn't it?

For the longest time, and heedless of the rain, Nelson just stood and stared at the waters.

They'd have to take him seriously, if somehow he was chosen for the King.

'Well,' he laughed out loud, 'ain't a boy allowed to dream?'

*May 1942*

# Chapter Fourteen

It wasn't so long ago that the beaches at Camber Sands were nothing but rolling pastures of gold, undulating dunes that stretched out to the sea. Now, as Raymond watched through the window of the taxicab he'd picked up in Rye, all he could see was barbed wire and fortifications. Pillboxes, half camouflaged, sat above the dunes, looking out to sea.

Had it really been only two years since he was stranded on the other side? Since he buried his brother six feet under the earth and somehow made it back across the Channel? He'd thought of it less and less as the months passed by but, now that he was here, it suddenly seemed so *present*.

Thank goodness, then, that he was almost at his destination: the mansion on the hill.

The taxicab had to stop at the bottom of the drive so that the driver could get out and open the gates, for the way up to the manor house was a private road, winding between resplendent lawns, the old gamekeeper's cottage, and an apple orchard just coming into full leaf. By the time they'd got halfway, with the manor house revealing itself beyond the glasshouses, Raymond thought he understood the appeal of a place like this. In here it was possible to believe the war did not go on at all.

And at least he wasn't coming here as Raymond de Guise, in the employ of MI5.

Here he could be Raymond de Guise, the dancer of old.

He got out of the taxicab, rang the little bell that hung above the door, and waited for it to open.

He'd thought she'd have a housekeeper – but no, there she was, the lady of the house herself, as resplendent as she'd been in their younger days, as glacially beautiful as she'd been looking out of the front cover of *Harper's Bazaar*.

As pale as the ghost who'd left the ballroom, and all her secrets, behind on the eve of war.

'Hélène,' he said, with the softest of smiles.

'Raymond de Guise,' said Hélène Marchmont. 'Of all the gentlemen and vagabonds I get knocking on this door, I never expected it to be you.'

Raymond bowed his head and flashed her a smile. 'I always liked to wrongfoot you, Miss Marchmont.'

Then he followed her within.


The Marchmont manor had been in Hélène's family for generations, but she had never expected it to be part of her future. Hélène had grown up with Raymond, forged a reputation in the clubs and competitions, been garlanded and praised, featured on the front pages of magazines and courted by countless producers to come to California – where the stars were lining up to give her a future on the silver screen – but she'd forsaken it all. The reason for that now hovered by a table in the sitting room, pencil in hand, under the tutelage of her elderly grandparents: Sybil, seven years old, and three years since Raymond last laid eyes on her. She looked up from the picture she was working on and considered him with suspicious eyes. She was growing into the long, lithe body of her mother, but still had her father's luminous eyes. Sidney, dead before she was born, lived in her even now.

'Sybil, do you remember Raymond?'

Sybil set down her pencils, picked herself up and pottered to a chest of drawers in the alcove by the room's great hearth. From here she unearthed a pile of old sketchpads and, upon locating one, opened it to reveal a pencil sketch of two dancers beneath a glittering chandelier. This was the hand of a child, thought Raymond, but someone who promised great things – an artist, just like her mother before her. Just like her father. 'You're the dancing man,' Sybil pronounced.

'You've captured our likeness perfectly,' said Raymond, who decided to ignore the bandiness of his legs in the drawing. 'Can you dance, Sybil?'

'Mama takes me for lessons, but... She shrugged, held up her drawings as if to declare this was what she liked best, then trotted back to her grandparents' side.

Then, with a certain practised look – the kind of imperceptible flicker that people only develop after countless years in each other's company – Hélène guided Raymond away, until they had settled, at last, in the back drawing room of the manor, where glass doors looked out over the grounds, with just a hint of the seascape beyond.

'She wants to dance,' Hélène explained, 'but she's born into an unfair world. How is a mother to tell her daughter: you won't have the same opportunities, darling; they won't let you follow your mother's path – and all because of the colour of your skin.'

Sybil's father, Sidney, had played trumpet in the Buckingham's orchestra, back when Raymond and Hélène first graced the Grand. If, back then, it had bordered on bad taste to have Black musicians in an orchestra of such high renown, it was at least permissible; but the scandal of a secret pregnancy, out of wedlock, between one of society's darlings and a man who didn't even have the decency to be white? It might have undermined the Grand forever – and so Hélène had retired from the ball, found herself a mother alone.

'The world changes, Hélène. There may be hope for her yet.'

'And for you, Raymond? Now that you're a father?'

'I believe there's hope for us all,' Raymond smiled – though, at times, he struggled to believe it. 'I'm back in the rank and file, Hélène.'

'Why did they send you home, Raymond?'

They'd been close, once upon a time – close in a way that lovers rarely are, close in a way that transcended simple friendship – but things had changed when Hélène left the ballroom. That was inevitable, for their partnership was based on common purpose, common ideals, and a treasure trove of shared endeavour. People who build worlds together are not easily divided – but then Hélène had revealed her child, Raymond had recited his wedding vows, war had come and the world was upended. Yet, when he started telling her all the lies he'd been spinning, he still felt as if he was betraying her, making a mockery of all they'd once shared. Lies, even lies told in the service of King and Country, somehow corroded a soul.

'Oh, but Raymond,' Hélène said, her heart swelling with feeling, 'can you even hear the music well enough?'

Raymond smiled wanly and said, 'We used to dance in silence. Do you remember? We'd simply count, beneath our breaths.'

'But that was rehearsing, Raymond. That was by rote. When we were *performing*, it was all about the music.'

That was the problem, thought Raymond. That was why Nancy was right. He wasn't leaning into the music at all. His loved ones thought it was because of his affliction – even Marcus thought as much – but in truth it was because of his mission.

Somehow, he supposed, he was going to have to find a way to marry the two together. Observe one, without ignoring the other.

That was why he was here.

By God he loved Nancy; she always knew what was right.

'Hélène, you've danced at the Royal Albert Hall.'

'A lifetime ago, Raymond. I was twenty-eight years old. I was—'

'Crowned champion, the last time the King held a contest.'

Hélène evidently hadn't heard of the Royal Dansant, for she screwed up her eyes in confusion and asked, 'What's this about, Raymond?'

'I want to feel like I'm worthy of the ballroom again. It hasn't been enough to dance in the Grand. I've felt like I don't belong.' *Like I'm not drawing the eye enough to do what's being asked of me. Like I won't last long enough in the troupe to fulfil my purpose.* 'In two months' time, the King is hosting an open competition at the Royal Albert Hall. A fourth of July spectacular, to celebrate the New World coming to the war. Nancy wants me to enter. I've been casting the idea aside, but the truth is, it's been growing on me. Nancy says it's about happiness, joy, finding purpose again – and she's right. I've lost something, Hélène. Between France and North Africa, and everything in between, some hunger or passion has bled out of me.' He stopped. 'So I'm going to enter the Royal Dansant, and I should like nothing more than for you to be my partner.'

Hélène was silent, stony-faced. 'Raymond, I haven't danced formally in years.'

Raymond just grinned, 'I'm a soldier with a soldier's physique, heavy in my tread and hard of hearing.' He shrugged. 'Just the thing to astonish the King. But Hélène, listen to me, what if it could be like those early days? What if stepping out together might feel like it did when the doors of the Grand first opened, and you and I sailed out together, to all that expectation, all that anticipation just bursting in the air around us?'

Hélène was still staring at him, those unreadable eyes so glassy and blue, when the drawing-room door opened a crack and Sybil appeared, brandishing a picture. 'Mama,' she ventured, 'it's for the man.'

And he turned to gracefully accept the illustration Sybil was presenting.

This was a more mature hand, its lines steadier, its shading more delicate and deliberate. Beneath a resplendent chandelier, two figures danced: the man, a mane of flowing black hair; his partner, a seven-year-old's study of her mother, perfect even down to the wintry eyes.

'Even when you draw, it's dancing on your mind?'

Raymond flashed a look back at Hélène, who still seemed to be brooding over his request. 'Perhaps, Sybil, you should show me how you dance.'

'You're too …' she waved her hand airily, '…up there …'

'We are indeed mismatched in size – but should we try?'

Already she was laying her picture carefully down so that she could step close to Raymond. If he could not hold her in any classical style, he could still take her by the hands. He started counting quietly, just loud enough that Sybil could hear – and led her in a simple box-step across the drawing-room rug. For her part, Sybil seemed to know what she was doing. By the time Raymond announced a turn, she was already bowing into it. 'Now the big finale!' Raymond announced – and, quite by surprise, he lifted Sybil up high and twirled her around.

'That's more for the dance halls than the ballrooms,' Raymond winked as he set her down. 'Dance changes, Sybil. Your father played trumpet in the greatest ballroom in London. To my mind, the very greatest in the world. The other week I saw a young

Black pianist transform the mood in the Ambergris Lounge by the sheer power of his playing. The Buckingham Hotel's orchestra is led by Max Allgood – a more talented man you'd never meet. I see no reason why you mightn't one day be dancing among them...'

Sybil's eyes lit up in wonder, but Hélène's had narrowed in caution.

'Now Raymond, she needs to know the real world isn't as easy as a dream. You know that, better than any.'

'I think we all have to start dreaming a little again. It can't wait forever. It can't wait until the war is done.'

'I want you and mama to dance,' Sybil declared.

Hélène looked like a trapped animal, but Sybil was already tumbling towards a gramophone player in the corner. The song she put on was hardly modern – just one of Jack Hylton's old standards – but Raymond and Hélène had performed to it, once upon a time. As Hélène sashayed towards Raymond, he could remember it vividly.

He remembered this too.

Hélène presented herself, and he took her in a simple hold, regal yet loose.

Strange how, however much the years changed a person, two old dancers could still slide back together.

He'd missed this.

To dance with Hélène again might be just the tonic he needed.

Just the counterweight to the lies he was telling and the tension he carried as he danced in the Grand.

'Shall we?' he asked.

Sybil was already clapping.

So how could they not?

\*

The feeling of dancing with Hélène stayed with Raymond as he caught the train back into London. Tonight, the Grand beckoned. Marcus, no doubt, would have sidelined him again. But Raymond didn't mind, not now that he had a *plan*.

He'd forgotten how much it mattered, but in convincing Hélène he'd somehow convinced himself. To dance was to live, and to live was the only thing that mattered.

The taxicab dropped him at the bottom of Berkeley Square, in exactly the same moment that Max Allgood emerged from a taxicab of his own, to huff and puff across the green expanse in the middle of the square. The bandleader lifted his crumpled brown homburg hat at Raymond as they came together. 'Six weeks until the Summer Serenade, Mr de Guise. How's that body bearing up?'

'I'll be fighting fit, Mr Allgood.' Then he had a sudden thought. 'Have you found your pianist, yet? For the Summer Serenade?'

'All the pianists in London are keeping their powder dry. Nobody's gonna commit until they've announced who's playing at the Albert Hall.' He paused. 'Ray, I'm having a hell of a time. But we've had it worse before. Most folks can play a bit of piano, if the piano's not the heart of the thing.'

'Marcus will want it to be the heart.'

'Mr Arbuthnot will know what he wants when he hears it,' Max grinned. 'But we'll need to find someone.'

Raymond was about to follow Max into the Mews but, at the last minute, he paused. Standing in the shadow of the townhouse that neighboured the Buckingham Hotel, holding an unlit cigar while propping himself up on the open door, was a man with a jowly, hangdog countenance. His eyes bored into Raymond's. He beckoned him near.

'Pardon me, sir, spare a match?'

Raymond recognised that look.

A feeling like gravity blossomed inside him.

'I'm afraid not, sir,' Raymond replied.

'Then perhaps you ought to go looking,' the man replied, and slid back inside his taxicab.

Raymond watched the taxicab wheel away.

He glanced upwards, at the darkening skies.

*Pardon me, sir, spare a match? No? Then perhaps you ought to go looking.* The simplest of words, but they were meant as a summons – and, in Raymond's new business, when your paymaster whistled, you answered the call.

How much time was there before the first trumpets sounded in the Grand? Enough, evidently, to get to the Deacon club and back – for Maynard Charles would not want to risk Raymond's position in the ballroom.

Collar turned up, head down, Raymond turned away from the Buckingham Hotel and bowed into the gathering darkness over Berkeley Square. In but ten minutes, he was knocking the familiar pattern upon the little nondescript door along Piccadilly. A few moments later, one of the concierges was escorting him upstairs, into a bustling, smoky bar room – where, among two dozen other patrons and a Greek chorus of whispered conversation, Maynard Charles was sitting with his White Owl cigar.

Maynard greeted him like an old friend – though, of course, so much of this was an act.

'Mr Charles,' Raymond ventured, 'I'm expected in the Grand.'

'And you'll be there on time,' remarked Maynard, shepherding him onward, away from the bustle of the bar, into one of the echoing back corridors beyond. 'I won't put Mr Arbuthnot's nose out of joint more than it already is. You're risking his ire enough with this talk of the Royal Dansant and recapturing the glory days of your partnership with Hélène.'

Raymond stared, in both accusation and disbelief.

'Don't think we don't know what you do and where you go, Raymond. As it happens, I should be glad of you being at the Albert Hall this summer. We may have need of you – and, if you win plaudits, well, how could they ever eject a man celebrated by his King from the Buckingham Hotel? Marcus would have to make accommodations for you then. He'd have to treat you as his star. Your position would not be in doubt, and we could all stop walking on eggshells and get on with the task at hand.'

'Then what am I doing here, sir?'

Maynard Charles tramped forward, his head shrouded in cigar smoke, and gently pushed open an office door. Inside, a refined-looking gentleman with wisps of auburn hair, his shirtsleeves rolled up to reveal meaty forearms generously covered in freckles, looked up and nodded.

'Raymond, I should like you to meet Mr Jack Ambler.'

Jack Ambler stood up, reaching out a hand to clasp Raymond's own.

'Jack, this is Raymond – our man in the Buckingham Hotel.'

Raymond shook his hand.

'And Raymond, this is Jack Ambler. His department is going to be of critical importance to your endeavour.' Maynard Charles gestured for Raymond to sit. 'Mr Ambler here is the head of the British Gestapo, and he has something he needs to say.'

# Chapter Fifteen

'The British Gestapo?' Raymond ventured.

It was as if he'd passed into some strange world, somewhere on the other side of the looking glass. Never had two words fitted more poorly together than these two. He sank into his seat with an otherworldly feeling. Jack Ambler did not seem like a man in the employ of that scurrilous Nazi organisation.

A drink was poured. Raymond just held on to it, waiting for the pieces to slot into place.

'You might be able to tell, Mr Ambler, that de Guise is an honest, upstanding man. But what he lacks in duplicity and guile, Raymond makes up for in intelligence and courage. He'll just need a little convincing.'

Jack Ambler topped up Raymond's brandy from a decanter, even though Raymond had not touched a drop. 'Rest assured,' he said, 'I am no Nazi.'

'Raymond,' Maynard Charles weighed in. 'There are more malcontents and seditionists in London than a good, loyal Englishman can bear. Oh, we speak of British pluck and British resilience – and there is plenty of that old bulldog spirit abounding in London right now – but, look a little further, and you'll find there's a certain type of Englishman who sees common purpose with Mr Hitler's henchmen. Make no mistake about it: were Britain to fall to the Reich, were Mr Churchill deposed and somebody like Domville put in charge, there would be plenty among us who'd turn collaborator. We British like to think ourselves apart. But all you need to do is take a look at Paris to know how many of your neighbours would run into their arms.'

'My job is to document them,' said Ambler. 'We keep files on these people so that, should Britain fall, our resistance would know who the most eager collaborators might be. Most are petty thugs, criminals, the sort of downtrodden souls who refuse to be saved by taking the King's shilling – and would rather get their own back at the country instead. Most of these are harmless. Others,' Ambler went on, 'are a little more active. They push at the edges of what might be permissible. They dance around sedition, like you might in your ballroom. My job, Mr de Guise, is to entrap them.'

'You're not Gestapo,' said Raymond. 'It's a set-up.'

Maynard Charles smiled, and tapped out the ash of his cigar. 'I told you he had nous, Jack.'

'The Office needed a simpler way of tracking these seditionists than sending agents out to keep eyes and ears on every single one. We are severely understaffed and under-resourced, Raymond. The government is stretched in fighting its real wars, which leaves us in want, fighting this war in the shadows. So a plan was hatched.' Ambler smiled in pride; it seemed, then, that the plan had been Ambler's own. 'Rather than go out and find these traitors, we would simply bring them to us. To you, Raymond, my name is Jack Ambler, agent of military intelligence. To them, I am Jack Morgenroth – and I have been living in London since the days of the Beer Hall Putsch, awaiting an assignment just like this. I am the head of the underground British Gestapo. When Britain falls to the Reich, I will be elevated to the head of its secret police, based here in London – but, until then, I am their conduit back to the Reich.'

'You're a shopfront,' Raymond said, 'with nothing behind it. They come to you to contact the Reich, and you spin lies for them, to make them part of it. Then you know who they are. Then you can follow their trails.'

'The project has been enormously successful,' Maynard Charles chipped in, 'and approved by Mr Churchill himself. Not only do we now have a directory of British collaborators – but, on several occasions, we have been able to stop the sale of sensitive documents to the Reich, and all because of the work Mr Ambler has been putting in.'

'What clearances does Mr de Guise have, Maynard?'

'We may speak freely in here.'

Jack Ambler made a steeple of his hands and said, 'Last year, the British Gestapo were in receipt of a file detailing a tactic the RAF have developed for neutralising an enemy's air defences. My contact sought to sell this document to Reichsmarschall Göring, and to use me as his intermediary. Of course, he believes he was successful. But do you think the RAF would right now be pursuing their thousand bomber raids on Continental targets if this was so? This work will win the war, Raymond. Great Britain is not impregnable, but it may last long enough if we head these traitors off – and leave them thinking they have won.'

Maynard Charles drank his brandy and said, 'Which rather brings us on to your visit here tonight.'

'One of the more permanent associates of our British Gestapo is a man named Angus Kemp. He is an impressive man – or would have been, in peacetime. A moneyed man, Raymond. You'll know the sort. He has various industrial concerns across the southeast. He has done handsomely from this war, as rich men often will. But he is also a virulent seditionist. He does not believe in Britain – and for some time he has believed he is a princeling, waiting to be anointed by Nazi high command when they eventually rule these shores.'

'What is he to do with me, sir?'

'I'm getting to that,' said Ambler. 'Kemp reports that he has received an overture from St John Bancroft – whose wife, apparently, you know well. A business proposal, so I'm told – though that is how all these things start. Bancroft appears to have invited him to cocktails and cards at the Candlelight Club at the Buckingham Hotel.'

'We're allowing the gambling to proliferate as much as we can,' Maynard interjected. 'It's helpful to the cause.'

'A week from today, St John Bancroft has organised for his wife to accompany Susannah Guthrie to the Guthries' estate in Scotland – a little respite from London, and all its terrors. The two couples, it would appear, have become great acquaintances through their stay at the hotel.'

'And as we know, they hold other interests in common as well.'

'The ladies will be in Scotland, and the men will meet to play cards, make merry... and speak *business*.' Ambler stopped. 'You're to join the card game, Mr de Guise. I daresay it shan't be easy, given Bancroft's enmity towards you, but you'll find a way. Befriend them, let them bankrupt you at the card table, and report back on everything you glean. Is that understood?'

'Forgive me, sir,' said Raymond, 'but Kemp's conduit to the Nazis doesn't exist. If Bancroft is romancing him because he thinks he can help him make contact with the enemy – well, won't it come to you anyway?'

'That's only one of several eventualities,' Ambler explained, more sternly now, 'and we must cover every one. I want to know why Bancroft is seducing Kemp.'

Raymond stood and lifted his hand to his brow in salute. 'Understood, sir.'

Moments later, he was perambulating Piccadilly, then returning to the shadows of Mayfair. From one world, he stepped into another. And yet... the border between worlds had blurred. He stood on Berkeley Square and thought: the Buckingham, that shining bastion of British resolve, had become but a boarding house for untouchable aristocrats with designs on being honoured by the Nazis when they came.

How he was going to get into that card game, he did not know.

It was easier when all he had to do was march.


Raymond hurried through the tradesman's entrance, through the warren of higgledy-piggledy halls hidden behind the Buckingham's lavish mask, until he had reached the dressing rooms behind the Grand.

To his horror, the rooms were barren.

Through the dance-floor doors he could hear the pounding of piano, the soulful swoop and glide of Max's trombone. When he dared to push the doors open, just a crack, he could see Frank and Mathilde turning, Marcus and Karina dominating the dance floor. His heart stilled a little, then; it was still only the showpiece dance that signified the start of every evening. He hadn't missed anything yet, for Marcus had still ('regrettably, Raymond') found no place for him in the choreography.

The song was reaching its finale. Quickly, he scanned the dressing tables, screens and booths. There, folded neatly beside Marcus's day clothes, was the roster for the evening's dances.

His eyes flashed over it.

There, his first dance of the night: Susannah Guthrie.

His lips twitched in a smile.

Out in the ballroom, the song came to its end. Applause filled up the Grand Ballroom. Raymond threw himself at his dresser, donned his suit of midnight blue. The band were already striking up as he opened the dance-floor doors, stood there like a returning King, and surveyed the ballroom. There was Susannah Guthrie, up by the balustrade, waiting for him. The Scottish laird lingered behind, looking imperiously on.

She must have asked for me by name, thought Raymond. Good. *One step closer to joining the fray.*

He made eye contact with her across the dance floor, and watched as her face lit up. Then he started wending his way towards her.

He was halfway there when Marcus, similarly en route to meet his first guest for the night, took him casually by the arm. To any outsider, they looked like brothers in arms, sharing a quiet word before the festivities began. But in a low whisper, Marcus said, 'Don't show us up, Raymond. The rest of the troupe were here on time, as they always are. If you want to be part of us, you must win their hearts – the same as you must win mine.'

Raymond remembered *deference*. It was the only way back in. 'Marcus, my apologies,' he said. 'I'm afraid there was an unavoidable delay. You know how London is these days.'

'An unavoidable delay on your way back from Rye, to meet with Hélène Marchmont?' Marcus released Raymond's arm and shook his head witheringly. 'I'm afraid Frank explained – though the boy had loyalty enough to you to feel shamefaced about it afterwards. You promised me, Raymond, that this troupe would be your devotion – and now ... the Royal Dansant? I myself am not competing, because I know where I am needed.'

Raymond paused.

He was normally able to control his temper, unlike his brother Artie. And yet ...

'Marcus, you'll have to forgive me. All the background noise in the ballroom, I can hardly…' He smiled, softly. 'Perhaps we can speak about it later? When our guests are not waiting?'

They held each other's gaze for only a moment; then each man spiralled away to meet his guest by the balustrade steps.

Before Raymond could get there, Frank – himself crossing the dance floor to meet his guest – reached his side. 'I'm sorry, Raymond. A slip of the tongue. I hope I didn't…'

Raymond flashed a look back at Marcus. At least the broad, blond titan was now otherwise engaged, enveloping his guest – an elegant young woman in crimson chiffon – in his syrupy charm.

'It wasn't a secret, Frank. How could it be? Mr Arbuthnot is acting out of insecurity. Strange as it may seem, it's a plague that afflicts the talented most of all. He's worried I'll upstage him. But I have to do this, Frank. I want to know that it *matters* again.' He paused. A thought had entered his head – and, though he knew it would be playing with fire, he could not push it away, because it was *right*. 'Frank, you've never competed in dance. You entered the ballroom world so differently to me and Hélène.'

'Mr Arbuthnot said that, after the war was done, he might tutor me. That there might be a future in the competitions.'

'It sets a dancer up, Frank – to be garlanded, to be praised, to be written about in the Society Pages or the *Dancing Times*.' He flashed another look at Marcus. Was he doing this just to bait the gentleman dancer, or because it was good for Frank? It was, he later reflected, a little of both – but, now that he'd had the idea, he could hardly leave it alone. 'The Royal Dansant is an open competition, Frank. You and Mathilde might shine.'

Frank looked stupefied. 'Really, Raymond?'

Up on stage, the guest pianist rolled his wrists up and down the ivories, building a succession of chords.

The song was about to begin.

'We'll talk more, Frank,' said Raymond. Then he marched on, until he stood at the bottom of the balustrade steps, looking at Susannah Guthrie above.

'You enjoy keeping a lady waiting, do you, de Guise?'

'Mrs Guthrie, it fills my heart to dance with you this night,' Raymond began, as he took her hand.

It really did, he thought, as he led her onto the dance floor, turned her suddenly around and took her in hold.

Because here was his chance.

By the end of the night, he intended to be in the very heart of her family – and, by this time next week, when she was in Scotland entertaining Jane Bancroft at her husband's estate, he would be sitting quietly at the card table, absorbing every word, understanding every silence, learning what manner of treachery he had been commissioned to unpick.

# Chapter Sixteen

The Queen's Gate Concert Hall dominated a Kensington crossroads, half hidden by the scaffolds erected in the reconstruction of a neighbouring church. Word had rippled around London some days before that this was to be the venue where the orchestra playing at the Royal Dansant was assembled. Barry Pike, that esteemed Englishman (and personal choice of the King) who had led the BBC Symphony Orchestra for so many years, had been chosen as conductor – and, consequently, as the man who would be assembling the band. 'It's an open call,' they'd said in the Midnight Rooms, the Ambergris, the Starlight Lounge, and all those other illustrious London venues at which Nelson now hawked his talents. While he hadn't made a connection, loitering by the bar and drinking away what little money he had, he had at least picked up on the gossip.

An orchestra, to be assembled for the King.

An orchestra in celebration of the United States joining the war.

An orchestra like that just *had* to have an opening for somebody like Nelson.

And wouldn't that stick it to Uncle Max, and all his rules and regulations?

Yet, from the moment the auditions began and Nelson joined the line outside the Queen's Gate Concert Hall on a crisp May morning, he knew it wasn't going to be so easy. The sheer multitude of musicians told him that. So too did the colour of their skin, the cut of their jib. Apparently the war had summoned most of London's younger musicians to its service, because the men gathered here – carrying their trumpets, their violins, their cornets and bassoons and French horns – were uniformly of Freddie Riordan's generation. Indeed, there was Freddie, standing among them – surrounded by a horde of greying forty and fifty-somethings. What was worse, they were all dolled up as if they were about to step onto the stage at the Royal Albert Hall itself. Nobody had given Nelson the memorandum, because while they wore smart jackets, belts and braces, shirts with silver cufflinks and neckties sporting the colours of the Union Jack, he wore a ragged pair of slacks, a creased shirt with its collar button missing, and shoes threadbare enough that he could feel the contours of the street as he walked.

It was hopeless.

There wasn't a city in the world, it seemed, where music mattered as much as it did in New York. Here in London, it came second to refinement. Here in London, it was too easy to be out*classed*.

Five minutes in the queue was all he could take. Hands shoved in pockets, muttering darkly under his breath, he abandoned his place and started marching away.

Then a hand took hold of his arm – and he looked up to find a group of other Black performers who'd been standing in the queue somewhere behind him.

'Where are you going, son?' said one of the older musicians, a short, round man bedecked in a grey suit that matched the hue of his whiskers. 'They haven't heard you yet.'

Nelson looked this group up and down. There were five of them, all twice his age – and all ten times as smart. Apparently he was the only musician in the whole of London who hadn't understood that, to play for the King, you had to dress like one.

'You look like you were up all night,' one of the others said, slapping Nelson on the shoulder. 'Did you sleep in a hedgerow?'

'I slept in the Midnight Rooms,' Nelson countered. 'It was a wild night.'

Nelson had taken an extra shift mopping floors after the music was done. He'd done it, at first, to ensure that he didn't get drawn into any nasty card games after the performance was through – and the consequence was that, sometimes, he got to curl up in a booth and just sleep there all night.

'You smell like it too. Do you *want* to get through those doors?'

Nelson took a moment to decide whether these men were roasting him or not. Part of him wanted to tell them to go to hell – but that was the devil on one shoulder talking. Nelson decided to listen to the angel on the other before he said, 'It's why I'm here. I can *play.*'

'When a boy turns up to audition for the King looking like he's been laying in a latrine, you got to hope he can,' said the elder musician. 'Listen, you need to get sharpened up – and quick. This queue's *marching.*'

One of the other musicians had a spare jacket that was quickly slipped over Nelson's ragged shirt. Another had a necktie, which hid the missing buttons at his collar. Somebody had a little tin of shoeshine, which went some way to smartening the frayed, shabby brogues Nelson was wearing. After they were done – and Nelson was liberally applying the pomade somebody had provided to his hair – he looked half presentable. 'It might be enough to get you through the doors,' said the elder musician. 'After that, son, it's every musician for himself.'

'Ain't it always?' Nelson grinned.

'That's the spirit!' one of them laughed. 'Hey, how'd you even get here anyway? You hardly look old enough to be off your mother's knee.'

'I came to be with my Uncle Max. Max Allgood – you heard of him?'

The musicians looked at each other in surprise.

'Oh, of *course* you've heard of him,' Nelson grinned. 'But you wait until I get myself in there. You haven't heard anything yet.'

Nelson thought his heart had never beaten so fast as when he reached the door and felt the appraising eyes of the doormen all over him. But, the next moment, he was being shepherded through to take his seat, among a crowd of other musicians, in the auditorium hall.

The chairs were quickly filling up at the Queen's Gate Concert Hall. On the stage at the front of the hall sat the seats for an orchestra. A baby grand piano sat centre stage and, arrayed around it, all the places where the trumpeters, percussionists, saxophonist and more would sit. In the seats in front, dozens of musicians waited their turn. The tall, lithe gentleman with burnished gold hair standing by the stage must be Barry Pike – the man everyone was set on impressing – but the men flitting around him seemed to have a say in proceedings as well.

Nelson fidgeted nervously in his seat and tried to keep the piece he intended to play in mind, drumming his fingers on his knees as if his piano was right here in front of him.

This was easier said than done. Holding on to any sense of melody or rhythm was nearly impossible when, time and time again, the concert hall was being filled with the sounds of trumpets, saxophone, and other piano players.

Yet Barry Pike seemed to approve of them all.

He nodded, shook hands and made congenial comments to every single one of them.

When Nelson's name was called, two whole hours of fidgeting and distraction later, he picked himself up and vaulted onto the stage. He took a seat at the piano, and tested the weight of the keys.

'We all ready?' he said, grinning wolfishly at the conductor.

Barry Pike had the kind of voice that New Yorkers put on when they wanted to make a mockery of an Englishman. It was almost musical, thought Nelson, in its 'uppercrustedness'. Airily, the man said, 'Play on, good sir,' and closed his eyes to listen.

Nelson approved of that.

It meant the man wanted to *hear*, and that could only be a good thing.

So he started playing.

It was his own song. The song was called 'Helpless', a proper paean to those times when you fell hook, line and sinker for someone. It started a little mournful – but then the left hand kicked in, and built a rhythm like a rising storm. A song for a quickstep, but one that had its own three specific movements. Well, the composers of old used to write in *movements* – why should it be any different for the dance-hall era? The first movement built the storm. The second came crashing over the dancers, heightening the dance. The third was when the whole thing fell apart, in the messiest, most glorious way. He'd have Princess Elizabeth jitterbugging yet, he thought.

'That will be enough,' announced the rich baritone of Barry Pike, before his eyes dipped back to his clipboard.

'Is that it?' Nelson ventured.

But Barry Pike had already begun to announce the next name on his roster.

Now, the royal retainers were extending their arms, as if to guide Nelson off the stage. Not truly understanding what had happened, he followed them.

'Mr Pike?' Nelson said, as he was escorted past. 'Mr Pike, didn't you *listen?*'

The old conductor had kindly eyes as, just a little exasperated, he took in Nelson and said, 'Young man, you do have a talent – but we're looking for something a little less about *you*, and a little more about *us*. Keep practising, young man. You'll get there.'

Those three words, meant with such genuine encouragement, stung Nelson more than any he'd ever heard. *You'll get there.* He already was *there*. *There* was wherever he, Nelson Allgood, sat down and played.

What was the point?

What was the point in even trying?

They didn't want something daring. They hardly wanted something memorable at all. What they wanted was something *safe*. Some old standards, played with boldness but not with brio, to fill the Royal Albert Hall and then be forgotten.

God damn them – wasn't this for the *King?*

Wasn't this for the *war?*

Nelson was already one foot out of the door when the feeling got on top of him. There was only so much willpower a young man could have, and it seemed he'd already used up his reserves. Unable to douse the fire a second longer, he turned on his heel, ready to bellow out – and froze when he saw that the Black musician who'd just got up on stage (and whose jacket Nelson now remembered he was wearing), had returned to its edge, crouched down, and was sharing a private word with Barry Pike.

Barry's haughty, imperious face seemed to crease suddenly in surprise. Then he turned to stare directly at Nelson, extended a long arm and beckoned him to return with a single crooked finger.

Nelson shoved his hands in his pockets, if only to control his fury, and tramped halfway back towards the stage.

'Young man, what did you say your name was again?'

'Nelson,' he mumbled.

'Nelson...?'

'Nelson Allgood,' he replied. 'It's right there on your paper.'

Barry Pike considered his clipboard one final time. 'So it is,' he mused. 'And am I to understand that you're *Max* Allgood's nephew?'

*June 1942*

# Chapter Seventeen

Dawn crept over the rooftops of Mayfair, the sun's pale fingers lighting up the townhouses one by one. There'd been a time when the view from the observation post on the rooftop of the Buckingham Hotel induced panic and dread – from here you could see the pillars of smoke rising from the devastation in the east, the cradles of fire pockmarking London after every night of battle in the skies above – but, this year, a tentative peace prevailed. Spring was turning towards summer, the night had been balmy – and dawn brought not only a soft, buttery light, revealing all the beauty and majesty of London, but Rosa, climbing through the trapdoor to find Frank at his post.

She'd brought hot buttered toast, marmalade and the Buckingham's signature greengage preserve. She did the same every morning after Frank's long night on duty.

'I can't stay Frankie. Nance has got us all down in the Grand before we're out on the suites.'

'Rosa, listen – tonight, I'm going to …'

But Rosa didn't have the time. 'Frankie, I can't wait – right now, I've got chandeliers to polish.' And she left him with a kiss that tasted of crumpets and jam.

Nancy gave her a mildly admonishing look as she joined the girls in the Grand, and Rosa whispered her apologies. She had to be careful with Nance. She was 'Mrs de Guise' when in the hotel, and 'Nancy' out of it – but somehow, though she'd started out as a friend, a chambermaid just like all the rest, she was always her 'boss'. It would probably be that way even after she and Frankie were married…

She stopped that thought dead.

Where *had* it come from?

Was it just the inevitability of it? She'd been stepping out with Frank for some time now, but they'd never actually talked about marriage. Never talked about the future at all, as it happened – but perhaps that was as much a symptom of the war as the nature of their relationship. Nor was Rosa like lots of other girls. Yes, she wanted to be married one day – and yes, she wanted a family of her own, and a house, and perhaps not to have to change some debauched lordling's bedsheets every morning.

But… Frank?

Was she *really* thinking about that with Frank?

'Girls,' Mrs de Guise was announcing, 'this isn't your first time in the Grand, so let's get all the gawping out of the way sharpish.'

Rosa looked round – it was true, the girls did like a good gawp at the ostentatious fittings of the Grand Ballroom. The run-up to the Buckingham's fêted Summer and Christmas Balls was the only chance they got to catch a glimpse inside – for, right now, workmen were on ladders, servicing the pulleys that lowered the three great chandeliers, and eight smaller ones, to the ground, and it was to be the girls' job to polish them. Annie Brogan was in charge of the trolley of vinegar, lemons and salts.

'You're back on rooms and suites at eleven, so there isn't much time to make a good job of this. Rosa, I want you marshalling one team with the big chandeliers. Mary-Louise, you're on the smaller ones. Annie, you're mixing the solutions. I'll be back to check on you at eleven. Don't let me down.'

Rosa watched as she left. It wasn't often that it smarted that Nancy was now her boss – but right now, for some reason, she got to thinking about how *she'd* been a fixture of the Buckingham Hotel long before Nancy. In that time, Nancy had got married, had a baby, been promoted – and then promoted again. And what had Rosa done? Scarcely a thing, not since she'd started stepping out with Frank.

Was it right that she'd just been drifting, from one year to the next?

Wasn't a girl supposed to *get on*?

The thought needled at her as they started on the chandeliers. How many times had she done this now? It wasn't that the Grand had lost its allure – Rosa was enjoying gawping just as much as the rest – and it wasn't that she didn't grin, from ear to ear, when two of the girls started waltzing around the dance floor to the amusement of the workmen on the ladders above. It was just a sudden feeling that she was being left behind. The world was changing, more rapidly and dramatically than it had ever changed before. Every day, the headlines screamed of some new victory or some fresh calamity. Lives were being lost, stories were being told, heroes were being made out on the battlefields and in the war rooms – and Rosa was perfecting her polishing technique, teaching it to a gaggle of chambermaids who, she suddenly realised, were much younger than her.

'Is this how your Frank does it?' grinned one of the girls. She'd permitted one of the workmen to take her in hold – and now, with rigid backs and preposterous postures, they were spinning around the dance floor with their noses pushed in the air, each trying to outdo the other with the haughtiness of their expressions.

'Give over,' said Rosa, polishing the chandelier more furiously still. 'My Frank's got more style than any of them dancing in this ballroom. You've seen him out in the clubs. He just has to keep it restrained in here. He has to do what he's told.' She looked up. All the girls were staring. 'What?' she exclaimed. 'It's too stuffy in here. Too aristocratic! And I, for one, want something a bit more *lively*. I want a little excitement. No, scratch that – I want a lot of excitement, and I want it fast, or else I'm going to ... burst!'

She saw the other girls quietly studying her as if not quite sure what she might do. 'You know what we really need, girls?'

'An extra pair of hands?' asked Mary-Louise, who had re-focused her attention on the chandeliers.

'Another wild night. Frankie and I are meant to go to the pictures tonight, just the two of us – but here's what I say. All of us at the Ambergris Lounge at eight. I'm sick of this war, and I'm sick of this hotel. I want to do some *living*.' She gazed around. 'Now, who's with me?'

Nancy was grateful for the quiet in the Housekeeping Lounge. The extra duties assigned to Housekeeping in the run-up to every ball always made a mess of the department's rosters, but with a couple of hours' quiet study, she would be able to resolve it. The real problem was that the department was perennially understaffed. She was going to have to speak to Mr Hastings about how best to retain new girls.

As if merely thinking of the man was enough to summon him, there came a knock at the Lounge door. Nancy called out, 'Come in,' and was surprised to see Mr Hastings sliding through.

'Mrs de Guise, I'm glad I could catch you. I wonder if we might have a quiet word? It's about Raymond.'

For the first time, Nancy grew nervous as to where this conversation was going. 'Sir?'

'I was in the ballroom on Saturday night. Raymond performed admirably with the guests, but his star has been kept in check. He isn't featuring in Mr Arbuthnot's showpiece dances – and he isn't attracting as many requests among the guests as I might have hoped. In part, I believe that's because he isn't being shown off by Mr Arbuthnot. There is, shall we say, some professional rivalry latent in the ballroom. That's fine. Competition breeds quality. But I'm concerned that Raymond may be masking the damage done to him in Africa. That, perhaps, the injury he sustained has impacted his appreciation of music, and therefore his ability in the ballroom, an inordinate amount.'

'I see.'

'I want to enlist Doctor Moore to appraise him and make a recommendation – all at the hotel's expense, of course. I know he has been under the care of military medics, but perhaps there's more that can be done.'

Nancy said, 'I don't know if you're right, sir. I've wondered if it's more about finding his place again – working out where he belongs.' She paused. 'I'm grateful you released him to compete at the Royal Dansant, sir. It might be the thing that reminds him why we dance.'

'I know he is making a great effort to romance our guests. I'm told he's even joining Mr Bancroft and Laird Guthrie for cocktails and canapes at the Candlelight Club tonight. Even so, I should like it if you would broach the matter of Doctor Moore with him. Can I trust you with that?'

At that moment the clock on the office wall started chiming 11 a.m.

185

'Sir, I must go to my girls.' Nancy marched with him to the door of the Lounge. 'I'll speak with Raymond. I promise. But – Mr Hastings?'

'Yes, Nancy?'

'Trust him too. Raymond loves this hotel more than any. If he thought he couldn't play his part here, I believe he'd tender his resignation in a second.'

The thought of Doctor Moore appraising Raymond wasn't a terrible one – but Nancy couldn't help thinking it was wrong, as she made her way back to the Grand. The remedy lay not in the body, she thought, but in the mind. Hélène would be good for him. The Albert Hall might bring him back to life.

Strange, but he hadn't told her about cocktails and canapes with those two aristocratic guests. Perhaps, in all the chaos of hotel and home life, it had simply slipped his mind – or perhaps Mr Hastings was mistaken.

Into the Grand she came. 'A fine job, girls,' she pronounced. 'But I'm afraid we must march on with the day. We have twenty minutes for elevenses in the Housekeeping Lounge. The rosters are already on the wall.' She clapped hard. 'Onward, girls! We mustn't let service slip, even for a second!'

*We mustn't let service slip*. Nancy was good at inspiring the younger girls, but Rosa could see through it. What did it really matter if some lordship didn't have his pillows plumped in precisely the way he wanted? It was all just an act – and Rosa was dog-tired of acting. Right now, she just wanted to play.

The war was like a cage.

So too was the Buckingham Hotel.

Both of them, just boxing you in, telling you where you could go, what you could do, who you had to be. You could get along with it if you tried – but sometimes, you just needed to let off some steam.

Now that she'd mooted the idea, she just couldn't wait for tonight.

'Give me five minutes, Nance,' she said, grabbing a biscuit from the table in the Housekeeping Lounge. 'I'll be back before rounds start, I promise.'

Then she darted away, made haste up the service stairs, and scrambled into the attics where the chambermaids were quartered.

Frank was sleeping on the hard-worn sofa in the chambermaids' kitchenette when Rosa appeared. The moment she saw him, some of the wildness that had been building in her since the Grand seemed to be tamed. He always looked so content when he was sleeping – and, as soon as she'd thought of that, she started thinking about their future again, and marrying him, and how he might look every morning when he awoke. Solid, dependable Frank Nettleton.

Was this what the future had in store?

Sometimes, a girl who liked things wild needed a gentleman to keep her grounded.

It had worked until now, hadn't it?

And, besides, Frank definitely had a wild side too. She saw it every time he took her out onto a dance floor. He could have the devil in him when the music was right...

'Frankie,' she said, rousing him gently. 'Dust yourself down, back to your duties – and then... I've been talking to the girls. We fancy a proper night tonight. Well, we can do the pictures any time, can't we? *Mrs. Miniver* can wait! I was thinking... back to the Ambergris? Or even the Midnight Rooms, if there's a band playing. God, Frank, I feel ready to burst. I feel like I could just tear myself open.' Rosa rocked backwards and laughed.

'God, I almost feel like burning everything down and starting again. I know I sound silly, Frank. I was just polishing the chandeliers, over and over and over again, and I couldn't help thinking: why does it *matter*? Don't you ever get that feeling, that none of it really *matters*?'

Frank grinned and took her hand. 'You're having a mad day.'

Rosa grinned too. 'But a drink and a dance, Frank, that's the thing to shake it all off.' She kissed him on the cheek. 'Until it happens again – and then, I suppose, you just keep dancing.'

'Oh, but Rosa,' Frank called out.

Rosa turned.

'Rosa, I can't tonight – not tonight. I've been trying to tell you. It was Raymond's idea really. Well, Mr Arbuthnot had been talking about it – the idea that, after the war, Mathilde and I might start competing. Properly competing, like Raymond and Hélène Marchmont used to do! And maybe we'd win garlands, or – or rosettes, and then we'd be ... well, champions I suppose!' Frank paused; he wasn't sure how to read the curious expression on Rosa's face, as if she might either be excited or disappointed, or perhaps both at the very same time. 'Then Raymond started talking about the Royal Dansant – and how it's an open competition. All you really need is a sponsor, somebody to put in a good word and tell them you're not a rank amateur. So me and Mathilde ...' Frank couldn't stop himself beaming. He rushed across the kitchenette, sending the breakfast plates spinning, and grabbed Rosa. 'We're going to dance at the Albert Hall! Me and Mathilde – for the King!'

Rosa was suddenly brittle. 'You and Mathilde, Frankie?'

Frank always started stuttering when he felt uncertain. He had to grapple with his words before he said, 'R-Rosa, it's b-because we're a partnership in the Grand. Me and Mathilde, it's a p-professional partnership. We could go places. Raymond said it himself and …'

At last, Rosa returned the embrace – but it felt limp to Frank, somehow. 'But you can still dance with *me* tonight, can't you, Frankie? It isn't the Royal Dansant, not until July.'

'B-but that's just the thing. Raymond got where he is because he had a mentor. He's put in a good word. His old mentor's going to train us for the Royal Dansant. Georges de la Motte.'

Rosa hadn't heard of the name, so the smile she put on was entirely fake.

'Our first session's tonight. There's so little time left. But I think we can do it, Rosa. Not win, perhaps – but win *something*. Good comments from the judges. Maybe even a rosette. It could start us on our way – and then, when the war's done, maybe we'll be like Raymond used to be. Dancing in Paris. Dancing in Rome …'

Rosa looked at him. 'That's brilliant, Frankie!' she thrilled, and kissed him again.

The girls were still in Housekeeping when she burst through the doors.

'The Ambergris,' she declared. 'Half past seven. No men allowed. This night's for us. Let the lords and ladies waltz all they want in the Grand. Let the *proper* dancers practise and preen and pray someone tells them how talented they are. They might be our betters – but *we* know how to have a better time. And tonight, girls, I'm going to prove it.'

# Chapter Eighteen

John Hastings arrived back at his office to find the door standing ajar – and, just inside, Max Allgood shifting nervously from foot to foot, his trombone case in hand.

This had the look of *another* problem, he thought.

Max Allgood started and wheeled round. 'Mr Hastings,' he said, 'you caught me off guard there. Have you got a moment?'

A moment was the last thing Hastings had. He picked his way to his desk, all the thousand issues of the day clamouring to be heard in his head.

'Mr Allgood, what can I do for you? Have a seat.'

At least sitting down settled Max's nerves. He clung on to Lucille as he settled.

'Mr Hastings, I've got myself something of a conundrum. A few days ago, I got myself a *proposition* ... You've heard of the Royal Dansant?'

Mr Hastings replied, 'The event of the season? The King's dance for his American cousins? A celebration of Old World and New? Yes, Mr Allgood, I may have caught wind of it.'

Max wasn't quite sure if Mr Hastings was joking with him or not. 'Well, sir, the first thing I got to say is: I didn't audition. On my life, sir. I know you've given Mr de Guise permission to go off dancing in the contest – but me, I know where my bread's buttered, and I know I got work to do steadying the ship in the Grand.' He paused. 'But they...'

It was painful watching him squirm – and John Hastings had never been the sort of boy who liked pulling the wings off insects. Not unkindly, he said, 'Am I to understand they approached you, Mr Allgood?'

Max breathed a deep sigh of relief. He'd been trying to find the right words – and there they were, coming out of John Hastings' mouth. 'They've invited me and Lucille to join 'em, down at the Albert Hall. Now, of course I said no, no way – I got my working life in *order* – but... They've been petitioning me, sir. I've had letters. I've had visits. They threatened to come straight to you, sir – and that's when I said: Max, you've got to ask him yourself. So here I am, Mr Hastings. Now, it won't worry me if you say no – it won't put my nose out of joint if you send me outta here with a flea in my ear, and tell me to get back to the Grand. But I needed to ask because they won't take my word for it any longer.'

John Hastings held his silence only momentarily before he said, 'Max Allgood, you are to go to these people directly and tell them that yes, you are to play for the King.'

Max was already sitting down – but, if it had been possible to topple over right then, that is what he would have done. 'Sir?'

'I don't know why you would even hesitate. Anything that elevates you, elevates this hotel. Have I not been clear about our mission? We are to win as much of the custom coming out of the United States as possible. When our countrymen require suites in London, they are not to think of the Imperial, the Ritz, the Savoy. Our name is to come to mind before any others.' He paused, if only to let the sentiment seep in. 'Mr Allgood, here's a ball, a festival, a competition, hosted by royalty in honour of the United States – and you were thinking about excusing yourself?'

Max ran a finger around his collar. 'So I have your permission?'

'You don't just have my permission. You have my *order*. Jump to it, Mr Allgood – before they hire somebody else in your stead.'

After that, Max barely took a breath until he was waddling out of the Hotel Director's office, through the labyrinth of corridors and up along Michaelmas Mews.

The Royal Dansant. Well, here was a 'turn-up for the books', as the English were prone to say. No doubt Marcus would be sceptical once Max announced the news tomorrow, but he'd just have to make it work. Two weeks separated the Buckingham's Summer Serenade from the spectacular at the Albert Hall, and the clock was already counting down towards both. He'd have to work doubly hard to make sure they were each the talk of the town.

A taxicab was waiting out on Berkeley Square. Some time later, it sailed through the Houses of Parliament and crossed the grey waters of the Thames, depositing Max among the construction works at the end of Albert Yard.

When he opened the door of No 62, the smell of Orla Brogan's freshly baked scones washed over him. And there was Ava, helping her in the kitchen, while Nelson just sat in front of the fire.

The moment Max appeared, Nelson sprang to his feet.

'Well?' he said, with sudden urgency.

Max just waddled forward, as if he hadn't heard. In the kitchen, he picked up one of the scones and started juggling it from hand to hand.

'That's just come out of a hot oven,' Orla Brogan said.

Nelson appeared in the kitchen door. 'Well, Uncle Max? How'd it go?'

Max was silent, for he was already burning the inside of his mouth with some of the scone.

'Uncle Max,' Nelson exclaimed, 'tell me!'

Max pointedly finished his mouthful. Then he looked squarely at Nelson and said, 'Lucille and me, we're going to sing for the King.'

'Holy cow, Uncle Max!' Nelson looked as if he was about to embrace his uncle – but then he saw the older man's staunch appearance and faltered. 'So? You talked to them yet? You talked to Barry Pike?'

'I'm going down there tomorrow to tell 'em I got the blessing of the Buckingham.'

'*And?*' Nelson went on, loading the word with meaning.

'Max,' Ava interjected, 'put the boy out his misery, one way or another.'

There was a moment in which Max seemed to think twice. A moment in which he looked about to break some solemn promise, or else break the boy's heart.

Because he hadn't told Mr Hastings the full truth. He'd only told him that he was being courted. He hadn't told him about the devil's pact he'd walked into, the promise in which he'd found himself entrapped, the promise that was already eating him up, making him wonder if he'd done the right thing.

He hadn't told them about Nelson…

Then he sighed and said, 'I'll tell him, Nelson. Mr Pike, I'll say, I'm game for it. I got the blessing of the Buckingham Board and me and Lucille'll slide right into whatever orchestra you're cooking up. We'll make your orchestra fit for the King – but, if you want me, there's something I want in return. Mr Pike, I got a *condition*.'

'Yeah?' Nelson went on, his face split apart by his grin.

'I'll play for you, Mr Pike, but you got to let my nephew play too.'

This time, Nelson couldn't bridle his excitement. He flung his arms around Max and held on tight.

'I don't know how your mother convinced me – but there it is, boy,' said Max, when he could finally extricate himself from the embrace. 'It's yours to embrace or it's yours to stuff up. I don't know how much they'll let you play. Maybe it's ten songs. Maybe it's one. But, whatever it is, it's *your* chance. Take hold of it, boy. Don't mess it up.' The scone had lost some of its heat now. Max started chomping on the rest. 'It ain't the Buckingham Hotel, but I've put myself on the line for you, Nelson. It's the gig of a lifetime for any musician, and it's coming your way. What happens next? Well, that's up to you. But Nelson Allgood, count your lucky stars – you're going to play for the King.'

# Chapter Nineteen

From the wide-open terrace of the Candlelight Club, Raymond de Guise gazed over the verdant oasis of Berkeley Square.

The truth was, he had never quite developed a taste for the martini he held in his hand. Raymond de Guise might have been the sort of man who appreciated fine wines and a masterfully made cocktail – but Ray Cohen had been raised on the stout and pale ales of his forefathers in Stepney Green, and he still had to *pretend*. How many layers of deceit did he indulge in now? Too many to care about or count – that was for sure.

He glanced back through the open terrace doors, framed by potted ferns and palms, and saw that the club was filling up. The Buckingham's rarefied guests were gathering for early-evening aperitifs. Ladies in expensive finery accompanied their husbands to the booths. One of the old Flemish princelings, visiting London from the Oxfordshire estate where he was living while his homeland was overrun, occupied the back wall, playing host to his English cousins. Mr David Margesson, one of Mr Churchill's parliamentary allies who had since fallen from governmental grace, took drinks with a party of investors with whom, it seemed, he was to forge a new career.

And there, entering the club right now, was St John Bancroft, his simple white dinner jacket and formal black trousers making him stand out in a sea of colour.

'Mr de Guise, I'm afraid I must ask you to step inside.'

Raymond turned. Ramon had been managing the Candlelight Club for as long as it existed: a methodical man, given to a certain flamboyance, he considered the club his own private fiefdom within the Buckingham's walls – and, while its profits remained so high, management had never seen fit to disabuse him of the notion.

'The blackout is coming, sir. I must insist.'

Raymond stepped back inside the club, then felt the darkness close over him as Ramon closed the terrace doors. The lamps over each of the club's tables lent the place a shadowy, intimate aura. Smoke billowed and curled in the air. Two waiters, in pure white and gold brocade, skipped through like circus acts, balancing a multitude of trays laden with drinks. In the corner, one of Max's guest pianists had taken up his station at the upright Steinway and begun to play soft, lilting background music.

'I believe your party is already assembled, Mr de Guise,' said Ramon as he brushed past. 'They're gathered in the Fairfax.'

The Fairfax Lounge, one of several private rooms on the edges of the Candlelight Club. Mr Churchill had gathered potential members of his war cabinet here in the days when Parliament was still wrangling over who was the right man to lead the nation through war. Now, it occurred to Raymond that a room that had once played host to the men bent on saving Great Britain was hosting a group of men who plotted its betrayal.

He held his head up high and stepped through the doors.

'Mr de Guise, fashionably late to the party,' declared Bancroft, rising to his feet. 'Gentlemen, this is the dancing chap I was telling you about. A decorated veteran, on battlefield and ballroom floor. His money's as good as any.'

Inside the Fairfax Lounge, eight men were arrayed around a long card table. One after another, they rose to greet the newcomer, then made space for him to sit down.

It hadn't been easy to gain admittance to the game. He'd tried three times to get himself invited into the parties in the ballroom, and each time found St John eager to rebuff him. 'You may dance with my wife, but only so that I don't have to,' he'd said, on one occasion. Jane had been withering about her husband's response. 'Oh yes, because men like my husband have *much* more important things to do than show their wives that they matter,' she'd said wryly, when he took her to the dance floor.

In the end, it had been Susannah Guthrie's intervention that truly opened the door to his presence here at the card game. 'You ought to learn something from the Buckingham Hotel, Douglas,' she'd said at the end of a long night in the Grand. 'These business meetings of yours – they're too dry! You need *glamour*. Why host a meeting at the Buckingham Hotel if you're not going to take full advantage of what it offers? De Guise is a chap worth befriending. While we're in Scotland, you might indulge him a little.'

Raymond didn't mind if the reason he was here was to add glamour to a business deal.

He just wanted to know what that business deal was.

As the cards were dealt, he looked around the room. St John Bancroft was evidently the head of proceedings, with Douglas Guthrie at his right-hand side. Apart from these two, Raymond recognised only one other man: a junior diplomat who worked among the Free French, responsible for sourcing the funds that kept the exiled government alive. What that man could possibly be doing fraternising with men whose public record was so damning, he did not know; this was certainly worth reporting to the Deacon Club – but perhaps the young man was just a rich fool, prone to losing at cards. The other men all had the jowly appearance of men wealthy enough not to have to live off ration-books – men of industry and finance, Raymond supposed.

'I wouldn't want a man like this entertaining any wife of *mine*, St John,' a porcine man at the end of the table snorted. In less well-kept clothing he might have looked like a brutish railway worker, with meaty forearms and a perpetual scowl – but this man was immaculately dressed, silver cufflinks sparkling in the low lamplight. 'She's liable to start having ideas if she's off gallivanting with a dancer.'

'Jane likes to have a pet,' Bancroft remarked. Then, dealing the cards, he inclined his head towards Raymond. 'You'll have to forgive some light rough-housing tonight, de Guise. We're not dancing men. Indeed, we're not artistic men at all – so I'm afraid you're rather at a disadvantage. Angus there wouldn't even grace a ballroom floor – but then again, he's unmarried, so he doesn't have to.'

*Angus.* So that was Angus Kemp, thought Raymond, the man who believed himself an ally of the British Gestapo. He looked so ordinary. Brutish and short – like life on the battlefield – but *ordinary* nevertheless. Not for the first time, Raymond lingered on his recollection of what Maynard Charles had said about Paris and the propensity for collaboration. How many of the people he knew and loved would be brave enough to set themselves apart, if the Nazis marched through London? How many would quietly look the other way?

How many would make a *deal*?

'Mr Kemp, I'm sure the delights of the ballroom will entice you one day,' Raymond ventured. It was important to say something to the man, important to make some connection, important to look him in the eye. 'The Buckingham's Summer Ball is coming. Perhaps you might like an invitation?'

'Pah!' Kemp snorted. 'I'm sure I shall be perfectly happy without. I *was* married, once upon a time. I shan't make that mistake again. Nowadays I prefer cold hard cash to a woman's touch.' His eyes glittered darkly. 'At least with money, you know where you are.'

The laughter around the table perhaps indicated some private joke to which Raymond was not privy.

'Susannah reports you a very capable dancer, Mr de Guise,' chipped in Douglas Guthrie, as he too studied his cards.

'Aye,' one of the other men laughed, 'and she'll need some dancing and romancing now your eye's elsewhere, Douglas. What's this woman called again?'

Douglas Guthrie eyeballed his opponent severely. 'That *woman* is a lady – by title as well as in character – and you'll steady your tone, good man. That is, unless you would like to air your own marital complications?'

The other man raised his hand, proffering peace.

There was hardly a hesitation – apparently Douglas Guthrie's infidelity was an open secret around the table – before the game began, but a dozen disordered thoughts started hurtling through Raymond's mind. The Buckingham Hotel had hosted a thousand upper-crust infidelities across the years. If the walls of this hotel could speak, they would lay bare a hundred thousand secrets. That the Guthries didn't share the purest of marriages came as no surprise to Raymond – but perhaps it would be of note to Maynard Charles. As he folded in the first hand – 'The dancing man holds no aces!' Bancroft was pleased to pronounce – he resolved to make it part of his debrief at the Deacon Club by the end of the evening.

Raymond was no veteran of the gambling dens, but he knew enough to hold his own. This particular talent came courtesy of his wayward brother, who had frequented every gambling den in the Limehouse basin, growing fat off his winnings, then destitute the very next day. By the fourth hand it occurred to Raymond that the game he was playing right now was no different from those games Artie had dragged him to in Shadwell, or down by the Wapping dock. Gangs of ruffians were not so different from gangs of businessmen. In the East End, cards were just an excuse to get together, to drink and be merry, and for Artie's friends to talk about whatever skulduggery they might get up to next. Here, there was Champagne where Artie drank pale ale; here, there was talk of business and investment instead of housebreaking and where to steal the best copper wire; but that was just aesthetics. Men the world over, whether rich or poor, seemed to have the same drives and ambition.

'And how are the factory lines, Angus?'

Angus Kemp betrayed himself with a smile. 'Bancroft, let's just say that this war has been very kind to me. We exist in a kind of partnership, this war and I. People malign it. They tell us war is bad for our nation. Well, what's bad for one is good for another. There are balances in life. There will always be money in munitions.'

'Opportunities too, I shouldn't wonder?'

Angus Kemp opened up his hand. The two red kings he revealed sent groans around the table. Soon, he was collecting yet more tokens to add to the teetering pile at his side.

'What are you getting at, Bancroft?' Angus wagged his finger at St John, like an admonishing teacher. 'You know, I did think it was out of the ordinary to be invited here tonight. I did wonder if there was some ulterior motive. Just what are you after?'

'We are all men of business, Angus.' St John Bancroft just shrugged, and dealt another hand. 'It would be remiss of me not to explore opportunities whenever they arose. Money makes the world go round.'

Kemp studied his winnings. 'Indeed it does.'

'Douglas, you're a man in need of somewhere to put your money, aren't you?'

Raymond's eyes darted. There was something almost practised about this, he thought. Something almost theatrical. He watched as Douglas Guthrie took his new set of cards, studied them in silence, then lifted his eyes and said, 'I happen to have come into some unexpected wealth. Not, I hasten to add, by design. Certain estates I owned have been stolen from under my feet. Our government, people, is not to be trusted. Lands that had been in my family for generations – mine one day, gone the next. A "forced purchase", they're calling it. Well, they can compensate me for the land's monetary value, but they can't compensate me for its real, familial worth.' The anger had been rising in his voice as he spoke. Now, with trembling hand, he conquered it, and went on, 'It leaves me with reserves that need investing. I don't trust money, gentlemen, not in its raw form. No, I want to direct this money to a place it can do some good – and, Mr Kemp, a place where I might see a return on my investment.'

At this point, St John Bancroft chipped in, 'Just a thought for the night, gentlemen. I'll leave you to pursue it at your own pleasure. Right now, I should very much like to win some of my money back…'

Angus Kemp tapped his cards playfully on the table. 'Gentlemen,' he grinned, 'you're making me blush. I've spent much of my life a solitary wolf. It makes a man shudder to feel so wanted.' Then he tossed a token into the centre of the table to get the next round started, and flashed a devilish, almost flirtatious look at Raymond de Guise. 'What do you think, dancing man?'

Raymond adopted the most syrupy smile he could imagine and answered, 'Think, Mr Kemp?'

'Well, this is your sort of thing, isn't it? Being the star attraction? All those ladies, fawning over you down in the Grand?' Angus Kemp brayed with laughter. 'All of a sudden, I'm the belle of the ball.'

It was almost midnight by the time Raymond got to the Deacon Club. Upstairs, the dining room was emptying – though, in the club's innumerable nooks and crannies, a motley collection of drinkers remained. Maynard Charles was not at his ordinary table; nor did the waiting staff know how to alert him – so, for some time, all Raymond could do was sit and nurse a whisky in the corner. Waiting. So much of his new role involved *waiting*.

Midnight passed, and he knew he ought to leave. Home was where he ought to be. Yet something kept him pinned in place – and, when Maynard Charles finally appeared at 1 a.m., he was on his feet in seconds, following the older man into one of the cramped back rooms.

'Sir, I'd been expecting you at night's end.'

Maynard Charles had hardly taken off his jacket, a White Owl cigar already lit and rolling between his teeth, but something in Raymond's tone obviously irked him. His eyes flared. Raymond remembered that look only too well from his days at the hotel: the sudden incandescent fury of a man whose inferiors had misinterpreted his willingness to converse with a kind of brotherly love. One look was all it took to dispel any idea Raymond had had that the two of them were working *together*.

'Don't allow yourself to think, Raymond, that you are my only concern in this city tonight. Nor that you are the only agent I have kept waiting.' He took a lungful of smoke and luxuriated in it before he went on. 'Report then, Raymond. Your night might be coming to its close, but mine goes on.'

'Sir, tonight's meeting might have been instigated by Bancroft – but that wasn't its aim. Bancroft didn't invite Kemp to the Candlelight Club tonight to further any interests of his own. He was acting as an intermediary.'

'Go on...'

'The purpose of tonight was to introduce Angus Kemp and the Scottish laird Guthrie. Guthrie asked Bancroft to effect an introduction. They're to follow up tonight with private meetings, a private dinner – private business of their own.'

'Guthrie is a wealthy man,' Maynard mused. 'He could provide Kemp with significant funds, for whatever this endeavour is.'

'The way he described it, the British government have taken control of his family estates – robbed him, or so he said. A forced purchase.'

This seemed more interesting to Maynard Charles. He made a hurried note, chewing on the end of his cigar. 'It's in the government's purview, of course. There have been innumerable forced purchases since this war began. Military training grounds all over the country.' He hesitated. 'Other... secret installations.'

'That isn't all. Sir, I believe Douglas Guthrie is keeping a mistress.'

Maynard Charles rolled his eyes. 'Welcome to the aristocracy, Raymond. Have your years at the Buckingham Hotel taught you nothing? Raymond, people born to money do not subscribe to the same familial arrangements as those born into privation. The poor must ration everything: butter, flour, bacon, *love*. For the rich, these things exist in bounty. A rich man can't possibly only have *one* wife – so he collects half a dozen. Our laws forbid him from marrying them, but he can still keep private penthouses for them all. These are the private pacts our overlords make. It is quite likely his wife is aware of the arrangements.'

Raymond nodded. 'I thought it might be significant, sir.'

'It may yet be.'

'And sir, there was another man at the game. A young man, a frequent visitor to the Buckingham Hotel. A clerk with the Free French.'

'Yes,' Maynard said. 'His name is Lionel. He's acting on de Gaulle's orders, if our intelligence is correct.' Maynard Charles stopped. 'Well, you didn't think the French don't also have their intelligence officers working the Buckingham Hotel, did you? You didn't think we pooled resources with them?'

'They're our allies, sir.'

'Half of them willingly took the Führer's schilling the moment tanks lined up on their lawns, Raymond. No, we share with the French only that which we must share. They *are* our allies,' he laughed, 'but not our bed-mates. And besides... a man like young Lionel is hardly capable of doing what I must now ask of you.'

Raymond's head was spinning. Perhaps, one day, he could understand why allies were not necessarily friends; why partners must be held at arm's length; why suspicion must be cultivated, and how untruths could be honourable. But that day was not today.

'What do you need of me, sir?'

'I need you to seduce Susannah Guthrie.'

There was silence in the office.

'If Douglas Guthrie is keeping mistresses,' said Maynard Charles, 'there's every chance Susannah could turn on him. Oh, it needn't be openly. She needn't know that's what she's doing. A wife will often enter into a willing fiction – she'll tell herself that, as long as it's not happening in broad daylight, she can glide through life oblivious, holding her head up high. But when that fiction is exposed, she will often snap. My working life depends on these fascinating facets of human behaviour, Raymond – so you'll have to trust me on this. Confront her with the fiction of her life, and it may open her to manipulation.'

'But seduce her, Mr Charles? I'm a married man. I'm a father. I'm—'

'Under my employ, Raymond – or have you forgotten?'

For the first time Raymond realised that, in a sense, he too had been seduced: seduced into thinking that this was a partnership; seduced into thinking that he had been given a gift by being brought home – that he could slide back into his ordinary life, and yet serve King and Country at the very same time.

'What did you think you were here for, Raymond? What did you think your job was going to be? *Anything, whatever it takes, to serve your King.*' Maynard Charles paused, to luxuriate in yet more of his cigar. 'I'm sorry, Raymond. You don't get to be taken from the battlefields of North Africa and deployed in a ballroom without a cost. I want to know what manner of deal Douglas Guthrie is striking with Angus Kemp, and to what end. If it takes you breaking your marital vows to accomplish it, that's how it will be. Lives will be saved. The cause of this war pushed further towards victory. We all must make sacrifices if we're to come through, and ... you're serving your King now, Raymond, not just dancing for him.'

'I understand that, sir, but—'

Maynard Charles held up his hand, commanding Raymond's silence.

'You didn't really think you were going to get to keep your hands clean, did you? There's a war to win – and it isn't just won out there, in the deserts, on the seas, under the sky. It's won right here, with dirty hands ... and dirty reputations.' Maynard ground out the end of his cigar, peeled back the corner of the blackout blind, and looked down on Piccadilly. 'It's time to come to the party, Mr de Guise. I expect your report on my desk by the night of the Summer Ball.'

# Chapter Twenty

'She's looking lively already,' said Mary-Louise as the Buckingham girls scurried through the London sunset, rounding the construction works outside the Ambergris Lounge. Rosa had been marching ahead ever since Berkeley Square, declaring that they had to reach the club before the blackout came into force (as if there was any danger of that on this luminous summer night) – but really, as all the girls knew, she was just eager to let the night begin. 'You'll have to keep an eye on her, Annie. She's liable to do herself some mischief,' said Mary-Louise – as, up ahead, Rosa slipped past the doorman in front of the club.

'Me?' Annie asked, startled. 'Why me?'

'Somebody's got to,' said Mary-Louise, skipping forward in Rosa's wake, 'and I want to dance.'

Annie remained, crestfallen, on the pavement – wasn't it always the way that the youngest, most junior chambermaid got the worst jobs? – but the feeling quickly passed, for there, waiting by the construction works, was her sweetheart Victor, who worked in the Queen Mary kitchens. 'You should have waited inside,' said Annie, gambolling into his arms. 'Rosa told us no boys tonight. The girls reckon she's had a barney with Frank. She'll have my guts if she thinks I've brought you along.

I told you – just be there by *coincidence*. Then we can have a dance.'

At that moment, another figure rounded the corner.

Billy Brogan sidled into view and declared, 'Now Annie, a big night out, is it? We could all do with one of those.'

Annie's heart stilled. She'd been keeping her distance from Billy wherever she possibly could. It wasn't that she didn't love her brother – familial love was infuriatingly eternal – but the bonds of that love had been tested of late. Billy had always salvaged a few odds and ends from the Buckingham's refuse – things a fine lord or lady might throw away, but which still had value to somebody beyond the esteemed hotel's walls – but, last year, he'd pushed his enterprise a little further, actively seeking out things to steal from the hotel's many stores. He provided those goods, now, to a number of corner shops in Camden town – and, worse, he'd had Annie and Victor working for him for months. Soaps and lotions, handkerchiefs and bath towels from the Housekeeping stores; wines, steaks, butter, lard and flour from the Queen Mary kitchens. The Buckingham was a bounty, and Billy Brogan plundered it wherever he could.

Victor looked a little shamefaced at Billy's arrival, but he didn't dare breathe a word of it, not until Billy – who still walked with a vague limp after the devastations at Dunkirk – slipped ahead, straight through the Ambergris doors.

'He was coming down to the kitchens to check on me as I was leaving. I'm sorry, Annie – as soon as he knew where I was going, he said he ought to come along.' Victor paused, for when Annie was silent, it always meant she was upset.

She hated pinching things for Billy. And yes, he was right – the poor had nothing in London, while in the Buckingham Hotel they still had oranges! – but stealing was stealing, wasn't it?

'I'd better catch up with the girls,' Annie said, and leant up to plant a consolatory kiss on Victor's cheek. 'If they see me come in with you, they'll know what I did.'

When Annie got into the Ambergris Lounge, the music was already pounding. She hadn't seen this band before – the banner above the stage read 'The Moonlighters' – and they didn't have the same wild, American sound that had pulsed in here the last time the girls came dancing. Perhaps that was a good thing – that music had very nearly incited a riot, and Annie was squeamish when it came to fighting.

She saw that the club was filled with American soldiers. Mary-Louise was already on the dance floor, dancing with one, while the other girls occupied one of the booths.

Suddenly, Billy was beside her.

'Exciting, isn't it?' he said. 'It's like the world's changing, all around us. Every season brings something new.'

Annie had never heard anybody quite as excited about wartime as Billy had been in the last six months. 'I'm glad they're here but I wish they didn't need to be. Aren't you tired of the war, Bill?'

Billy shrugged. 'The war doesn't care if we're tired of it or not. It'll be over one day, Annie. But we've got to make the best of it while we can.' His eyes scoured the room – almost greedily, thought Annie. Then he landed on a group of American infantrymen in one of the booths on the other side of the dance floor and he lit up. 'Opportunities, Annie – everywhere you look. These Americans have got a bit of dough – that's what they call it, isn't it? *Dough*. Well, maybe they can help us out. Keep those shelves stocked for us, what do you think?'

Annie just shrugged. The less she knew about Billy's business endeavours, the better. She watched as he introduced himself – with characteristic flair – to the group of American GIs on the other side of the club. At least he wouldn't be on the dance floor tonight. Billy never liked dancing, not even before his leg was injured. Pretty soon, she'd be able to step out there with Victor and forget her brother was here at all.

Then, Victor was at her side.

'Fancy seeing you here,' he said, with a shy smile.

She took his hand. 'Billy's off making business out of it,' she said, glumly.

'I know one way to stop you thinking about *that*,' said Victor.

As he led her onto the dance floor, Annie looked up and saw Rosa staring at her from the railing, shaking her head. 'Just ignore her,' Victor said. 'Just ignore all of them. Let's have a dance.'

At that moment, one song came to its climax and the band launched directly into another.

American voices hollered and cheered on every side.

'No fighting tonight,' Victor grinned, 'only *this!*'

He wasn't much good at dancing. But that only added to his charm.

'I knew she couldn't resist it,' said Rosa up above, as Mary-Louise returned from the dance floor, sweat glistening on her brow. 'That Annie – she *had* to bring her kitchen boy along. Hasn't he got pots that need washing?'

'I don't think he came with her,' Mary-Louise said darkly. 'Billy's over there, talking to some Yanks. I reckon he dragged the kitchen boy along.'

Rosa shook her head. 'She isn't one of us, that Annie. This was meant to be for us girls to get a little wild.'

Wildness was certainly what Rosa had in mind. She'd already convinced one of the barmen to pour them brandy and lemonades, and was slurping at hers greedily. 'Well, who's going to dance?'

The other girls wanted a little more time to assess the situation – and their potential partners – before they went out looking. 'Nobody's asked yet,' said one of the girls – and Rosa only snorted again, 'Who are *we*, to wait around and be asked? No, girls, if you wait for a boy, he'll only keep you hanging on. Probably he's got something *better* to do with his time. Probably he thinks this is too downmarket for him – when he's ... when he's destined for the stars!'

At this, Rosa drained her drink and marched off in search of a partner.

'Do we think she really did have a barney with Frank, then?' asked one of the girls.

Mary-Louise nodded. 'I doubt whether Frank knows he's upset her, but this club's going to find out tonight. Go on, drink up, girls. We may as well have some fun while we're here.'

Billy was happy to have found a likely group of Americans so early in the evening. It was no secret that a club like the Ambergris was not his natural environment, so when he'd heard Victor was sloping off to spend the night dancing, it hadn't been the lure of the music that tempted him. No, Billy Brogan was more interested in *opportunities* than having a night to remember – and, now that the Americans had come to London, there were surely opportunities too many to mention. There was wealth in the pockets of every American serviceman – and, if Billy was wily enough, he could help spread some of it around.

'Razor blades,' he was saying. 'There's people out here looking practically indecent for work, wearing thick stubble and shaving cuts, and that's on account of a lack of razor blades. Well, I heard you boys have got mountains of them back at your bases – and

I'm just saying that, if a few boxes happened to go missing from the quartermaster's stores, well, I could quite easily find a home for them. The same goes for soap.'

The Americans seemed to find Billy little more than an amusing annoyance, until he suggested a stiff drink might grease the wheels of business. 'These are on me, lads,' he said, rising up. 'Whiskies, I reckon, by the look of you. Just something to show you I can be a good friend. Then we can talk about these *nylons* I keep hearing about. You know, they banned silk stockings here more than a year ago. Just think how much those nylons are needed out here...' He'd heard they might be able to get hold of cigarettes as well. And *sweets*. The corner shops all needed sweets – and why should a London kid go in want of chocolate, when these servicemen were eating it every night?

He turned on his heel, meaning to go to the bar, and there stood Rosa, looking as fiery as he'd ever seen her.

'Billy,' she said, stiffly.

'Rosa, I didn't reckon on seeing you here. Where's my Frankie?'

'*My* Frankie is off gallivanting with Mathilde tonight, when he ought to have been taking me to the cinema. So I'm here to have a good time.' And she bustled Billy aside, to look down upon the American infantrymen. She was about to introduce herself and demand the first willing gentleman take her to dance, when suddenly she recognised the group of faces staring back at her. 'You boys must come here often, then? I hope there aren't going to be any more fisticuffs tonight?'

The foursome looked at her curiously.

'Fisticuffs,' she said, and mimed the most ridiculous right hook any of the soldiers had ever seen. 'You know, fighting – right there on the dance floor, with that poor piano player?'

The burliest of the infantrymen – Rosa thought she remembered him being called Rick – just grunted. 'Animals, ma'am.

We're good folks our side of the world, but we do get our share of animals too.' And he inclined his head, as if bowing. 'I'm sorry you had to see that.'

Rosa just shrugged. 'Boys play differently to girls. But I don't see him here tonight. And I should like to dance.'

She surveyed each of the young men in turn, then extended her hand.

She didn't have any of the boys in mind, not particularly. Nevertheless, she had to admit she felt some sense of disappointment when it was Rick who took her hand. He dwarfed her, and no doubt that would make it ungainly on the dance floor. Nor did it help that he was the most brutish-looking of the four. Still, at least he was *nothing* like her Frank. That made it a little easier as they waded onto the dance floor and Rosa allowed him to take her in hold. 'Just close your eyes and *go* for it,' she laughed. 'I can tell this one's going to be wild!'

By the time Billy got back from the bar, balancing a tray full of drinks, the dancing was well under way – but, much to Billy's chagrin, the American boys were in no mood to talk about business. All of his questions about candy, Hershey's chocolate bars, and razor blades just fell by the wayside – because, down on the dance floor, their old friend Rick was making a fool out of himself with quite the prettiest English girl in the whole of the Ambergris, and the night couldn't have been going better.

'She's getting a bit turbulent down there,' said Annie nervously, moments after she and Victor had left the dance floor and climbed to the booth up above. 'She's been dancing an hour now. Don't you think she's had enough?'

'Do you want to be the one to tell her?' said Mary-Louise.

Annie looked back sheepishly. Victor was standing at the railing around the dance floor, along with Billy Brogan and the group of American boys. Rosa seemed to have had a dance with all of them now.

'I just think maybe she should... slow down.'

'She's just enjoying the night.'

'I think she's enjoying all those brandy and lemonades as well. Shouldn't we... *stop her?*'

Mary-Louise sighed. 'There's only one thing that's going to stop her, Annie, and that's *morning*. You're better off just enjoying your night.'

But Annie wasn't so sure. She was even less sure an hour later, when Rosa was still dancing – and even less sure than that as the next hour flashed by and her dancing became sluggish, off-pace, as ungainly as any drunk from the streets.

'All right, Annie,' grinned Mary-Louise, who had had her fill of dancing half an hour ago, '*now* it's time. Go and tell her, we're getting our coats.'

Annie scurried to Victor, still drinking with Billy by the dance floor, and squeezed his hand. 'Get my coat too, will you?' she said, after telling him they were leaving. 'I won't be a minute.'

She waited for a break in the songs to seize her opportunity. By then, the rest of the girls had already collected their coats and were gathered above the balustrade, eager for Annie and Rosa to join them so that they could skedaddle back into the night.

Annie took a breath and reached for Rosa's hand. 'Rosa, it's *time*.'

But Rosa shook Annie off so fiercely that the girl staggered backwards.

'Rosa!' Annie gasped.

'I'm sorry, Annie, but *really?* The music hasn't stopped yet. The night isn't over. You take off if you want to, but who made you queen of the dance floor? Coming down here, telling me when it's *time* like you're Nancy de Guise? Good Lord, Annie, don't be such a *bore*. I want to keep dancing.'

Annie looked back. Up above, the girls seemed to understand what was going on – but just shrugged idly, as if to wash their hands of the problem.

Annie turned back to Rosa. 'Rosa, the girls are all leaving.'

'Let them leave,' Rosa shrugged. 'You're not my keeper, Annie Brogan, you don't have to stand there gawping.'

At that moment, Victor appeared at Annie's side, her coat draped over his arm.

'Pot wash is here to chaperone you home,' Rosa squawked, 'but you don't need to chaperone me. The Buckingham's hardly miles away.'

Annie flashed a lost look at Victor. 'We can't just *leave* her,' she whispered, 'not in this state …'

Rosa rolled her eyes dramatically. 'What state would that be, Annie? Having a good time? Blowing away some cobwebs? Living a little, while we still can? Good Lord, Annie, you're eighteen years old – not eighty!'

Victor took a step backwards, trying to coax Annie with him, but she was rooted to the spot.

'Ma'am,' came a confident baritone, from the edge of the dance floor.

Annie turned to see one of the infantrymen striding towards her. She recognised this one instantly. He'd been the one to see sense, the last night they'd been in the Ambergris, the one to break up the fight with the piano player instead of goading it on. Kaplan, she thought. That was his name. Joel Kaplan. He was holding himself with the bearing of a true soldier, solid and statuesque. She'd seen him dancing tonight, that was for sure, but he didn't look as if he'd touched a drop of drink – even though he carried a half-empty glass in his hand. Some folk,

Annie thought, with a worried look at Rosa, just bore their alcohol better than others.

'You don't need to worry about your friend, ma'am,' Joel said, 'she's in good hands here. Let her dance. We'll make sure she gets home safely. *I'll* make sure of it. You have my personal guarantee.'

Rosa abandoned her partner and strode to Joel's side. 'A *personal* guarantee, Annie.' Then she looked Joel up and down. 'Not that I need a guardian angel, Private.'

'That's Corporal Kaplan to you,' Joel smiled.

'You see, Annie?' Rosa grinned, victorious. 'I've got a private corporal to march me home, so I won't get lost. You run along to bed now, won't you? Let the grown-ups finish the night in style.'

There seemed little point in remaining; little point in doing anything but taking Victor's hand and walking with him to the railing above the dance floor where the other girls were congregated.

'She's having a good time,' said Mary-Louise, upon seeing the conflicted look on Annie's face. 'You can't stop a whirlwind, Annie. You've just got to let it peter out.'

Even so, there seemed something wrong about leaving Rosa here – so, back at the Buckingham Hotel, Annie refused to go to bed. Instead, long after the other girls had retired, she sat up in the kitchenette, leafing through old *Reader's Digest*s, drinking hot tea and nibbling at buttered toast – until, some time after midnight (and surely long after last dances at the Ambergris Lounge), she heard the clatter of footsteps on the rickety chambermaids' stairs, and heard Rosa laughing and humming to herself as she palmed drunkenly along the corridor, then stumbled directly into her room.

At least she was safe, thought Annie.

At least the whirlwind had petered out.

But what she'd been doing all those hours, in the blacked-out city with Corporal Joel Kaplan, Annie could not say.

# Chapter Twenty-One

The Royal Albert Hall: even Madison Square Garden didn't quite compare to this.

It would be wrong to say that Max Allgood was doing this for Nelson alone. He'd been putting the thought of the Royal Dansant out of his mind, telling himself over and over again that he had to steady the ship at the Buckingham Hotel, that he had to cement his place as bandleader for a decade to come, but whenever he heard another musician speak of the Royal Dansant, fireworks had gone off in his mind. Now, as he stepped out of the taxicab and gazed up at the imposing dome of the Hall, he felt a little like he had when he'd first won his place in the Creole Jazz Band back in Chicago: like a hand had reached down from the heavens and anointed him from on high. Max Allgood, penniless trombone player, was *going places*. He hadn't thought to have this feeling again in his life. Even his ascension to the Grand had been plagued with uncertainty and doubt. But this?

This felt like *fate*.

He grinned to himself as he waddled to the single stage door, where a prim English doorman was admitting the musicians. He seemed to know who Max was before he'd even introduced himself. He knew who Lucille was too. 'It's an honour to have you join us, Mr Allgood sir,' he said.

The Royal Albert Hall was everything he expected it to be. Its heart had already been arranged for the Dansant, with a sparkling dance floor where the stalls of a theatre would be, and various musicians, technicians and King's men gathered in the galleries of seats above. The hall was bustling with lighting engineers, sound technicians and general staff. Scaffolds had been erected to arrange the lights, a cleaning crew was making a reconnaissance visit, and the front of house manager was busily barracking one of his juniors about security arrangements – but Max and Lucille drifted through it until their chaperone had delivered them safely to the stage.

Barry Pike was here to welcome them. The man was as stuffy and English as Max had expected, but that only added to the aura around him. Even now, some weeks before the performance, he was dressed as he would on the night itself: his black evening jacket offset only by a golden bow tie, its colour matched perfectly with his burnished hair.

'Mr Allgood, when the news reached me that you had accepted our summons, it made my heart soar,' said Mr Pike. 'We have assembled an orchestra of the finest musicians in our land – but what we were lacking was a little American *panache*. For an evening that celebrates the arrival of the New World, I felt we needed New York personified among us. And here you are. Play something for me, Mr Allgood.'

Max rarely needed an excuse to let Lucille fly free. 'Come on girl, let's show him what we've got,' he said, lifting her high and putting her to his lips.

The room stopped when Max played.

He didn't notice, for his eyes were closed as all the other musicians turned to him, grinning and nodding approvingly.

When Lucille was done, Max opened his eyes to find Mr Pike nodding sagely along. 'American panache indeed,' he said, good-naturedly. 'But you may need a little corralling, Mr Allgood. We have to avoid this being recollected as the Max Allgood show – be wild, be free, but be part of the whole; and always, above all, remember this is on behalf of our King. There is, of course, a little room in this orchestra for some adventure – we need spirit, Mr Allgood, and passion and drama, just like all the best! – but not, I have to add, for somebody who, as you Americans would say, goes *completely* off the reservation...'

Max smiled, but only because Barry Pike was smiling.

There had been good humour in those words, but there'd been a warning too.

And suddenly Max was thinking of the only payment he would take to join the orchestra here, the risk taken to make sure he played here.

The deal that seemed more devilish every time he thought about it.

Max scanned the Royal Albert Hall.

Nelson, he supposed, ought to be here any minute.

Nelson Allgood at the Albert Hall. Sweet Christ, it was going to feel good tonight when he told those blowhards at the Midnight Rooms what he'd been doing all day. 'You're gonna have to start paying me double time,' he'd tell them, 'on account of who my ordinary clientele is. You want a prince of the piano? By God, you've got to *pay!*'

They'd summoned him for three o'clock, which left Nelson half the day to while away. His mother reckoned there ought to be some extra work he could pull in during the days – but why bother when his future was already rampaging towards him?

On a summer's day like this, there were *girls* out here in Hyde Park. Granted, most of them only had eyes for the soldiers in the park – but Nelson didn't mind. As long as he could go on looking, he was satisfied.

There'd be love enough after the show was done.

When noon had passed, and 3 p.m. sailing through the sky, Nelson picked himself up and followed the trail to the south lawns, dropping from there beyond the boundary of Hyde Park. The Royal Albert Hall certainly was an impressive institution, bold and stark against the cyan sky, but it didn't daunt Nelson Allgood. The Royal Albert Hall was made for a moment like this.

He'd even dressed up for the occasion. He'd borrowed one of Mr Brogan's shirts (he was sure Mr Brogan wouldn't mind), slipped into a pair of Billy Brogan's trousers (what he didn't know wouldn't hurt him), and used some of Orla Brogan's boot polish to smarten his shoes. Now, he looked like he meant business.

'I'm Nelson Allgood,' he announced to the doorman. 'I've come to make some noise.'

The doorman consulted his list. 'This way, young man. Mr Pike's expecting you.'

'I know it,' Nelson beamed.

He was beaming still when the doorman ushered him into the concert hall's central auditorium, where joiners were hard at work fitting in the last tiles of the dance floor, and a cleaning crew was filling the circle above with great reefs of vinegary steam. Up above, lighting engineers dangled in the rigging; down below, the venue's acoustics expert paced around in solitude, a single triangle and metal beater in hand. And there, on stage, were the pieces of Barry Pike's orchestra. There, among the trumpets and horns, the bassoon and clarinet, the strings and flautists and percussionists at the back, sat the most spectacular piano Nelson had ever seen. Uncle Max hovered beside it, but Nelson didn't care about that. He'd played on fine pianos before, but never like this. It was, he believed, constructed from pure ebony. Yes, Barry Pike's orchestra might be composed of the finest players in the land – but none would upstage whoever sat at this piano.

Nelson knew he wasn't the only one. Uncle Max had been clear about that. He also knew, however much he believed he belonged here, that he was really here because of the deal Uncle Max had struck. Well, if that was how he had to get his foot in the door, so be it. Connections. The whole world ran on *connections*. But once you'd made that connection, you had to make it count.

Here was Nelson's chance.

If he conjured a storm up there, maybe Barry Pike wouldn't use his other pianists at all.

He thrust out his hand towards Barry Pike. 'You won't regret this, sir.'

He slid onto the piano stool, cracked his knuckles over the keys and looked at the sheet music laid out on the stand. 'All right, all right, I can see it,' he said, bobbing his head. 'Want me to start, or are we waiting for somebody?'

Barry Pike circled the piano, gestured to the musicians to line up and declared, 'We have six piano players joining us for stints at the Dansant. What I'm hoping today will lead me to is how precisely we are sharing these pieces. But let's take it one step at a time. Mr Allgood?'

'Yeah?' Nelson piped up, still embroiled in the sheet music.

'I think he meant me, boy,' came Uncle Max's voice.

Nelson didn't care. While Barry Pike was issuing instructions, talking around the song, speaking of its feelings and peaks and troughs, he was listening to the music in his head. He'd been able to do it ever since he was tiny – just sit with the notation and listen to the piece coming to life. He could feel its depths and its shallows. This was a decent piece of music. It was the bedrock of something great. A few little frills, a little wayward energy, and people might *dance* to this. His fingers reached for the first chord.

The orchestra swelled around him. Nelson followed the music, his wrists rolling from one movement into the next, until – halfway through the first piece – he was following by intuition alone. He closed his eyes, the better to feel where the music was going. Barry Pike was an efficient conductor. He marshalled all the musicians superbly – and the fact was, it was novel for Nelson to be playing with an orchestra of such range and depth. Back home he'd played with percussionists and trumpeters, saxophonists and even guitarists – but he couldn't remember ever hearing a woodwind section dovetailing with the piano he played, nor a string section as sweeping as this. He *liked* it. The double bass kept things rolling along, so it wasn't all down to his own left hand, and the drummer kept a rhythm that didn't seem military at all. Nelson bet that, if that guy let loose, he could make an avalanche all on his own.

Thinking about these things kept Nelson from straying too far. By the time they'd reached the end of the first piece, the temptation to rip up the music and just follow his nose had been kept at bay by the sheer novelty of it.

It was the second piece that was harder.

This one, he decided, didn't have the same merit as the first. It was a little bit sombre – and when the finale turned out to be a big band rendition of the 'Star Spangled Banner', Nelson felt as if he ought to just throw the song out and start again. He'd never liked that number. Land of the Free, Home of the Brave. Well, it depended who you were. Depended on the colour of your skin. They'd announced, back when he was a boy, that it was to be the United States' very own national anthem. Well, it wasn't *his*.

But he got to the end of the song without complaint. His fingers rebelled against it, just like his heart, but without a cherry brandy inside him, he'd managed to keep his wilder impulses under control.

'Let's run one more piece,' Barry Pike announced. Nelson saw him giving Max an approving nod across the top of the piano, and something wrenched inside him; Uncle Max might have made some introductions, but he wasn't his keeper. Nelson had had a manager once, one of those back-room blackguards who ran the music scene in New York, and he hadn't liked it one bit. 'I'm hoping this piece will conclude the festivities,' Barry Pike went on. 'The Dansant's very last dance – perhaps even the moment we welcome the Princess Elizabeth to the floor. Let's take it from the top.'

Nelson turned the sheet music.

His heart sank.

In the United States they called this melody 'My Country 'Tis of Thee'. Here in Great Britain they called it 'God Save the King'. As for Nelson – well, he just called it *rot*. If he'd wanted to play hymns, he'd have played the organ in a church back home.

His stomach knotted as he tried to play. *This*, to close the evening? *This*, to get people dancing? By God, this lot knew nothing about putting on a show. It was all about honour and duty and genuflecting, wasn't it? But this was a *dance*, by God! What about wild abandon? What about *fun*? The King might have been a stuffy old man, but Nelson was damn sure his children would want to dance.

'My country 'tis of thee,' Nelson muttered, 'Sweet land of liberty... Yeah, but not for people like *me*...'

That was when his fingers found a different way.

That was when the walls came down and the music roared.

It was still the same melody. The chords still rolled in the same order, to the same rhythm, the same count. But Nelson knew how to put some passion in a song. Even a funeral dirge could become a dance when Nelson played. Up it went, up and further up. Then, down it came, crashing back to Earth like a fighter jet on fire – only to be rescued at the last moment by bouncing chords and strutting rhythm.

The other musicians tried to keep up. Above them all, Nelson heard his uncle's trombone Lucille swooping around the melody he drove. No doubt Uncle Max was trying to mask whatever Nelson was doing – trying to make it sound dignified, planned, *acceptable*. But Nelson knew about acceptability – and acceptability was not what the public wanted. They wanted the daring, the tumultuous, the unexpected. God damn it, they wanted *adventure*.

He brought the song to its end with fists raining down.

Then he stood up and took a bow.

He was panting, gasping for breath, as he looked around. That had felt good.

The other musicians were staring. Uncle Max looked stricken. Then, as Nelson stared, his face turned to thunder.

Uncle Max looked almost *comical* when he was angry.

Then Nelson turned to Barry Pike. The man had always had a severe expression, but now it looked more severe than ever.

'I think, young man, that that might be considered *traitorous*.' He shook his head. 'Although, since I'm not sure whose nation it was most traitorous to, I think we had better perhaps consider it on its musical merits. And ...'

Here it came, thought Nelson.

They were all as bad as one another in this country.

Not one of them wanted anything new. They just wanted to live in the past.

'I can't say I didn't like it,' pronounced Barry Pike.

It took Nelson a moment to understand what the elder statesman had said. Barry Pike wasn't furious. He was begrudging, and perhaps bewildered, but he wasn't cross.

'You need to remember, young man, that this isn't a dance hall. This is serious.'

'It's music, Mr Pike, it's not meant to be—'

Before Nelson could finish what he was saying, Uncle Max had crashed over and almost barrelled him out of the way. 'He just needs a bit of refinement, Mr Pike,' Max interjected. 'But the basics are there. And you – you can't say it wasn't *memorable*.'

Mr Pike shook his head. 'I'll have to consider this carefully. The last thing the Royal Dansant needs is a firestorm. There's enough uncertainty out there every night without us having to spirit up more in here. Young man, I need to know I can trust you to do what we ask of you.'

Nelson felt his uncle's hand grip his arm, fingers gouging into his flesh until he yelped out, 'Yes, sir!'

'But this is, after all, meant to be about our two nations colliding,' Barry Pike observed. 'Musically, culturally, body and soul. Young man, if I'm to permit playing like this in my orchestra, I need to know it's coming – and I need to know it's at my command. Am I clear?'

Nelson said nothing, until another sharp jab in the side from Max made him fling up his arm in salute. 'Yes, sir!'

'Very well then. So be it. Ladies and gentlemen, I think we have our last dance.'

# Chapter Twenty-Two

In a palatial Bloomsbury townhouse, overlooking a square untouched by scaffolds and bombs, Frank Nettleton took his partner Mathilde in hold and prepared to dance.

'Let's pause for just a moment,' intoned the aged, authoritative voice on the edge of the room.

*Pause?* thought Frank. The truth was, he wasn't aware they'd started.

Georges de la Motte. Frank had often heard the name, for he was close to being a legend in the story of Raymond's lifetime, but until Raymond had breathed those words, he hadn't once dreamt about the opportunity to study with him. He was an aged man, though he'd been as broad and statuesque as Mr Arbuthnot in his time, his hair like grey waves crested in white, his voice still thick with the accent of his French boyhood. That his war was to be spent in this Bloomsbury townhouse, far away from the Paris he'd once called home – and the golden sands of California, where he had latterly hung his hat – was pure coincidence, but also Frank's good fortune. And this, their second visit to take Georges's instruction, made him feel more fortunate than ever – for nobody of Georges's stature would have continued tutoring a dance partnership if he thought they were hopeless.

'As with every journey, the first step is the most important,' Georges intoned. 'Before you can move as one, you must *become* one. I can see the connection in you. But Frank, you bow over her – just a fraction of an inch, I admit, but you bow over her nonetheless. A judge will spot this in an instant. To the trained eye, you hunch over Mathilde as if you own her, as if you *possess*. But this is not the meaning of the dance. You must lead, confidently and unambiguously, Frank – but Mathilde's response must be willing. Only in this is there meaning and romance. She is not yours to dance with. You dance *together*.'

Frank thought he understood. He'd never been very good at school – but this felt different. Until now, he'd danced by instinct. Yes, Raymond had shown him the formalities – and yes, Marcus was a fountain of advice – but interrogating his technique, looking at it from an outsider's angle, trying to perceive what a judge might perceive, was a new experience.

'What we're looking for,' Georges went on, 'is both connection *and* separation. Both of you must be in full command of your bodies. Your frames must be held so confidently that, even if I were to click my fingers and spirit one of you away, you would remain in position. And yet ... your bodies must fit together as well. They must line up. Think of the shoulders, the hips – these are our points of connection. Two bodies, one shape.' He paused. 'Dance for me.'

The music began, just a gentle waltz emanating from the gramophone in the corner. 'Shall we?' Frank grinned at Mathilde – and together they slid into the dance.

Almost immediately, Georges lifted the needle from the recording and said, 'Perhaps the occasion has got the better of you – but would you look each other in the eye like this in the ballroom?'

'Sometimes the guests need it,' Frank shrugged. 'They're not always confident.'

Georges paced. 'What works for the Grand may not be correct for the Royal Dansant. Remember – this is a competition. You are being judged. When you look into the eyes of your partner, something takes over. We are drawn towards the eyes. If you gaze too deeply, your frame will collapse. Look to your left, Frank. Look to *your* left, Mathilde. This space between your partner's head and your own shoulder? This is the portal through which you must be gazing as you let the music take control...'

Frank and Mathilde had knocked, full of nervous excitement, at the townhouse door in mid-afternoon, as soon as the demonstration dances were over in the Grand – but they did not leave until the summer sun was already setting, and rehearsals were about to begin back at the Buckingham Hotel. 'It's only a week until the Summer Ball,' Frank had told Georges. 'That means only three weeks until the Royal Dansant,' Mathilde had added.

So it was down to business. Georges was never cruel with Frank, nor Mathilde, but nor did he sugarcoat his words. Each song seemed to last half an hour, as he repeatedly stopped the recording, instructed them on some finer point of movement, rhythm and poise, then sent them back to their task.

'You mustn't let your arm droop, Mr Nettleton. The moment you lose the position, your connection is gone. Now – dance on!'

'Your hand is climbing Mr Nettleton's back, Miss Bourchier. Arrest it! To an eagle-eyed judge, it will seem you are hanging from your partner. Now – dance on!'

By the time sunset threatened the rooftops over London, Frank was near exhausted – and yet Marcus and Max would be waiting in the Grand, marshalling the troupe for the Summer Serenade to come. Frank had seen the decorations going up in the Grand this morning, Rosa and all the other chambermaids let loose with bunting to festoon the walls, the balustrade, the stage and bar.

'Mr Nettleton, a quiet word, perhaps?'

Frank and Mathilde were already making their goodbyes when Georges said, 'Mathilde, I shan't keep your proud partner more than a moment,' and led Frank off, into a little side hall. Then, with his voice dropping low, he went on, 'I'm worried for Raymond. I was grateful to hear from him, and nothing gives me more pleasure than knowing he's passing on the lessons I taught – but I'm led to believe he's been back in London all year, and he hasn't once been to see me.' Georges paused. 'He tells me that he has been invalided home.'

Frank tried to explain, in his own faltering way, 'He can still dance – he seems to feel enough of the music to carry him through. Mr Arbuthnot keeps him in place in the ballroom – and he's rustier than he used to be – but he's still Raymond. Nancy encouraged Raymond to enter the Dansant. He's dancing with Hélène again. It might be the thing to bring him back to life.'

'Mr Arbuthnot needs to deploy him properly in the Grand.'

Frank felt almost treacherous, because what he wanted to say was 'Mr Arbuthnot's afraid.' Instead, he just shrugged. 'Do you think we can do it, Monsieur de la Motte? Me and Mathilde, at the Albert Hall?'

'Make the best show of yourself that you can, Mr Nettleton. You and Miss Bourchier both. Some day soon, the world is going to change again. You'll want to be ready when it does.' Then he marched out into the hall, placed a kiss on the back of Mathilde's hand, and opened the door to the coming twilight. 'Watch the skies, my young friends. And stay safe until I see you again.'

There was a certain crispness to the June evening, but Frank barely felt it as he and Mathilde hurried over the high road at Holborn, and into the snaking streets of Covent Garden. 'I don't think I've ever felt so weary from just dancing,' Frank laughed.

'It's the concentration,' Mathilde grinned. 'Have you ever *thought* about dancing as intensely as just then?'

'I don't know if I'll remember it all. My body remembers the steps, but can my mind keep up?'

They reached, at last, the great expanse of Leicester Square. The theatre on the corner was still in ruins, half-hidden behind hoardings and scaffolds, the reconstruction trucks out front. A little further along, beside the site of the demolished Alhambra, the Odeon Luxe cinema still stood defiant. Its doors were open, the blackout not quite in place, and streams of guests were already wandering through to await the evening show. On the billboard above, the faces of Greer Garson and Walter Pidgeon gazed out, clasping each other against a bucolic country backdrop. *MRS. MINIVER*, it read, in giant scarlet lettering.

'Frank,' Mathilde said, her voice suddenly uncertain, 'isn't that... your Rosa?'

Frank was still gazing at the poster, but now his eyes drifted down to the front of the cinema and the crowd gathering outside. Most of the guests were slipping straight into the building, but several just lingered under the awnings, gazing out over the square.

That *was* Rosa.

She was wearing her grey woollen coat, with a paper rose in her hair.

Red lipstick, like she wore when they went out dancing.

Frank's heart sank.

'I promised her we'd go and see it together,' he said, still staring. 'Then she wanted to go out dancing instead and I... It was our first night with Georges. I never did find another night. I suppose she really *did* want to see it.'

Mathilde said, 'Then go to her. Frank, she'll be glad to see you.'

Frank froze. 'Marcus is waiting.'

'I could make some excuse. Tell him you pulled a muscle or strained your side. I could still dance, Frank. Raymond's in want of a partner. Hey, it might be quite something to dance with the fabulous de Guise!'

She was baiting him, her eyes twinkling – and Frank might even have played along, if only he hadn't seen Rosa lifting her hand to wave. He lifted his too – but, too late, he realised she wasn't waving at him at all. Feeling like a fool, he let his arm drop at his side and watched as another figure approached Rosa. A solid, square-built young man with a short military haircut, dressed in brown slacks and a pale yellow shirt, had emerged out of the crowd. Frank watched as Rosa skipped the few steps between them, and greeted him by threading her arm with his own.

'I know that man,' Frank whispered.

The smile vanished from Mathilde's face. She seized Frank's arm and tried to draw him away but Frank would not be led. 'We met him at the Ambergris Lounge. He's the one who broke up that fight. Joel Kaplan. American infantry.'

Mathilde whispered, 'Are they friends, Frank?'

'She's never once mentioned his name.' Frank stared, ashen-faced, as Joel Kaplan led his sweetheart Rosa into the cinema.

'Frank, they might just be friends. Look at us, Frank – me and you, partners and friends. Think of Raymond and Hélène. It's friendship, Frank That's all it is. And you said it yourself – you've been so busy with the ball and the Dansant and... maybe she just found somebody to go with.'

Frank had already started drifting towards the cinema.

'Frank, you can't. You mustn't.' Mathilde took three faltering steps after him. 'Marcus is waiting. The ball's nearly here. He'll be incandescent if you aren't there. I was only joking about dancing with Raymond. It wouldn't work! We wouldn't fit. I need you, Frank. You're meant to be there.'

Frank's throat was dry. 'I'll make it,' he said – though both he and Mathilde knew it was a lie. 'I've just got to know.' Then he looked over his shoulder. 'Go,' he told her. 'What would Georges say? Dance, dance, dance!'

Frank only had a few pennies in his pocket, but it was enough to get a ticket. He found his seat, sandwiched between two couples on one of the shadowy back rows, and tried to settle down – but his heart was racing, and try as hard as he might, he could hardly focus on the story unfolding above. Up there, the Miniver family were calmly facing the war with all the determination and stoicism Frank had seen unfolding around him in the past few years. Kay Miniver was the very spirit of hope and resistance. She waved to her son, a Royal Air Force pilot, who dipped his wings in the skies above the rolling fields for her to see. She welcomed his lover, Carol, to the bosom of her family. When a German pilot crash-landed in her garden and marched her inside at the point of his gun, she calmly waited until his injuries overcame him, took his gun, and summoned the police.

Frank scoured the crowd. But the theatre was too dark. Only when some moment of brightness exploded on the screen above could he dare to hope he'd find Rosa and Joel among the cinemagoers.

He rose in his seat.

Somebody told him to get down.

He craned left to right.

Somebody told him to sit still.

And there...

*There they were.*

Up on screen, a German plane banked over the bucolic English village. Machine-gun fire rang out – and the younger Mrs Miniver lay dying on the English earth.

Six rows in front of Frank, Rosa sobbed.

She sobbed with her head on Joel Kaplan's shoulder.

Frank thought he'd seen enough. He was up on his feet, trying to march away – but, although voices harried him to sit back down, he couldn't tear his eyes away.

Joel Kaplan's arm tightened around her.

He was loving this, thought Frank.

Acting the protector. Playing the hero.

Rosa melted into his side.

Joel planted a single, tender kiss on top of her head.

At last, Frank ripped himself away. Boos and jeers chased him as he stumbled down the row, tangling with other people's legs as he staggered – as ungainly as a man who'd never danced before – into the aisle, out of the cinema, and into the night falling over Leicester Square.

He'd hoped that his heart might have stopped racing by the time he reached Berkeley Square, but even as he floated along Michaelmas Mews it was like thunder in his breast. When he arrived, he hurried along the back halls until he was stumbling into the dressing rooms behind the Grand.

In the ballroom, the rehearsal was already gathering pace. Frank gave himself but a moment, staring at his harrowed, darting eyes in one of the dressing-room mirrors, before he flung open the dance-floor doors to join the troupe.

The rehearsal had reached a hiatus. Up on stage, the musicians had gathered together – Max leading them through some points in the song they'd just performed – while the dancers assembled at the balustrade steps, Marcus rhapsodising his sense of ambition for the ball to come. Mathilde, it seemed, had been dancing with Raymond after all. She gave Frank a sheepish smile as he approached.

'Mr Nettleton, are you sure you're feeling quite up to this?' Marcus declared, breaking off from whatever speech he'd prepared.

Frank's eyes flashed to Mathilde.

'Are you still feeling nauseous, Frank?'

So that was what she'd told them. But the fact was he really *was* feeling nauseous. He slid alongside her, whispering his apologies to Raymond, who slipped out of the way.

'I know what the day has held in store for some of you,' Marcus proclaimed. 'I know that there are those among us whose hearts have been captured by the Royal Dansant.' At this, he gazed first at Raymond – but then at Mathilde and Frank, his eyes excoriating them with the intensity of their stare. 'I will say only this: it is a fine, fine thing to dance for the royal household. But our duty, first and foremost, is to the Buckingham Hotel. We precious few have been chosen as servants of the Grand – and, while there is breath left in my body, we will serve her well. I am, regrettably, informed by the hotel's management that it does our reputation no harm to host dancers who excel this summer at the Albert Hall. But I will insist that, for the next week, our focus is on nothing but the Buckingham's Summer Serenade. We are not the warm-up act for the Albert Hall. This hotel has celebrated the summer in its own magnificent way ever since the Grand's inaugural year – and Mr Hastings has set us the challenge of winning all the custom flooding in from the New World. While I lead in this ballroom – and I *do* lead – we will not let him down.' He turned his gaze to the stage. 'Mr Allgood, are we ready to go?'

'Ready as ever, Marcus, my boy.'

Marcus swept Karina back to the dance floor and took her in hold. 'I'm sorry Raymond – Frank has no need of an understudy any longer. But perhaps you could watch from above, and make what suggestions you will?'

Frank muttered his apologies to Raymond and took Mathilde in hold.

'Did you see her, Frank?' she whispered as the dancing began. 'Did you talk to her?'

Frank shook his head, swept Mathilde onward, bowed into the first steps of the showpiece.

'Frank?' Mathilde said. 'Frank, what happened?'

Suddenly, Frank broke out of hold.

But he had no words for Mathilde.

'I'm sorry, Mr Arbuthnot,' he said, 'I'm just too sick…'

And, without another word, he took flight from the Grand.

# Chapter Twenty-Three

The moment Max returned home to Albert Yard, he knew something was wrong. Ava was waiting for him on the doorstep and he'd rarely seen his cousin flustered. But this was panic, pure and simple.

Was he right, or did she even seem a little *scared* as Max approached?

'Now, Max, first you got to listen,' Ava said as he came through the gate.

Max stood stock still. 'Where is he? Is he inside?'

'He ain't well, Max.'

Max didn't like being the sort of man who bustled a woman out of the way, so he left it to Lucille to push bodily past Ava and into the house.

Ava was indomitable. Ava was a rock. But the one thing she'd never been able to be ruthless with was her son Nelson – and there he lay, splayed out on the sofa in front of the Brogans' fire, his face a bloody pulp where fists and boots had piled into him; his nose flat to his face, his ears swollen like a veteran boxer's, his hair matted and dark.

One of his eyes was swollen shut.

The other was refusing to look at his Uncle Max.

'What in hell have you done?' Max gasped, falling at the stricken boy's side.

'That's a fine way to start, Max Allgood,' Ava intoned. 'Your nephew's taken a hiding, and without a breath, you think it's all down to him.'

'It's all good, Uncle Max,' Nelson croaked, the sentiment completely at odds with his bloody repose. 'I got it. Head's pounding, but when ain't it? I'm good, Uncle Max. I just need to sleep it off.' And he patted Max's hand with a bloodstained paw. 'Trust in me. It's all workin' out.'

Max reeled back, disgusted more by the boy's words than his sticky touch. He glared, in righteous fury, at Ava. So this was what it felt like to feel on fire. Max had never really felt it before. Anger had eluded him almost all of his life – until now.

Ava said, 'Max, he stayed out all night. Couldn't bear to show his face when you were around, so he slept in some gutter until he knew you were gone.'

'Damn right too,' Max fumed. 'You damn fool, Nelson. You'll never learn. *This*, *this* is why I don't trust the kid. Sweet Jesus, he's meant to be back at the Hall tomorrow. I'm up at the Buckingham, setting up for the show – and he's meant to be with Mr Pike and all the others, running the numbers.' Max rounded on Nelson. 'What in hell are you mixed up in this time?'

'I told you, I'm good.' Nelson tried to sit up, but some pain in his ribs wouldn't let him. 'I can still play, Uncle Max. They didn't break my fingers.' Then he stopped. 'Not this time.'

'This time?' Max breathed. '*This* time?'

In reply, Nelson only started coughing.

'I told you, boy. I *told* you. Keep your head down, I said. Keep your eyes peeled and your hands clean. These English might not put us in different buses. They might not kick us out of their restaurants and train carriages. But it's still in them. There's still hate around. What is it Orla Brogan said? NO IRISH, NO DOGS, NO BLACKS... And you? You incite 'em, boy! I seen you do it. It's your speciality. Second only to playing the piano – and who's gonna have you now? I told you – you doff your cap, and you pay 'em deference. It's what the English *know!*'

'English?' Nelson snorted, spitting into a bucket at his side. 'Hell, Uncle Max, it wasn't the English did this. You've got to run into some of our own good old countrymen for this kind of a whippin'.

Some of the fury faded from Max. He went to Nelson's side, slumped down beside the bloodied boy and heaved a sigh.

'Oh no, Uncle Max,' Nelson grinned, darkly, 'it ain't just the jitterbug and the jive those GIs have brought with 'em. It ain't just money and nylon stockings and chocolate for all the girls. They brought some good ol' Southern charm with 'em as well – and look at me, here I am, the very *beneficiary* of it!'

It had started the moment he left the rehearsal and went to join Freddie Riordan's crew at the Midnight Rooms. He was full of himself, flying high on the events of the day – certain in the knowledge that soon he'd be leaving the clubs behind and setting sail on his true course in life. They'd started calling him 'the King's Man' that night – and, as a matter of fact, Nelson *liked* it. He knew, on some level, that they were teasing him. But he could also see, in their eyes, a kind of admiration as well.

In fact, he felt so good about life that when they'd suggested a little card game – well, he'd thought, why the devil *not?*

And he'd been right as well: his good fortune at the Albert Hall had carried him into the small hours of the evening, as a teetering tower of winnings piled up. It had been with him the following night as well, when Freddie Riordan's band played at the Starlight – and, three days after that, when they were back at the Ambergris Lounge and the club was a heady paradise of wild dancing, showmanship and style. The card game that night was wild. Nelson risked big, but won big as well.

Nothing could stop him now.

That was when Freddie said, 'You know, we ought to open these games up a bit. There's a group of likely lads in the Lounge tonight. They look flush – well, Americans always do, don't they? I'd bet you could soak some winnings up out of them, Nelson. Listen, why don't I go and see who's interested? We'll play the second half, then we'll bring them back here.'

Nelson liked the idea of this. The fact was, the King's Man was getting tired of taking money off the same old bunch. It was, to coin a phrase, getting to be like taking candy off a baby.

The thought of the game geed Nelson up as he played the second set of the night. When the finale came round, the expectation was positively coursing through him, shooting out of his fingers to animate the piano keys. By now, he'd got used to playing his wild rendition of 'My Country 'Tis of Thee' at the end of each night. He fancied some of the revellers here even expected it – and the roar that went up when he hit that first chord was nothing short of electric.

The adrenaline was still surging through him when the show came to its end and the cards started being dealt backstage. 'The American boys have asked for higher stakes,' said Freddie Riordan casually, 'so this game's only for those that can afford it.' One after another, the trumpeters declared their intention to sit the first hands out. A handful of Freddie's musicians were game, and Freddie declared himself good for one or two hands; then he met Nelson's eyes and said, 'Of course, the King's Man's got enough winnings to give these American boys a battle. Look, here they come now...'

The stage doors had opened up – and through the black curtains came a quartet of thick-set infantrymen.

They were still filing through, shaking hands and clinking glasses with the musicians, when Nelson realised he recognised one of these Southern types.

Right out there, on the Ambergris dance floor, in the very same spot where he had landed Nelson a blow, was that redneck bastard.

But he was the King's Man now – and revenge wouldn't come in a hailstorm of open-palmed blows, but in cold hard cash.

'You want to shake my hand before I rob you?' Nelson grinned, up on his feet.

The infantryman recognised Nelson now. He lowered himself to the table with the rest of his crew and said, 'Just deal 'em. I'll deal with you later. Right now, I'm playing cards.'

And the game began.

Back in Albert Yard, Nelson paused in the telling. His bottom lip had started oozing again, he winced as he spoke – but when Ava held up a mug of cold water and let him take a few sips, he could at least carry on.

'You never told us you got into a fight before,' Max sighed.

'I been in a hundred fights. It don't mean nothing.'

'It means *something*, boy. Look at the state of you!'

'Well, see, I'm getting to that. Because that game, Uncle Max, it started good and it went even better. Those Southern boys, they was jawing and hawing and guffawing with the band like they'd been brought up in the same damn town – they were so distracted they hardly even cared about the game. No, for them, it was just an excuse to be out drinking and gallivanting, without even thinking, for a second, that they're here to win this war. Uncle Max, I robbed 'em *blind*. There was only that boy Rick who even paid attention by the end of the first hour. The rest was just having a good time. And boy, when someone's having a good time, you can skin 'em alive. And that's what I did, Uncle Max. I took just about every penny...'

'Then where is it now?'

Nelson could tell that Max was seething, but he felt his mama's hand on his shoulder and went on, 'I was strong though, Uncle Max. I looked at what I had and I reckoned it was thirty pounds – and I thought, hell, there's no way I'm losing this! So I stood up and I said: see you later, boys. I'm done. Game over. I'm *out.*' He grinned, bloody and demented, as if somebody ought to have given him a medal. 'And I would have been, as well, if only I'd got to that door. I'd have been home and dry – and *rich*, Uncle Max! – if only one of those infantrymen hadn't spotted what was going on and tried to stop me. Because suddenly he was in my face, Uncle Max. Suddenly he was telling me those weren't the rules, that the game wasn't over until it was over, that I wasn't allowed to just walk away.'

'You can always walk away, boy. It's called willpower.'

'Ah, but Uncle Max – you see, they was *persuasive...*'

Nelson was at the door, meaning to march off across the Ambergris Lounge with all his winnings, when one of the infantrymen threw himself into his path. Nelson couldn't re-member what this one was called, but he was the one who'd taken hold of him and wrestled him off his pig ignorant pal over there. 'Hey, you don't need to get nasty about this,' Nelson remarked. 'It's all fair and square. It ain't my fault if your buddies aren't paying attention.'

'Now, Nelson,' Freddie Riordan began, 'it's hardly fair to call time on the game before it's through, is it, now? Don't these boys have the right to win their money back?'

'It's called *willpower*, Fred. You got to know when to walk away. Me? I been practisin' it all year – and look where it's got me. Off to play for the King, with a pocketful of money. I'll be eating fine off you boys for the next month. Good God, I'll be eating like a King myself! So hands off me, Private – I've got a long walk home.'

The infantryman just looked him in the eye.

'You're chicken-shit, that's what you are. Three months ago, you're out there knocking about a man who's had so much to drink he can hardly stand – and now you're taking his hard-earned money, without even giving him a chance to win it back.'

The King's Man suddenly looked a lot more feral than he had mere moments ago. 'You want to watch your mouth. *Hard-earned* money? As far as I can see, you young bucks are just sitting around in barracks, marching on parade, idling around drinking and gambling. Outta my way, horse-shit, I'm not doin' nothing wrong.'

Then Freddie Riordan's voice rang out across the back room: 'One more hand, Nelson. You owe them that.'

Nelson, who didn't think he owed anybody anything, threw himself back towards the table and reclaimed his seat, his body filled with fire. 'One more game, and I'm done with you lot.' He picked up his cards. 'Oh, I fold,' he grinned. 'Game over.' But when he tried to stand, Freddie took hold of him by the forearm and hissed, 'Just play the game, Nelson. Keep the punters happy. There's no honour walking out early. Everyone's here just to have a good time.'

'Yeah, and so am I,' said Nelson. 'So just deal the god damn cards and let me be on my way.'

The next hand was not kind to Nelson, but that didn't matter; a few shillings lost on a hand of cards was no great loss to him – and, the more hands he folded, the more he protected the winnings at his side, the greater the anger that boiled in the infantrymen dominating the table.

'Just raise the stakes, piano man,' the infantryman named Joel snapped, as one game ended and another began. 'This is meant to be a *game*.'

'And I'm playing to win,' said Nelson. He looked at his hand. Two kings was surely a winning hand, but a wicked part of him decided that to fold would be better. The clock on the wall had already gone past 1 a.m. Just a little longer and it would be over.

One after another, the players tossed in their coins.

'I'm out of this one,' Nelson declared.

The hand went to Rick. With a grizzled look, he swept up his winnings, then revealed his hand.

Just a queen high.

Nelson's two kings would have beaten it. He flipped them over. 'Sorry guys, it's just not my night.'

Rick rose to his feet in fury. 'You're not playing the game, you rat. You're sitting there on your hoard, just stringing us along. That was a good hand you got. If you were playing for real, you would have gone all in.'

Nelson stood. 'I played it your way. I done what you said. But it's 1 a.m. now, and past our bedtimes. You grunts have probably got marches in the morning.' He turned and shook Freddie's hand. 'Fred, we got another show at the weekend, right? But after that, I'm done. I'm playing for the King, and then it's on to the Promised Land. Off to join the orchestra at the Buckingham Hotel, and to hell with the rest of it.' He winked, theatrically. 'See you later, cowboys.'

This time, nobody stopped him.

This time, he marched straight through the door, off across the Ambergris Lounge, and out into a dewy summer's night.

Had Nelson Allgood ever felt better than he did right then? Money in his pocket, vengeance in his wake, all the hope and glory of the Royal Dansant up ahead?

It felt as if London belonged to him. The way back to Lambeth was long and dark, but suddenly, the air was filled with his song. 'My Country 'Tis of Thee,' he sang. But then: 'Nah, forget it. God save the King!' he whooped, and his voice echoed through the empty boulevards, all the way to Oxford Street and beyond.

New York had taken so much from Nelson and his family.

But London?

London gave everything back, and heaped a mountain of interest on top.

He hadn't gone far, still whistling to himself, when he saw shadows up ahead.

Four silhouettes stepped out of the scaffolds that surrounded the old John Lewis store. In seconds, they surrounded him on every side.

No guesses who these were. 'Hello boys,' said Nelson. Quietly, he reached into his back pocket, where his winnings were weighing him down. 'I guess you're finished playing fair?'


'So they beat you for the money,' Max sighed, his head buried in his hands. 'Nelson, you fool. You goaded them. You baited and poked at them. You *asked* for it.'

'Funny, Uncle Max, 'cause that's what they said too.'

Max's eyes flared. 'You got nothing to show for the night, boy. Your winnings went right back to them. It's a wonder they didn't break your fingers.'

Nelson wiggled them, to show he could still play. 'Who said they got my winnings, Uncle Max?'

*

As Nelson careened into an alleyway, staggering through the bins at the back of a shadowy little canteen, his heart sank. He'd felt like the King of Soho, felt like this was his territory, his home turf – and he'd blindly run himself into a dead end.

Up ahead, the alley was bordered by walls on every side.

Rats scattered in the shadows.

'God damn,' he muttered. Nowhere to run, nowhere to hide.

'You want this?' Nelson declared. He plunged his hand into his back pocket, brought out the fist full of coins and crumpled notes. Pennies scattered at his feet, but he didn't care about them. 'Come and get it.'

His eyes scoured the darkness at his feet. There, against the wall, water pooling in the broken cobbles, lay exactly what he wanted:

A sewer drain, ripe with the scent of below.

'If you played the game fair, it wouldn't have to be like this, King's Man.'

The infantrymen sidled down the alleyway, drawing near.

'I wasn't holding fake cards. I had luck with me tonight. I had *fate.*'

'Oh yeah?' snarled the one named Rick. 'Well, what does fate have in store for you now?'

'I don't know,' smirked Nelson, 'but I think she's still smiling.' He opened his hand.

Down rained the coins, down fell the crumpled notes, down into the gutter at his feet, down through the grate, into the sewer below.

A single pound note floated in the effluent for just a moment, as if saluting him farewell; then it too was sucked down below.

By instinct, the infantrymen clattered forward.

'Sorry, boys,' said Nelson, 'but that money was mine to do with what I wished. Spend it, donate it, waste it – it's all the same to you, because it wasn't yours. It stopped being yours when you got lazy at the table. Couldn't let you take it off me, not like this, boys – so how about we call it evens and ...'

That was when the first fist struck him.

Nelson was on the ground, his face pressed into the drain, in an instant. The boots were in his side, the fists were in his face, his arm was wrenched behind his back and the world was spinning – but it didn't matter, not really. The way Nelson remembered it, he'd even been laughing as they kicked ten bells out of him. Every blow they struck was just another reminder: he'd won, and he would go on winning; there wasn't a thing these blowhards could do about it.

'Win?' Max snapped. 'You didn't win nothing. You're a wreck. You're ruined. I bought you a chance at the big time, and you've squandered it – squandered it like I knew you would.'

'Hey, I can still *play*,' Nelson declared.

'You think they let guttersnipes looking like you play for the King? It won't matter a thing what you sound like, when you look like *that*. Boy, it's hard enough looking like we look, all three of us, without looking like a piece of rancid meat from a butcher's hook. You want to play for kings? You don't look good enough to play for beggars.'

Max groaned, wild and long. 'Here's what's going to happen. I'm sending excuses to Barry Pike. There's no chance you're rehearsing with 'em now. I'm telling him you're laid out – yellow fever, scarlet fever, some damn fever no fool's ever heard of! – and he'll have to muddle through. And you? You're not moving from this house. You're not stepping outside. You're not playing gigs, you're not raising hell, you're not strutting around London telling everyone you've got it made. You sit where you are and you drink your mother's soup, and you pray to God that your face looks halfway handsome by the time the Royal Dansant comes around. I staked my reputation on you, Nelson. I knew I couldn't risk it in the Grand, but I gave you a chance. You want to throw it away, that's on you – but you won't make me look a fool as well.'

Nelson started to put up a protest – but Max would hear no more. He marched out of the room.

Ava grabbed Nelson by the shoulders and looked into his one good eye.

'It's not over yet, boy,' she told him, with the kind of conviction and commitment only a mother ever musters. 'But he's right. You can't leave this house. You play with fire too much. It's what makes you so good up on stage, but it's what's going to destroy you too. I'll look after you, Nelson. I always did. I'll get you back on your feet. I'll clean you up. There's still time. But Max is right. You're not to leave my sight.'

Nelson slumped.

It was strange to see the fire go out of him.

Ava drew herself closer. Only when she wrapped her arms around him did she realise that her son was sobbing.

'Ma, you don't understand. It was before those cowboys left me in the gutter. They had my arms behind my back. Let's break his fingers, they said. They would have done it too; I could feel 'em straining. But – no, said another. He's going to need those. Then they knelt down right beside me and said...'

Nelson could still feel the warmth of that boy's breath on his ear.

The self-satisfied smirk on his face.

*'You're gonna need those, King's Man, because you owe us every last penny. And if we don't get it...'*

Nelson mimed each of his fingers snapping, just so there wasn't any doubt that his mother understood.

*'And don't think you can escape us. Don't forget – on Independence Day, we know exactly where you're gonna be . . .'*

# Chapter Twenty-Four

John Hastings hadn't seen his wife and family in three days. For most men of his stature, with a portfolio of business interests so varied and wide, this wasn't unusual. But ever since he swapped New York for London, Hastings had been determined to live by his family's routine. His wife Sarah kept their apartment in Baker Street pristine, and every evening he repaired there to take supper with her and the children, to forget about business and embroil himself in the minutiae of their days.

Tonight, however, was the night of the Buckingham's Summer Ball, and his first as Hotel Director. Here was the hotel's chance to authoritatively declare: we are open for American business.

All his pieces were in place:

Max Allgood, a bona fide American star, lending the Grand a wilder, more daring air than its adversaries.

Himself: a native New Yorker at the helm of this quintessentially British institution.

The guests confirmed in attendance: the exiled King Zog of Albania and his entourage; Crown Prince Olav of Norway; the formidable Queen Wilhemina of the Netherlands – a genuine coup for the Buckingham Hotel, for she was due to set sail for the Americas in days and, out of all the ball's highborn guests, she was the only one not attending the Royal Dansant.

And there, at the heart of everything: his company of star dancers.

Marcus Arbuthnot: the proud leader of his dignified troupe. Frank Nettleton, whose star was in the ascendant. And Raymond de Guise, his wildcard, his soldier returned from the war; the evening's enigmatic romance.

On paper, it looked perfect.

And yet...

He'd been to see the final rehearsals. He'd seen Raymond standing on the sidelines. He'd watched Frank dancing with his beautiful partner Mathilde – and even John Hastings, never a dancing man, had seen him distracted, discombobulated, as if he wasn't quite in the room.

He'd seen Marcus's brow furrowing as he fussed with the dancers, poked at the choreography, chopped and changed and pivoted around – as if something in the ballroom just didn't seem quite *right*.

The clock on the wall turned its hands towards 1 p.m. Lunch was being served in the Queen Mary, and John Hastings' presence had been requested. He strode off to meet his public.

In the house on Blomfield Road, Raymond peered into the crib where Arthur was sleeping and softly drew the blanket around him.

'You know, he'll get too warm,' came Vivienne's voice, from somewhere behind. 'He'll tell me if he's cold.'

Raymond was so fixated on his son that he didn't turn round as he said, 'I wouldn't dream of overruling you. He just looks so ... peaceful.'

Too late, Raymond realised what he'd done. A voice as soft as Vivienne's ought to have been on the very edges of his hearing. He turned, hoping she'd made no connection – but he'd made the same mistake with Vivienne before, and he could see some hint of suspicion in her eyes. 'It's getting better, isn't it?' she asked him. 'Your hearing?'

Raymond remembered his paymasters' advice: ambiguity, opacity – these were the best friends for a spy. 'I feel I should be able to dance at my best this evening,' he replied. 'Sometimes it feels like emerging from the water. You've been swimming in some lake, and suddenly you break through the surface – and everything's distinct.' He winked at Vivienne. 'You mustn't spread it too widely, Vivienne. I fear they'll send me back to the front.'

Then he slipped past, out of the nursery and along the hall.

As he marched the long route to the Buckingham Hotel, taking in the rolling green of Hyde Park, he found that he could no longer sidestep thinking about the order from Maynard Charles. In just a few short hours, he would be stepping onto the dance floor at the Buckingham Hotel. There, he'd lead Susannah Guthrie down the balustrade steps, look longingly into her eyes and say, 'Shall we?', with all the nuance and undertone that Maynard required.

He'd felt it needling at him ever since Mr Charles's command. The thought had weighed on him as he lay with Nancy at night, or woke in the morning to find her already brushing her hair in the long mirror. That wedding vows meant nothing to Maynard Charles was no surprise; that he expected Raymond to accept the same so willingly still made him numb.

There had to be another way.

And yet...

If he disobeyed the order and, further down the line, Douglas Guthrie struck some nefarious deal with Kemp, what might that mean for the war?

What might it mean for Raymond himself?

What did a man do when doing the honourable thing required *dishonour*?

The thoughts were still turning around in his mind when he reached the Buckingham Hotel. He could sense, already, the anticipation in the air. Concierges nodded knowingly as he drifted through. One of the pages scuttled past and remarked, 'Good luck tonight, Mr de Guise!' The Queen Mary restaurant throbbed with its early dinner service, the eager hum emanating out and filling the hotel reception.

Some of the musicians were already backstage. As Raymond marched past, he could hear the evening's guest pianist working through his numbers, keeping a steady beat. Past them he marched, until at last he slipped into the Housekeeping hall. The chambermaids were just coming off shift. Most of the staff at the Buckingham only ever heard about its fêted balls, but these nights were occasions for all; when Raymond stepped into the Housekeeping Lounge, he found that Nancy was already reorganising it for the evening – when her girls would be permitted to host revelries of their own, the hotel swept into the same air of celebration that rippled out of the Grand.

'I wondered if you might use some help, Mrs de Guise?'

'I'm not sure I can face a party,' she grinned. 'If there's one thing being a mother does to you, it makes you hate a late night. But I can't leave the girls to it. I don't trust them enough. Come on, you can help me with these tables. They can have some space for dancing, and we'll set up the gramophone.'

It was good to work with Nancy. As they organised the Lounge, they got to speaking of Arthur and Stan, of Vivienne – of *home* – and it eased the tension in Raymond's mind. It was only when the work was done, and his thoughts returned to the evening ahead (the thought of Susannah Guthrie in his arms, how he might charm information out of her without having to lead her to bed), that Nancy saw the lines deepening on his face.

'Just embrace it,' she told him, squeezing his hand.

Raymond was almost startled out of his skin – but, of course, Nancy knew nothing of what was going through his mind. She was still swept up in the thought of his injury, how distant he seemed from the Raymond of old, his hesitation on the dance floor. All of her empathy for him, based on lies. Once more, the falsity stung him. Perhaps it would be better, right now, if he just let rip with the truth.

He opened his lips to reply.

But... wasn't that *dishonour* as well?

In the end, it was Nancy who saved him. It always was. Raymond was ready to tell her everything, when at last she said, 'It isn't your name at the head of the dance troupe tonight – but it's still your world. You know that, deep inside. Go out there, Raymond, and show them what they've missed. And then... the Royal Dansant is coming. The whole world's going to know who you are, who you *really* are.'

Nancy couldn't have known it, but those were the very words to bring him back to earth.

Yes, he thought, the whole world would know who he was.

Not a man who lived by falsehoods – for that was just a part of him now, and it wouldn't be forever.

He was Raymond de Guise, the former King of the Grand, and – no matter what else they asked of him – he would show them that tonight.

So he kissed Nancy, long and hard.

'Save a dance for me, after it's done,' he told her.

And as he walked away, he remembered:

I've charmed a thousand guests in that ballroom. I've talked them into making the Buckingham Hotel their home away from home. I've sung to them and danced with them, and made them feel, for fleeting moments, as if they were the centre of the world.

What did a man need to seduce a woman for, when he had talents like that?

Yes, thought Raymond, *now* I remember...

It was getting busy backstage. Frank had arrived when it was still quiet, meeting with Mathilde in the little rehearsal studio behind the Grand, but now the hubbub was growing. At the practice piano, the guest pianist worked through his pieces; around him, the orchestra assembled. Frank only wished he could feel it. Mathilde kept geeing him on, but it made it worse that she knew what played on his mind. 'You've just got to embrace the evening. You're dancing with *me*, Frank.'

The clock on the wall announced it was barely an hour before the first dance.

'Don't worry, Mathilde. It'll be different when the music starts.'

That was when the door flew open, and Max Allgood stalked through. He waddled to the piano, rallied his musicians, and began to lead them through the set-list for a final time.

The clock ticked past the hour.

Fifty-nine minutes and counting...

'Have you talked to her about it?' Mathilde asked.

'I haven't seen her.'

'Now, Frank,' Mathilde chided, 'that's not true.'

There was enough truth in it, Frank decided. He'd been up in the kitchenette, and he'd sat with the girls and shared in tea and toast – and he'd seen her in the hallways and winked and smiled, like he always did – but the first time he'd tried to say anything, the words just died on his tongue. It was like they didn't want to be said – and, the longer the silence went on, the more unreal, improbable, imagined that moment in the Odeon seemed.

'I've been busy,' Frank snorted.

Then a dainty knock came at the rehearsal-room door. Moments later, Rosa stepped through with a small bouquet of lilies in her arms.

Mathilde caressed Frank's elbow, then skipped towards the dressing rooms – the very place where Frank wanted to be.

'I had to say good luck,' Rosa smiled, bowing apologies to the other dancers and musicians as she crossed the floor to greet Frank. 'I know it's silly, but ... lilies. I thought they were pretty.' Frank found himself taking them, even though his hands tried to rebel. 'You look nervous, Frank.'

'I *am* n-nervous,' he replied.

If only she knew *why*.

'Listen, Frankie – you've worked so hard for this. This and the Albert Hall.'

'Rosa, I've g-got to go.'

But he couldn't extricate himself, not before she had grabbed him and pressed her lips to his cheek.

She must have felt it, then.

His whole body, coiled and tensed.

'Have a stiff drink, Frankie,' she told him. Then she dazzled him with a smile and said, 'We're having the shindig, like ever, in the Housekeeping Lounge. Annie says Victor's been allowed to bring a half-bottle of brandy from the Queen Mary. Mr Hastings has set aside some bits and pieces for us too. We'll be there until late, Frankie. And even *later*, up in the kitchenette ...'

Rosa looked back before she left the rehearsal room. As for Frank, he was still staring. It wasn't until she was gone that he could bear to turn around and march into the dressing rooms. Immediately, he was met with Marcus's towering frame.

'Lilies, Frank?' Marcus beamed. 'Pour *moi*?'

'You're welcome to them, Mr Arbuthnot,' Frank said – though the moment Marcus took them, then presented them to Karina like some medieval courtier, he felt a sudden stab of guilt.

Silly, really, but he hadn't been able to stand their smell.

'Frank, are you OK?'

It was Mathilde's voice.

Frank looked at her through one of the dressing-room mirrors and nodded. 'I'm being c-cruel, Mathilde. I should just say it out loud. I should just t-tell her what I saw. It isn't fair to just keep a-avoiding her. She wonders what's wrong. She thinks I'm nervous of the dance.'

Mathilde drew closer to him and whispered, 'Only you, Frank Nettleton, could see what you saw and think *you're* the one being cruel. And, if you're not being fair to anyone, you're not being fair to yourself…'

The dressing-room door opened.

In strode Raymond de Guise.

'Mr de Guise,' Marcus announced, 'I'm glad you could join us.'

Frank looked at the clock on the wall. Half an hour separated them from the opening number. Out there, the ballroom doors were opening up for guests to claim tables, raise their first cocktails, to allow the anticipation to build – but Raymond was far from being late.

'Let us rally, ladies and gentlemen!' Marcus announced. 'The Summer Serenade is about to begin!'

John Hastings walked, his good lady wife Sarah on his arm, down the gently inclining corridor that led to the Grand. Through the marble arch they came, through the open doors, and hovered – for only a moment, since other guests were following close behind – on the threshold.

'You were right, John,' Sarah whispered. 'It looks spectacular.'

'I couldn't hang the Stars and Stripes,' John whispered, 'but it'll feel like a New York City gala once the music starts playing.'

'Don't be fooled, John, that what Americans want is America. I fancy every American with money really wishes he was an old English lord – with his castle and his keep, and his manor house in the country...'

'Every century has its own kinds of gentry,' John winked, and whisked his wife on.

Sarah was more adept at society than John. While she left his side to parley with the other wives of the Hotel Board members, he charted a path through the guests, greeting them each by name, marvelling together at the flags, the bunting in summer colours, the flowers – supplied at considerable expense from the royal floriculturists at Kew – that adorned every table. Tonight, the Buckingham smelt not of beeswax and varnish, but of a meadow at the very height of summer.

Soon, John Hastings was standing at the dance-floor railing, watching as the doors opened up, revealing Max Allgood to the crowd. In the few minutes he'd spent hobnobbing with guests, the Grand had filled up around him. The applause crashed over him like a tumultuous wave, spilling out over the dance floor and enveloping the orchestra as Max Allgood led them out.

'I do enjoy the way he looks as if nobody's ever applauded him before,' Mr Hastings remarked to the gentleman at his side. 'The bravest, freshest, most original bandleader in London – and he's still astounded that people greet him in such raptures.' He smiled. 'That's not *often* the way of my fellow American, you know.'

'Oh, I *do* know,' said the Scottish laird Guthrie. Tonight, he was dressed in a simple black dinner jacket, his moustache perfectly tamed into two tight curls. 'I've done much business with your countrymen, Hastings. You're not generally a humble type.' He tapped his unlit cigar on the balustrade and added, 'I happen to think my countrymen could have learnt a thing or two from yours. You value your freedoms. I like that in a nation.'

'Well you may celebrate that tonight, Lord Guthrie. A waltz, perhaps, with one of our fine ladies.'

Up on stage, Max Allgood bowed to the crowd, turned promptly to his orchestra and signalled for them to begin.

The pianist hit the first chord.

The trumpets sounded.

On the dance floor, the doors opened up, revealing Marcus Arbuthnot and Karina Kainz in all their glory.

As the dancers fanned out and the evening's first showpiece began, Lord Guthrie smiled sardonically and lit his cigar. 'I'll leave the dancing to my wife, Hastings. The ballroom is but business for a man like me.'

Backstage, Frank and Mathilde waited their turn, then sallied out to join the troupe on the dance floor. Behind them, the doors fell shut – and Raymond was alone.

Swiftly, he scoured the roster pinned to the dressing-room wall. Susannah Guthrie had reserved dances with Marcus to begin the evening, but some time after that – before the evening's first intermission – she would be in Raymond's arms. Perhaps that timing was for the best. By the time he marched with her across the dance floor – to the fiery gale of Max Allgood's 'This One's For Me', perhaps the wildest waltz of the ball's first half – she would have imbibed two or three cocktails from the bar. Tonight, the Grand was specialising in cocktails that brought to mind the pleasure palaces of New York City and Hollywood. Out there, English lords were raising Brown Derbys – that famous staple of the Vendome Café in Los Angeles – and Old Fashioneds, made with deep, amber American rye whiskey. With a few drinks warming her, Susannah might speak more freely.

Out in the Grand, the band reached the climax of the very first song. Wild applause filled the ballroom, the showpiece coming to its end. Raymond remembered the thrill of those moments well. The bitter hand of nostalgia – perhaps even jealousy? – took hold of him, but the feeling was only fleeting; he was about to stride into the ballroom with a higher purpose in mind. Even so, when he stole to the dance-floor doors and pushed them open just a crack, just enough that he could catch a glimpse of the dance troupe taking their bows, he was filled with a *longing*. Right now, watching Marcus take his ostentatious bow, his face lit up by the chandeliers from above, then stepping aside to present Karina to the ballroom, he was filled with memories of when he and Hélène had done the same.

Those were simpler times, of course.

A time before secrets.

A time before family.

A time before war.

Raymond steeled himself.

Out there, the dancers fanned out to meet their first reservations for the night.

So Raymond did the same. He strode to the balustrade to meet Jane Bancroft. As she took his hand, he gazed into her eyes and said, 'It has been too long since we danced.'

'Before Scotland,' Jane said, allowing Raymond to lead her to the floor.

'Well, London has missed you.'

'I have to admit, sir, that I missed it as well. The far north holds little interest for a lady.'

'You travelled farther than I thought.'

Jane Bancroft shook her head and grinned wickedly. 'The Guthries act as if they own half of Edinburgh, but – between you and me – their riches extend to hill farms too lonely and steep for most sheep. No, give me the glamour of the Grand Ballroom above all that. Let the bombs rain down, Mr de Guise. At least I shan't die of boredom.'

Jane danced elegantly. Perhaps it was only that she'd been starved of music in her Scottish sojourn, but she leant into each number and Raymond was glad to be leading her along, rising and falling with the wild cadences of Max's music. One dance blurred into a second. The second exploded quickly into a third. In the corners of his vision, Raymond saw Marcus leading Susannah Guthrie on a merry dance of her own – but, for the first time since his meeting with Maynard, he found that his mind was not whirling with thoughts of how he might inveigle his way further into her life. The music was doing what it used to do in days gone by: it was transporting him, lifting him from this place and planting him in another world. Very soon he would have to come back to earth, but right now it felt good. It felt like taking flight. If he could reach this perfect feeling when he danced at the Albert Hall, then perhaps he really could end the evening accepting a trophy from the King.

The music came to a close. Raymond's time with Jane Bancroft was over. He watched as she weaved her way back to St John, who was jawing with some other industrialist among the guests up above.

There was no time to linger. Raymond marched to the balustrade, where Susannah Guthrie was draining the last of her scarlet cocktail, served in a tall champagne coupe.

'Blood and Sand,' she said as she took his hand. 'I believe you may have stolen this one from the Savoy.'

'Impossible, my lady. The Buckingham is first in all the finest things.' Then he dropped his voice to a whisper. 'I shan't breathe a word if you don't.'

He didn't feel this dance as effortlessly as he had done with Jane Bancroft. The touch of her body reminded him of his instruction; the warmth of her caress brought only Nancy to mind. Max's next song encouraged closer dancing yet, and when she lifted her lips to his ear to congratulate him at the end of the number, he felt the possibility opening up in front of him. Seduction itself was a kind of dance.

And when their time dancing together came to an end, Raymond left it unspoken in the air between them. 'I wish that were not the end of our time this evening, Susannah.' He paused. 'May I call you Susannah?'

'You may,' she replied, 'and you may also entertain me after the intermission. I fear I shan't convince Douglas to the dance floor. He's several decades past the point of indulging his wife.'

Raymond let her go for only a moment. Then, catching her arm – and allowing his fingers to slide along her wrist, just a fraction of a moment too long – he said, 'I'm reserved after the intermission – but perhaps ... a cocktail, while the band takes its break? That is,' and his eyes flashed again at Douglas Guthrie, 'if the good laird would not object.'

Susannah rolled her eyes. 'The good laird will be otherwise occupied, so my time is my own. As it happens, Mr de Guise, the good laird is otherwise occupied much of the time. Sending me back to Scotland, so he can spend time with one of his kept women?' Susannah shook her head wryly. 'My husband may have his pets in secret, but he won't stop me from taking a few dance tips from a champion artiste in sight.'

Raymond stared at her, trying to process the fact that Susannah Guthrie really did know about her husband's infidelities. What was it Maynard Charles had said? *These are the private pacts our overlords make. It is quite likely his wife is aware of the arrangements.*

'A cocktail, then. I shall look forward to it.'

The moment Max Allgood thrust Lucille aloft and declared the end of the ball's first act – 'But don't you go anywhere, ladies and gentlemen! Me and the boys, we're just getting started!' – the Grand erupted in raptures. The rolling waves of applause were enough to make the hanging crystals of the chandeliers tremble, making delicate music of their own.

Off went the dancers.

Off went the musicians.

And, as one, a phalanx of waiters marched out to fill every glass in the Grand.

Backstage, Frank returned quickly back to his station and splashed cold water all over his face. Moments later, looking up to dry his face in the mirror, he saw Marcus cutting a swathe through the resting dancers. His face, which had been etched in such practised magic and wonder in the Grand, transformed in an instant to a thunderous mask.

'Must Karina and I carry this night alone?' he exclaimed. 'Or do my eyes deceive me? Do the rest of us not *know* what night this is? Have we so easily forgotten, while we dream of His Majesty and the Royal Albert Hall, what an honour it is to dance right here, in the Buckingham Hotel? Are we all so inured to its splendours that we take it for *granted*?' He turned a perfect pivot on his heel, taking in the whole of the dressing room, dancers and musicians alike, until his eyes fixed upon Frank. 'Well, Mr Nettleton? Can you look me in the eye and tell me that you were *present* for the guests tonight? Or were you like a metronome, just keeping beat, just counting the steps?'

Frank turned his face away.

'Frank, you seem to have forgotten the chance at your feet. You seem to have forsaken your dignity and pride. Tonight is the most important night in your young dancing life, and there you are, on the dance floor, as if this is some ... dress rehearsal? There is but one chance of redemption tonight, Mr Nettleton. In tonight's second half, you will put thoughts of the Royal Dansant from your mind, and you will do justice to the ballroom which has nurtured you and given you the opportunity for a life beyond your wildest—'

'Mr Arbuthnot, *please!*'

It was Mathilde who had spoken out. Every eye backstage turned towards her.

'It isn't the Albert Hall preying on Frank. I happened to think that Frank danced with—'

'I'll brook no argument,' Marcus announced. 'I have been slaving to put on a spectacle for this ballroom all year long, and we must not fall at the last hurdle. Frank, I expected better of you. I expect you to remedy this immediately and ...'

'You don't know what's going on, Mr Arbuthnot. Frank's hardly just forgotten. He's—'

But Frank reached up and took Mathilde's hand.

Softly, he shook his head.

'It's all right. I'll do better, Mr Arbuthnot. I just ... It wasn't coming together. But it will. I promise.'

'I respect a man by his promises, Mr Nettleton – but you've broken yours already, by dithering in my ballroom. We have a mission, people. We are at war for American custom. I demand rigour from each and every one of you, and—'

'Marcus, everyone hears it,' came Raymond's sudden voice. 'We're not on a battleground. We're in a ballroom. Get them there by wonder, not by the whip.'

The silence garnered a new, more mortified quality now, as Marcus pivoted again, this time to look Raymond de Guise squarely in the eye. 'You and I shall talk about this at length, Mr de Guise, at a time and place of my choosing. Your ambition undermines everything we have achieved in this ballroom since the war came down. You spread its seed. Everyone's focus is on the Albert Hall, for personal glory and fame, instead of the fortunes of this troupe, this hotel, our own Grand Ballroom. So I ask you now, and I ask you to declare it in front of one and all: who leads this troupe? Who is responsible for the elegance and splendour of nights like these? On whose head lies the reputation of the Grand?'

Raymond's eyes flashed around the room.

Every piece of him wanted to rail at Marcus, to tell him he was sacrificing his authority by losing his temper. The man was a giant of the ballroom world, but vanity twisted a legend.

'It's your troupe,' Raymond said, 'but it's everyone's responsibility to conjure magic out there. It's down to every last one of us – and, where one of us falters, the others will rally. Because we're a troupe, and it falls to us all.'

Then Raymond inclined his head towards Marcus and, with a single step backwards, slipped out of the dressing rooms, back to the Grand.

In the backstage area, Marcus looked around.

Now it was his turn to flush red, to look shamefaced – though he did a better job than Frank in hiding it well.

'We return to the fray in but fifteen minutes. People, summon all the majesty you can.'

*

Out in the Grand Ballroom, above the balustrade, Susannah Guthrie was waiting.

'I took the liberty of summoning you a drink,' she said as Raymond drew near. 'How does a Tom Collins sound?'

'I drank these when I danced in New York,' Raymond remarked, holding the glass up high to catch the crystalline light. Their glasses chimed and, exchanging glances over the rims, they drank. 'You must tell me about Scotland, Susannah. I haven't been further than Glasgow – but I've danced at the Barrowland Ballroom.'

'Oh, you'll have to excuse me – but if I speak of Scotland once more, I shall scream. The one thing that doesn't occur to you when you take a wealthy Scotsman's hand in marriage is that you'll swiftly be leaving society behind – if not *civilisation*.'

'Thank goodness for the war then.'

'What do you mean?'

'I understood the war had been kind to your husband's estate. That it had left him in something of a prosperous position.'

'Prosperous enough to throw a lot of money away at cards, you mean?' Susannah must have thought Raymond caught off-guard, for a moment later she touched his hand and smiled, 'Oh don't worry, Mr de Guise. I am well aware why Douglas sent Jane and me north of the border. He wanted time with his ladies, and time with his gentlemen, and I am but a hindrance.'

'You almost sound unhappy, Susannah.'

'I wouldn't characterise it as such. But, no, my life has not followed the path I perhaps hoped it might.' She drained her drink. 'Well, we all make accommodations, don't we? Look at you – back in the ranks of the ballroom you once ruled. I made a similar kind of pact. I enjoy the finer things in life, Douglas can provide them for me.'

'And more so than ever, now that the war smiles on him.'

'If only he saw it like that.'

'Isn't he enjoying speculating on the war?'

'Raymond, my husband enjoys *winning*.'

'I saw as much at our card game. There was a gentleman there, a Mr Kemp I believe – your husband was very keen to make his acquaintance.'

'Oh, to watch him fawning over men with money, it's quite sickening! Have you ever watched a lovelorn fourteen-year-old try and win the heart of some girl he's sweet on?' Susannah grinned. 'My husband is much the same.'

'At the card game, he was talking about the lands he lost to the military.'

'A sore subject,' Susannah warned him. 'He claims the loss is sentimental, but in fact he feels he was short-changed.'

'I can only imagine.'

'He isn't the only one. There's a group of families much the same. The highlands and islands – what the British military want with them, I can only imagine. Gruinard Island, for goodness' sake – what use is it to anybody? Douglas did try and rally the families together to resist the sale – but the Scots can no more resist the King than they could in the sixteenth century, so I'm afraid it was lost.' She paused. 'Anyway, Mr de Guise, the upshot is that we have spent much of this spring in London, while my husband hunts for opportunities – with this odious Kemp fellow that you met.'

'Will it keep you here for long, Susannah?'

Susannah's eyes twinkled. 'That's an intriguing question.'

Raymond just shrugged. 'A gentleman can ask. A lady doesn't have to tell, but a gentleman likes to know.'

'A little while longer, at least. My husband is meeting his new friend Kemp on the first of July, I believe.'

The first of July, thought Raymond. Scarcely a week away.

'Let him play as long as he likes. Personally, I have found it a boon to be back in civilised society. It makes a woman realise what she's been missing.' She looked down, studying Raymond's hand. 'I see you wear a wedding band, Mr de Guise.'

By instinct, Raymond covered it. The falsity of what he was doing stung him once more; as soon as Nancy was in his mind, he could hardly shake her image.

'It has been difficult, to return from the war. I'm sure you can imagine – even if, perhaps, you can't understand.'

Susannah said, 'Not all marriages make sense. I've already told you of mine.'

The dance-floor doors opened up, and in their frame Max Allgood appeared. Soon, the ballroom's attention turned towards him. One after another, the musicians returned to the Grand, assembling up on stage to herald the second act.

The music struck up.

The dancers fanned out.

From above, Raymond watched as the night's second show-piece began. It was difficult to believe that, only a short time ago, Marcus's face had been wrenched into such righteous fury backstage. Now he looked as serene and invincible as ever, his head held high, Karina connecting perfectly with his body as they led the dance.

'I should like to dance with you, Susannah. I think, perhaps, I could … adjust my reservation.'

Susannah touched his arm. 'Mightn't that upset the delicate balance?'

Raymond just smiled. There was so much more he wanted to ask her, before the night was through. Douglas's planned meeting with Kemp was only the beginning. If there was some way that meeting might be held right here, at the Grand, might he be able to get even closer?

'Oh, I think the balance is worth upsetting, don't you?' Raymond smiled.

The showpiece dance had reached its end. As the applause filled the Grand once more, Raymond hurried Susannah to the dance floor. 'One little waltz, before my duties drag me away.'

'Lead on, Mr de Guise.'

Yes, thought Raymond, lead on and ever onward – until he was at the heart of whatever this plot might be.

For the first time that night, catching the scent of his quarry, Raymond started to wonder if this life of subterfuge and deceit might suit him after all.

Even before the applause had died down at the end of the night, even before the last of the musicians had taken their bows and left the stage, Frank Nettleton was tearing off his bow tie, kicking his dancing brogues back into the dresser, and hurtling out of the dressing rooms. Marcus's voice chased after him – 'You embraced the second half, Mr Nettleton, you rose to the challenge!' – but Frank didn't care. Falsity suited some people. It didn't suit Frank Nettleton. For the last hour he'd faked wonder, faked majesty, faked magic – but it had been at a cost. He felt sick with himself, rotten down to the core – and, as he ran, he realised it was all because of the falsity he'd been carrying with him for days.

He had to purge it, from body and mind.

Knowing that any hesitation would let the doubts creep in, Frank hustled his way to the Housekeeping Lounge. He could hear the music from halfway along, old swing records from Archie Adams' time in charge of the orchestra here.

He remembered the first time he'd joined a shindig in the Housekeeping Lounge. It had, he remembered with a mounting sense of regret and heartache, been through this door that he'd first *tried* to dance. Until that moment, the little boy from Lancashire, desperately grateful just to be a page at the Buckingham Hotel, hadn't even dreamed of the future that had come to dominate his days. The thought of how beautiful that moment had been, all the potential and possibility it contained, was almost enough to keep him from opening that door.

But open it he did – and, two footsteps further along, when he had closed the door behind him, all the girls in the Housekeeping Lounge were cheering his arrival.

'Frankie!' Annie Brogan grinned, grabbing him by the hand to haul him into the dance.

There was Victor, and there was Billy. There was Mary-Louise – and there, right there, was Rosa herself. She'd been dancing gaily, glass in hand, bouncing and kicking just like in the jives he'd taught her – leading a pack of other girls, porters from the kitchen, pages and concierges, their clamour enough that the whole Lounge seemed to be shaking.

In the middle of the dancing, Rosa was the eye of the storm. She kicked and skipped around until she was facing Frank.

Her eyes lit up.

Her smile blossomed.

'Frankie,' she cried out, 'get in here!'

But Frank held fast, his feet rooted to the spot.

His heart was pulling him into the dance.

It was his head that would have to keep him out of it – for the moment he entered that maelstrom, he'd be lost, the music coursing through him, Rosa in his arms, his mind playing that most dastardly of tricks: telling him that what he'd seen wasn't true, that it hadn't really happened, to cling on to what he wanted instead of what he had.

'Rosa, I need to talk to you.'

'Frankie, let's *dance!*'

'Rosa,' he said, 'please.'

She must have sensed something different in him then – because, although the music and dancing went on around her, at once Rosa seemed locked in a bubble of silence. Quietly, she lifted herself out of the dance. There was a moment in which it seemed she knew what he had come here to say, because their eyes met and the silence between them was pregnant with all their squandered potential. Then she seemed to break out of the spell; she skipped to Frank's side and allowed him to lead her back across the Lounge.

'What is it, Frankie?'

Frank said nothing, not until they were in the Housekeeping hall, away from eager, eavesdropping ears. Through the walls, the music still pulsed.

'I'm sorry I didn't take you to see *Mrs. Miniver,*' he said.

Rosa rocked backwards on her heels. 'Frankie, it doesn't matter. We can go another time. I didn't mind. I know you've been preparing for the ...'

Frank couldn't look at her as he said, 'I c-couldn't go again.'

Rosa was silent.

Then, at last, Frank looked up.

'I wish you'd told me. I wish you'd just said: Frank, this just isn't what I want, not any more. I would have been shocked. I would have been upset – but I'd have understood. I'd have picked myself up and dusted myself down and g-got on w-with it l-like everyone d-does when there's b-bad news.' He stopped, if only to gather his thoughts, his breath, his courage. 'I saw you with him, Rosa. We were coming back to the hotel from tuition and you were standing outside the Odeon on Leicester Square – and I thought, gosh, Frank, you've let her down. You've let her down and she's going to see the film on her own. Except… you weren't. I saw him meeting you there, just like you must have arranged. Joel Kaplan, that infantryman from the Ambergris Lounge.'

Rosa reached for his hand, but Frank drew away.

'How many times have you seen him?'

Rosa just stared.

'Rosa, please?'

'Frankie, it isn't like you think. We were out dancing with some of the girls, that first night you went to Georges. The boys were there and Joel said – well, he wanted to see the film too. It's just friends, Frankie. That's… all… it…'

But even as she said the words, she was faltering.

Frank turned away. Of all the cruel things right now, he didn't want her to see him cry.

'I went into the picturehouse too,' he said, with voice breaking apart.

He didn't need to say anything more. He just pushed his hands into his pockets and started walking away, lengthening his stride when he heard her faltering footsteps coming after.

'You've been so busy, Frankie.'

The soft, plaintive words followed after Frank, but they didn't catch him. By the time they petered into silence, he was already halfway along the Housekeeping corridor – and he and Rosa, and everything he'd hoped they would be, were finished.

*July 1942*

# Chapter Twenty-Five

Maynard Charles was almost twenty-four hours without sleep and starting to feel the fatigue when the knock came at his office door and the department secretary appeared with the file.

On the front, the stencilled letters: R#4861.

De Guise was a capable agent, and it had been the right decision to bring him back from North Africa, but rumours of the man's relentless principles had been spreading of late. That was Maynard's fault, of course – it had been wrong to discuss with his staff his agent's tendency to moralise – but it didn't change the department's opinion of the man. That de Guise was their only asset capable of inserting himself into the Buckingham's ballroom was not a matter of debate; that he was the sort of man who would gladly get his hands dirty and soil his own morals was a more nuanced matter. Maynard contended that, when the time was right, de Guise would do as he was asked.

Others were not of the same opinion.

You had to accommodate different personalities in this trade, of course. The perfect spy did not exist. Amoral men could make excellent spies – and poor men even better, for there is little a man will not do to put bread on the table for his family. But de Guise? Well, the case for de Guise was not so clear-cut. The man would have died for his country on the battlefield. No doubt he had already killed in his King's name. But lies took a toll on some men, and so it was with de Guise.

Maynard read and reread the file in front of him.

He'd been useful so far. If his return to the Grand had not run as smoothly as might have been hoped – and what hope was there, really, when the egos of artists were involved? – he had, at least, secured his position. He had inserted himself in Bancroft's parlour games; he had befriended Guthrie's wife.

And now, because of information gleaned, a security operation was about to take place.

The telephone on his desk rang, as if to summon him from his brooding.

'What's the update?' he asked, when he answered it.

A voice on the other end said, 'It's just as de Guise said. They're in the restaurant now.'

Maynard Charles nodded. 'I'm going to attend this one. Send a car.'

The car arrived swiftly, though in truth there wasn't far to travel. The little restaurant in Covent Garden was a favourite spot of the Office – and, indeed, one of the waiting staff already took their coin. By the time Maynard Charles arrived, both parties were seated. 'They're having the oysters, sir,' said one of the junior staff when he stepped out of the car.

'No expenses spared,' Maynard replied. 'Who have we got in there?'

'We're watching front and back, sir. Carlson's at the neigh-bouring table.'

'I want my own eyes on these bastards,' Maynard replied. He approached the restaurant from the front, took the homburg hat off his head, and ventured through the doors.

A drink at the bar would be enough. Plenty of gentlemen of his generation took solitary drinks on a lonesome night. He occupied a spot in the corner, then glanced over to where his colleague Carlson was sitting.

At the neighbouring table, Douglas Guthrie and Angus Kemp were deep in conversation.

Thank goodness for de Guise, he thought.

A few moments later, when the oysters were finished, Maynard Charles drained the cognac he'd ordered and returned to the night.

'Is everything to your satisfaction, sir?' one of the underlings asked, as Maynard slipped back into the car.

'Do we know where Susannah Guthrie is tonight?'

'She's at the Buckingham Hotel, sir – playing the loyal wife, while her husband does business.'

Maynard nodded.

'To the office, and make it quick,' he instructed the chauffeur. 'We're going to test the edges of this thing tonight – and there's a call I must make.'

At the house in Maida Vale, Raymond de Guise released Hélène from hold and stood back to appraise her.

'How does it feel?'

To Raymond, Hélène had felt as light as she did when they had soared across the dance floor at the Grand, elegant and nymph-like despite the years she'd spent away.

Hélène, evidently, was less sure. 'Too rigid, perhaps? And too ... expected? It's missing something. Missing the—'

'Magic,' proclaimed Nancy.

She'd been watching from the armchair by the fire, and now she brandished the copy of the *Radio Times* she'd picked up from the newsagents that morning. In simple black and white on the front cover, beneath the red lettering *RADIO TIMES*, was an artist's impression of the Albert Hall. 'WELCOME TO THE ROYAL DANSANT!' read the legend.

Nancy had opened the listings magazine, where four pages were dedicated to the upcoming celebration and its coverage by the BBC.

'It's right here,' she declared. 'Among the participants in the upper stages of the professional competition will be veterans of the ballroom Raymond de Guise and, for one night only, his partner Hélène Marchmont – who has come out of retirement especially for the event. Expect great things from a partnership who were once known as "the magic of Mayfair".'

'You get a mention in the *Dancing Times* too,' said Frank. He had appeared in the sitting-room doorway, cup of steaming tea in his hand. Freshly back from another session dancing with Mathilde under the watchful eyes of Georges de la Motte, he seemed more buoyant than he had in the days since the Summer Serenade. 'It's right here – there's even a picture of you, from the first night in the Grand!'

Frank brought the magazine into the sitting room – and, by the fire's paling light, they gathered to look at the image of Raymond and Hélène as they'd once been, that summer's evening more than ten years ago, when the Grand had first opened its doors.

'I think we can still conjure a little magic,' said Raymond.

On the stand out in the hall, the telephone started buzzing.

It was Frank who picked up the receiver. Moments later, his brow furrowing – for he was certain he recognised this voice – he said, 'They're asking for Mr de Guise.'

Raymond went out into the hall.

'De Guise,' said the voice, 'you're needed.'

Maynard Charles rarely called Raymond at home.

'The Buckingham Hotel, de Guise. I'm going to need you on the ground.'

Raymond flashed a look through the sitting-room door. Hélène was waiting. Nancy and Frank were waiting. Scarcely three nights separated them from the Royal Dansant.

And yet...

'I'm sending a car. You're to meet it on the corner by the North Gate Entrance at Lord's.'

Raymond took a breath. This was the pact he had made in returning to London, but there was no denying that it stung to let his family down. 'What's the duty, sir?'

'I need Susannah Guthrie occupied and out of the Continental Suite within the hour. Do you understand? The Candlelight Club should suffice. Take her to a private booth. Romance her a little more.'

'Sir...'

'I'm not telling you to take her to bed, de Guise. In fact, I'm instructing you to keep her away from her suite. I have a detachment of officers standing by to search it while Guthrie's at dinner. Don't let me down.'

Then the line went dead.

Raymond's mind whirled. The smells of Vivienne's lamb broth were steaming in from the kitchen. There stood Hélène, ready for more dance. The night stretched in front of them, to be filled with laughter and chatter, anticipation for the Albert Hall.

'I'm sorry,' he said wanly, as he came back into the room, 'duty calls. And... Max Allgood's asked to see me, up in the Grand.'

The lie was paper-thin, but it was all Raymond had. That was something he'd have to work on: building a roster of lies he could summon up at a moment's notice, anything to help extricate him from the family home. Every lie told was a little easier to stomach. He supposed that was how professionals did it; when you lived your life by lying, eventually it barely touched you at all.

The car was waiting just a short walk away, by the gates of the towering cricket ground. It was a silent ride through the blackout until they reached Berkeley Square. Raymond slipped out with only a whispered thanks, then straightened himself and marched along Michaelmas Mews.

Something in this felt like donning his suit of midnight blue, that moment before every dance where he ceased being himself and became the debonair de Guise. Now, every time he stepped into the Buckingham Hotel, it was like donning another disguise. His stride lengthened; he held his head up high; he strode through the storerooms by the tradesman's entrance knowing he was a cuckoo in the nest.

Somewhere up above, Susannah Guthrie was waiting.

He wondered how pleased she'd be when he knocked on the door.

As he stepped into the golden cage of the guest elevator and greeted the attendant, his eyes flashed about reception, wondering for the first time where the surveillance officers Maynard Charles had mentioned might be.

When the elevator deposited him on the fifth storey, Raymond thanked the attendant and marched out. It was better not to think about Nancy, nor the lie he'd had to spin.

He knocked on the door.

There was only silence within.

He knocked again.

Slowly, the door opened.

Susannah Guthrie looked, perhaps, even more striking without make-up. Sixty years old, dignified in the lines and creases that marked her face, she was wearing a simple cream house dress, a pale yellow shawl around her shoulders. Pearls hung loosely around her neck. A silver bracelet of tiny chains sparkled at her wrist.

Her wedding ring flashed – not from her finger, but from the dresser, where spectacles and an open envelope lay alongside the book she'd evidently been reading.

'Mr de Guise?' Susannah stepped out and looked, curiously, up and down the corridor. 'You have a habit of making unexpected appearances – but this one, I have to say, is more unexpected than any.'

There was little point wending his way slowly into this lie.

It was better, when lying, to be brassy and bold.

'I remembered what you told me. How the good laird is indulging his business interests tonight.'

A smile played on Susannah's lips. 'The good laird indulges his business interests most nights.'

'But tonight he dines with Kemp. Tonight he isn't at the Buckingham Hotel.'

'And here we are.'

Raymond just smiled.

'Do you want to come in, Mr de Guise?'

Raymond stalled. It would have been easy, right now, to slide into the room alongside her, to close the door to the outside world, to lie down and occupy her time. But that was not Raymond's duty – and, if it were, he could not possibly have done it.

Better, then, that he simply take her hand, as he did now, and draw her close, bowing his head so that he could whisper the words directly to her ear: 'I was wondering, first, if you might enjoy some private tuition, Susannah?'

'Oh yes?' she smiled.

'The ballroom stands empty tonight. I might light the chandelier – just a single one, dazzling over the dance floor.'

'I'm not dressed for the dance floor.'

'Do you see me in midnight blue?'

Susannah looked him up and down. 'You'll have to wait a few moments. I won't be seen in the hotel like this. There are standards to maintain.' She paused. 'Close the door, Raymond. I shan't bite.'

As soon as the door was closed, Raymond could feel his heart pounding. Susannah disappeared into the bathroom; the sound of water running masked all else as she readied herself for the evening. He fancied he could already see shadows crowding at the closed door, the footsteps of Mr Charles's agents out in the hall. 'Susannah, we mustn't tarry.'

She emerged, looking resplendent in an ivory-white evening dress. 'I wouldn't worry, Raymond. I don't expect Douglas to return this evening. He ordinarily needs to toast a successful evening's work. A handshake isn't enough for Douglas.' She waved airily at the dresser, the wedding ring she didn't wear, the envelope and book. 'I'm sure he'll find a bed for the evening. He ordinarily does. But you can guarantee it shan't be this one.'

'Oh, Susannah…'

She disappeared behind a screen, bowing down to tie the ribbons of her shoes.

'There's no need for pity, Mr de Guise. These are the pacts that we make.'

Raymond gravitated to the dresser. Was there any more tangible sign of a faithless marriage than the wedding ring, set down on the dresser alone? He felt for the band on his own finger. When, he wondered, did betrayal begin? If Nancy knew the truth, right now, would she take his hand and tell him: do what you must? Would she understand that he was here at all? When he took Susannah to dance, was it treachery, even if your lips never touched, even if you never whispered about love, even if your clothes never lay entangled on the bedroom floor?

Was there treachery in *pretending* to betray?

The envelope wasn't sealed. It was just a simple Buckingham envelope, cream with the hotel's royal insignia on the lip, like some medieval seal. Checking first that Susannah was still occupied, he prised it open and looked within.

Not a letter, just a compliment slip courtesy of the Buckingham Hotel. 'As Requested,' it read, 'Billy.' And folded inside, a ticket for a first-class carriage to Liverpool on the 1 p.m. service, three days hence.

Liverpool, Raymond thought, almost wistfully. It seemed so long since he'd come into port to march straight into this new, strange life. There was probably money to be made in Liverpool. When a city was razed, there were always speculators ready to stake out their ground. That could probably be a place the good laird could multiply what capital he had.

Or else: the home, perhaps, of one of the laird's lovers?

He noted, with sadness, that it was a ticket for one person alone.

Raymond had only just stepped back from the dresser when Susannah emerged from behind the screen, a silver fox stole around her shoulders.

She really did look stunning, thought Raymond.

They said that money didn't buy you happiness, but it bought so much besides. On the streets of Whitechapel, there were women twenty years younger who didn't look as bright, effervescent, alive.

The words felt treacherous when they came to his lips, but he'd said them so many times – what difference did one more make?

'Shall we?' he asked, and took her by the arm.

In the attic room of the house at No 62 Albert Yard, Nelson looked at himself in the mirror and poked at the swelling just underneath his eye.

'I'm telling you, Ma, it's almost gone. I can see out of it. See how many fingers I'm holding up?'

Ava said, severely, 'Two, Nelson.'

'That's damn right, and that's how many I'll be showing to Uncle Max if he don't let me go rehearsin' today.'

Nelson was up and at the door before his mother could stop him. Moments later, he was out in the hall and hammering at the door behind which Max Allgood was snoozing, his trombone Lucille in the case by the bedside.

It was never a good thing to wake an elderly musician from his slumber. Max looked like a bear just woken from hibernation when he opened the door.

'Uncle Max, you've got to take me with you when the rehearsals begin. I can't miss it. I got to be there. You want me to dazzle 'em? Uncle Max, I got to *be there*.'

Max rubbed his eyes, then peered at Nelson. 'You look like you got hit by a car.'

'That's right – and, one week ago, I looked like I got hit by an airplane, so things are looking up.'

Max just glared. 'NO,' he pronounced.

Then he closed the door.

Nelson looked at his mother with a world weariness entirely at odds with his age, rolled his one good eye, and started knocking again. 'Now, Uncle Max, you know it's right. How can I put this straight if you won't let me rehearse? How can I get on the straight and narrow if I can't even be there?'

The door flew open. Max strode out. He lifted a thick finger and prodded it in Nelson's chest, so that the young man staggered backwards, wincing with the pain of his broken ribs.

'You've got three nights to look like you didn't take a hiding. Three nights to just about pass muster. They're breathing down my neck out there, boy. They're asking where you're at. And I'm telling them – he's just about better, but this damn pneumonia, wretched luck as it is, it got a hold of him. But he'll play. He'll play because I promised he'll play – and I won't be made a fool of. You hear me?'

'Uncle Max,' Nelson relented, 'I said I was sorry.'

Max closed the door.

'Playing like a whirlwind will give a man a good life,' he said from within, 'but living like he got a whirlwind inside of him – well, that's ruined us before, and it isn't gonna ruin us now. They expect more of me now. It's the way this city works. It's the way of society. And I'm not taking my chances.'

Raymond noticed nothing untoward as he led Susannah down through the Buckingham Hotel. If Maynard Charles's security team roamed the hotel, they did so in near silence, with only the softest of footfalls on the very edge of his hearing, shadows flitting beyond the limits of his sight. Arm in arm, he led Susannah into the guest elevator – took her across the bustling reception hall, winding with her through the backstage doors into the dressing rooms behind the Grand.

'It isn't nearly as ostentatious in here as it is out there,' Susannah remarked.

'So it is in all the old theatres and dance halls,' Raymond returned. 'But what happens back here is hardly important. It's what happens out there that matters.'

He pushed open the dance-floor doors.

They stepped into the cavernous Grand.

'A private kingdom, all to ourselves,' Raymond smiled.

He knew the Grand like some old haunt from childhood. In moments, he was operating the winch that lowered the central chandelier, then turning the valves that lit each of the gas-lamps inside its crystalline crown. When it hung in place again, it illuminated a circle in the heart of the dance floor, the light rippling and dancing as the chandelier settled into place. Next, he climbed onto the stage. Raymond was no seasoned musician, but he'd learnt a little over the years. He ran his hands up the piano – 'In another life, I might have serenaded you' – before he opened the trap in the stage where the rehearsal gramophones were stored. The song he chose was a fast one. 'Shep Fields,' he said. 'He's already such a star in New York.'

'Moonlight and Shadows' started playing.

Yes, this would work, thought Raymond.

He could make her *feel* something with this. He might begin a dance that lasted for hours ...

'Lean into me,' he told her. 'First time round, let's just listen to the music. By the second time you listen, you won't be able to hold yourself so still. You see, dance – it's all about anticipation ...'

He had just taken her in hold when the doors of the Grand opened. There stood John Hastings, Marcus Arbuthnot at his side.

Upon seeing Raymond and Susannah, they stalled.

'You see, Mr Hastings,' Marcus sighed, 'this is precisely to my point. Here we are, discussing ambitions for the Grand, expectations for the troupe, our thoughts already turning towards Christmas and balls to come – and here stands Mr de Guise, treating the ballroom, this hotel's crowning glory, as his own private parlour.' Marcus threw his arms in the air. 'We have to discuss this. I'm held to ransom, in the very troupe you asked me to lead. I've done my utmost. I've made room for the man – and yet he undermines me at every opportunity. There's discomfort in my troupe. There's imbalance – and here, sir, right *here*, is the perfect example. This ballroom does not belong to de Guise. He treats it like it's his.'

Raymond blanched. Releasing Susannah from hold, he said, 'You may need to excuse me, for just a moment.'

'Perhaps I should simply see you ... upstairs, Mr de Guise?'

Susannah was drawing away, but Raymond gripped her – quite fiercely – by the wrist. 'Stay,' he told her. 'We'll dance.'

'Gentlemen,' Mr Hastings began, 'it seems we have much to discuss.' As he reached the balustrade, he smiled at Susannah and said, 'Mrs Guthrie, far be it for me to disappoint a guest in her – private tuition, I think? – but might I borrow Mr de Guise, for just a moment?'

'Wait for me,' Raymond whispered to her.

But Susannah's eyes seemed suddenly to lack the magic that had glittered in them some time before. She stepped backwards, collecting the fox fur stole from where she'd left it on the very edge of the stage and said, 'Another night, perhaps.'

Then Raymond could do nothing but watch her go, back through the dance-floor doors through which they'd come.

'Gentlemen,' John Hastings resumed, though Raymond's eyes were still on the closing door, though every piece of him told him to follow, to unleash thunder at Marcus, to tell him there wasn't time, that things much more important than rivalry in the Grand were taking place tonight. 'I understand things have not been easy this year. But if I have a problem in my ballroom, I need to resolve it.'

'The man's eye is drawn elsewhere,' Marcus declared. 'The Royal Dansant might be a boon for this nation, but it's no boon for my ballroom. He's spread its poison. Nettleton and his partner have their eyes on the same prize. Our Summer Serenade was...'

'Quite spectacular, Marcus,' John Hastings intervened.

The compliment stalled Marcus for only a moment. Then he went on, 'Even Max Allgood is lured by the call of the Albert Hall. It has made us an aperitif for something greater – and I will not have it. You enlisted me, Mr Hastings, to carry this ballroom through the war. Well, I agreed on the presumption that I would not simply ensure its survival. I would ensure its glory. And that is what I want – a team around me with the very same ambition. Anything less will not do.' Marcus paused. 'Look at him, Mr Hastings. His eyes keep flashing at the door. He doesn't want to be here, even now – not even as we try and right this listing ship and—'

'Oh Marcus, stop!' Raymond thundered.

His voice filled the cavernous Grand, even as the Shep Fields recording came to its close.

'I've told you, time and again, Mr Arbuthnot – the troupe is yours. I'm a private here, nothing else. Deploy me as you will. You already keep me out of your showpieces. You already stand me to the side. I utter no complaint – not one.'

Raymond fixed his eyes, now, on John Hastings. 'Mr Hastings, we waste our time embroiled in petty drama, while the world burns. I have your permission to dance at the Albert Hall. Mr Allgood took your instruction to do the same. We draw attention to the Buckingham Hotel. If there's personal glory in it, then it only adds to the reputation you're building here. It isn't this that divides us.' He paused. 'It's you, Mr Arbuthnot. You decided I was a cuckoo. That I'd come to supplant you. Well, it wasn't my choice to come back to London. The hand of fate, as you would say, took me in its hold and tossed me back – with nowhere to go, except here. And I'll serve you,' Raymond railed, 'I'll serve this place as a footman, just as I served it when I was in your shoes. It's bigger than us, Marcus. The Buckingham's bigger than us all. But you have to stop. It's like a magic trick – you summon the drama on this dance floor, but you summon it backstage as well.'

As loud and ferocious as Raymond had been, the silence that followed was louder still.

Raymond stepped backwards.

If he didn't leave this ballroom soon, Susannah would get back to her suite.

Mr Charles's agents might still be there.

'I'll resign if you ask it of me, Mr Hastings,' he said, with a finality he himself had not expected. 'But I won't play parlour games any more. When you look for enemies, Mr Arbuthnot, invariably you find them – and they're out there, closer than you think. But this one? This one's just in your head.'

Mr Hastings looked like he was about to say something. Marcus stood stunned, without a breath left in his body – but the silence lingered just long enough for Raymond to take advantage.

In seconds, he was tumbling back through the dance-floor doors. In the dressing rooms backstage, Susannah Guthrie was nowhere to be found.

He started to run.

*

In the restaurant in Covent Garden, the fine wine was flowing and the lamb shank served up. At the table beside Douglas Guthrie and Angus Kemp, Maynard Charles's man Carlson poked at his plate of pork chops and listened...

Business, all night long.

Just factories and munitions, profits and losses, the vague opportunities for the hundred different futures that might unfold.

'We have to be prepared for every eventuality, of course,' said Kemp. 'That's been my principle from the beginning. Wars are won and lost by governments and armies – but that isn't *us*, that isn't the *people*. A government has one advantage over its people. A government can dissolve. We, the people, have to go on.'

'Indeed,' said Guthrie, his Scottish purr becoming even more pronounced as the wine warmed him through, 'and we the people must thrive.' He paused. 'I intend to thrive, Mr Kemp.'

'Then are we agreed?'

Guthrie sat back and lifted his glass. 'I have everything you might need. It's all waiting in my suite, back at the Buckingham Hotel...'

In the chambermaids' kitchenette, high up in the rafters of the Buckingham Hotel, Rosa sat in the window. At this late hour, most of the girls had already retired – so she thought nothing of rolling up the blackout blind and gazing out over the rooftops of Mayfair.

The reflection in the darkling glass revealed the tears she'd been trying desperately not to shed, already streaming down her cheeks.

'Rosa, you ought to go to bed.'

It was Annie Brogan's voice. The redhead had appeared in the shadowy kitchenette doorway. One after another, she took tentative steps towards Rosa.

'What happened, Rosa? What did he say?'

Rosa determinedly stared out of the window. 'I don't know what you're talking about, Annie.'

'It's all the other girls have been talking about. It's ever since the night of the Serenade. Ever since Frankie came to find you. You haven't been the same.'

The teacup trembled in Rosa's hand. Scalding hot tea splashed her on the wrist. Mouthing unutterable curses, Rosa leapt up and cast the crockery into the little tin sink, where it smashed into a dozen different shards.

'Rosa!' Annie gasped.

But when she rushed to Rosa's side, the older girl just pushed her aside, and marched out of the kitchenette.

'Rosa, we're just worried about you,' Annie cried after her. 'That's all.'

'Well, you don't have to worry. It's my mess. I'll deal with it.'

Then she was gone, her tears chasing after her, and Annie was left at the sink with all its broken pieces of teacup, thinking: well, actually, it looks like *I'll* be dealing with it after all.

And, unless she was very sorely mistaken, this tea had been laced with a healthy glug of gin.

Shadows dressed as concierges moved through the Continental Suite: two men sweeping the dresser, the bedstead, the armoire, while another stood with his foot bracing the door, guarding against discovery.

Through every drawer they combed, through every suitcase and clutch bag.

Under the mattresses, the sheepskin rug, every loose floorboard and cavity in the skirting.

Every suite in the Buckingham Hotel had its own safe, and the Continental's was half hidden at the back of the deep walk-in wardrobe. Nestled among Susannah Guthrie's gowns and furs, the shadow-men set to work.

Combinations like these might have kept opportunistic thieves or scurrilous chambermaids at bay, but the men of Maynard Charles's office made short work of the mechanism. With practised ease, they waited for the teeth inside the lock to line up. A gentle hiss of air announced their success. Next moment, the safe was sliding open – and narrow beams of electric torchlight danced upon whatever was lying within.

Just a simple brown envelope, lying there stark and alone.

One of the shadow concierges reached in to take it.

Fat and ripe, he thought.

Ripe with the scent of secrets...

In the golden cage of the guest elevator, Susannah Guthrie's face was set in a stricken mask. She looked almost furious with herself, thought the attendant, the lines around her eyes deepening as the floors flew by.

When the elevator came to a stop on the fifth floor, off she strode, head held high, back bolt upright, away from the elevators and along the hall.

The Continental Suite was only a quick march further along, through the doors at the end and round the corner.

She was almost at those doors when a girl appeared out of nowhere, tears streaking her face, and crashed directly into her.

Susannah was holding herself steadfast enough not to stumble – but the same could not be said for the girl. Moments later, she was in a tangled heap on the floor.

'I'm sorry ma'am,' Rosa spluttered, as she picked herself up. 'You'll have to forgive me, ma'am.'

The smell on her was gin – Susannah was certain of that. 'Whatever's the matter with you, girl?'

Rosa stumbled on. 'You wouldn't care, ma'am.'

'A gentleman, then.'

'Oh, not for the likes of me. Never for the likes of me. You and your type get your gentlemen, but for me it's just...' Rosa stopped. 'I *did* have gentle – but... but I don't want gentle, ma'am. That's the problem. I want to live while I still can. And damn it, why shouldn't I? There's good and kind, and that's well and good, but then there's...'

'Has somebody done you a wrong turn, girl?'

'No, ma'am. It's me. I *am* the wrong turn – and I'm sorry for the hurt and I'm sorry for the pain... but, by God, I *enjoy* it!'

By the time Raymond burst into the reception hall, Marcus's petulant protest still echoing in his ears, Susannah Guthrie was nowhere to be seen. Nor was the golden cage of the guest elevator, for it was already soaring through the floors above. His eyes flashed around. He hurtled towards the guest stairs and started to run.

By brute force, legs pumping like pistons underneath him, he made it to the second floor. There was every chance he was already too late. Every chance Susannah Guthrie had slipped back into her suite to find it crawling with whatever security specialists Maynard Charles had dispatched. If it was so, he had failed in his mission. If that was happening, he had forfeited it all. What use was their man in the Buckingham if he let them down at the first opportunity?

With heart pounding, he reached the third floor.

Breathlessly, he hit the fourth.

He crashed through the doors onto the fifth-floor corridor without a breath left in his body.

And there, just beyond the closed elevator grille, stood Susannah Guthrie, her hand on the shoulder of some sobbing girl.

'Rosa?' Raymond whispered, as he approached.

Rosa wheeled round. The tears were real, but he realised now that her face was wide open in braying laughter as well. The two emotions made a horrible rictus of her face – but, upon seeing him, she drew away from Susannah, started staggering up the corridor, past Raymond. 'I'm sorry, Mr de Guise. Please don't tell Nancy. I know I oughtn't to be out here. It was an accident. I didn't mean it to happen this way. It was all an...'

Still blathering, she banked round the bend in the corridor, and then she was gone.

'What happened?' Raymond breathed.

'Some affair of the heart, as I understand. Do you know, Raymond, that girl's plight makes it all so clear, the bind we women still live in. My husband will have his frolics tonight and think nothing of it. It wouldn't occur to him to feel guilt, and it wouldn't occur to me to feel put out by it. It's just the way of things. And yet... were it to be *me*, having my frolics – perhaps beginning by dancing with a suitor, alone in the Grand – the stain it would leave on my life would be irreparable. Where men shrug their shoulders, women feel guilt. Is it just? Is it fair? Not in the slightest – but here we are.'

Raymond took a step towards her, 'Come and dance with me, Susannah.'

His eyes flashed over her shoulder.

The Continental Suite was just round the corner.

'Raymond, stop,' she declared. 'The ring on your finger, does it mean nothing to you?'

*It means everything.*

'The vows you made, did they not count?'

*I live my life by them.*

'Go home, Mr de Guise – go home, while you still can. I'm not sure why you knocked on my door tonight, what you had hoped for, what you were expecting – but the moment has passed. I'm retiring – and, with a little luck, I'll be gone from the Buckingham Hotel forever by the time you step out to dance for the King.'

Susannah turned and strode towards the Continental Suite.

'A drink,' Raymond cried out, chasing after her. As she rounded the corner, the Continental just ahead, he grappled for her hand. 'The Candlelight Club, a martini apiece. I owe you that much, at least.'

His eyes flashed to the door, his mind a tumult as he dared to imagine what was happening on the other side.

'You owe me nothing, Raymond.'

She took out her key.

She turned it in the lock.

Raymond's blood ran cold as the door opened.

But through the frame all he could see was the suite exactly as they'd left it, with no shadows lurking, no officers caught in the act, no dresser upturned or armoire torn apart.

'Goodbye, Raymond,' she said.

As she closed the door on his face, he finally took a breath.

Maynard Charles was already at the Deacon Club by the time his officers arrived. De Guise, it seemed, had done an estimable job in the end. That would go on his record. It hadn't been easy to bring the man back from Cairo, but at least it meant this Buckingham business had been worth something, in the end.

As soon as the brown paper envelope was in his hands, Maynard dismissed the officers, closed the door of the private chamber where he was seated, and slit it open.

Some time later, one of his subordinates found him still studying the pages from the package. The look of consternation that coloured his face had rarely been seen upon Maynard Charles. Maynard was known as an impassive officer, an old-fashioned stoic, a man who would no more betray an emotion than he would his King and Country – but tonight he looked alarmed.

'Sir?' said his subordinate.

Maynard shuffled the papers back into the envelope and rose to his feet.

'I'll not leave this one in play,' he said, coldly. 'Sometimes, in this game, you make a sacrifice. You let something slip past, simply to maintain your cover. You let a knight walk to its death, so that your pawn might reach the end of the board. But not tonight.'

He handed the envelope to his subordinate, whose eyes roamed each page in mounting unease.

'Sir?' he whispered.

'I know – and if his plan is to sell this through Kemp, what other secrets does he hold? What other access has he gained?' Maynard reached for his coat. 'We won't wait for a warrant. Let's take him the moment he leaves the restaurant tonight. Let Kemp go, but put watchers on him as well.' They walked out of the door, across the barren club floor, and out into the darkness of Piccadilly. 'You're to oversee this personally. Escort him directly to the office.' Maynard turned up his collar and started to march. 'I'll interrogate this one myself.'

# Chapter Twenty-Six

Bright, buttery sunshine spilled its glow over London on the morning of the Royal Dansant. And, in the hearts and minds of every musician and dancer taking part, true anticipation had begun.

Raymond had been awake since the smallest hours, pacing the halls, dancing with an imaginary partner in his arms. By the time Nancy stirred, he was already donning his charcoal slacks, sliding his belt through its loops, and fastening the cufflinks of his shirt.

'Already, Raymond?' Nancy purred, rolling over in the tangled sheets.

'Arthur's still sleeping,' he said, bowing down to kiss her on the brow. 'So should you.'

Rare were the mornings when Nancy wasn't leaving the house just after the sunrise, making her way to the Buckingham Hotel to rally her girls. Raymond was right. And yet, 'Where are you going?' she asked him.

'To shake out the cobwebs before the day truly begins,' he told her. 'But I'll be back before the Dansant.'

Now that Nancy was awake, she could hardly let herself drift back beneath the covers, no matter how inviting they seemed. She watched Raymond go from the window, then drew her robe around her and went to lift Arthur from his crib. Sleep was precious, but so were mornings like these, when she was free to just sit with her son in her arms.

When she carried him downstairs, it was to find that Vivienne and Stan were already slumped at the kitchen table. Vivienne had the old, exhausted look in her eyes; Stan didn't need the sirens to wake in the dead of night, for he himself was the siren, sounding every time Vivienne closed her eyes.

'Raymond's already gone?' Vivienne asked, curiously.

'He's like you. He couldn't sleep.'

Vivienne had set a teapot to brew. She poured dark tea for Nancy, then drizzled in what little milk they had. 'Do you think he's ... the *same*, Nancy? Since he came back?'

At first, Nancy didn't answer. Then, as she said, 'I don't think any of us are the same from one season to the next,' there were yet more footsteps behind them – and Frank emerged from the sitting room where he'd been sleeping. He too was already dressed, as if ready for the competition ahead. His hair was skewed, sleep still beaded in the corner of his eyes, but he'd donned his black brogues and held his evening jacket over his shoulder.

'Here, Frankie, let me,' said Nancy – and, having first settled Arthur in the highchair at the table, she rushed out into the hall to run a brush through his hair, to flatten down his creases, just as she'd once done every morning, after getting him up and ready for school. 'You're nervous, Frank. I can feel it. You're so ... tense!'

Frank shrugged. It was always a nice feeling, to be cosseted and clucked around by Nancy – but today it made him feel small, somehow, almost as if he didn't deserve it. Or as if he really ought to have outgrown it. He was a grown man, wasn't he? Did other grown men sleep on their sister's sofa? Did other grown men let their sisters straighten their collars as Nancy was doing now?

'Nance,' he ventured, 'do you think I'm a coward?'

Of all the things he might have said, this was the least expected. 'What's brought this on, Frankie?'

He looked at himself in the mirror that hung in the hall. He'd looked exhausted before, especially after those long nights on the watch-tower up on the hotel roof, but he'd never looked quite as inward and drawn as he did right now.

'It's just... well, I didn't get to join the war, did I? And I know it wasn't my fault. I did try. And I do my bit for London, and I went out to Dunkirk, and I ...'

'Frankie, what *happened?*'

He couldn't catch her eye, not even through the reflection in the mirror.

With a wan smile, he slipped away and sauntered down the hall. 'I suppose it's just these Americans, all over London. Sweeping in like heroes,' he said, 'catching the eye of everyone, catching the eye of...' But he stopped before he said what he was truly thinking. 'I'm dancing to celebrate them tonight. I suppose I just feel a bit of a fraud.'

'Frank Nettleton,' Nancy declared, 'you look at me now. You're dancing for your own future tonight. You aren't just dancing for the nation. You aren't just dancing for the King. You're dancing so you can say that you, Frank Nettleton, were garlanded by King George at the Royal Dansant. So you can rise above your station after the war. And if that isn't enough – well, Frankie, you're doing it for me, and you're doing it for Dad, and you're doing it for the mother you didn't know, so they can all look down on you and smile and say: Frank Nettleton, he kept his heart, even when the world was turning to ruin around him.'

She meant the war – of course she meant the war – but in that moment Frank couldn't help discerning some different meaning in Nancy's words.

'Thank you, big sister,' he said.

Then he followed where Raymond had gone, out into the day of the Dansant.

And left behind, in the hall, Nancy couldn't resist the one thought that had started rising up in her mind:

She hadn't seen Frankie and Rosa together in *weeks*.

London was just stirring when Raymond arrived at the Deacon Club to be admitted within by a taciturn fellow with the hangdog expression of a permanent night manager. Sullenly, he took Raymond upstairs, depositing him in the smoke-filled room where Maynard Charles had evidently spent his night.

'Sir,' Raymond began.

'Sit down, de Guise. I hardly know where to begin.'

The truth was, Raymond wasn't yet sure whether he was here to receive a dismissal or a commendation. The last he'd heard of the whole sorry affair was when Susannah Guthrie slammed the door in his face, seeming – in her own haughtily bitter way – to be closing the door on their fledgling relationship as well. It would be wrong to say he was not grateful, for he'd skirted as close to betraying Nancy as his body and mind would permit – and, if Maynard had pressed him yet further, he wasn't sure what he would do. Yet a part of him had felt a failure as well, as if he'd left the job half done, as if he'd abandoned ship in the middle of some fateful endeavour.

'The Guthries are gone, sir. Their residency at the Buckingham Hotel comes to its end this morning.'

Maynard Charles nodded. 'Douglas Guthrie is in our custody, de Guise, and has been since the night of our endeavour.'

Raymond took a breath. 'I didn't realise, sir. When I didn't hear from you, I feared I had let you down.'

'On the contrary, de Guise. Our officers were able to access the Continental Suite while you led Susannah Guthrie on a merry dance. The information we uncovered there could only be countered by the laird's immediate incarceration. Of course, he rejects our accusations – but the evidence speaks for itself.'

'What did you uncover, sir?'

Maynard Charles appraised him closely. 'I didn't bring you here to debrief you, de Guise. Your position does not necessitate you seeing more of the picture than the little piece in front of you. I brought you here because there is no rest for the wicked. By the week's end, a detachment of American financiers will be taking up a three-week residency at the Buckingham Hotel. Our information points to them seeking to speculate on the war – though not, perhaps, in the way the good laird Guthrie did. They seek to build connections with the exiled French and Dutch governments, in the hope of opening up opportunities for themselves once the war is won. Now, we at the office admire this confidence – but, of course, they would not be competent businessmen if they were not, in some way, hedging their bets against the Continent's permanent fall. And the profile we built of one among them, a man of certain Confederate tendencies, suggests he would happily build bridges with the enemy, if it secured him contracts at some future date. His name is MacLean. I'm asking you to …'

Raymond threw up his hand in salute. 'I understand, sir.'

Then he turned to leave.

It was only at the threshold that he stopped and said, 'Sir, Susannah Guthrie … is she aware of what's become of her husband?'

Maynard said, 'It is not our policy to debrief loved ones, Raymond.'

'And her husband, he'll be held for some time?'

'You sound like you really did develop a soft spot for this woman.'

Raymond shook his head. 'It doesn't feel right, to use people like I used her. It leaves a stain on a man's soul.'

Maynard shook his head. 'That stain would be more easily wiped clean if you knew what your actions have prevented, de Guise.' At once, he put down his cigar, marched to the door – and then, having first opened it to make sure no eavesdroppers lurked outside, whispered, 'You should understand that, if you were to divulge any of this, there would be a strong case of treason laid against you, de Guise. I'm not permitted to tell you everything, but what you are doing for us *matters* – and you need to know it, before you let that foolish, moralistic head of yours start to dictate.'

Now he paced the room, cigar between his lips. 'We had been working under the assumption that the good laird Guthrie was seeking an investment opportunity – that the wealth he'd garnered from the forced acquisitions of those estates, up in Scotland, was going to be put to some nefarious use. Kemp's the man to speak to about it. Many men know how to get rich out of suffering, but Kemp's a prince among them. He's biding his time, cultivating his connections, waiting for his associates across the water to succeed. Once Britain is a protectorate of the Reich, or so the theory goes, they'll need homegrown munitions factories and military outfitters to keep the British SS in power. Well, Guthrie, we thought, wanted a piece of the action.'

'Were you wrong, sir?'

'De Guise, it is worse than we had ever imagined.'

The silence was thick and heavy in the smoke-filled room.

'We have spoken, already, about the many reasons the Department might requisition land.'

'For military purposes, sir. For training ranges and barracks. For—'

'Research facilities. Oh, the Department doesn't advertise it – but war is built upon research. Mark my words – this war won't be won in the shadows; it will be won by the scientists. Our job is to buy them a little time. And it just so happens that, at the start of this year, the Department decreed that the island of Gruinard, off the far north of Scotland, was the perfect site for a scheme they had in mind.'

'Let me guess – this island, was it owned by Guthrie?'

'Alas, it was not. We are yet to establish how and who else was involved, but Douglas Guthrie came into possession of certain information pertaining to the experiments being carried out on Gruinard Island.'

'He hosted a supper, sir – he drew together others whose lands had been taken. Susannah let it slip. Perhaps he made some contact?'

'We'll push him on that. Until we know who colluded with him, this case is not complete. What we do know, however, is enough to run a conviction. The simple fact that that file was waiting in the safe in the Buckingham Hotel is evidence enough. OPERATION VEGETARIAN, they called it. Well, the Department has never liked an histrionic name. When I tell you, Raymond, that certain scientists working for His Majesty's government have bent all their energies on devising weapons that might end this war without a single bomb being dropped, you will think me a fantasist. Except that is exactly what was being planned up on Gruinard Island.'

'But *how*, sir?'

Maynard shook his head. 'Loose lips sink ships, Mr de Guise – and this ship is already taking on far too much water.'

'Have we bailed quickly enough, sir?'

'I believe so. Guthrie was in possession of research papers dated June – that they were stolen as recently as this gives us all a little hope. Guthrie learned, via Bancroft we can only assume, that Kemp was the sort of man who could introduce him to those who would spirit his information over the sea. After Bancroft made the introductions at the card game you attended, Guthrie set about his romance. Tonight, he meant to broker the deal.' He stopped. 'Guthrie denies it, of course. He insists he was simply looking to invest wealth. But the presence of those documents is proof enough of his treachery. Raymond de Guise, a man who would sell out his own King and Country has been removed from the war this week – and it's in large part down to the cunning and guile you provide in the Buckingham Hotel.'

By now, Maynard Charles's cigar had burned down to its stub.

'I need you back in play by tomorrow evening, de Guise. This war is not yet won.' He paused. 'But for now, you may go and dance for the King.'

Raymond lifted his hand in salute.

'Sir,' he said as he retreated, back across the room, 'what will become of Guthrie's wife?'

'You may keep your marriage vows for now, Raymond, if that is what you mean.'

'Sir, I rather meant ... what becomes of those who get left behind, in moments like these?'

'Raymond, it may end up being an estimable outcome for the poor woman. Freedom from a faithless marriage, Guthrie's legal assets left to her control ... I'm quite certain she'll find her way. As you proved this summer, Raymond, she is not without guile of her own.'

By the time Raymond emerged onto Piccadilly, the city was awake. London buses coasted past. A dark green Rolls Royce drew into the bays at the front of the Ritz to disgorge its elegant passengers. City clerks rose up from the Underground at Green Park; the Lyon's teashop filled up for its first service of the morning; all of London, ignorant to the treasons, big and small, being committed on its streets. Raymond felt the weight of them as he marched into Mayfair, but he felt the lightness of being released as well.

For one day, at least, there would be no lies to tell.

Tonight, he was free to dance.

Hélène was waiting at the Buckingham Hotel. When Raymond entered via Michaelmas Mews, she had already been shepherded to the Grand by one of the concierges – and there she stood, in the heart of the dance floor that was once her own.

'It suits you, Miss Marchmont,' Raymond said as he glided through. 'Shall we dance?'

Five hours until the Albert Hall welcomed its competitors. Six hours until the band struck up. Perhaps there was no use in rehearsing again – except that it wasn't really *for* the footwork. It wasn't for the balance, the poise, the pivots and turns. It was just for the simple feeling of it. What better way to prepare for the dance of a lifetime, than to spend those hours rehearsing with the partner with whom you'd shared your dancing life?

The doors to the Grand opened.

Footsteps tolled.

And Marcus Arbuthnot's voice rang out, 'Perhaps I could be of some assistance?'

Raymond's body tensed at his voice – but the russet-haired titan of the Grand was sweeping towards them, not with fire in his eyes, but a muted sense of welcome. When he reached the balustrade and crossed the dance floor, he took Hélène's hand

and half bowed. 'Miss Marchmont, it must be fifteen years since our paths last crossed.'

Marcus released his hold of her hand and turned to Raymond. 'The last time we stood here, I was too free with my emotions. Mr de Guise, believe it or not, I am grateful for what you said. This year has been a tempest for us all – but for you more than I, and in my desperation to succeed in this ballroom, I lost sight of that.'

Raymond looked at him with furrowed, suspicious eyes. 'Why the change of heart?'

Marcus simply replied, 'Because a heart can change.'

Perhaps it was because this seemed wise and true, or perhaps it was because Raymond was weary of living his life with such suspicion, but in that moment he wanted so eagerly to believe their enmity was gone that he took Marcus by the hand.

'I thought, perhaps, that I might offer some observations as you dance. My gesture, to the two of you, before you rise to this evening's challenge.' He paused. 'Well, it's been a long time since either of you took tuition – and my sources tell me you lent your old mentor to young Nettleton. What do you think?'

Raymond looked at Hélène. The Ice Queen of the Grand was hardly smiling, but her eyes seemed to suggest she was game.

'You've been on the longest of journeys, Mr de Guise,' Marcus announced. 'But a tale that began with you coming to shore in the ruins of Liverpool will come to its climax tonight, as you waltz to victory at the Albert Hall. And for you, Hélène,' he went on, turning, 'another story unfolds. Summoned back to the dance, a starlet who feared her days on the dance floor were gone must step out onto the grandest stage of them all, and dance for an audience like no other. Raymond, Hélène, show me what you have…'

A smile graced Hélène's lips – that rarest of things – only because, in all her dancing days, she had never met anyone with the theatrical pomp of Marcus Arbuthnot. She winked at Raymond. 'Shall we?' she whispered – but, for some reason she could not decipher, Raymond seemed suddenly a hundred miles away.

*Liverpool...*

The moment Marcus had mentioned the city, Raymond could see it: the tumbledown terraces framed in black, reefs of orange and red lighting up the cityscape in fiery array as conical searchlights lit up the heavens above.

*Liverpool...*

That mad, urgent flight from the city, Raymond bustled into the back of the Ministry's car, hurtling through the blackout as the bombs rained down.

*Liverpool...*

That ticket he'd seen, on the dresser in the Continental Suite.

He hadn't thought of it until this very moment, but it had only been for one.

He'd thought it was Douglas, scouting out some other investment opportunity – or else travelling to see some mistress he kept on the dockside out there.

*But what if...*

He turned on the spot, but he wasn't really in the ballroom at all. Hélène and Marcus were staring at him with mounting incredulity, but right now they were just like ghosts, phantoms he was staring straight through to the truth on the other side. What was it Maynard Charles had said? 'Guthrie was in possession of research papers dated as recently as this June.' But, by then, hadn't he already made his overtures to meet Kemp? By then, hadn't he already enlisted Bancroft to make an introduction?

Or might Maynard Charles and his officers have missed the truth that was staring them in the face?

Because only one Guthrie had been in Scotland at the time those research papers were stolen.

One Guthrie had been in London, playing at cards, visiting his mistress, speaking of investment opportunities and romancing Angus Kemp.

While the other had been in Scotland – banished, she said, to the family estate.

But what if...

*Could it be?*

Raymond closed his eyes and summoned that envelope on the dresser to his mind. He saw the Buckingham insignia, like a medieval seal. He reached inside, drawing out the compliment slip and the message neatly printed upon it:

AS REQUESTED. BILLY.

'Hélène,' he said. Then, 'Marcus,' he added, with a bow. 'Perhaps you could work together, for just a few short moments? I'll be back before you know it. And then – Hélène, we'll soar.'

Their incredulity reached a new zenith as Raymond started running. Through the dressing rooms he charged, out and along the Housekeeping hall. By the time he reached the hotel post room, buried at the back of Housekeeping, his mind was a tumult. All thoughts of the Royal Dansant had vanished.

He careened through the post-room door without pausing to knock.

Billy Brogan almost jumped out of his skin at Raymond's approach. The younger man might have been a veteran of France, but he had the look of a guilty schoolboy as he flurried up from the seat at his desk, burying whatever ledger book he'd been writing in.

'Mr de Guise!' he declared. 'What's happened, sir? You look like you've seen a ghost.'

Raymond staggered to the desk where Billy was desperately organising his papers – another man might have thought the boy looked *shifty*, but Billy had always had that tendency, ever since his days running unsavoury errands as a hotel page – and braced him by the shoulders.

'You're still doing odd jobs, aren't you? For the guests?'

'Whenever I'm asked, Mr de Guise. I'm a man of many faces, as you know.'

'And you organised a train ticket, to be sent to the Continental Suite.'

Billy shook away Raymond's hands. 'Of course I did. It's all part of the job. At your service, m'lord! At your service, ma'am! They like to think they keep servants, Mr de Guise. Doff your cap, call them "sire", anything they want.'

'Billy, it's very important you remember this right. It's very important you're focused and clear. Was it the laird who asked for that ticket, Billy, or was it his—'

'Oh, it was his wife, sir.' Billy said it so nonchalantly, oblivious to the fact that, with those few words, everything changed. 'She came to me herself. It was straight after she sent the telegram to the Adelphi.'

'The Adelphi Hotel – that's in Liverpool too?'

'I daresay they didn't barrack you *there*, sir, when they brought you home. Far too fancy for a poor infantryman, I'm sure! It would be like sending some navvy lads to sleep right here at the Buckingham. Well, I sent the telegram and, while she was here, she asked if I'd do her a service and organise a ticket.' Billy paused. 'Have I done something wrong, Mr de Guise?'

'No, Billy – no, not you...'

Raymond had that strange, faraway look in his eyes again. As for Billy, he had no idea why the older man was suddenly so silent. He just kept staring, until at last Raymond himself broke the spell.

'Billy, can you recall what that telegram said?'

'It was just a confirmation, sir. Just to say she'd meet him there.'

'Who, Billy? Meet *who*?'

Billy opened his palms. 'You know we don't keep tabs on our guests, sir. What they get up to behind closed doors, well—'

'Billy Brogan, don't tell me you've never eavesdropped in this hotel.'

Billy sighed. 'I think his name was Wright, sir – but... why is it so important?'

Without reply, Raymond reached for the telephone receiver sitting on Billy's desk. Billy himself started sweeping papers away, burying them in his drawers, as if there were things he couldn't bear Raymond to see – but he needn't have bothered; Raymond's eyes were fixed on the telephone alone. 'Billy, I'm going to need you to leave the room.'

'Mr de Guise, this is the hotel post room! This is my—'

'Out, Billy!' Raymond snarled.

Billy had rarely seen Raymond as defiant, not even on the beaches at Dunkirk where the boys from the Buckingham had found themselves stranded together. With a grunt, he lifted himself and limped to the post-room door.

As soon as he was alone, Raymond dialled the number. The man on the other end of the line announced himself as the concierge of the Deacon Club.

'I need Maynard Charles, and I need him now.'

'Sir?'

'Maynard Charles. He was with you but an hour ago.'

'One moment sir.'

Raymond waited impatiently, beating his palm upon Billy's table. Some moments later, just as his impatience was beginning to boil, the voice returned.

'Mr Charles vacated the Club twenty minutes ago, sir.'

'Then I need you to get him a message.'

'Sir?'

Raymond was tired of these parlour games. 'Do you know how to send a message to Mr Charles or not? It pertains to national security!'

At once, the voice changed. The plummy baritone vanished; in its place, a nasal voice seethed, 'Those matters, sir, are not to be conducted across telephone lines.'

Raymond felt so furious he might rip the telephone from the wall.

'If he truly isn't there, then I'm laying it on you. Tell him...' Raymond took a breath. 'Tell him it wasn't the laird. Tell him it was his wife. Tell him it was Susannah Guthrie – and tell him she's getting away with it right now!'

## Chapter Twenty-Seven

So there it stood: the Royal Albert Hall.

The crowd was already gathering at the cordons the security officers had put in place, so the London bus which brought Frank from the corner of Oxford Circus, through the Marble Arch and around the fortifications of Hyde Park, slowed to a crawl almost as soon as it reached the wider boulevard of Kensington Gore. From the window, Frank watched the crowds deepening. It had been a long time since he'd seen so many people in one place, and longer still since he'd seen them gather in such joy. Union Jacks rippled from every flagpole. Bunting in red, blue and white garlanded every lamp post and telegraph pole along the edge of the park. Not even the shadows of the barrage balloons could blot out the magnificence of the morning.

Nancy was right.

Today mattered.

And that thing she'd said, about rising above his station after the war? Well, Frank liked the sound of it. After the war, there'd be chances for a young dancer to climb, to compete, to grow into his talent. All those stories Raymond told of his grand tours of Europe – well, that could be Frank as well.

Lives went in different directions, didn't they?

Had Rosa *really* been going to follow him into that world?

Wasn't it just the hand of fate?

But the moment the bus came to its stop and he forced his way out into the crowds, he caught sight of the Housekeeping girls from the Buckingham Hotel – and all the ways he'd been trying to buoy himself just withered. There was no reasoning with matters of the heart. He wanted Rosa. It was as simple as that. She was as much a part of him as the ballroom. And there she was, laughing among the other Housekeeping girls, Annie Brogan up on her shoulders keeping lookout for the golden carriage that would deliver the King.

It wasn't easy to reach the cordon. It was harder still to do it without looking back and trying to catch a glimpse of Rosa one more time. But Frank fixed his gaze on the imposing dome of the Albert Hall and picked his way through the onlookers, until at last he was giving his name to a towering security officer, appraised from head to toe, then admitted over the line.

It was open ground between here and the Albert Hall. The spectacle of the building was awe-inspiring, even to a boy inured to the delights of the Buckingham Hotel. King's guardsmen stood at the entrance to the auditorium. Union Jacks rippled from poles outside the many windows and galleries. He stopped momentarily on the verdant green lawns that surrounded the amphitheatre and just stared. His first competition, not in some provincial church hall – but here, in front of the entire nation? It hadn't seemed overwhelming until this very moment.

He wanted to look back. Perhaps Rosa had spotted him from the crowds on Kensington Gore. Perhaps she'd wave to him, wish him good luck, mouth out the words 'I'll see you after the show'. But something inside made him resist the temptation. You didn't look backwards, not in dance. If you made a misstep, if you found yourself on the wrong foot, you couldn't spool backwards in time and undo it. You simply had to sail forward, letting the music take you, and make sure you didn't stumble again. It would have to be the same today.

'I'm F-Frank N-Nettleton,' he stammered to the doorman. 'I'm here to d-dance.'

The doorman consulted his notes, found Frank's name among all the other competitors, and said in his silky baritone, 'Follow me please, sir. Your partner is awaiting you.'

The outer ring of the Albert Hall, into which he'd stepped, was as busy as the Buckingham reception, with men in black bustling backwards and forwards, velveteen ropes cordoning off doors, ushers and security guards assembling – and a good number of guardsmen, dressed in scarlet red just as if they were marching up and down Horse Guards Parade, standing sentry.

'Competitors are being held backstage until they're ready for you in the auditorium,' the gentleman escorting Frank explained. 'I'm afraid there's plenty of you, so you'll find the holding area a little cramped. I'm sure the magnificence of the show will more than make up for some momentary discomfort.'

Frank hardly cared. He just longed to catch a glimpse of the main auditorium, the dance floor, the stage. They seemed to be circumnavigating it now, following a long circular corridor, then slipping through a side door and down narrow stairs.

'You're seeing a part of the hall few guests ever get to see, sir.' Frank's escort led him on, into a subterranean darkness lit by a multitude of electric lights. 'We're passing under the stage right now. You'll have to forgive the bustle – as you can imagine, we have a veritable legion of hospitality staff this evening.'

This was no exaggeration: every hallway down here bustled with kitchen staff, silver service staff, lighting crew and technicians. The dancers and musicians, it seemed, were only the smallest part of this endeavour. There seemed as many staff working tonight as there were guests at the Buckingham Hotel: the Albert Hall was an entire town's-worth of industry, all working towards the same magnificent goal.

'Through here's the holding bay where you'll gather before the band strikes up – but don't worry about timings; our stage managers will be shepherding you. All you need to do is dance.' They banked round a corner, through a clot of yet more stage technicians, and came along a hall flanked with dozens of dressing-room doors. 'Men are through here. I'm afraid it's six to a dresser, but you'll make it work. The ladies are on the other side, but...' The gentleman stalled. '...it appears one is waiting for you now. Your partner, sir?'

The bustling staff came apart – and there, standing at the third door along the row, was Mathilde.

'Thank you, sir,' Frank said to the gentleman who was drawing away.

'You have one hour until the first call. That's the tour to familiarise yourselves with the layout. It will be your only chance. Doors open half an hour after that. Show time is in two and a half.' The gentleman slipped back his black calfskin gloves and checked the golden watch at his wrist. 'We're running a tight schedule to sew up proceedings before the blackout takes effect, so be prepared. Good luck, sir.' He inclined his head at Mathilde. 'Good luck, ma'am.'

Frank joined Mathilde outside the dressing-room doors. 'I'm sorry,' he stuttered, 'I meant to be here sooner. I was going to find you at the doors. But... the bus.' He shrugged, sheepishly.

'Frank Nettleton, you must be the only man who caught a bus to dance before the King.'

At least Mathilde was smiling. Frank took some cheer from that.

'I'm nervous, Frank,' she admitted. 'It's been two years since I competed. Everyone in my dresser – well, they're as elegant as Hélène Marchmont.'

Frank squeezed her hand for good luck. 'I know I'm not the most glamorous here. I know I dress up like a gentleman but end up looking like a Lancashire pit boy in some landowner's stolen clothes. And I...' Frank took a breath. 'I know I'm not as flash and exciting as all those Americans out there, the ones we're meant to be dancing for. But I – I want to be myself. I do want to win, but I want to do it my way. *Our* way, Mathilde.'

Mathilde grinned, 'I'm not so sure Georges de la Motte would quite approve.'

'Back straight, shoulders square,' Frank replied. 'I won't look you in the eyes at all, Mathilde. We'll do everything he said – but let's just... let's just dance, and see where it takes us.'

Mathilde lifted herself to kiss him on the cheek. 'I'm glad you made it, Frank,' she whispered. Then, with a last squeeze of his hand, she brushed past, meaning to return to her own dressing room.

'I told her,' Frank blurted out, once Mathilde was almost swallowed up by the bustling staff. 'I saw Rosa, on the night of the ball. I told her what I knew, and she...' Words failed him at that point. Some other staff member crossed his path, blotting out his view of Mathilde for only a moment. When she reappeared, her eyes were shining wet for him. 'But like I say, let's just dance.'

'Those Americans have got nothing on you, Frank,' said Mathilde – and then she was gone.

Frank stood alone, steadying his breaths.

Two hours until the lights went up.

Two hours until the evening's first dance.

The clock was already counting down.

*

Raymond flew through the tradesman's entrance, reached the top of Michaelmas Mews and erupted out onto Berkeley Square.

The sun was already directly overhead.

A hot July morning had turned towards midday.

That left him one hour until Susannah Guthrie's train departed the station.

Two hours until the musicians and competitors were due to be registered at the Albert Hall.

It hadn't been easy to tell Hélène. It hadn't been easy to look her in the face, tell her, 'Rehearsal's over – I'll have to meet you at the Albert Hall,' and then take flight. The withering look on Marcus's face suggested he took it as a personal affront, but Raymond had no time to mollify him now. That could come later. Right now, the clock was ticking. Right now, he needed to fly. He hailed the first cab he saw, threw himself into the back seat and urged the driver on. 'King's Cross station,' he cried, 'and make it quick. I'll pay you double. I'll pay you whatever it takes.'

By the time he burst out of the taxicab into the frozen traffic on Euston Road, half an hour had passed him by. Calling back, 'Charge it to the Buckingham Hotel!', he thundered through the clerks and shoppers, the flood of day-trippers pouring out of King's Cross station to take in the day's spectacle. More than one cried out in alarm – somebody muttered a vicious oath as Raymond flew by – but the debonair dancer did not stop. It wasn't music that carried him forward today – not yet. No, it was pure and utter desperation that drove him through the station arches, under the flickering departure boards, past the piles of luggage, the exasperated attendants, the platform sweepers and ticket vendors, until he reached an information desk.

A gaggle of day-trippers, talking animatedly about the procession into Kensington, were already making enquiries. Raymond scoured the departure boards above – but, seeing no sign of the

Liverpool train, bustled to the front of the queue. An Englishman hates a queue jumper almost as much as he hates a Nazi – but Raymond weathered the storm of insults ('For shame, sir!') flurrying around him, and reached the counter. 'There's a train heading to Liverpool,' he declared. 'Please – which platform?'

'That's on Two, sir – but the gates have already closed. She's due to leave any minute.'

Raymond turned and ran.

There were conductors waiting on the platform's edge. Some of them were hurrying up and down the carriages, securing windows and doors, but as soon as Raymond reached the platform one hailed him, asking for a ticket. Raymond was as fleet of mind as he was of foot. Without breaking his stride, he cried out, 'My wife waits on board, sir!' and clawed his way in through the first open door he could find. The conductor who had just been wrestling it shut asked again for a ticket, but Raymond simply bowed in response, then turned and burst into the first carriage.

The cheap seats were jam-packed. Not everyone, it seemed, was so enamoured of the Royal Dansant that they had chosen to flood the streets of London; here, it seemed, there were many hundreds eager to get away. By the looks of them, most were office workers, clerks and underlings from the City of London. Raymond cut a swathe up the train, unlocking outer doors, sliding through over the clasps between carriages, scouring each seat as he went.

Outside, on the platform, a shrill whistle screamed.

Raymond burst into the dining carriage. Some more refined passengers were already taking tea at the tables – but no Susannah Guthrie.

A carriage further along, the cheap seats gave way to carriages filled with private rooms. Raymond forced his way up the narrow aisle, spreading himself against the wall to let a middle-aged conductor squeeze past, then dared to push open the first door along. Inside, a pair of dejected-looking clerks in dowdy suits and bowler hats shuffled up, as if to make room – but Raymond quickly made his apologies and marched on. In the second room he dared open, a pair of grandparents with three children immediately began to protest that they had reserved every seat; in the next, a rather hopeful young lady appraised him with doe-like eyes and seemed to suggest he sit down. Nevertheless, Raymond marched on.

He was just opening the door to the fourth compartment when another whistle sounded and, with a terrible grating sound, the carriages shifted underneath him. Very slowly, the platform at King's Cross station started to glide by outside the window.

Raymond froze, his hand hovering over the door handle.

'Tickets please,' halloed a voice from somewhere deeper in the train.

Even now, the dancers would be gathering backstage at the Royal Albert Hall.

Hélène herself would be anxiously awaiting him.

Perhaps she was being shown around; perhaps she, Frank and Mathilde were among all the other competitors, getting the feeling of the especially laid dance floor before the first guests arrived.

Raymond supposed there'd be no dancing now.

There'd be more lies to tell.

But this, Maynard Charles would have told him, was what he was paid for.

He opened the door.

And there was Susannah Guthrie.

She looked at him with the most incredulous eyes.

*

Nelson Allgood was sick of pacing. Pacing and prowling – that was all he seemed to have done for two solid weeks.

Well, now it was coming to an end.

With one last look in the mirror – the eye hadn't quite healed, but to any onlooker he just looked ugly, not beaten up – he tightened the blood-red bow tie at his collar, brushed down his pinstriped jacket, and bolted out of the door.

The touch of the sun – now, that was what he needed. It lit him up as he cantered down the steps at Albert Yard, through the iron gate and out into the obliterated street. The Brogans' house still seemed the only one that had been fully reconstructed. All the others stood behind scaffolds and hoardings, families camping in them like modern-day cavemen.

'Just wait for the taxicab,' his mother called after him.

Nelson looked back. Poor Ava had been standing sentry all day. Why that woman had suddenly decided to come over meek and obey Uncle Max's every command, Nelson would never know. There'd been a time, not so long ago, when it was Max in hock to her, not the other way round. Perhaps something had changed since Max took up at the Buckingham Hotel, but Nelson wanted *that* woman back. *That* woman wouldn't have taken part in locking him up these past weeks, not when there were shows to play – not when there was a debt that needed paying to these American blowhards.

'I'm gonna walk, Ma,' he called back. 'I gotta get rid of *this*.' And he shook his arms at her viciously, as if to show just how much energy was pent up within him. 'I'll make a mess of my playing, if I can't get on top of it. A caged dog wants to run, Ma.'

Ava rushed down the stairs and grabbed her son by the shoulders. 'You go out there and you play like your life depends on it, Nelson – because it does.'

'I'm aware of it, Ma. I've been doing it ever since I came to town.'

Ava softened. She stroked the side of his face, moving her fingertip around the faded abrasions where those infantrymen had left their impressions. 'This one wasn't on you, Nelson – but Max is right. You're a magnet to trouble. You're like gravity, drawing it in. But listen to me: after tonight, maybe you don't need Uncle Max. Maybe you don't need the Buckingham Hotel. One night for King and Country, one night only, and…' She let him go. 'You'll be a magnet for a different kind of attention.'

Nelson liked that. His ma was backing away from him, but he followed her and wrapped her in arms. 'I'm gonna give 'em hell, Ma. They're gonna remember who I am.'

'I never doubted it.'

While they had been talking, the taxicab had appeared. Moments later, Max Allgood himself emerged from the house – and crab-walked his way to the roadside to clamber in.

'You ready for this, boy?'

Nelson declared, 'I've been sitting there ready for weeks, Uncle Max. I've done nothing but be ready. I've been playing my set over and over in my head, every hour of every stinkin' day.'

The taxi rolled forward.

'Nelson, boy, you never did jail time – but trust me, you've got *nothing* to carp about. A couple of weeks out of trouble never did anybody any harm.' Max stopped. 'Tonight's your night. Make a good show of it, stay on point, and there's a good chance you won't have to run with the ruffians ever again. There's a good chance you can *stay* out of trouble. Make a meal of it, though, and…' Max shrugged. 'If you ain't gonna do it for yourself, do it for your mother.'

Nelson threw himself back in his seat like a tantrumming toddler. 'I'm gonna do it for the world, Uncle Max. I'm gonna do it for the King of England and all his glory.'

In the seat in front of them, the taximan grinned. 'Big day, is it?' he asked.

'My friend,' Max drawled, 'it's gonna be the *biggest*.'

'But Mr de Guise,' said Susannah, her intonation high with surprise, 'I don't understand. Please don't tell me they send ballroom dancers after a guest who's forgotten something at the Buckingham Hotel, do they? I know your Hotel Director prides himself on service, but it seems rather...'

Raymond closed the door behind him.

Susannah Guthrie was alone.

He ran his hands through his hair, threw himself into the seat opposite, then dazzled her with a smile.

'I'm afraid I've committed a mortal sin, Mrs Guthrie.' He pitched forward. 'I didn't buy a ticket. You'll simply have to shelter me here.'

'But sir, *what* for?' Susannah paused. 'Am I to understand that you are speculating further upon romance, Mr de Guise? And that you... followed me here?'

Yes, thought Raymond, the woman certainly had guile. Her face seemed impassive; she betrayed no whisper of suspicion, though her heart must have been full of it.

'I couldn't let you go, Susannah, not with the rumours abounding.' Deceit was Raymond's profession now, but the best deceits relied on truths at their core. What value was there in hiding this now? Susannah Guthrie knew what had become of her husband; she knew because she had willed it to happen. What better disguise for a treachery than lining up some useful fool to take the blame? 'There's talk all over the Buckingham Hotel that your husband was arrested under a defence regulation. That they took him, and Angus Kemp as well.'

Susannah was silent.

She stared.

And in that stare, thought Raymond, was some realisation of a sort; as if, at last, she knew what Raymond really was and why he was really here.

'My husband has always made poor choices in his life. That he made one more came as no surprise to me. But you mistake me, Raymond, if you think I am bemoaning his fate. You know what my husband was to me. My keeper. Nothing else. It is not a life I chose, to be some old fool's trophy – to hang on his arm in the Grand Ballroom, while he indulges his private interests, be they business or carnal.' She paused. 'You needn't have come, Raymond. I'm not sure why you did. I need no knight in shining armour – or have I not been clear about that?'

Raymond met her steely gaze with one of his own. 'You were very clear, Susannah.'

'Then why behave as if I am some poor damsel in need of your rescue?' She laughed, darkly. 'You men do indulge your fantasies of heroism. I rather hoped you were different – that you had exorcised that need to be a hero on the battlefield, and come back a different man. Do you know, we *might* have some fun, you and I – but, in the end, Raymond, if I am to indulge that side of life again, it will not be because I have fallen into some hero's arms. It will be because *he* has fallen into mine.' She sat back. 'I suggest you just get off this train before you are missed.' Then she paused. 'As a matter of fact, isn't there somewhere you're meant to be, right now?'

Raymond had no answer.

On the other side of London, the royal procession had already left Buckingham Palace to make its way, through streets filled with well-wishers, to the Albert Hall.

'Raymond,' Susannah ventured, with fresh fire in her voice, 'what has *really* made you come here? You're due to dance for the King.'

It was a hot July day, the sun at its zenith above London, but in the carriage, all felt deathly cold.

'No more lies, Mrs Guthrie,' Raymond said, at last. Then he was on his feet, looming above Susannah. Moments later, having first tried to seem insouciant, she rose too. Raymond was aware of how much bigger he was – but, somehow, she was the one who seemed to fill up the carriage. Was it just the knowledge of who she was, and what she was doing? Or was it the fact that, for the first time, each one knew what the other had known all along? There was a release that came with the death of a lie. At least Raymond had to pretend no longer. 'I doubt your husband is an innocent man. I'll shed no tears for a man of his sympathies, a man who helped fund the Link. Hitler's Man in the Highlands – did you know that's how he's known?'

'A lot of baseless accusations have been levelled at my husband, Raymond, but I am not him.'

'No, Susannah – you're worse.' Raymond paused. Outside the window, the blur of greys and browns of outer London gathered pace. 'The laird's an opportunist. He's like those sitting pretty in Paris, safe from the Nazis only because they work with them. Marshall Pétain and the rest at Vichy. Or the Quislings in Norway. Your husband's a sympathiser, yes, but he's been arrested for so much more. He's been arrested, Susannah, for selling government secrets. He's been arrested for trying to fence research and plans to the enemy. But he's innocent of that, isn't he? He really did go to Angus Kemp just looking to invest his windfall from the forced purchase. It's *you*, Susannah, who's doing more.'

'Raymond, let's sit down and speak about this—'

'How did you do it, Susannah? I know it happened when you were in Scotland. Did Douglas really send you there, or had you engineered it all along? I know your husband had already gathered together all the landowners who lost their estates. I know that, among them, was the family who owned Gruinard Island. How did you get access? Did you romance someone? Make some contact, after that gathering, and then sweep in when you went back north? It can't have been easy, Susannah – but I already know what you're capable of. And I know what they were doing out there, on Gruinard. I know it was meant to change the course of the war—'

'You've no idea what they were doing, you fool,' Susannah spat, her voice laced with venom.

'Operation Vegetarian,' Raymond whispered.

'And have you any idea what it is? Have you?'

Raymond's silence betrayed him. Inwardly, he cursed – for the smile in the corner of Susannah's lips betrayed the fact that he had let his ignorance slip.

'A weapon to win the war,' Raymond began. 'A weapon to bring it to its end, without bombs, without—'

'It's called anthrax, Raymond – and whoever you're working for evidently didn't think to apprise you of that fact, which suggests to me you're on the lowest rung of some ladder, just cannon fodder for men who couldn't care less if you lived or died.' Susannah shook her head. 'Anthrax, Raymond, do you even know what it is?'

'It's a government secret, and you're trying to sell it.'

'It's a deadly infection. It's a painful, horrific way to die – and your countrymen plot to use it to end this war. What did you think this war was? Just soldiers lining up, Queensbury rules, and may the best man win? No, Raymond – it's a dirty, nasty business, where life is cheap and the cheaper the better. Your countrymen plot to lace linseed cakes with anthrax spores. They plot to drop them all across the Fatherland, to infect millions of grazing cattle. How many people do you think might die from eating that meat, Raymond? How much death might be caused in whatever famine ensues?'

'You say they're *my* countrymen, Susannah – but they're *yours* as well. How many thousands have already died in this war? How many more have to, before it comes to an end?'

'This country is mine in name only.'

'Why?' Raymond demanded. 'Why, Susannah?'

'Because Great Britain is going to fall, and I intend to be on the right side when history is done with it.' She stopped. 'And there you were, crawling around me, seeking to entrap my husband, when all along—'

'What does it matter now, Susannah? The documents are gone.'

Susannah just smiled, 'Yes, I see it now. Your little parlay in the ballroom. How desperate you were to dance! They were in my suite then, weren't they? They opened the safe. My poor husband's fate was sealed while I was lamenting with that unfortunate chambermaid in the hall.' She paused. 'Did you really think they were the only copies?'

'You're too clever for that. He's waiting for you right now, isn't he? At the Adelphi in Liverpool? What's his name... Wright?'

It was the first time Susannah seemed caught off guard. 'You really have done your homework. But his name is hardly Wright, Raymond.'

'I suppose every officer of the Reich needs his nom de plume... but what's he going to do if you don't deliver?'

Susannah only had a small bag at her side – not big enough to carry a file filled with documents, thought Raymond, but the suitcases in the rack above were big enough. He lunged for the first one, heaved it down and set it aside. Then he lunged for the second. Was it strange that Susannah put up no protest? Was it strange that she just stood back and watched as he tore each of them open, covering the compartment with her gowns, nightdresses, toiletries and more?

'Where is it?' Raymond demanded, at last. 'What have you done?'

He looked her up and down.

'Do you keep it on your person, Susannah?'

She waved her hand. 'I keep it *in* me, Raymond. I've already told you – your presumptions about the sort of woman I am betray you for the very same kind of fool as my husband. I am no trophy to be carried around. I am no pretty passenger in my husband's life. I am not some simpering debutante of the kind you indulge in your ballrooms. You want to destroy the research I carry with me, Raymond? Well, then, you're going to have to kill me. I am no biologist, I am no researcher, I am no engineer – but memory is a muscle, Raymond, just like deceit, and mine is more formidable than any.' She opened her arms. 'So come on then – kill me, if that's what you're here for.'

'I don't need to kill you,' Raymond breathed, 'all I need to do is stop you before you reach the Adelphi.'

'And how are you going to do that?'

'Susannah, do you really think I came here alone?'

Susannah's eyes darted to the door. Panic flashed in her eyes, then faded almost as instantly as it came.

'Nice try, Raymond – but you're cannon fodder, a soldier on the front line. They didn't send you here. Perhaps you summoned them, but they're not on this train. You're alone with your enemy.

Which means...' She seemed to be weighing something up. Raymond could almost see a decision being made. Her calmness was bone deep, the composure of pure logic and reason. 'It means you're a violent soldier, who just burst into a lone woman's carriage and started tearing apart her luggage – and she's standing there terrified, not knowing what you might do next, needing – oh yes, *actually needing* – a knight in shining armour after all.' She paused. 'I'm sorry, Raymond, but it's game over. At least this next part ought to be fun.'

Susannah Guthrie opened her mouth and started to scream.

'Help!' Her voice, suddenly shivering and shrill, reached far beyond the carriage door. 'Somebody – help me – please!'

# Chapter Twenty-Eight

'Here they are,' Rosa thrilled. 'Girls, they're coming...'

The crowds on Kensington Gore had grown so deep and dense that the Housekeeping girls could hardly move – but at least they'd staked out their position early, in full view of the Albert Hall. Behind them, the crowds reached back as far as the first trees of Hyde Park. Further still, the park itself was a swarm of Londoners and day-trippers who'd turned out just to be part of the moment. Even they must have felt the atmosphere change when the King's procession came into view. Wonder and joy had a ripple effect. Rosa had felt it coming even before she caught sight of the carriage itself.

'I can't see,' Annie Brogan exclaimed. 'Come on, Rosa, help me up!'

'Up on my shoulders, Annie,' Rosa grinned. Annie never minded being treated like a little sister; in seconds, she was scaling Rosa like the trees she used to climb with her brother Billy. 'Can you see them yet? Are they there?'

The carriage door was opening. Somehow, Rosa and Annie forced their way another step forward – and, sandwiched between two burly women (old enough to have seen a good number of kings and queens go by), they saw the royal carriage draw down in front of the Albert Hall.

'That's her,' Annie grinned, 'that's the princess...' Then she stopped. 'Which one is it?'

'That's Princess Margaret, Annie,' Rosa said, with just a hint of admonishment. 'Look, don't be treacherous.'

'I'm not treacherous. I'm...'

'Irish,' Rosa laughed. 'Look, here comes Princess Elizabeth!'

The King's eldest daughter was being helped out of the carriage by a footman. At sixteen years old, she already looked so regal. The city loved her. She was one of them, on the front line, already signed up for vital war work in the storm-ravaged city. And there she stood, waving to the crowd as her father appeared behind her, her mother on his arm.

It wasn't often that you stood so close to your own kings and queens. Rosa had changed the bedsheets of Continental princes, but nothing felt quite like this. The King raised his hand to acknowledge his subjects, then allowed his entourage to lap around him, escorting him towards the Albert Hall like knights of old.

'I bet you can't believe it,' Annie thrilled, still balancing precariously up on Rosa's shoulders.

'Believe what?'

'That your Frankie's going to be dancing for him, right through there!'

Rosa froze.

'Maybe you better get down now, Annie? My shoulders can't take no more.'

Annie didn't mind; she'd had the best view at the very best moment. Down she scrambled, until she was again at Rosa's side, sandwiched tightly between the other girls.

'Imagine if he wins, Rosa – you'll be so proud!'

But Rosa didn't answer. Her eyes had already been drawn further along the cordon, where the hordes of onlookers were separating, just slightly, now that the royal party had passed. There was still plenty to see – hardly any of the Dansant's great guests had arrived – but as the royal fervour ebbed, gaps appeared in the crowd, and through one of them Rosa caught sight of *him*, standing with his comrades.

Joel Kaplan, tall and dark, his military buzzcut just growing into a dark stubble that made him look more rugged still. There he stood, proud among his fellow soldiers, the lumbering Rick a good distance further along, talking to some girl in the crowd. Rosa knew what they said about American soldiers – that they were flashy fly-by-nights, that they only impressed because they had money, nylons, chocolate, all the things Great Britain had been doing without. And maybe it was true – because Joel had brought her all those things and more, extra bacon from his ration packs, glass bottles of Coca Cola from his billet down in Sutton – but what did that matter? Excitement was excitement, wasn't it? You felt it, deep in your bones.

It was just *life*.

And there he was, tall and dark and bathed in summer sun.

'He's going to do us *all* proud,' she said at last, and squeezed Annie by the arm.

And she really wanted him to, as well. A rosette at the Royal Dansant might be just the thing for Frank. It might be the start of something.

Rosa returned her eyes to Joel. This time, it seemed, he had seen her too.

Perhaps *this* might be the start of something for Rosa as well.

Screams filled the carriage.

Susannah was practised at this. Her screaming went on and on. Pinned into place by that terrified wailing, Raymond had no idea what to do. He reached for her, braced her by the shoulders.

'Stop it, Susannah,' he barked – but Susannah wrenched herself away. 'Keep your hands off me!' she screamed. 'Conductor – conductor!'

In seconds, she had flung herself at the compartment door, heaving it open to reel out into the narrow corridor. Raymond lunged after her, desperate to drag her back inside – but by now the screams had flooded the corridor. The conductor, an elderly fellow with a beak nose and fat grey eyebrows beneath his cap, was hurrying along, punctuating the screaming with blasts on his whistle.

Raymond snatched hold of Susannah's wrist.

'Unhand me!' she screamed. 'Sir, unhand me!'

The conductor fell upon them. 'Hands off the lady, sir. This is a civilised service, and the police are just a station away. I've no intent to get involved in a marital dispute, sir, but I can't have violence on my service.'

Susannah broke free of Raymond's grasp and scrambled past the conductor. Cowering behind his back, she fixed Raymond with a knowing look and said, 'The man isn't my husband. He's – he's a dancer, that's all, a dancer from the hotel where I've been staying and he … he's been pursuing me, sir. He followed me here. I'm a lady travelling alone and …'

The conductor looked Raymond up and down. 'How's about you take a few steps backwards now, sir?'

Raymond faltered.

'I have to insist, sir. You've got the devil in you. I can see it in your eyes. Now, I don't know what's going on here – but there'll be no skulduggery on my service. Ladies travelling alone ought to feel safe on our railways. Back, sir. Back, I said!'

'She's lying to you,' Raymond insisted.

'What I can see with my own eyes is bad enough.' He craned to look inside the compartment. 'Dear God, man – have you been tearing through this lady's cases?' He put the whistle to his lips and three short blasts sounded out. Moments later, the staff from the dining compartment had arrived in the company of another conductor, to see what was going on. 'I need your help, Reg. I need your help, Dick. This gentleman's accosting this lady – I'm going to take her to the conductors' corner, help her to calm down. Her bags will need packing up. And as for this gentleman...'

'We'll deal with him, sir.'

Raymond watched, in mounting horror, as the first conductor led Susannah away. The moment they vanished into the vestibule at the end of the carriage, the others crowded the corridor in front of him. By now, passengers were craning out of the compartments further along, eager to catch some glimpse of whatever this disturbance might be – but soon even they were obfuscated from Raymond's view, for the train staff were battling him backwards, into the compartment where Susannah's cases were splayed open wide. As the dining-carriage staff started packing them up to cart away, the second conductor forced him into the corner.

'You look like a decent man,' he said, solidly, 'so let's not make this worse than it already is.'

*It's you who's making it worse*, Raymond seethed, inwardly. *It's you who's letting her go.*

But how to say it?

How to make his case without betraying what he knew?

Telling them who he really was?

'Can I see your ticket, sir?'

Raymond almost smiled. Of all the things to undo him, this would be the most laughable. 'Sir, I came onto this train to—'

'Accost the gentlewoman,' the conductor concluded, 'and with the temerity to not even buy a ticket. I'm sorry, sir. You don't leave me with any choice. You'll be ejected from this train when we reach the next siding.'

Something inside Raymond snapped. He tried to hustle the conductor back, but immediately the dining-car staff leapt to his defence. Behind their barricade of suitcases, now packed and shut tight, they started barracking him.

'I'm going to have to lock you in, sir, if you won't put down your fists.'

'I'm trying to appeal to your better nature, gentlemen. That lady isn't who she says she is.'

The three men looked at each other grimly. 'They never are, sir, but there's not one of us followed a lady onto a train and forced our way into her private carriage. You ought to be ashamed.' As one, they stepped backwards, out of the door. 'Stay where you are, sir.'

Raymond watched, blankly, as they slipped into the corridor, then closed the door to seal him inside.

Seconds later, a key turned in the lock.

And the train hurtled on.

It ought to have been a sense of homecoming that washed over Hélène as she stepped out of the car in front of the Albert Hall, and was shepherded through the crowd, across the cordon, and into the building's grand stage door – but she couldn't keep the feeling of unease at bay as they led her into the labyrinthine complex beneath the auditorium, where hospitality staff swarmed like ants in a nest. Hélène was not given to nerves – she never had been; perhaps it was why they once called her the Ice Queen – but she felt Raymond's absence keenly as she stepped into the dressing rooms and arranged her gown at her station. Soon she was arranging Raymond's suit of midnight blue as well. How empty it looked, without him inside it – like the shell of Raymond de Guise. Some of the other girls crowded around to admire it – but none of them had lost their partners, none of them were riven with doubts that they'd even get to dance, and Hélène worked hard not to explain it. 'My partner is running late,' she told the stage managers when they came to take the dancers on their tour of the auditorium above. 'He'll be along in a moment.'

Even so, she joined the other dancers as the stagehands introduced them to the cavernous auditorium. The dance floor, ringed by tiers of seats stretching up into the gods, had been laid especially for the event; it felt new and delicate to touch. Hélène could already feel how beautifully the dancers would glide across a floor like this, how the springs beneath the interlocking wooden boards resisted the pressure *just enough* to encourage each step. Every dancer was in constant dialogue with the dance floor beneath them. If Hélène was right, this one would contribute to every graceful step she took. Its craftsmen had been masters of their trade, summoned – just like every dancer hereabout – to the call of the King.

An elderly gentlemen stood on the edge of the dance floor, cane in his hand, soaking up the anticipation in the air. 'Georges,' she breathed, and soared to his side. Hélène had known Georges only fleetingly – the mentor who had brought the ragged young Ray Cohen into the rarefied ballroom world – but his face opened in a smile to see her. 'I didn't think we'd see the two of you dancing again, Miss Marchmont,' he beamed, 'but what a spectacle it will be ...'

Together, they looked up. The great dome of the Albert Hall was a frame of iron and plate glass, the most ambitious in the world, but right now it was painted as black as a starless sky. Enemy bombers were known to use the Albert Hall to orientate themselves when dropping their loads across London, but so far it had escaped direct attack. The black paint made Hélène feel as if it was already night-time. They would dance beneath bright sunlight, but in the Albert Hall it would be a different place, a different time.

'But Hélène,' Georges said, 'I don't see Raymond anywhere.' Hélène took his hand.

'He'll be here,' she whispered. 'He promised he'd be here.'

And Raymond de Guise had never broken a promise in all of his life.

The crowds were almost impassable from the moment the taxicab brought Max and Nelson Allgood over the river. The bridge at Westminster, ordinarily choked with soldiers at the checkpoints, was the last stretch of open road. After that, all the taxi could do was crawl along the edge of St James's Park. The crowds which had gathered to see the royal procession leaving Buckingham Palace were hardly any less sparse than they had been when the King and his family rolled by.

Nelson kicked back in his seat, much to the taximan's chagrin. 'Come on, just drive through 'em! This show *matters*.'

'The man's not gonna go runnin' folks down just to get us to the Albert Hall on time,' said Max – but the truth was, he was nervous too. He cradled Lucille in his lap. 'We still got time. Show doesn't open for another hour.'

'It's all right for you Uncle Max,' Nelson groaned. 'You've already got where you're going. If I don't get to the Dansant and show 'em what I've got, I'm never gonna be up there at the Buckingham Hotel.'

Beside him, Uncle Max barely looked him in the eye.

'Well, I'm right, aren't I? It's the challenge you laid me. Dazzle 'em at the Dansant, and I'm the star of the Grand, aren't I?' Nelson paused. 'Well, aren't I, Uncle Max?'

'We're gonna talk about that after the show, Nelson.' Max stared resolutely out of the window, fingers drumming on Lucille's case.

'Uncle Max, don't hold out on me. It's what I'm here for. It's why I'm in London, isn't it?'

'You've been making hell, Nelson,' Max snapped.

'Hell's been coming after me and *I've* been outrunning it. Those hicks had it in for me from the start. It wasn't my fault. You're just gonna leave me in the gutter because of *that*?'

For the first time, Max wheeled round and looked at him. 'There's nobody leaving anybody in any gutters. You hear me? But it's one day at a time with you. Two weeks ago, you were crawling in with a smashed face from some gutter. You're lucky to be playing at all. I've near killed myself with promises to keep the slot for you. I've near choked on lies. But I can't do it for you all your days. And if you're gonna be in my orchestra, I got to trust you. It's too good a gig to ruin.'

'Ruin?' Nelson baulked. 'Ruin, Uncle Max?'

More calmly now, Max said, 'Boy, I've told you my life story time and time again. You know how hard I dragged myself up. Rising and falling and rising again. In and out of that penitentiary. In and out of good favour. But I'm getting old, boy. I feel heavier every time I wake up. The music's all I've got. Without it, it's a lice-infested flophouse and an early grave. The Buckingham Hotel's my saviour. The fact I'm there at all? Boy, the stars had to line up *just right!* And I can't risk it. I *won't* risk it. Not until I know for sure. Not until I know you're not gonna screw it up for me.'

Nelson threw open the taxicab door.

Next second, he was slamming it closed behind him.

'Nelson Allgood, get back in here. We've got a show to do!'

But Nelson just threw two crooked fingers at the window and said, 'I reckon I'm better off walking. If I'm gonna have to stand on my own two feet, I might as well start now.'

The fire didn't burn off even as he bobbed and weaved through the crowds flooding Birdcage Walk. Past the palace he went, into the verdant expanse of Green Park. Picnickers had turned the vast green lawns into a veritable festival, but Nelson stalked through them like a roiling black cloud. It wasn't his fault that somebody's picnic blanket got ruffled. It wasn't his fault that somebody's hamper got upturned, nor their dog's paw trodden on. All of *that* was because of Uncle Max. Because of false promises. Because of disrespect. Because everybody, whether they were family or not, wanted to get the best out of Nelson Allgood, use him for their own ends, and then just cut him loose.

'Hey, that's out of order!'

The voice chased after him. But Nelson was already imagining what it might be like to upstage Max once he reached the Albert Hall. Only there because of a family connection, was he? Well, just wait until they saw what he could do. Next time the King came calling, it would be Max Allgood begging Nelson for a place.

'Excuse me, sir – you owe the girls an apology!'

Nelson turned round.

He'd never seen these girls before. Just some lowly London types, who'd come out to see the King. But the voice had belonged to one of the men gathered with them around the picnicking blanket – apparently the very same picnicking blanket across which Nelson had just planted his boots. He'd heard that voice before. It was imprinted upon him, just the same as those fists and boots had been. An American voice, rich with the twang of Georgia.

'You,' said Rick Larkin, rising to his feet.

Nelson's heart sank, but at least he knew not to show it. 'Howdy boys.'

At once, the other three GIs were up on their feet. One of the girls piped up, 'He didn't mean anything by it, he just wasn't looking,' but another one of them grabbed her by the hand and said, 'Nonsense, Annie – he just marched on through like he's the only man in the world!'

'I'll handle this, Rosa,' said the one named Kaplan, Joel Kaplan. 'King's Man,' he cried out, 'you've been keeping yourself scarce.'

Nelson wiggled his fingers, playing on an imaginary piano. 'I've been busy.'

'Yeah?' Rick seethed, and closed the gap between them in one great stride. 'Busy healing that pretty face of yours, I reckon, because we haven't seen you out playing shows. You know, we've been asking around.'

'I been taking a sabbatical. Gotta keep it fresh, boys, when you're playing for the King.'

'A sabbatical,' Rick snorted. 'You know, King's Man, it's almost like you say these things deliberately. It's almost like you want more of what you got. Sabbatical,' he spat. 'King's Man, where's our money?'

Nelson took a step backwards. This didn't help his cause, because almost immediately he was trampling somebody else's picnic – but he hopped and jumped until he was on clear ground again and said, 'I still don't see how it's your money. And you know where it went. Straight down the drain.'

'Why do you say these things?' Joel asked, stepping out in front of Rick. 'You know what's good for you. You don't have to say a thing. And yet...'

The truth was, Nelson didn't know. It wasn't just the fire burning in him after what Uncle Max had said. It wasn't just a reminder of how *strong* he'd felt, even while their boots were piling into him, as he let the money sink deep into the drain. It was something else, something he'd been born with, something which pulsated in him, even now, with the Albert Hall only an hour away. It was the same thing, he knew now, which made the music take flight. The same instinct that drove him to wild flights of fancy on stage was driving him, right now, to taunt these boys even further, to goad and cajole until they snapped.

'Why are you girls lounging around here with these hicks,' Nelson grinned, 'when you could be coming to the show of your lives? I reckon I can sweet-talk those doormen. With a bit of luck, I could probably get you backstage, have you curtseying for the King. What do you say? Worth a chance? Or just sit around here all afternoon, with these donkeys, wondering what might have been?'

The girls didn't look tempted, even for a second – but Nelson didn't care about that. It was the looks on the infantrymen's faces that he was treasuring.

He even enjoyed it when one looked to the other and said, 'Boys, if he ain't got our money, he's still got to pay.'

Then, without another word – because Nelson Allgood had already said too much – he started to run, and to hell with any poor picnickers who got in the way.

Raymond wrenched at the door handle. He kicked at the frame. The train plunged into a tunnel, leaving him in nothing but the flickering electric light, then emerged again, to the first hints of green fields rushing by the window. Every moment took him further from London. Every minute, another mile from the Albert Hall. 'Let me out of here!' he thundered. He took three strides backwards, then ran full force at the door. The wood buckled, the metal lock groaned, but the frame held firm. 'Open... this... door!'

Raymond thrust out with the flat of his foot, and the door splintered outwards.

Out into the corridor he crashed, disentangling himself from the shattered wood. The passengers who'd been craning their heads out of the compartments further along the row quickly vanished back inside, but Raymond paid them no heed as he palmed his way past. In moments, he reached the end of the carriage, then levered himself through the door and into the next carriage along. In the brief moment between carriages, the wind caught hold of him, propelling him on. Through here, more passengers seemed to scatter at his approach. Doors slammed. Locks slotted into place. In the dining cart, diners watched him with a curious sense of unease. He bowed politely to each of them, but barely broke his stride – not until he was crashing into the final carriage, close enough to the locomotive to feel the tremble of its furnace, to smell the soot and smoke.

The conductors' compartment sat at the end of the carriage. Raymond reached for the handle.

The moment he opened the door, the conductor sprang up. Inside it was a cramped affair, half the size of a passenger compartment and most of that taken up with buckets, mops, boxes and crates. Susannah Guthrie sat by the window. To Raymond she scarcely looked distressed at all. She watched him enter coolly, even as the head conductor – his cap taken off, revealing a mottled, balding pate – swung round, seizing the mop to battle Raymond back. 'Sir, you take it too far.'

Raymond wanted no fight with the old man. Courage flared in his eyes, and that could only be an admirable thing. 'I'm sorry, Susannah,' he said, looking straight past the conductor, 'but you're coming with me.'

The emergency brake cord was high above, running along the topmost edge of the compartment – but Raymond reached it with ease. 'Sir!' the conductor barked and drove the mop like a spear straight into Raymond's breast. Raymond staggered back but, by then, his fingers had already curled around the cord. As he staggered, the cord remained in his hand – and the sudden hissing of steam releasing from valves, the screech of metal pressed suddenly against metal, told him the brake had been applied.

Raymond reached for the mop handle and, bowing his head in apology, used it to swing the man aside. 'You'll know, one day, it's for the good,' he declared – then reached out to grab Susannah's wrist.

The conductor had started blasting on his whistle, but at least that gave Raymond the few seconds he needed to haul Susannah from the compartment. 'It's over, Mrs Guthrie. We're getting off this train.'

The carriages still juddered around them. Now, at last, they came to a stop. With Susannah's arm pinioned behind her back, Raymond forced her on until they reached the first carriage door.

Whistles were still sounding. Footsteps rampaged along the carriages – no doubt the other conductors answering the call. It didn't matter any more. Raymond held Susannah against the wall while he reached out of the window and forced open the door. Moments later, he was spilling with her onto the edge of a lonely railway where hedgerows grew wild. 'Tell me what's in this for you,' he said through gritted teeth, compelling her through the hedgerow to some farmer's field, rippling in yellow oil-seed rape on the other side. 'How do you profit?'

'That's just like a hero,' she spat, 'to think his enemy can only be in it for personal gain. I profit when the world profits!'

The vivid yellow fields were broken below by the old stones and thatch of a farmhouse, its chimney trailing smoke. Raymond started propelling Susannah in that direction, even while he heard the flurry of whistles from behind.

'They think you're a blackguard, you know. They think you're insane. What's it going to look like, de Guise? Dancing man, veteran of Dunkirk and Tobruk, driven wild by...'

'Please don't, Mrs Guthrie. You're only making this worse.'

They reached the farmhouse with the conductors already flocking through the field to find them. A more picturesque sight it would have been impossible to find. The farmer had trained roses up the trellis outside his doorway. The thatch was full and dry. As Raymond thrust Susannah towards the door, a rooster squawked in either greeting or alarm, and the hens in an open barn started beating their wings furiously, as if at the appearance of some fox.

When nobody answered, Raymond did not hesitate. He kicked open the door, threw Susannah inside, and bolted it behind him.

'Hello?' he cried out. 'Hello?'

But there came no reply, and when Raymond forced Susannah into the bright, cheery farmhouse kitchen, it was to find the teapot cold, the range holding only dead embers, and mice the only living things in the building.

'No telephone,' he cursed, dragging Susannah from room to room.

'I hardly think you need one now,' Susannah laughed.

Raymond rushed to the kitchen window. Moments later he heard what Susannah had already perceived: out there, engines were roaring. A convoy of black Wolseleys were roaring up the farm road.

By the time Raymond ducked back inside, he had counted four cars, and a cloud of dust behind them that could only have meant five.

'But how?' he whispered, brokenly. 'How so soon?'

Susannah stood. 'I'm sorry, Raymond – but nobody questions a damsel in distress.'

As Raymond watched, Susannah threw herself back across the farmhouse, clamouring at the front door to lift up the latch. Moments later, before Raymond had summoned the wherewithal to follow, she was staggering out into the sunlit yard. The black cars were almost upon them now. The first slewed around in the farmyard, in the exact same moment that the train conductors erupted from the flamboyant yellow fields.

The sun beat down upon Raymond de Guise as he too raced back into the yard.

The second car cut an arc round the yard, then the third and the fourth. The fifth remained behind, blocking the farm track.

Strange, thought Raymond, but these were no village constables summoned by some clever conductor.

He put his hands in the air.

In the very same moment, Susannah started sobbing and threw herself onto the farmyard ground. Above her, the first car opened its door and its thick, heavyset driver stepped out.

'Please help me,' Susannah wailed. 'He's crazy. He won't stop. He's coming after me ...'

The second car opened its door, and the face that appeared snuffed out all the turmoil in Raymond's heart.

'I daresay he is coming after you,' Maynard Charles declared. 'It's what he's been paid to do.'

On the edge of the farmyard, the train conductors stuttered to a halt. With faces wrenched into paroxysms of surprise, they watched as Maynard Charles's men hoisted Susannah from the ground, then thrust her, like a trussed-up pig, into the back seat of one of the Wolseleys.

'Sir,' Raymond gasped.

As he rushed forward, two of Maynard's men were march-ing towards the conductors, compelling them back into the field. There would, it seemed, be a lot of tidying up to be done. Maynard took him by the hand and said, 'Of course, you *are* meant to work in the shadows.'

'I'm sorry, sir. I tried to send a message. But I knew what train she was on and—'

Maynard opened his palm and held it up, instructing Raymond to sink back into silence. 'Loose lips, sir.' Then he opened the car door and Raymond slipped inside. The driver bowed his head, practising obliviousness, as Maynard slid in beside Raymond and went on, 'Your message reached us too late. The train had already embarked. I ought to have known you were on board – but I must admit, I doubted you, de Guise.'

Only now did Raymond feel his heartbeat slowing. 'Her cover was better than mine, sir. I ought to have known from the start. It happened when she was in Scotland. The forced acquisitions, and the party Douglas Guthrie convened, and… I don't know if she planned for Douglas to take the blame, sir, but it worked for her. She—'

At this point, Maynard intervened: 'I'll require a full debrief from you soon, Raymond. I'll have to drag you before my su-periors. But right now…' He tapped his driver on the shoulder and asked, 'What time is it?'

The man consulted his watch. 'It's almost a quarter to two, sir.'

Maynard heaved a sigh. 'It's cutting it fine.'

'For what, sir?' Raymond asked.

Maynard barked, 'Start driving,' and gripped Raymond's arm. 'I believe you have a prior engagement, don't you, de Guise? And since you've single-handedly saved our bacon today, perhaps we ought to save yours.'

'But sir, Mrs Guthrie…'

Maynard opened the door and, as the engine burst to life, stepped out. 'She's in my custody now, de Guise. I must say, I feel rather sorry for the grilling I gave her husband – especially if it turns out he was telling the truth all along. Rotten little man that he is, it seems his wife's more riddled with it.' He closed the door, then bowed to the window. 'Good luck, de Guise. And, garlanded or not, I'll see you at the Deacon Club by nine.'

Nelson hit Constitution Hill at a run, weaving so frantically between the cars crawling along the thoroughfare that, more than once, he collided with a stalled taxicab and went sliding wildly over a bonnet. By the time he'd reached the Wellington Arch, he felt sure he'd lost the GIs somewhere behind – but the crowds up ahead made Hyde Park Corner almost impassable, and he'd evidently underestimated the bruises he still carried from his last hiding, because the pain in his side was intensifying with every step. His body was telling him to slow down, even while his heart kept up its insistent percussion. 'Pardon me,' he said, and started limping his way through the crowd. 'King's Man coming through,' he muttered to himself. Even now, the name appealed to him. That it incited those bastards even more just brought more pleasure to his mind.

All he had to do was reach the Albert Hall.

At the cordon he'd smile, stretch out his hand, announce who he was and why he was here.

The doors would open up, the crowd would roar; once he took to the stage, the King himself would be on his feet with his hands raised up in applause.

If only he could even get there...

Nelson looked over his shoulder. Across the sea of faces, he saw them coming. They seemed to see him too. There was no use denying it. Nelson extended his hand, gave them a dainty wave, then took off into the traffic.

If there was any way to lose them, it wasn't in the crowds of Kensington Gore. He could make better headway in the backstreets.

Of course, you couldn't really call these *backstreets*. He wasn't in Harlem now. This wasn't the Bowery. It wasn't Hell's Kitchen. But they would do, all the same. There were plenty of well-wishers here, but at least they didn't clog the arteries of the city. Nelson could feel the streets rushing by underneath him, the shopfronts and townhouses whistling by. He trusted to instinct, banked right to follow the line of Kensington Gore from below. The stitch in his side intensified, but the pain had a side effect too; it seemed to be sapping him of the anger that had been coursing out of him ever since the cab ride. When it got too much, he threw himself against the railings and braced himself there, gasping for breath, letting the anguish ease.

He turned round, looked up between the townhouses. The alley in front of him was a dead end, just a place for refuse and rats, but hanging over the rooftops was the magnificent dome of the Albert Hall.

Sometimes the stars really did line up.

Uncle Max was full of horseshit. Just the kind of man who made things difficult for himself. There were too many of that type in the world.

Nelson turned to follow the road round towards his destiny.

And there they stood, arrayed in a horseshoe around him.

Not one of them was smiling.

'We're not unreasonable people,' grunted the one named Rick. 'So – you give us our money and we won't break your hands.'

Nelson thought he'd heard rats more reasonable than this. 'How do you expect me to get that money if I can't get over there?' he said, and thrust his hand upwards, to the very place where the Albert Hall dominated the sky. 'You can have all the money you want, boys, once I'm top of the world.'

The infantrymen looked at one another. This time, even the one named Joel looked despairing as they closed in.

'It's funny, boys,' said Rick in his thick monotone, 'but I think we've heard that one before ...'

The black Wolseley had made swift work of the journey back into London.

It was the journey *through* London that was the problem.

As if it wasn't bad enough that the Luftwaffe had recast the map of the city, closing down crossroads, blocking off boulevards, mounting diversion upon diversion upon diversion as London was broken down and rebuilt, crowds of well-wishers clogged the West End. The closer Raymond's driver got to Hyde Park, the slower he crawled. By the time he reached Marble Arch, the road was almost impassable. Horns blared, drivers yelled, but the crowds had tumbled from the park into the boulevard and the minutes were flashing by.

'I'm going to take the small roads, sir,' the driver said when, at last, they came to the Wellington Arch, at the bottom of Constitution Hill. 'I'll not get through Knightsbridge like this. But the back of the Albert Hall's every bit as good as the front, sir.'

Raymond craned out of the window, to gaze up at the sky. There was the sun, already sinking past its zenith. At the Albert Hall, the seats would already be filled.

'I know what you're thinking, sir. You're thinking you're better off sprinting. But I'll get you there on time.'

The Wolseley kicked forward, cutting away from the Wellington Arch and into the luxurious boulevards of Belgravia.

Past the embassies of foreign governments they burst, round opulent gated gardens, the imposing outline of Harrod's department store hanging above. Cromwell Road, and the roads around the museums, were busier with traffic avoiding the hordes on Kensington Gore, but Raymond's driver knew instinctively which side-roads to take, which alleys he might pass, how to bully the other drivers without ever inciting their ire. By the time they reached Prince's Gardens, with its pristine white townhouses and emerald lawns, there was only empty road ahead.

That was when Raymond knew he was going to get there.

That was when he knew he was going to dance.

That was when he looked out of the window and saw the young Black man pressed up against the railings of a certain white townhouse, and the four other men ranged around him, tightening their ranks.

'Stop the car,' Raymond blurted out.

He'd seen that face before...

'Now boys, don't be so hasty,' Nelson said, his eyes flashing from left to right, feinting first one way, then the next, anything that might give him the opportunity to cut suddenly though their ranks and do what he did best: skedaddle. 'You break my fingers, how're you ever gonna get your money? We can come to some arrangement. That's what gentlemen do. Aren't we gentlemen, boys?'

The soldier named Rick drew back his fist.

He was tired of all the talking.

'First things first, even before those fingers, I'm gonna have to shut your—'

But Rick's fist couldn't fly forward, because suddenly hands were grasping his arm, wrestling him down.

As one, the infantrymen turned.

In the same moment that they'd been barracking the musician, a black car had ground to a halt on the street behind them. Now its back door stood open, and out of it a tall man with swept-back black hair and the look of a Roman general had emerged. Releasing Rick's arm, he looked imperiously over the heads of the infantrymen and eyeballed Nelson with something approaching disbelief.

'It feels like we've been here before, young man.'

Nelson threw back his head and howled. 'I got myself a knight in English armour!'

'What's this to you?' one of the infantrymen snarled, now that their surprise had worn away. 'This is a private affair between gentlemen. It's none of your business.'

Raymond strode between the infantrymen, opening a passage between them. Then he snatched Nelson's hand and hauled him bodily through, until the boy was standing at his side.

'There's four of you,' Raymond spat. 'And there's one of him. It started being my business the moment I saw it.'

For a moment, the infantrymen were silent. Raymond looked at each of their bristling faces in turn.

'Leave him,' said Joel, stoutly. 'The kid never could stand up for himself. He's a runner, boys. Every time he ought to stand, he bows out.'

Rick hawked thick phlegm from the back of his throat and spat it directly in front of Nelson's boots. 'You're just a chicken. Too chicken-shit for service, too chicken-shit to do what's right. You've got no courage, boy. You're yellow, through and through.'

Raymond had been trying to steer Nelson into the back of the car, but suddenly he froze.

'What did you say to me?' he whispered, turning back round.

'I called you out,' said Rick. 'Called you what you are. Nothing but a little boy, holding on to his papa's hand. Just a little boy, crying out for help whenever things get messy. Running and hiding, hiding and running. Just a little boy who needs his momma.'

Nelson lifted his chin.

He brushed Raymond to the side.

He looked the infantrymen up and down.

And everything he'd seen since landing in London, every rise and fall, every triumph and temptation, coursed through him: half a year in half an instant, and here it was.

His fingers flexed.

They curled into fists.

If these boys wanted a second round, why in hell not give it to them?

He stepped towards them.

'I'm no chicken,' he said, feeling the sudden fury of fire.

Then, just as the boys drew together, just as they raised their fists and readied themselves for the fight, Nelson's mind was filled with music.

He turned and slipped into the car. 'I'll see you boys on the other side of the war,' he said, and winked at them as Raymond slipped in beside him. 'Sir, you're my avenging angel – that's what you are.' The car had started moving, but Nelson flashed an urgent look through the glass. 'Those boys been plaguing me for months, sir.'

'Trouble loves you.'

'That ain't the problem. The problem is – *I* love *it*. And, sir, it's hard to fall out of love.'

There was something in this that felt unearthly and wise, though the urgency of the moment prevented Raymond from dwelling on it for too long. 'I'm afraid I can't take you very far,' he said. 'I'm already running out of time. You'll have to make your own way from there.'

'That's fine by me, sir. One step ahead of those blowhards is all I need.' Nelson paused. 'Where is it you're going?'

Raymond looked up, through the windscreen. 'There she sits. The Royal Albert Hall.'

A strange, delighted howling filled the car. When Raymond looked round, it was to discover the brightest, most effervescent of grins on the boy's startled face.

'Raymond,' Nelson began. 'It *is* Raymond, ain't it?'

'It is.'

'Well then, Raymond,' Nelson laughed, 'I reckon fate really has brought us together after all...'

# Chapter Twenty-Nine

In the sitting room at No 18 Blomfield Road, Nancy cradled Arthur to her shoulder while Vivienne chased Stan around the hearth. The radio receiver sitting in the alcove by the windows, where net curtains kept out the cascade of summer sunshine, crackled as the BBC announcer declared the Royal Dansant about to begin.

'Now comes the moment, ladies and gentlemen. King George has taken his seat in the box above the stage. As applause fills the Royal Albert Hall, three hundred of this nation's finest patrons rise to their feet to display their gratitude to the family who have weathered every storm alongside us. Up in the galleries, we can see Mr Cary Grant taking his seat. Across the auditorium, Mr Laurence Olivier – fresh from his success in Hollywood – sits but a stone's throw away from Mr Noel Coward. The great, the garlanded and good have come together tonight to show their appreciation for this once-in-a-lifetime event, held in honour of...'

Nancy whirled round. Behind her, Vivienne was still trying desperately to catch Stan – but, true to form, the little boy did not want to be caught. 'This is it, Vivienne. They're about to start.' Then she did a little box-stepping of her own, Arthur in her arms. 'Arthur, one day I'll tell you that *we* were waltzing on the day your father danced for the King...'

Arthur just gurgled.

'Wish him luck, my little man. It's about to begin...'

The lights went down

The band struck up.

From his place on the stage, Max Allgood turned round to see the entirety of the Royal Albert Hall on their feet, gallery upon gallery gazing down from the stands – and he, Max Allgood, standing centre stage.

The Royal Box was somewhere above, but Barry Pike had issued the declaration moments before they were due on stage: 'Nobody, not one of us, be they musician or dancer, is to look directly at the King.' Just peasants, Max thought to himself, that's all we are – but what fortunate peasants, to be invited to court!

As he lifted Lucille, her bell glinting in the brilliant stage lights, he looked at the piano. The night's first guest pianist was a middle-aged impresario, one who'd forged a brilliant partnership with Pike at the BBC Symphony Orchestra. Nelson wouldn't be needed for another forty-five minutes – but, of course, the boy was nowhere to be seen. Max tried not to think of it, nor any of the promises he'd blathered out to Barry Pike, as he led Lucille into the night's first number. This dreamy, faraway waltz was the evening's aperitif, meant to welcome the competitors of the first wave to the stage. Down below, the couples started to appear. One after another, they dotted the dance floor: twenty, thirty, forty of them, presenting themselves to the waves of applause. Lucille lulled him; what Nelson did, he told himself, was his own business.

Max had tried.

He'd kicked open doors.

He'd risked his reputation.

He just couldn't risk it *all* by promising him the Grand, and that's what Nelson didn't see.

Lucille's first flight touched down, and Max took his lips away from her mouthpiece. The dancing was yet to begin, but it would happen in moments. The evening's compère, the one and only George Black – impresario of London's fabulous theatres, and the man who'd marshalled every Royal Variety Performance since the days of the Depression – was waiting in the wings.

Max scoured the dancers. There stood the Buckingham's very own Frank Nettleton and Mathilde Bourchier. Mathilde looked like she *belonged* in a place like this – that was a talent in itself – but her partner looked almost overwhelmed, and the dancing hadn't yet begun. Even dressed to the nines, Nettleton looked just a *little* dishevelled – but nobody, yet, had seen him dance...

In the middle of the dance floor, bolt upright with Mathilde in his arms, Frank Nettleton closed his eyes.

The evening's compère, George Black, marched onto the stage and announced himself to the crowd, and still Frank kept his eyes closed. The Royal Albert Hall cheered for its orchestra, cheered for the King, cheered for the joining of Old World and New, an alliance of good against all that was wicked in the world – and still Frank remained safe, in his own little world, humming inaudibly as he tried to keep the nerves at bay.

'Frankie,' Mathilde whispered gently, 'open ... your ... eyes ...'

So he did.

From the dance floor to the cavernous vaults of the blacked-out dome above, stars seemed to be shimmering. The lights on each gallery flickered like constellations. Up there sat everyone who mattered in the gilded London firmament, the galleries filled with stars of the stage and screen – every one of them invited personally at the behest of the King. Gracie Fields and Leslie Howard, Cecil Lewis, George Bernard Shaw – so many names had whistled past Frank backstage that he hadn't been able to take them all in. Nor could he contemplate it right now, when all of their eyes were upon him.

'Don't think about it,' said Mathilde, looking him in the eye. 'Just hold on to me – and Frankie...' The trumpets sounded; the dancers readied; the band launched in. 'Let's dance.'

Hélène was still considering herself in the dressing-room mirror, waiting for the moment when she'd have to break the news to the stage director, when a knock came at the door. In the end, it was one of the other girls who answered it. Hélène just continued staring into the mirror, applying kohl to her eyes. No doubt some of the younger girls here found it old-fashioned, but that was just the way it had to be: if Hélène belonged to the past, she was going to be proud of it. The early 1930s had been a much simpler time.

She saw his reflection first.

There he was, just standing in the doorway, mouthing her name.

Hélène turned round, even as the girl who'd answered the door was coming to find her.

There stood Raymond de Guise, as nonchalant as if he'd been waiting in the hallway all this time. As he approached, he gave her one of the winsome smiles that had won over countless guests at the Buckingham Hotel. 'Forgive me?' he whispered.

Hélène shot back, 'I don't know if I can.' But the light in her eyes told a different story. 'Are you going to tell me where you've been?'

Was any lie good enough for this moment?

Raymond took Hélène in hold, bowed his head to her ear and simply whispered, 'No.'

Hélène was looking at him with incredulous eyes, wondering how on earth she could just sail into the dance with a man shrouded in secrets, when a fresh wave of applause set the Royal Albert Hall to shuddering. The boards above them started trembling, as cheers flooded the passageways and vaults underneath the auditorium itself.

When the applause had died away and some fresh song begun, she said, 'Raymond, you need to get changed.' Then she stepped aside, revealing his suit of midnight blue hanging against the bright white wall beside her mirror.

'Let's give them a show, Helene,' he smiled, and snatched the suit from the wall to hold it against him.

'Still as debonair as on the night the Grand opened.'

Raymond smiled. 'Do you remember it, Hélène? Coming through those doors for the first time, thinking – no, *knowing* – that this was it, the very height of what we could do? The whole of society lined up in front of us, and asking – no, *demanding* – that we entertain them, that we spin a little magic, that we show them how the world could be?'

The applause rolled through the Albert Hall again. The first phase of the competition, it seemed, was coming to an end.

'It seems like a lifetime ago.'

Raymond supposed it was. 'But today my son is listening.'

'Today, my daughter's at home with her grandparents. They're out on the lawns, with the radio playing through the summerhouse windows.'

'A lifetime ago is right,' said Raymond as he whisked away, 'but let's show them how it's done.'

Raymond marched out of the dressing room and hurried up the hall. Through one of the open doors he could see Nelson

357

lurching into his own dark, velveteen suit. 'I'm telling you,' the boy was remonstrating with some unseen stagehand, 'this is how it's going to be!' Two stagehands milled in mild panic, urging him into his brogues, telling him he was needed on stage. 'Mr Pike's already lined up an understudy, sir. If we don't get you to the wings, there's no way of knowing.'

Raymond careened round a corner – and there, just outside his dressing-room door, stood his old mentor, Georges de la Motte.

The older man had a wry look in his aged, weathered eyes as he said, 'I remember a night in Vienna when it was much the same. You'd been *elsewhere* with that rascal Lavigne, and I stood by the doors of the Vienna State Opera, the guests already arriving for the winter *Redoute* – and in you sashayed, as if your heart hadn't skipped a beat, as if you hadn't had an old man's heart in tumult.'

'Georges,' Raymond took his hand, 'I can assure you my heart was always panic personified.'

Georges looked him in the eye, dropping his voice to a whisper. His eyes radiated concern. 'I thought you might come to me, boy, when you came back from the front. I thought, if you were to return to the ballroom, you might yourself have need of a little… help. The counsel of an old mentor, perhaps, to set you back on your feet.' Georges paused. Until now, it had been concern for Raymond rippling out of him; now, it seemed like wounded pride. 'Nettleton tells me you needed ushering back into the dance, that if it hadn't been for Nancy you might not be here.'

Lies, thought Raymond. In moments like these, he was supposed to spin more lies. Instead, he said, 'I've missed you, Georges. But I haven't wanted to weigh you down. You carried me for so long.'

'I brought you into the ballroom. I would have done it again.'

Raymond released his hand. 'And here you are,' he said. 'Georges, wish me luck.'

In the dressing room, Raymond looked at himself in the mirror. It had been different, that first night in the Grand; his face had not been so lined, and his mind had not been so riven with the scars every little falsehood left behind. But there was much that was similar too. The sense of nervous excitement. The sense of occasion. Hélène at his side, and this suit – this very same suit – of midnight blue, made by a Savile Row tailor and gifted to him by Georges de la Motte himself.

Raymond slipped inside it, like he was slipping into his old self.

Not the veteran of France; not a lieutenant of the sun-burnished desert; not the spy sent back to infiltrate the very ballroom where he used to think only of wonder and joy.

Just Raymond de Guise, ready to go out there and steal some hearts as he danced.

Georges was waiting for him when he emerged from the dressing room. Hélène was waiting too. Further along, deeper inside this labyrinth of dressing rooms, the stage managers were rallying the competitors for the next phase of the contest.

Raymond opened his arm, allowing Hélène to thread hers through. Moments later, they were joining the procession of other couples being shepherded towards the auditorium. There were faces Raymond recognised here, couples from his old com-petition days, dancers from the other great ballrooms of London. 'The Savoy's here,' he whispered to Hélène. 'The Imperial too.'

Georges accompanied them to the end of the hall, where the stage managers had instructed they wait. 'The secret of the night,' he announced, 'is to pretend there's no competition whatsoever.

Let them dance around you. Out there, you compete only with yourselves – and your idea of what the dance might be.'

Raymond and Hélène shared a look. 'A world of our own,' said Hélène, 'just like that very first night...'

Nelson had been waiting for this. The stagehands had almost had to bridle him. By the edge of the stage, he watched as the orchestra reached the end of its song, as Barry Pike turned to bow to the stands and the couples on the dance floor below all stepped out of hold. George Black, the evening's compère, was already sallying out, his arms thrown wide to the heavens as he rhapsodised on all the beauty he'd just seen – but Nelson didn't care about any of that. All he wanted was to take his place.

'Go,' the stagehand whispered to him. 'Hands folded behind you, at a steady pace. Remember – their eyes are on Mr Black...'

'I hear it,' nodded Nelson. 'I'm not the star of this show. I get it.' But under his breath, as he took his first step, he whispered, 'But just wait until you hear me play...'

'Ladies and gentlemen, one last time for our competitors!'

Even as George Black led the applause, Nelson sauntered out to join the orchestra. As he reached the first musicians, Uncle Max caught his eye. Nelson just winked and sashayed on. As he approached the piano, Barry Pike's eyes flashed round – but Nelson just mouthed, 'Better late than never,' and slid onto the piano stool that the last pianist had just vacated.

This felt better.

This felt right.

At last, he could make it happen.

With an Englishman's determination to keep marching on and hoping for the best, Mr Pike started swinging his conductor's baton. Just a simple number, Nelson recalled – background music, while the wave of young dancers left the floor below and the next skipped out to confront the crowd. His fingers rolled into it, a rising cascade of major chords that welcomed in trumpets, guitars, Uncle Max's long, languorous swoon.

Just the calm before the storm, Nelson grinned.

He looked up.

Uncle Max was not grinning.

Just as Mr Pike swung his baton to pronounce the end of the number, Nelson's fingers relaxed. He stroked the top of the keys, making phantom chords without a sound. A Steinway, by God. The temptation to let loose with some ragtime on it, just for the cheap thrill, was almost overpowering – but instead he looked out, over the orchestra, up at the towering galleries, the starry constellations, the magnificence of it all. No, this wasn't any old Midnight Rooms or Ambergris Lounge. There were some things you couldn't cock a snook at.

Out on the dance floor, another constellation glittered: near a hundred dancers standing braced, ready for the music to begin. Nelson's eyes roamed over them until he saw Raymond de Guise, an elegant lady with white-blonde hair and a flowing satin gown in his arms. Now, *there* was elegance, thought Nelson. There was *class*.

He couldn't wait to play for them.

And here the moment came.


The song began in bombastic piano and rampant French horn.

'Here we go, Hélène.'

Raymond's hand, which had been poised in the small of Hélène's back, rose towards her shoulder. In reply, she gently rested her hand upon his upper arm. With their other hands clasped, they turned into the music.

How light it felt to dance with Hélène. How freeing, to glide across this dance floor with her, with the constellations looking down. Within three bars, Raymond had shed the day. The train ride, the farmhouse, the mounting panic of the swarming black cars; the deceit in the Buckingham, the deceit in the Grand, the deceit in his own home – all of it was as nothing, as the music took hold.

When they first left the ground together, it felt like they would never land.

When they turned and turned again, it felt like the Royal Albert Hall was for them alone.

The edges of the dance floor faded into a dreamscape; the galleries above really did become the clear night sky, devoid of conical searchlights and the comet trails of planes; the walls of the Albert Hall itself tumbled outwards, revealing the vast open world and its endlessly unfolding dance floor.

And that music, thought Raymond...

Thank God he really *could* hear that music.

One song turned to a third. A third turned to a fourth. The fifth began in muted piano, the brass leading the way, so Nelson closed his eyes and simply let his fingers do the work, high notes cascading like rainfall. Sixteen bars later, his left hand started drumming down low. There was double bass in the orchestra, and this propelled the song onward – but Nelson's left hand joined it in heavy rhythm. That felt good. He was like a locomotive, the engine room sending the song hurtling down the tracks.

He opened his eyes.

This was the last dance for these competitors. Below him, they pivoted and turned. There, in the heart of the dance floor: Raymond de Guise and Hélène Marchmont, their bodies parting, then coming back together in perfect time. Over and again they turned, soared on, then turned again. What would it be like, Nelson dreamt, to push them just a little bit further – to test the very edges of their elegance? What might it be like to light a fire underneath them? They'd been dancing long enough now. Their hearts were closed to everything but the music – and the music already had them in its grasp. All he'd have to do was ...

Nelson felt his left hand bouncing.

He didn't look at Barry Pike, for the conductor was still keeping time – and every twitching muscle in Nelson's body was telling him to throw off those shackles, to cast himself headlong into the song, to break free like a runaway train and drag all the other musicians, like helpless carriages, with him.

He rose to his haunches, hovering just above his piano stool, one foot still pounding the pedal.

Yes, *he* was in charge of this song now.

The Albert Hall, it wasn't so different from the Midnight Rooms after all.

The stage was bigger, the sound was bigger, but the music could be the same.

Nelson closed his eyes again. He didn't need to see Barry Pike. He didn't want to risk Uncle Max's disapproving eye. All he wanted to do was feel his way into the song. To hell with the lead sheets; to hell with the plan; music was meant to be wild and free, wasn't it? You were meant to follow it wherever it led. That was its joy.

His hands crashed down.

He threw back his head, as if he might howl.

Lord, how he wanted to howl ...

And an image crashed into his head:

There he was, in his mind's eye, back in the alley with those reprobate GIs closing in. Their faces set in scowls, their eyes blazing with hatred, they gave him one way out: the money, or your life.

But his hand hovered over the gutter, and when his fingers opened up, down the money rained, down through the sewer grate at his feet.

He opened his eyes.

The thrill of these moments, he realised now, was the same kind of thrill he'd got when he opened his fist to watch all that money vanish down the drain. It was the thrill of knowing what was good for you, yet knowing what was *fun*. It was the thrill of being told one thing and yet doing the other. The thrill of looking four bastards in the face and saying 'No'.

The thrill of just letting rip and to hell with the consequences.

The thrill of just being who you were.

It felt as if the whole of the Albert Hall was watching: Barry Pike, Uncle Max, all the great and the good – even King George himself... and he, Nelson Allgood, could take them wherever he wanted to go.

The howl was in his throat. The song was ready to seize.

But Nelson Allgood took a breath and let the moment pass.

Some moments later, now that the urge to rip down the Royal Albert Hall was fading, Nelson sat back on the stool, flourished his way to the end of the number, and looked up at Uncle Max. The older trombonist had just taken Lucille from his lips, but now he considered Nelson with a curious look, as if wondering what had happened, as if he couldn't quite believe the evidence of his own eyes:

Nelson Allgood was sitting daintily at the piano, his head bowed down, and his set had passed without wildfire.

The Royal Albert Hall exploded with applause.

And on the dance floor below, Raymond and Hélène took their bows.

*

364

In the living room at Blomfield Road, Stan had finally worn himself out. With summer sun streaming through the window panes, Nancy, Vivienne and their children sat together and listened as the Royal Dansant reached its final phase.

'Ladies and gentlemen,' came George Black's voice, crackling over the airwaves, 'our judges have deliberated long and hard and their decisions are made. In our amateur category, I am proud to say we have our winners – but first, the judges have three special commendations to hand out for couples whose promise has lit up this arena on this, our greatest of days... So, might I welcome to the stage, Mr Terence Macdonald and his partner, Miss Catherine Gray; Mr Billy Croft and his partner, Miss Penelope Warren; and...'

Nancy took Vivienne's hand.

'Mr Frank Nettleton and his partner, Miss Mathilde Bourchier!'

Nancy leapt up. 'Did you hear that?' she said, lifting up Arthur and whirling him around, face to face. 'Your Uncle Frank – garlanded at the Albert Hall!'

In reply, the baby just burped. In later years, Nancy decided, she would tell him that he'd been so excited he just couldn't keep it in. Right now, however, she simply held him to her shoulder, rubbed his back dutifully and grinned, 'If that's your reaction to Frankie, we better get ready for if your father wins...'

Standing in front of the stage at the Albert Hall, Frank could hardly hear it as his name was read out. It wasn't until Mathilde took his hand and whispered, 'Come on, Frankie, they're expecting us!' that he seemed to come to his senses. Even so, the world felt like a dream as he trailed after Mathilde, up onto the stage – where George Black, the judges, and the orchestra were assembled – and stood in line.

Applause like this was like a storm. Frankie felt caught in a headwind.

One after another, the runners-up bowed in front of George Black as the judges awarded them rosettes.

As Frank and Mathilde's turn came around, Mathilde turned to him and said, 'Frankie, if you can do this with your heart in such tumult, just think what you can do when you're at your best. Just think what we'll do after the war!'

But Frank wasn't thinking about the future, not as he bowed down his head for the emerald rosette to be pinned to his lapel. He wasn't thinking about what golden days there might be after the war, nor even that there might be so much more war left to come.

The only thing he was thinking was that his heart *hadn't* been in tumult, not as he danced.

And, for now, that was the most magical thing of all.

In the wings, Raymond watched rapt as Frank accepted his rosette and followed Mathilde to the front of the stage. Not certain his heart could feel fuller, even if it were he and Hélène taking their bows, he turned to take her hand – and instead saw the wild young pianist Nelson sauntering up to Max Allgood, with a look like victory plastered all over his face.

'Well, Uncle Max?' Nelson beamed. 'You didn't think I had it in me, did you? Didn't think I could just sit still and do what I was told? Didn't think I could *follow orders*. Well, now you see it, old man! I've been following orders like one of those grunts who keep chasin' me around town. You didn't think I was capable, but I *was*.'

Raymond didn't quite understand this – had the boy somehow contorted the simple act of being *obedient* into a rebellion? – but right now he was more flabbergasted that the two musicians seemed to know each other.

'You two are connected, Max?'

Max Allgood rolled his eyes. 'Mr de Guise, you better meet my cousin's boy Nelson.'

Nelson hawed and grabbed Raymond's hand. 'Me and the lieutenant already go a way back,' he grinned. 'Small world, ain't it, Uncle Max? It's almost like ... *fate*. That's right, the hand of fate, pushing us along, driving us where we're meant to go. So what do you say, Uncle Max? Is it mine? The place at the piano in the Grand?'

Even though the last waves of applause for the amateur category were breaking over the auditorium, and even though George Black was readying the judges and audience for the awards dished out to the professionals, the silence between Max and Nelson was overpowering.

'Raymond,' Hélène whispered, taking his hand, 'they want us all out on the dance floor.'

Moments after Raymond, Hélène and the other professional dancers sallied out, just as the amateurs – all the winners and runners-up together – were flocking backstage, Max took hold of Nelson's shoulder and declared, 'We'll talk about it, boy.'

'Talk about it, Uncle Max? Just talk about it?'

In an instant, Nelson could feel the fire he'd kept at bay on stage. He pulled backwards, brushed away Max's hand, rocked back on his heels, a coiled spring ready to burst.

'Is anything gonna be good enough, Uncle Max? Anything *ever*?'

Then, he turned and marched off into the warren of passageways underneath.

'Nelson,' Max called after him, 'it ain't that easy. There's folks I'd have to convince, and ... We can talk about it, boy. We can *talk!*'

But Nelson was already gone.

Down into the empty caverns beneath the auditorium. Down past the dressing rooms and hospitality stores, the practice rooms and countless other doors. Round and round in circles he stalked, desperate for the fire to ebb out of him, desperate for the anger to subside. Was that *it*? Had it really been for nothing? And now ... back to the clubs? Back to the Midnight Rooms and Ambergris, all the places those blowhards danced? What about destiny? What about fate?

Nelson was marching wildly down a long, barren corridor when he heard footsteps behind him.

'Uncle Max, I don't wanna talk,' he snarled, as he whirled round.

But it was not Uncle Max following him through the Albert Hall's subterranean labyrinth.

The man approaching Nelson was tall and lithe, a gentlemen dressed in a startling suit of forest green, with white-blonde hair and the look of royalty about him. His fingers were adorned in silver rings as he reached them out towards Nelson. His lips curled in a placatory smile.

'You'll have to forgive me. I'm afraid I rather overheard your tête-à-tête with Mr Allgood up there. Your uncle is a brilliant musician, one of your nation's finest, and it's well and good that he came to represent the New World today – but, I hope you don't mind me saying, he is not the greatest of leaders. A great leader makes room in their company for men of different character. A great leader knows that special dispensation must be given to those who bring to the party something that cannot be replaced. Max Allgood, it seems, favours safety over excitement. Well, it pains me to see somebody's talent go to waste because the people around them are *frightened*.'

Nelson grinned, 'Yeah, frightened – that's what it is. Frightened of me. Frightened I'll upstage him in his own ballroom, I bet that's it. You can't please that man. Be wild and exciting, Nelson – but not *that* wild and exciting. Learn to do what you're told, Nelson – yes, that's right, but it just ain't *enough*. I'm sick of the man. I'm sick of being held down. I want to – I want to break free!' Nelson stopped. He took a step closer to the man, inspected his extended hand curiously, then shook it. 'Who in hell are you, anyway?'

Nelson drew back his hand. Inside the man's palm had been a little ivory card. Nelson considered it now:

*LAURENCE JOHNS*

*TROUPE CHOREGRAPHER*

*IMPERIAL HOTEL*

'I've been here tonight to shepherd two of the Imperial Hotel's finest in the professional competition. Our director, Mr Gove, has been very clear with us all, that the Imperial must stake its claim to as much of the American custom flooding into London as possible. Our appearance here tonight will go some way to drawing the eye – but it occurred to me that to have a rising star, someone as unbridled and exciting as you, a star fresh from the Americas no less, might be just the thing our ballroom needed.'

'The Imperial Hotel,' Nelson read, eyes still flashing between Laurence and the card. 'Yeah, I get it. Some people *recognise* talent, right? Some people *see* it when it's right in front of them.'

The tall, willowy dancer inclined his head in a smile. 'I imagine the first step might be a meeting at our hotel – say Monday afternoon, at 2 p.m.? Just to explore the possibilities, you understand, and with no promises yet being made. But I imagine my director, my dance troupe – and indeed, my orchestra – will be intrigued to meet a young man of your startling character.'

Nelson just grinned.

'The Imperial Hotel needs to draw attention before the Savoy, the Buckingham, the Ritz take dominion. And what better way, young man, to draw the eye than with a bit of… rivalry?'

Then the lithe dancer bowed and marched away – and, in the echoing corridor, Nelson Allgood simply stared at the card, wondering at how the hand of fate operated.

'Ladies and gentlemen, might I invite our commended runners-up to the stage?' George Black paused; in the Albert Hall, the anticipation had never been higher. 'Mr Iain Armstrong and his partner Winifred MacLean, Mr Stewart Hobbs and his partner Josephine Hunt; Mr Kieran Mailer and his partner, Anna Reid!'

In the heart of the dance floor, Raymond stood tall, with Hélène on his arm. Above and around them, the applause rose and fell in great tidal waves of cheer. It was enough, he thought, just to be here. After everything, after France and Africa and the Buckingham Hotel, it was enough to hold his head high and say: yes, I am here; I am a father, I am alive, and I dance.

As the commended runners-up accepted their rosettes, George Black returned to centre stage.

'And now we come to our victors, ladies and gentlemen. Awarded our bronze medal, commended by the judges for perfect poise, please welcome Mr Alastair Shaw and his partner, Ashley Doyle!'

Raymond watched them soar onto the stage, their faces lit up in the lights from below. Photographers gathered. Camera bulbs flashed, then faded away.

'Awarded our silver medal,' George Black went on, 'and commended for the fluidity of their footwork, put your hands together for Mr Kieran Wood and his partner, Amy Ness!'

'They were brilliant,' Hélène whispered as the silver medallists took their bows. 'You'd have been proud to dance with them in the Grand. They had it all, Raymond – you know how two dancers just fit? Their bodies slide together. They were so calm, so collected, even when the music flew...'

Hélène's arm had been threaded through his; now that they came to the final reckoning, Raymond slid his hand further down, so that his fingers entwined with her own.

Win or lose, succeed or fail, it hardly mattered – he knew that in his head.

But oh, in his heart...

It felt good to *want* something so badly. After all the death and the killing, the ruin mankind was making of the world – the lies and deceit he'd promised to perpetrate, to help bring it to its end – it felt good to want something just for the sheer pleasure of it.

As a young man, it had been winning that convinced him this was the world where he belonged.

Right now, just a flicker of the same feeling would do.

'Ladies and gentlemen, our gold medallists – please welcome to the stage, Mr Raymond de Guise and Miss Hélène Marchmont!'

The applause folded inwards. From every gallery it crashed towards him, from every box and every seat – applause for them alone. Raymond rode its wave as he soared with Hélène to the edge of the stage, then up the steps to meet the judges. He lifted his hands skywards in appreciation of the crowd.

In the Buckingham Hotel, where John Hastings paced up and down by the wireless, a cheer went up for their champion.

In Maida Vale, where Vivienne still chased Stan, Nancy was breathless, whispering into her son's shell-like ear that his father had done it; that Raymond de Guise truly had returned.

In the wings at the Albert Hall, Frank swept up Mathilde – and in their excitement, they held on to each other just a little too long before sheepishly coming apart.

And up on stage, Raymond held his face to the bright white lights, forgot – for just a moment – what he was here in London to do, and allowed himself to imagine that this feeling, this feeling he had right now, would go on and on; that tomorrow, though there would be darknesses to face and terrors to contend with, this feeling would be his guiding light, his heavenly torch as he waded in the grubby mires of Hell.

From triumph to disaster and back again, all in the space of a day.

He looked up – and there, on their feet in their box, stood the royal party: the good King George and his wife, his daughters Elizabeth and Margaret, their hands raised to join the applause for the dancers below.

By evening, he would be back at the Deacon Club – but right now, he stood in heaven on Earth.

# Chapter Thirty

John Hastings threw his copy of the day-old *Sunday Times* to the desk with a victorious smile. If the Royal Dansant had been the talk of London for weeks, it would be the talk of the Buckingham Hotel for days to come – for there, captured in black and white, were his star dancer and his bandleader, and never had a newspaper poured more praise on an event since the World's Fair in '39.

'You see, Mr Allgood – this, right here, is precisely what I was looking for. Precisely what we needed. You play them, he dances to them – and the Buckingham Hotel is crowned twice over.'

Max Allgood, who had stumbled into Mr Hastings' office only moments ago, added, 'Don't forget Nettleton, sir. He's a commendable lad – and that has the King's seal of approval now. You can probably print it on tickets.'

Hastings smiled and invited Max to sit, though the elder man seemed to have little desire to take up the offer. Instead, he just bobbed from foot to foot, clinging to his trombone case like it was some religious icon.

'I'm glad we've done you proud, sir. It makes this easier, what I've got to ask.'

Until now, Hastings had been focused solely on the triumph and what it might mean for the hotel. This week, in the aftermath of both the ball and the Royal Dansant, the rest of the Hotel Board were due to meet for forecasting the year ahead. Predicting anything with a high degree of reliability was near impossible in a time of war, but Hastings had the mounting feeling that 1942 was going to look like a momentous year in the history of the Buckingham as well as the history of the war.

'Oh yes?' he asked, looking up.

'I've a nephew, sir. My cousin's boy. And I haven't got much family. Sir, he's a talent as well. He's raw and he can be a little... grandstanding, but he's got something good and he shone at the Dansant.' What Max wanted to say was: he didn't go *completely* wild; he didn't try and steal the show. The truth was, there'd been a moment when Max was certain Nelson was about to try and upstage them all; then the boy had taken a breath and brought himself back to earth, and nobody was any the wiser. 'Sir, I'd like to give him a slot, right here in the Grand. Just a few Saturday nights, to see how he copes.'

Hastings brooded on this a little. 'It's a hell of a thing, to give a place to family. They frown on it on Wall Street – though, of course, it happens all the time. The others around you get to thinking that you're doing favours.'

Max nodded, 'And I seen in the dance troupe how easy feathers get ruffled.' He paused. 'But a try-out, sir? I was think-ing, if the decision was yours, if it was taken out of my hands... maybe that'd make the whole thing more palatable.'

John Hastings sat back. The truth was, he was still more interested in the coverage of the Royal Dansant than he was in the inner machinations of the Buckingham orchestra – but time does not stop in a luxury hotel, and surely they would soon be looking towards Christmas and the winter ball to come. It would be advantageous to have a permanent pianist in place long before then – and an exciting young American, who had the pedigree of the Royal Dansant behind him, was surely a good place to start.

'I'll hear him play before we make any decisions, Mr Allgood,' John Hastings decided. 'Set it up.'

That same afternoon, in the sunlit garden behind No 18 Blomfield Road, the sprawling de Guise family gathered in celebration.

Nancy had decided that Vivienne was not to martyr herself in the kitchen today, so before dawn she had been awake, preparing the scones, the sandwiches, tidying up the portions of quiche they'd managed to liberate from going to waste at the Buckingham Hotel. Now she stood in the doorway, Arthur up against her shoulder, watching as Stan hurtled around the edges of the lawn – harried this time by Sybil instead of Vivienne, who reclined on the picnic blanket – and Hélène Marchmont listened to Frank's stuttering portrayal of the moment he and Mathilde had been summoned to the stage. In the background, one of Raymond's old Gershwin records was playing. Arthur liked these older ones; Nancy decided it was his mother's influence.

Nancy was still preparing the tea when the doorbell rang. Outside, the music was too loud, the conversation too convivial, for anyone else to hear – so, leaving the chaos of the kitchen, she hurried down the hall to answer the call.

On the doorstep stood Rosa, dressed in a glamorous spotted dress, a yellow rose pinned into her hair.

'Rosa,' she gasped, 'just the girl. I'm glad you could make it! Look, I need some help. Grab a drink – and there's fresh scones cooling – and help me cart some bits out to the garden.'

There was something almost sheepish about Rosa as she followed Nancy into the kitchen, then filled a tray to carry it out into the garden. As soon as she appeared on the sunlit lawn, a minor cheer went up. Raymond hurried to take the tray from her.

It was only Frank who seemed shocked to see her – but that was because, of everyone gathered at Blomfield Road today, he was the only one who *knew* he hadn't invited her.

To everyone else, she was just Rosa, Frank's sweetheart.

To everyone else, nothing had changed.

'Frankie,' Rosa exclaimed with a tremble in her tone, 'well done!'

She flung her arms around him and stayed there, saying it over and over again – even while the faces of everyone else in the garden creased in confusion. Had Frank really not gone to Rosa to celebrate his victory already? Had she really not been the first one he told?

Rosa lingered too long, dangling around Frank, so that when Frank finally extricated himself, an awkwardness had settled over the garden.

In the end, it was Rosa who tried to dispel it. 'Frankie, you must be so proud.'

Frank nodded mutely, then took a deep breath.

'Rosa,' he said, 'maybe we should go for a walk?'

Nelson Allgood was whistling to himself as he loped up the steps of the Underground at Hyde Park Corner, then gambolled into the park.

This, he supposed, was the scene of his most recent near-catastrophe, but it didn't feel like that today – not with his pockets fat and full, and not with the memory of the Royal Dansant still replaying in his mind. He'd asked around town, stuck his head into every beer hall and club, and he was certain they'd be here somewhere – but the day was so bright (as bright as his *future*, god damn it!) that he didn't care either way. Either he'd find them and this would be finished, or he'd not find them and he could just lounge here all afternoon, soaking up the sun. Good Lord, that would be a fine afternoon. All these passers-by would think he was a lazy good-for-nothing, but Nelson wouldn't care – because out of everyone in London, he alone knew what the future had in store.

In the end, they stuck out like a sore thumb. Blowhards always do. Nelson spotted them from a distance – or spotted one of them at least, the one named Joel. There he was, sitting on his lonesome by the edge of the glittering Serpentine Lake, a picnic blanket spread out in front of him. A red rose, by God, in a picnic cup.

'You shouldn't have,' said Nelson as he approached.

Joel, at least, was the most reasonable one. The bar was pretty low, but at least it had been Joel who'd tried to break up the ruckus that first night in the Ambergris Lounge. Nelson knew he ought not to taunt the man – those days were meant to be good and gone, weren't they? – but the temptation was too much. He caressed the rose, like some lover might caress the girl whose heart he'd just won.

'Hey, get your dirty hands away,' Joel snapped. 'Your dirty boots too. You know your problem? You just *love* trouble.'

'That problem's already been diagnosed,' Nelson grinned. Then, with a flourish, he pulled an envelope out of his back pocket and tossed it down disdainfully, to land between the sandwiches Joel had evidently taken care in preparing. 'It's all there. You can count it.'

Joel opened up the envelope in disbelief.

'Now, I still don't accept I owe you a penny. You gambled, fair and square – same as me. But I'm willing to be the bigger man. The bigger *gentleman*, as it happens. And if paying you off is gonna get you and your pighead friends away from me until you trot off to the war, well, I'm happy enough with that. Go on, take it. You don't even have to say thank you.' Then Nelson turned on his heel and began to march away. 'I don't need it. There's plenty more where that came from. I'm never gonna be playing for you blowhards again. I got myself a new *position!*'

Little victories mattered, in life as well as war. Nelson was still effervescent with the triumph of it when he returned to his lodgings at No 62 Albert Yard, to the scent of freshly baked bread in the kitchen (Billy Brogan had, as ever, delivered another off-ration sack full of flour), and his mother's proud eyes. 'Come through, Nelson,' Ava said, zealously. 'Uncle Max has got something he wants to tell you.'

Max was waiting in the kitchen, taking a taste of the bread just come out of the oven. Evidently it was too hot, because the old man started bopping and scatting like he was a vocalist performing in some jazz club back home.

'Now Nelson,' Max began, blowing on his scalded fingers, 'I know we've been rubbing each other up the wrong way. I know we've been locking horns. I know we haven't exactly been seeing eye to eye. But I also know that I was young once, and I got myself in a whole heap of trouble, and I know I've been hard on you. It's only because I know how hard it is to prove yourself for folks like us. And, Nelson, there ain't no doubt you proved yourself on Saturday night at the Royal Dansant. That's why, this morning, I sat down with Mr John Hastings and he's agreed that you can do a try-out at the Buckingham Hotel. Now, don't get ahead of yourself yet – it's just to play for Mr Hastings and a few select others. But if they like what they see – and they *will* – there could be a slot for you on a Saturday night in the Grand. And if *they* like what they see – well, let's just say, I reckon that the future might open up. They'll be talking about Christmas soon. A winter ball . . .'

'And you, Nelson,' Ava enthused, 'right where we promised you'd be – right in the heart of the Grand!'

Nelson grabbed a hot bread roll from Mrs Brogan's tray, held it up to the light, then tore a chunk off with his teeth and started chewing.

'Oh, don't worry about all that, Uncle Max,' he said with a knowing grin, 'I already got myself something sorted.' Then he turned and, still chomping on the bread, began to saunter away. 'You don't need to worry about me any more. I got the message – a man's gotta stand up for himself in this world. And that's exactly what I'm doing. You're gonna be so proud of me – both of you are!' He turned back with a devilish wink. 'I'm gonna be lead pianist at the Imperial Hotel.'

The cherry blossoms were in full colour along Blomfield Road. Underneath their radiant blooms, Frank walked with Rosa, each of them on one side of the pavement so that a yard-wide gulf of stone lay between them. When the cherry blossoms floated down, they seemed to make a beautiful pink, twirling veil that separated one from the other.

'I'm – I'm sorry, Frank.'

Such a simple sentiment, so very few words, but until that moment Frank didn't know that he'd been longing to hear them. At first, he could say nothing. He stammered three times, then folded his hands like a penitent. The silence of the last weeks had been cruel, but it was easier than this.

'I don't know what happened. I didn't mean it. It wasn't something I planned or thought about or ... We were just pottering along, Frank, you and me, and it wasn't even as if I was thinking about anything else. It wasn't as if I was even unhappy.' She paused. 'But then I met Joel.'

Still, Frank said nothing. He wasn't sure what it was all for. He wasn't sure why the excavation mattered, what it might change for either of them. He smiled and nodded and after some time he said, 'You fell in love.'

The words poleaxed Rosa, but only because he was right.

'I'm sorry.'

Frank inched a little closer to her, even while the tumbling cherry blossoms half obscured her face. 'I know it.'

'It's this damn war, Frank. It's been doing things to me from the beginning. And I didn't mean it, I promise I didn't – I wasn't unhappy, and I might have pottered along forever, but then... then it hits you, like a bolt out of the blue. *This, this* is what life is for.' She stopped. 'That day at the cinema. I'm sorry you saw that.'

'I know.'

'I would have told you.'

'I know.'

This time, it was all he could think to say – but he wasn't sure whether he believed it. He wasn't sure that it even mattered. The dance was already over, wasn't it? What difference did it make whether it ended in honesty or deceit? Either way, the music had stopped; the band had left the stage. Some dances wound down towards gentle stillness; others ended in a wild, dramatic climax. He said, 'Why did you come here, Rosa?'

'You've been ignoring me. Avoiding me at the hotel. I know why, Frank. I haven't been good, and I didn't want to hurt you, and I've made a mess of it all... but I don't want to lose you, Frankie. You've been such a big part of my life.'

Rosa had carried on walking, but Frank stopped dead. It was only some strides further along that Rosa realised Frank wasn't at her side. She turned back, the gulf between them even wider now. Her face fell. She'd hoped it had been narrowing, if only just a little.

'I don't think that's fair, Rosa.'

Frank stood fast – and, though he couldn't say why, it was Mathilde's words that were ricocheting through him. 'If you're not being fair to anyone,' she had said, 'you're not being fair to yourself.'

'Frankie?'

Frank buried his hands in his pockets. He wanted so much to bridle his emotion, but it was already breaking free of what constraints he had left. His eyes shimmered with tears, obscuring Rosa even further.

'I don't think you get to choose which parts of someone you keep and which you push away,' he said. 'I'm not sure that's how this works.' Then he stopped – and, because he was still Frank Nettleton, he added, 'I'm sorry, Rosa. I'm not trying to be cruel.'

This time, it was Rosa's turn to say, 'I know,' before the long silence returned.

'Frankie,' Rosa said at last, 'do they know? Nancy and Raymond and all of the rest? The way they looked at me, it was like they didn't *know*.'

'I haven't told them.'

Nervously, Rosa said, 'But you'll have to.'

'I will.'

How had conversation become so difficult, so different, so stilted? How did two people go from intertwined to exiled in such a short time? Was this just the natural end of love? Two people spent every day together, thinking the same thoughts, burrowing through the back roads of each other's minds, inhabiting the past, the present, the future – until, one day, they just stopped, and went on as if none of it had happened at all. Could that possibly be real?

'Frankie,' Rosa sobbed, 'I need my job.'

It was those words, puncturing the silence, that brought Frank back from whatever morass he'd been trapped within. Suddenly, he understood. It wasn't that she hadn't come here to make her apologies, because he knew they were sincere – but this other thing had been playing on her mind throughout, and now that she'd blurted it out it couldn't be pushed back in.

Frank looked up and down Blomfield Road. The pull of his family was strong, but he was rooted to the ground. 'I have to tell them, Rosa, but I don't have to tell them it all.'

Rosa took three stuttering steps towards him. 'Really, Frankie? You'd do that?'

'Rosa,' Frank said, 'please could you just call me *Frank*?'

Rosa nodded, suddenly chastened, suddenly hurt – though that wasn't what Frank had wanted.

'I know how much the Buckingham means,' he went on. 'I know you need it.'

'I send money back home,' Rosa whispered.

'I know it.'

'Then you won't say, about Joel, and what I did...'

Frank shook his head. 'I'll tell them we chose it together. I'll tell them it just wasn't to be.' He rocked, sadly, from foot to foot. 'I've never told a lie to my sister before – never, since the day I was born.'

Rosa's voice was so feathery and broken it was almost mute: 'I'm sorry.'

Frank nodded. Then, at last, he began to walk away, 'I hope he's nice to you, Rosa. I hope he takes you dancing.'

By the time Frank got back to the house, he had almost dried his eyes – but evidently the red rawness of them still showed, because when he floated through the door and picked his way out to the garden, Nancy could tell straight away that something was wrong.

'What is it, Frank?'

So then, it was time to say it out loud.

For a moment he took stock, gazing around the garden. There was such joy here, the ripple effect of the Royal Dansant, that it seemed a shame to have to break it. And yet, that was real life, wasn't it? The rough came with the smooth. People got married, gave birth, confessed their love, on the same day that the bombs rained down. Nothing good lasted forever, but everything that was wicked moved on as well.

'It's me and Rosa,' he said, trying his best to keep the words from fraying apart, 'we're not going to be seeing so much of each other any more. We've decided it's time.'

Across the garden, the adults turned as one. Nancy had wrapped her arms around him in seconds; then came Raymond, and Vivienne – and Hélène as well. In the background, Sybil and Stan charged on – but there, on the back doorstep, the family simply *gathered*.

'It's OK, Nance,' Frank said, once the moment had passed. 'I think I knew it wasn't forever.'

So there it was: the very first lie he'd told his sister.

It didn't feel good, but it didn't feel *awful* either. And it was kind, wasn't it? To protect Rosa's position, even after what she'd done? Was it even her fault that she'd fallen in love? Or was love like a wave moving silently, unseen but inexorable, catching unsuspecting people in its currents, just like the music of a dance?

He looked at Raymond, with Arthur in his arms. Raymond would understand. Raymond, he felt certain, had never lied to Nancy either. But perhaps one little lie could be forgiven in a time of war. There were so many bigger ones being told in the world. If one little lie eased someone's burden, did that really matter?

Raymond had gripped him by the shoulder. 'Frank, it might feel grave today, but tomorrow things change, and then they change again. For now, it's a grief. But trust me – grief has other victims waiting. It moves on.'

In the hall, the telephone rang. Vivienne, detaching herself from the group with a final squeeze of Frank's hand, hurried off to answer it.

'And you mustn't forget yesterday, Frank,' Raymond went on. 'Perhaps it's just that your story took a different turn to hers.'

'I'll be all right, Raymond. It just winds you a little, that's all.'

'Raymond,' Vivienne called, 'it's for you.'

Raymond left Frank to be coddled by his sister, then – with Arthur still in his arms – loped up the hallway to take the receiver. 'Raymond de Guise speaking, how may I help?'

'De Guise, I imagine you're celebrating now – but I'm afraid you're needed.'

Maynard Charles. Raymond felt a chill like ice coursing through his veins. He juggled the receiver, Arthur wriggling in his arms and said, 'Sir, what is it?'

'It isn't often that a man in your position benefits from publicity, Raymond, but the department has decided we can turn this to our advantage. Thanks to the Royal Dansant, your star is in the ascendant again. Your face splashed all over the newspapers – it appeals to a certain sort of vanity in a man.' He paused. 'I need you at the hotel, Raymond. The American contingent we spoke of have come to London early. The reservations are displaced. They'll arrive at the Buckingham by this evening – and I want you on the ground when they arrive. First contact, de Guise, with the man named MacLean. Hastings, we believe, could be convinced to host an evening of cocktails to welcome them. You're to organise and encourage those drinks, to romance them with stories of the Royal Dansant, to speak to them of the King and his daughters. And then, once the channels of communication are clear, you're to find out what they're up to. I want to know where their money is going, and to whom.'

Raymond glanced up and down the hallway. At its end, glorious sunlight still spilled over the garden – and there were his family, all of them lounging on the picnic blankets stretched out across the lawn, everyone together at last.

'Sir,' he dared to venture, 'I wonder if this one is better approached more gently. If I pounce on them the moment they arrive, mightn't they find it suspicious?'

Laughter burst up in the garden. Stan, it seemed, was suddenly performing a serenade for his crowd.

'De Guise?' Maynard growled, guardedly.

'I'm ready for the next fight, sir. I know what my job is now. I've seen it at its worst – but I've seen what I can do as well.' *And I know what I'm fighting for*, he thought, as Arthur grappled for the telephone receiver. *I know why it matters, why every little lie will be worth it in the end. It's for them, out there, right now: families, however they might look, coming through this war together.* 'But my family need me too. They deserve just a little of my time before I come back to the battle. And sir … these stories of the Royal Dansant, they're not going away quickly. I can still tell stories of the King tomorrow, and the day after that.'

Down the line came only the crackling static of silence and deep thought. Raymond could quite imagine the defiant look on Maynard Charles's face, his fury at Raymond's impertinence.

'We're grateful for your service in the Guthrie affair, de Guise,' he grunted. 'So I'll see you for breakfast at the Deacon Club tomorrow. Don't be late.'

Then the line went dead.

Back in the garden, the music was playing. Hélène had cajoled Frank into a little light waltzing, while Sybil eagerly tried to take an unabashedly uninterested Stan into hold.

'Allow me,' Raymond said, handing Arthur to Nancy and stepping into Stan's place. Then he looked down at Sybil and, with a mounting smile, said, 'Shall we?'

And so, he thought, the dance went on.

The lies as well.

But, in the end, it was the dancing that mattered.

# Acknowledgements

Thank you to everyone who worked on *A Dance for the King*.

Thank you to my manager and friend, Melissa Chappell. A huge thank you to Kerr MacRae, my literary agent.

Thank you to my editor at Orion, Sam Eades, and to my long-time writing partner Robert Dinsdale.

And to booksellers and readers all over the world. Thank you for being such wonderful supporters of my books. I am so grateful for your support.

And a special thank you to my wife, Hannah, my children, George and Henrietta, and my family. I love you!

# Credits

Anton Du Beke and Orion Fiction would like to thank everyone at Orion who worked on the publication of *A Dance for the King* in the UK.

**Editorial**
Sam Eades
Anshuman Yadav

**Copyeditor**
Francine Brody

**Proofreader**
Kim Bishop

**Audio**
Paul Stark
Louise Richardson

**Contracts**
Dan Herron
Ellie Bowker
Oliver Chacon

**Design**
Charlotte Abrams-Simpson

**Editorial Management**
Charlie Panayiotou
Jane Hughes
Bartley Shaw
Lucy Bilton

**Finance**
Jasdip Nandra
Nick Gibson
Sue Baker

**Publicity**
Francesca Pearce
Sarah Lundy

**Marketing**
Yadira da Trindade

**Production**
Ruth Sharvell
Fiona McIntosh

**Operations**
Jo Jacobs
Sharon Willis

**Sales**
Jen Wilson
Esther Waters
Victoria Laws
Toluwalope Ayo-Ajala
Rachael Hum
Anna Egelstaff
Sinead White
Georgina Cutler

# Don't miss the new novel by Anton du Beke, *Monte Carlo in the Moonlight*!

*By Royal Invitation,*
*Prodigal son and loyal daughter…*

Ed Forsyth has brought the Forsyth Varieties to Monaco to perform at the open-air Fort Antoine, at the personal request of Princess Grace. In a former life, of course, Grace Kelly was a bona fide star of the silver screen – and it was in this role that she first came across the Forsyth Varieties, the Forsyths having been hired to perform in one of her early movie's frenetic crowd scenes. On set, the future princess grew particularly fond of Ed's wife Bella. Bella has since passed away, but Grace has always held the Company in great esteem and is pleased to welcome them to the principality.

In Monaco, preparations are under way for both the Grand Prix, and a festival which Princess Grace has arranged at which the Forsyths are to be the defining stars.

The return to Monaco is an emotional one for Ed, who has always associated the principality with Bella – but it is a trip filled with potential for his children. Cal's youthful love affair with an older, married woman brings back ghosts of the past. Evie is looking for a fresh start when she meets French Formula 1 driver, Charles, whose own tragic past only serves to enthral Evie even more.

Cal tragically dies in a supposed accident on the Grand Prix circuit – an event reminiscent of James Dean's untimely death – and one that spurs Ed and Evie to uncover Cal's killer. Who could have wanted Cal dead? Does the answer lie in the rivalries and jealousies on the movie set where Cal was working? Does it lie in the old love affair he had in the principality? Or is it, in some way, connected to the mistrust and conflict brewing in the Formula 1 fraternity?

**AVAILABLE AUGUST 5, 2025.**

**PRE-ORDER NOW!**